A Mother's Courage

Dilly Court grew up in North East London and began her career in television, writing scripts for commercials. She is married with two grown-up children and three grandchildren, and now lives in Dorset on the beautiful Jurassic Coast with her husband and a large, yellow Labrador called Archie. She is also the author of *Mermaids Singing, The Dollmaker's Daughters, Tilly True, The Best of Sisters* and *The Cockney Sparrow*.

D1047869

Also by Dilly Court

Dilly Court

A Mother's Courage

arrow books

Published by Arrow Books 2008

18

Copyright © Dilly Court 2007

Dilly Court has asserted her right under the Copyright, Designs and
Patents Act 1988 to be identified as the author of this work

This novel is a work of fiction. Names and characters are the product
of the author's imagination and any resemblance to actual persons,
living or dead, is entirely coincidental

This book is sold subject to the condition that it shall not, by way of
trade or otherwise, be lent, resold, hired out, or otherwise circulated
without the publisher's prior consent in any form of binding or
cover other than that in which it is published and without a
similar condition including this condition being imposed on the
subsequent purchaser

First published in Great Britain in 2007 by
Century
Random House, 20 Vauxhall Bridge Road,
London, SW1V 2SA

www.rbooks.co.uk

Addresses for companies within The Random House Group Limited
can be found at: www.randomhouse.co.uk/offices.htm

The Random House Group Limited Reg. No. 954009

A CIP catalogue record for this book
is available from the British Library

Penguin Random House is committed to a sustainable future for
our business, our readers and our planet. This book is made from
Forest Stewardship Council® certified paper.

MIX
Paper from
responsible sources
FSC® C018179

Printed and bound in Great Britain by Clays Ltd, St Ives plc

Typeset by SX Composing DTP, Rayleigh, Essex

For Simon, Marian, Sarah, Julia and Jean in
New Zealand

Acknowledgements

Although the characters and the events in the Foundling Hospital are entirely fictional, the Foundling Hospital did exist. It was founded in 1739 by Captain Thomas Coram as a home and educational establishment for children abandoned on the streets of London. Although the building was demolished in the early 20th century, the charity, now known as the Coram Family, still continues its good work in improving the emotional health and life prospects of children.

Chapter One

East London, January 1879

A crowd of women had gathered outside the shipping office in Eastcheap, their pale faces masked with dread as they huddled together against the biting east wind. A sleety rain tumbled from a pewter sky pitter-pattering softly on the cobblestones, but not a sound could be heard from those patiently waiting for news of their loved ones, except for the chattering of teeth and the occasional muffled sob.

Eloise Cribb stood a little apart from them, but it was not that as an officer's wife she considered herself to be a cut above the rest. She was no snob, and her strict moral upbringing as the daughter of a clergyman had taught her that all men were equal, but she was uncomfortably aware that her elegant mantle trimmed with fur, and the pert little matching hat, were in sharp contrast to the shabby clothes worn by wives of the crew. She had scanned the gathering for the familiar face of the captain's wife, but she was not there. Eloise knew that the poor lady was in an advanced state of pregnancy, and her heart went out to her. How awful not to know the fate of your beloved husband when you were about to give birth to his child. The wives of the second and third mate were clinging together for comfort, and, as she hardly knew them, Eloise had acknowledged them with an attempt at a smile and then moved away.

She wiped a strand of long dark hair from her forehead, blinking away the raindrops that trickled down her face like tears. In her heart she knew the answer even before the heavy oak door opened and a whey-faced official representing the shipping company appeared at the top of the stone steps. One look at his pinched features confirmed her worst fears. There was an audible intake of breath as the wives, sweethearts, mothers and sisters waited for the inevitable announcement that the *Hellebore*, which had now been overdue for several weeks, was lost at sea. A long drawn out groan of despair was torn from the women's lips as the official read out the company's statement in a voice choked with emotion. Eloise listened but the only words that registered were those she had dreaded the most. 'The management regrets to inform you that the tea clipper *Hellebore* went down during a typhoon in the China Sea with the loss of all hands.'

A loud animal-like howl of pain was ripped from a pregnant woman's throat and several others fainted or collapsed in the arms of their friends and relatives. Eloise stood quite still, totally silent, unable even to cry. Her brief marriage to First Officer Ronald Cribb had not been perfect, but she had loved him dearly. The long months of enforced separation had been hard to bear, but it had made their reunion all the sweeter when at last he came home on leave. She shivered convulsively as the harsh fact dawned on her that her two children, Joseph who would be three in June and Elizabeth, a babe in arms not quite four months old, were now fatherless. She was a widow, and she was virtually penniless. Stunned and too shocked to feel either grief or pain, she waited in line while the counting house clerk handed out the allotments to the distraught widows. Eloise could tell by his tight-lipped expression that he was close to tears himself, and she felt vaguely sorry for him in his onerous task, but her mind seemed to be detached from her body as she held out her hand to receive the small brown envelope. The clerk murmured condolences, but he could not look her in the eyes and she saw that his hands shook as he fumbled for the next pay packet. Eloise moved away from the head of the queue like an automaton, putting one foot in front of the other and yet barely conscious of what she was doing or which way she was going. All she knew was that she must get home to her babies: poor fatherless little mites, who now depended on her for everything.

Blinded by the rain and tasting the salt tears that were flooding down her cheeks, she stumbled over the wet cobblestones as she headed off in the direction of Shoreditch. It was a long walk to Myrtle Street but she did not want to waste money on the bus fare, and she needed time in which to compose herself. Her heart might be broken into shards, but she must not let the little ones sense her despair. At least they were warm and dry at home, safe in the care of her neighbour's eldest daughter, Mary, who was a stolid reliable sort of child, and could be trusted not to leave Joss and Beth unattended.

Eloise headed north towards Bishopsgate, barely noticing the crowds of workers who were hurrying homewards. She was soaked to the skin and her feet were blistered and sore, but she was oblivious to physical pain or discomfort and she quickened her pace. She wanted to be at home with her children. She longed to hold them in her arms and to inhale their sweet, baby fragrance. Joss and Beth were her last link with Ronald. Her breath caught on a sob as the harsh truth dawned upon her. She would never see him again. She would never have the chance to kiss him goodbye, or even have the small comfort of seeing him laid to rest in a leafy cemetery where she might lay flowers on his grave. She stumbled on through the rain-soaked streets ignoring the curious looks of passers-by, but after a while a painful stitch in her side forced her to stop and lean against a shop window gasping for breath. As the pain ebbed away, Eloise made a concerted effort to be calm. She must try to think clearly. She must not panic. As her breathing slowed down and the fog of misery began to clear from her brain, she knew what she must do. She would collect the children and take them home to the vicarage and to Mother. Mama would make things right again. She always knew what to do for the best.

Gaining strength from the thought of her mother's comforting presence and the familiar surroundings of her old home, Eloise started off again, edging her way through the slowly moving forest of black umbrellas. She tried to focus her thoughts on happier times, recalling her first meeting with Ronnie and the heady days of their whirlwind romance. They had met at a church social during one of his infrequent shore leaves. Ronnie was not a religious man but, having nothing better to do, he had accompanied one of his shipmates to the social evening, and he had always teased her about the way they met, declaring that it was the 'best worst evening of his life'. Eloise was not fooled by his levity; she had known the first moment she had set eyes on him in the church hall that he was the one for her, and she knew that Ronnie had felt the same. He had charmed her with his dazzling smile and craggy good looks. She had noticed particularly how his bright blue eyes were crinkled at the corners, caused no doubt by years of gazing across vast oceans into the far horizon, and his lively sense of humour had quickly overcome her initial shyness. They had danced every dance to the rather out of tune notes of Miss Brompton on the pianoforte. They had sipped the fruit cup, which was so well diluted that there was barely a trace of alcohol in the over-sweet drink, and they had eaten fairy cakes baked by the Misses Bragg, two maiden ladies who owned a millinery in Pear Tree Lane.

'Oy, look where you're going, ducks.' The strident voice of a costermonger whose barrow she had bumped against brought Eloise back to reality with a jerk. She bent down to retrieve the oranges that had bounced into the gutter, which was oozing with muddy rainwater mixed with straw and detritus from the streets. She gave them back to him with a murmured apology.

He squinted short-sightedly into her face. 'I should get home and out of them wet duds if I was you, miss. You'll end up with lung fever if you're not careful.'

Eloise managed a wobbly smile and went on her way. Battling against the wind and rain, it took her over half an hour to reach Myrtle Street. It was not the most spiritually uplifting of places in which to live, but the rent was reasonably cheap, which was essential as they always seemed to be short of money. Although Ronnie earned a good wage he was a spendthrift by nature, and no matter how many times she had tried to make him live within their means he had never complied, laughing at her attempts to balance the housekeeping, and telling her that 'there was plenty more where that came from'.

Cold, wet and tired, Eloise quickened her pace as she walked down the narrow street lined with red-brick terraced houses which had been built half a century ago to house the navigators, mostly Irish immigrants, who were needed to construct the vast network of railways. They had long since moved on, following the progress of the railways and canals. Now these two up and two down dwellings were crowded with people of all nationalities, sometimes two or three different families sharing one house and a single privy in the back yard. Eloise knew she ought to be thankful to have the house to herself, but living in this deprived area had been a shock after the relative comfort of the large vicarage in Dorset where she had grown up. Papa had not been happy when he was given a parish in Clerkenwell, but he had seen it to be his duty and had moved his family from the country to London. Eloise had been just sixteen then, fresh from Miss Mason's Academy for Young Ladies, and hoping that she might go on to become a teacher, but Papa had insisted that she should stay at home and assist her mother with her parish duties. It had not occurred to her to flout his wishes, and it was no hardship as Eloise adored her gentle mother; they were the best of friends, more like sisters, so other people had often remarked, than mother and daughter.

As Eloise opened the front door, she had one thought uppermost in her mind. She would put the children in the perambulator that Ronnie had bought when Joss was born, and she would take them home to Mother. She stepped into the front room and shivered as the warmth enveloped her. A coal fire was burning brightly in the grate and beside it sat Mary, with Joss dandled on her knee. She stopped in the middle of the nursery rhyme she had been reciting to him and stared at Eloise with large brown eyes that were too knowing for her tender years. 'Is it bad news then, missis?'

Eloise took off her sodden, and probably ruined, fur hat. Rainwater was dripping from her clothes staining the floorboards on which she had expended much time and energy, polishing them until they gleamed like satin. She nodded, momentarily unable to speak. Joss was holding his arms out to her, smiling with delight. 'Mama, Mama.'

She bent down to kiss his curly blond head. 'In a moment, darling. Mama needs to change out of her wet clothes.'

'He's not coming home then?' Mary said in a matter-of-fact voice.

The harsh reality of Mary's words struck Eloise like a blow, but she bit back a sharp retort. The child was merely stating the truth. There were many seafarers' families who lived in the area, and there were few who had not been touched by some sort of disaster be it death by drowning or crippling accidents. She shook her head. 'No, Mary. I fear not.'

'You go upstairs and change out of them wet things then, or you'll be next. I don't mind staying on for a bit with young Joss, and the baby is still asleep.'

Eloise made her way slowly up the narrow staircase; the boards creaked beneath her feet and her high button boots squelched, leaving little pools of water on the bare treads. In the bedroom at the front of the house, Beth lay sleeping in her cradle, her thick golden eyelashes forming crescents on her rosy cheeks. Her breathing was so soft that Eloise had to resist the temptation to touch her, just to make sure she was still alive, but then the baby stirred slightly in her sleep and Eloise began to breathe again, but her relief was tinged with bitterness. It was so unfair that Ronnie would never see his beautiful daughter and that Beth would grow up without knowing her father. Eloise bit back a sob, and she was trembling as she stripped off

9

her wet clothes and towelled her skin until it glowed pink. Her breasts were engorged with milk and tingling. Soon it would be time to feed Beth, and she must do this before she could even think of leaving the house. She must focus on practical things; it was the only way to keep going.

She put on a clean shift and her only other pair of stays, lacing them as best she could with fingers that burned painfully now that the feeling was returning to her extremities. She took a clean white cotton blouse from the cupboard and a plain navy-blue serge skirt. She took off her wet stockings and dried the inside of her boots as best she could with the end of the towel. She would have to put them on again as her old boots had worn out months ago, and although her mama would gladly have bought her a new pair it was more than just pride that prevented Eloise from asking for help. Papa was not exactly mean, but he kept a tight hold on the purse strings, and Eloise knew that when Mama gave her money or bought her clothes it came out of her own allowance, which was not over-generous.

She sighed as she pulled on a dry pair of much-darned stockings. Money had been tight since Ronnie's last leave. He had come home hell bent on enjoying himself and had taken her to the music halls, theatres, Cremorne Gardens and the

Zoological Gardens. They had eaten out almost every night, either taking Joss with them or leaving him with Mary's mother, Fanny, who was pleased to oblige for a mere penny or twopence. No matter how much Eloise had protested that they could not afford such a lifestyle, Ronnie had merely laughed. If she closed her eyes she could still see the merry gleam in his blue eyes and hear the infectious sound of his laughter. 'If I can't take my lovely wife out and show her off when I come home on leave, then it ain't worth the pain and trouble of separation.' She could hear him now. 'Don't worry, my love. I'll send more funds when I get to my next port of call. I promise you that.' But like the rest of his promises, that one was never kept.

Beth stirred again and opened her blue eyes, so like her father's. She began to whimper and Eloise scooped her up in her arms. 'Oh, my little treasure, what am I going to do? How will we manage on our own?' She sat down on the edge of her bed and undid the buttons of her blouse, putting the baby to her breast. 'We will go and see your grandmama; she will know what to do.'

It had stopped raining, and Myrtle Street was cloaked in darkness when Eloise finally left the house with both children tucked up together in the perambulator. It was bitterly cold and the air

11

smelt of soot with a hint of snow to come. Eloise wrapped her muffler a little tighter around her neck and she stepped out briskly, heading towards City Road. The streets were quiet at this time on a freezing January evening, and she was able to pass unnoticed in the shadows between the pools of flickering yellow gaslight. Her breath curled like smoke around her face and head, but the two children slept peacefully in the warm cocoon of blankets in the perambulator. Her heart ached as she looked down at their innocent faces. How she would manage she did not know. Ronnie had never saved a penny in his life, nor had he thought to take out life insurance. She would have to find work, and quickly too. Mother would help. Mother would know exactly what to do. Eloise quickened her pace, breathing more easily as she saw the spire of her father's church looming above the pall of smoke that always hung over this part of the city.

There was light shining from the vicarage windows and Eloise sighed with relief. She had not stopped to wonder if her parents might be out at a church meeting or a social; she had just followed her instinct to fly home where she knew she would be safe. She knocked on the door, muffling the sound of the iron door knocker with her hand lest it should wake the babies. She listened for the sound of approaching footsteps on the encaustic tiled floor and her throat tightened with unshed tears when finally the door opened and she saw her mother's slender figure silhouetted against the gaslight in the hall.

'Eloise! My darling girl. What brings you out on a night like this? And with the babies too.' Grace Monkham held the door open wide. 'Bring them in out of the cold.'

Eloise pushed the perambulator into the porch and collapsed in tears in her mother's arms.

Grace stroked her hair, holding her daughter to her bosom. 'Oh, no, Ellie. It isn't – it can't be . . .'

'Ronnie's dead, Mama. His sh-ship went d-down with all hands in the Ch-China Sea.'

'What's wrong, Grace?' Jacob Monkham came out of his study, holding a copy of *The Times* in his hand. 'What's happened?'

Grace held up her hand. 'It's Ronnie. There's been a terrible disaster at sea. Have we got any medicinal brandy, Jacob?'

'I'll see if there is any in the chiffonier. Take her into the parlour and sit her by the fire. She looks perished.' Jacob disappeared into the dining room on the far side of the hall.

'There, there, darling,' Grace murmured, leading Eloise into the welcoming warmth of the parlour. 'Sit by the fire and Papa will bring you something to make you feel better.'

Eloise collapsed into the comfort of a red-velvet wingback chair by the fire, 'My babies, Mama. It's too cold for them in the porch.'

'Don't worry, my dear. Janet will look after them. It's you I'm more concerned with at the moment.' Grace tugged at an embroidered bell pull. 'Do you feel up to talking, Ellie?'

Eloise fished in her pocket for a handkerchief, and realising that she had forgotten to bring one, she looked to her mother. Without the need to be asked, Grace took a clean square of white lawn from her pocket and pressed it into Eloise's hand with a rueful smile. 'In all your life, Eloise, I have never known you to have a hanky when you needed one. You were always like that even as a child.'

Eloise blew her nose and was composing herself to tell her mother everything when Janet, the cook-general, put her head round the door. She glanced at Eloise and her sandy eyebrows shot up to her hairline. She cast a questioning glance at Grace. 'What's up?'

Grace hurried over to her, lowering her voice. 'There's been a tragic loss at sea, Janet. Will you take the babies upstairs and put them to bed in Ellie's old room?'

Eloise attempted to raise herself from the chair but her legs would not support her. She gulped and sniffed. 'Mama, they cannot sleep in a proper bed. They'll roll out and hurt themselves, besides which I really ought to take them home.'

14

'Nonsense, I won't hear of it. This is still your home, and you must stay for tonight at least. You are in no fit state to be alone, darling.' Grace motioned to Janet to go about her business. 'You know what to do, don't you, Janet?'

'I should think I ought to, ma'am. Having looked after you since you was a girl and Miss Eloise since the day she was born, I think I can still remember how to make up a bed for the little ones in drawers from the chest.' Janet tossed her head and her white mobcap wobbled dangerously on top of her frizzy, pepper and salt curls. 'Leave it to me, Miss Eloise, and don't you fret.'

She bustled out of the room, passing Jacob in the doorway. He carried a brandy bottle in one hand and three small glasses in the other. He put them down on an occasional table and poured out three tots, handing one to Eloise and one to his wife. He downed the third in one gulp. His bushy white eyebrows knotted together over the top of his aquiline nose. 'So there's no hope then, Eloise?'

She sipped the brandy and the fiery spirit caught her at the back of her throat, making her cough. 'N-none at all, Papa. The *Hellebore* went down in a t-typhoon with the loss of all h-hands.' She mopped her eyes with the hanky. 'I'm sorry, I c-can't stop crying.'

'I am sorry, my dear.' Jacob patted her awkwardly on the shoulder. 'You know that I didn't approve of your marriage to Ronald, but I am grieved by your loss. However, in time I am sure that . . .'

Grace laid her hand on his arm. 'Not now, Jacob. Eloise does not need a sermon at this moment in time.'

'I only meant to offer words of comfort, Grace.'

'Perhaps they will be more welcome tomorrow, my dear, after the poor girl has had a good night's sleep. Why don't you go back to reading your newspaper and leave her to me.' Grace reached up to kiss him on his whiskery cheek.

'Very well, but tomorrow I will offer up prayers in church for the departed.'

Grace pushed him gently towards the doorway. 'Of course you will, dear. But right now I think that Eloise's physical needs are more important. I doubt if she's had supper, or if she's had anything to eat at all today.'

His stern countenance melted just a fraction. 'Trust you to be practical, Grace. I'll be in my study if you need me.' He left the room, casting an anxious glance at Eloise and shaking his head. 'Very sad, very sad indeed.'

'Now, darling,' Grace said gently. 'Everything will be taken care of. Take off your boots and I'll fetch a warm mustard bath for your feet, and Janet will make you some supper when she's seen to the children.'

'Thank you, Mama, but I couldn't eat a thing.'

'You must keep your strength up, if only for the children's sake.' Grace paused with her hand on the doorknob. 'I can only imagine how you must be feeling at the moment, Ellie, darling. But the pain will grow less in time, believe me.'

Eloise managed a weak smile. 'I expect you're right, Mama. But part of me just refuses to believe that Ronnie is gone forever.'

Grace's dark eyes filled with tears and her lips trembled. She nodded her head and slipped quickly out of the room.

For the rest of the evening, Eloise drifted between disbelief and despair. She seemed to have regressed into childhood again as Grace and Janet fussed over her with tempting little dishes of food, a hot mustard bath for her icy feet, and a warm crocheted blanket to wrap around her shoulders. The interior of the old vicarage was slightly shabby and the furniture might not be in the latest fashion, but it was a warm and welcoming home filled with many memories, most of them happy. When it was time for bed Eloise was touched to find that Janet had warmed the sheets with two stone hot water bottles, and one of her mother's frilled lawn nightdresses had been laid out on the satin coverlet. A coal fire burned brightly in the grate, making companionable crackling sounds, and the air in the room was fragrant with the scent of dried lavender.

Joss and Beth were sleeping peacefully in two large drawers taken from the oak tallboy, and Eloise leaned over to kiss their plump cheeks before climbing into her old bed. She turned off the gaslight and snuggled down beneath the covers, watching the shadows on the walls created by the flickering firelight. She could smell her mother's scent in the fabric of the nightgown, and the starched white sheets were as smooth as glass. It was all so familiar and comforting, but Eloise knew there was no going back. She was not the young girl who had dreamt of becoming a teacher, of love and romance with a fairytale ending when she married her prince. She was the widowed mother of two very young children; she had a home of her own and she must now make a life for herself. She knew that she could rely on her parents for help, although if the truth were told she had always been a little scared of Papa, whose mind seemed to be on a loftier plane than that of ordinary secular folk. Eloise closed her eyes, but she was certain that she would not sleep a wink.

When the sound of a baby crying awakened her, Eloise sat bolt upright in bed. At first she could not remember where she was, and when she recognised the room she could not think why she was here. Then it all came flooding back to her and it was not just the bitter chill of the

January night that made her shiver. Beth's cries were becoming more insistent and Eloise swung her legs over the edge of the bed, moving carefully so as not to disturb Joss, and she lifted Beth up in her arms. Wrapping her shawl around her shoulders, she returned to the warmth of her bed, where she sat propped up on pillows while Beth suckled hungrily. Eloise closed her eyes, comforted by the physical closeness of her baby and the feeling of the small mouth tugging insistently at her nipple. Whatever happened, she would protect her children. Things might look bleak now, in the small hours of the morning, but she would find a way to support both them and herself. If she could get some kind of teaching post in the church school, perhaps Mama and Janet would help look after the children in the daytime. They could return home to Myrtle Street at night, and she would not be completely dependent on her parents. She would talk it over with them in the morning.

Next morning at breakfast, Eloise broached the subject but the reaction she received was far different to the one she had anticipated. Mama looked stricken and Papa pushed his plate of buttered eggs and bacon to one side, barely touched. He cleared his throat and rose from the table, pacing the floor with his hands clasped behind his back. 'This comes at a most unfortunate time, Eloise.'

'I don't understand, Papa.'

Grace reached out to touch Eloise's hand. 'Your father has something to tell you, Ellie. We weren't going to mention it yet. I mean, with things as they are . . .' Her voice trailed off and she cast a beseeching look at her husband. 'Jacob, I think you ought to tell her exactly what you plan to do.'

Eloise looked from one to the other and cold fingers of fear clutched at her heart. 'What have you to tell me? Please, just say it, Papa.'

Jacob came to a halt by his chair and he sat down suddenly, as if his legs had given way beneath him. 'There's no easy way to say this, particularly at a time when you are not quite yourself. But you must know that I have not been particularly happy working here in London. I didn't want to leave my parish in Dorset but I did my duty and uprooted us all to come here to this filthy, vice-ridden place.'

Grace frowned at him. 'Just tell her, Jacob.'

'Some time ago, Eloise, I applied to the Missionary Society for a posting to Africa. Nothing came of it for a while, and then I heard recently that I had been accepted. To put it briefly, in two weeks' time your mother and I are leaving on a ship bound for Mombasa. We will be gone for at least two years before we are eligible for home leave, and it could be even longer.' Jacob picked up his teacup and took a mouthful of tea, which he swallowed convulsively. 'I have been called, Eloise. I have to go.'

Stunned and disbelieving, Eloise looked to her mother for help. 'No, surely not. I can't believe that you would both go so far away, especially now.'

'My dear, I don't want to leave you, but I have no choice.' Grace bowed her head and her fingers plucked at the starched napkin lying on her lap. 'I have to go, my love.'

Eloise leapt to her feet. 'But I need you here, Mama. You can't desert me.'

A broken sob escaped from Grace's lips. 'Oh, Ellie. If only things were different.'

Jacob glared at Eloise, his brows lowered. 'That's enough, Eloise. Your mother must do her duty and accompany me on my mission. I cannot abandon my calling just because you have lost your husband. I warned you against marrying him, but you wouldn't listen to me. Now you must live with the consequences of your foolish liaison.'

'Papa!' Shocked by his violent tone, Eloise could only stare at him in dismay. 'How can you speak to me like that?'

'Jacob, please.' Grace held her hand out to him. 'You're making things worse.'

'Eloise is a grown woman now. She has children of her own and she will have to follow the path in life which she has chosen. You have another family, Eloise. Your children have grandparents in Yorkshire. They must take some responsibility for their son's wife and children.'

Eloise faced her father across the breakfast table. 'I would sooner die than go to live with them, Papa. Ronnie's mother hates me, I know she does.'

'Really, Eloise. Don't be so dramatic,' Jacob retorted angrily. 'When we met at the wedding I thought she was a sensible, down to earth woman, and she went out of her way to be pleasant.'

'Maybe to you, but I know that she would rather that Ronnie had married a plain Yorkshire girl, not a soft southerner.'

Jacob rose to his feet, scowling. 'This is hysterical nonsense. You are overwrought.'

Grace pushed her chair back from the table and she went to stand beside Eloise. 'Stop it, both of you. This is all wrong. We should be helping our daughter, Jacob. We should be comforting her in her loss, not abandoning her to the care of strangers.' She wrapped her arms around Eloise and hugged her. 'My poor girl, it will break my heart to leave you.'

'Stay with me, Mama. Don't follow him to the wilds of the Dark Continent. Stay with me and the children. I can find work. We'll manage somehow.'

Jacob thumped his hand down on the table,

causing the crockery and cutlery to bounce and jiggle. 'That's enough, Eloise. Your mother knows her duty and that is to accompany me on my mission. You are an ungrateful girl and a wicked daughter to try to turn her against me.'

Eloise glared at him over her mother's bent head. They were both sobbing now, but she was also furious. 'How can you stand there and pretend you are a man of God when you treat your wife and daughter like this? You call me wicked, Papa, but I think it is you who are bad and unfeeling, and unchristian.'

'That's enough.' Jacob strode round the table and he caught his wife by the shoulders, dragging her away from Eloise. 'This behaviour will stop now. Grace, I expect better from you. This sort of outburst is unseemly in a woman of your age and station in life. You are behaving like the lowest of the low slum women who rant and rave quite out of control. This sordid, godforsaken part of London has had a terrible effect on both of you, and you will be better off away from here.'

Grace tried to break free from him, but he held her by the wrist. 'Jacob, let me go. You're hurting me. In all our years of married life I have never gone against your wishes, I have followed you wherever your calling led us, but I think you are quite wrong in this. You are putting the needs of others above those of our daughter.'

'I am doing God's will, Grace. You will come with me, and Eloise will go to Yorkshire to live with her in-laws. I am going to my study to write them a letter explaining the situation, and I hope by the time I am done you will have composed yourself and remembered your duty to me.' He slammed out of the room.

Eloise and Grace stood in shocked silence staring at the closed door. Eloise was the first to recover and she placed her arm around her mother's shoulders. 'I am so sorry, Mama. I didn't mean to come between you and Papa. I just can't bear the thought of you being so far away, especially when I need you so much.'

'My darling girl, I would give anything to change the situation, but your father is a stubborn man. Once he has made his mind up to something, I don't think even God himself could dissuade him from his purpose.' Grace's brown eyes were magnified by unshed tears, but her lips quivered in a wry smile.

'Don't go with him, Mama. Stay here with me. I'll work my fingers to the bone to keep us all.'

'I wish it were that simple, but your father needs me and, whether I like it or not, my place is at his side. I just hope that if he finds missionary work not to his liking he will agree to return home. You can be certain that I will do everything in my power to persuade him to come back to England. I wouldn't mind living in the poorest parish in the land if I could be near you and my grandchildren.'

Eloise laid her head on her mother's shoulder, too distraught even to cry. 'Oh, Mama, what shall I do without you?'

Grace hugged her fiercely. 'You will go on for your children, Ellie. As I will go on for you, and one day we will be reunited, I promise you that.'

'Oh, Mama, I wish I was as brave and strong as you. But whatever happens, I'll keep my children with me and I won't go and live with the hateful Cribbs in Yorkshire. I would rather die.'

Chapter Two

Perhaps it was a pang of conscience that had led him to be so unusually generous, but her father had elected to purchase a first class ticket for Eloise and the children. The 'Ladies Only' compartment was reasonably comfortable but Joss was fretful and soon grew tired of standing on the seat to look out of the window. He wanted to toddle about, but not all their fellow passengers appreciated a small child clutching at their knees or falling against them when the train picked up speed or rattled over the points. The clickety-clack of the iron wheels on the rails had lulled Beth to sleep, and as she cradled her in her arms Eloise was thankful for this slight respite as the other ladies in the compartment did not seem to enjoy travelling with small children. Despite her papa's undoubtedly well-intentioned purchase of a first class ticket, Eloise was now wishing that they had travelled second or even third class, where perhaps the other passengers might have been more tolerant. She knew that Beth would be hungry when she woke up, but she was anxious about breastfeeding her baby in the present company. One lady in particular kept sighing and tut-tutting when Joss staggered about in the swaying carriage. Eloise tried to make him sit beside her on the seat, but he soon tired of this and his natural curiosity made him want to explore this strange new environment. The toffee-nosed lady twitched her skirts away from his outstretched hands as he toddled towards her. She glared at Eloise. 'Can't you keep that child under control, young woman?'

'I'm sorry, ma'am,' Eloise said, beckoning to Joss. 'Come here, darling. Come and sit by Mama.'

One of the other ladies murmured something under her breath to her well-dressed companion, and Eloise shot her a darkling look as she reached out to catch hold of Joss's arm. 'He's just a baby,' she said defiantly. 'If you have children of your own you must know what it's like when they are this young.'

The toffee-nosed lady eyed her disdainfully. 'My children had a nanny to look after them.'

A murmur of assent from the other two women acknowledged this barb.

Eloise opened her mouth to retort, but at that moment Beth woke up and began to whimper. Eloise rocked her gently hoping that she would go back to sleep, but Beth was hungry and unwilling to be pacified. Her lips trembled and Eloise could see that she was gathering momentum to scream. The train began to slow down and Eloise prayed that at least some of the ladies would get off at the next station. To her intense relief, they all began to gather their belongings, and when the train ground to a halt they stepped onto the platform in a flurry of starched petticoats, fur and feathers. For a moment Eloise thought she might have the compartment to herself for the remainder of the journey, but a plump, pleasant-faced country woman climbed in at the last moment. She had obviously had to hurry in order to catch the train and she subsided onto the seat, red in the face and gasping for breath. 'That was a close one,' she said, fanning her hot cheeks with her hand. 'I had to run for it and that were an effort for a woman of my size I can tell you.' She settled herself more comfortably in the corner seat. 'You'd think they would put on more carriages when the train was full, wouldn't you? To tell the truth, my dear, I've only got a third class ticket, but all the other compartments were crammed full. You don't mind if I stay here, do you?'

'No, of course not,' Eloise said smiling, but her words were drowned by Beth's angry howls which were now reaching a crescendo and Joss was also beginning to cry.

'Go on, love,' the woman said, nodding at Beth. 'Give Baby what she wants. I've had ten kids of my own so you won't shock me. I'm

Gladys, by the way. Gladys Danby.'

'I'm Eloise Cribb. How do you do?' Eloise hesitated, biting her lip. 'Supposing the guard comes along to check the tickets? It would be so embarrassing.'

'Don't worry, love,' Gladys said, chuckling. 'The guard is my second cousin. He's a married man himself.'

Eloise managed a weary smile. Her nerves were already stretched as taut as violin strings at the prospect of facing her in-laws, whom she had met only once, and that was at her wedding three years ago. Papa had been adamant that she should take her children up to Yorkshire, and, in the end, she had had no choice. When she had returned to the house in Myrtle Street, Eloise had discovered that the landlord had changed the locks and the bailiffs had seized what little furniture she owned. Fanny Higgins had managed to save her clothes and books, which were of little second-hand value, but everything else had been taken in lieu of outstanding rent. It was the final blow that had convinced Papa that the only solution was to send Eloise and her babies to live with Ronnie's parents in their vast Gothic house on the outskirts of Scarborough.

'You can borrow my shawl, love,' Gladys said, heaving her heavy body from the seat. She plucked the shawl from round her shoulders, passing it to Eloise. 'That'll save your modesty.'

Beth's cries were so insistent and real tears were oozing from her eyes, that Eloise felt she had little alternative. She took the shawl and rearranged her clothing so that Beth could suckle. 'Thank you, Mrs er . . .'

'Call me Gladys, if you please. Mrs Danby sounds so formal. My hubby and me have a farm outside of Driffield. Where are you going then?'

Eloise was unused to such open curiosity. People in London were not usually so forthcoming, or so nosey. She was temporarily saved from answering by Joss, who was apparently tired of being well behaved and had decided that Mrs Danby's wicker basket was much more interesting than the view from the window. 'Joss, leave the lady alone.'

Gladys chuckled and lowered the basket so that he could peep inside. 'Don't scold him. He's just curious.' She delved in and pulled out a brown paper bag. 'I've got a buttered bread cake in here. Just the thing to keep a small boy quiet for a bit.' Without waiting to see if Eloise minded or not, she proceeded to break off small pieces and feed them to Joss, who stood by her side opening his mouth to receive the crumbs like a hungry baby bird.

'That's very kind of you,' Eloise murmured, shifting Beth to her right breast and readjusting the shawl.

'Have you come far then, love?' Gladys's

beady brown eyes were alive with curiosity. 'You're not a Yorkshire lass, I can tell that. So where are you headed?'

Eloise hadn't intended to tell her inquisitor anything, but Gladys was undeniably friendly and it was a relief to speak of her troubles openly and without fear of hurting anyone's feelings. The last couple of weeks had been so traumatic and fraught with emotion that Eloise was left feeling drained and exhausted. She found herself telling Gladys about Ronnie's untimely death, and how her home had been snatched from her, of her father's intractable attitude and her mother's grief-stricken tears when they had parted on Euston station. Somehow it was easier to unburden her feelings to a complete stranger than it would have been to a close friend, not that she had any friends other than Fanny. All her girlhood companions and school friends had been left behind in Dorset, and when she was living at home Eloise had been content to keep her mother company. Papa had always been rather stern and aloof, but his attitude had only strengthened the bond between mother and daughter.

Then there had been Janet, who was not only a servant but also an integral part of the family. Janet had been with them for as long as Eloise could remember. The vicarage kitchen in Dorset had been a place of refuge when she had transgressed any of Papa's strict rules or infringed his moral code by truanting from Sunday school or eating chocolate during Evensong. Janet had always been there to spoil her with tasty treats from the larder, or to bandage a scraped knee when Eloise had fallen over in the garden. It had been Janet who had helped her creep out of the house to meet Ronnie without her parents knowing. That had been the first and only time that Eloise had done anything behind her mother's back, and at the start it had only been a bit of fun, an escape from the rather dull routine of daily life. Then she realised that she had fallen madly in love with him, but she also knew that Papa did not approve of the young merchant navy officer, and had hoped that she might marry someone like their staid young curate. Eloise had confessed the whole thing to her mother, desperate to gain her approval, and she had not been disappointed. Mama had understood and had told her to follow her heart – and she had done just that.

Ronnie had made everything so exciting and he had enthralled her with tales of his sea voyages and the foreign lands he had visited. She could still recall the first time he had kissed her. It had been on a starry night beneath a huge harvest moon, although they had been sitting on a gravestone in the churchyard, which was not quite so romantic, but his kiss had set her pulses racing and left her aching for more. A shooting star had pierced the black velvet sky. She had known it was an omen. They were meant for each other and would never be parted. Eloise sighed at the memory.

'I think Baby's had her fill, love,' Gladys said, setting Joss down on the seat beside her. She leaned over to take the sleeping baby from Eloise's arms while she adjusted her clothing. 'The precious little mite! So, you're going to live with your hubby's parents, are you? I don't envy you, lass. I never got on with my mother-in-law, but of course you may be different. It wouldn't do if we was all alike, now would it?'

Eloise snapped back to reality. In her mind she had been reliving the first heady days of discovering love with Ronnie. Gladys's brisk tone brought her down to earth with a bump. She gazed dismally out of the window at bare brown fields flashing past and flicks of white snow piled up in the hedgerows. 'It will be all right,' she said, swallowing a lump in her throat the size of a pigeon's egg. 'I'm sure we'll get by.'

Gladys placed Beth back in Eloise's arms and she retrieved her shawl, hitching it over her shoulders. 'Well, at least you'll be well fed, love.'

Eloise stared at her nonplussed. 'I'm sorry?'

'Well, you would be, wouldn't you? I mean folk round these parts all know about Cribb's meat pies and sausages. A pie and pea supper wouldn't be the same without their tasty steak pies with lashings of good gravy.'

'Meat pies?' Eloise stared at her in surprise. She knew that Ronnie's parents were in trade, but he had never mentioned pies and sausages. In fact he rarely spoke about his family at all. He had gone to sea when he was just fourteen and did not appear to have spent much time at home in the ensuing years.

'You didn't know?' Gladys went back to her seat, chuckling. 'They're famous throughout the East Riding and the whole of Yorkshire come to that. Don't they have Cribb's pies where you come from?'

'I – I'm not sure.'

Gladys picked up Joss and sat him on her knee. 'I think I've got a slice of lardy cake in the bottom of my basket. Shall we see if we can find it?' She allowed Joss to rifle round until he found it, and she broke off a piece for him. 'You don't know much about your in-laws then?'

Eloise shook her head. 'We only met once, and that was at the wedding.'

'Not that I'm one to gossip, but I grew up on a farm near Ganton, which is just a few miles from Scarborough, and folk round there remember when old man Cribb started. He had a pork butcher's shop on the outskirts of the town and then he went on to making meat pies. He's done well for himself has Harcourt Cribb. He's got plenty of brass, so you and the little ones will be seen right.'

Eloise wiped a trickle of milk from Beth's lips. 'I'm sure we will.' Somehow Gladys's words were not much of a comfort to her. If Ronnie's parents were so wealthy, why hadn't he asked them for money when they had needed it so badly? Now there were more unanswered questions buzzing around in her brain. Fortunately Gladys was too busy feeding Joss to carry on with the conversation and they lapsed into silence until the train once again began to slow down.

Gladys wiped Joss's sticky hands and face with the cloth which had covered her basket. 'This is my station coming up, love. I hope it works out for you, I really do. But if ever you need a shoulder to cry on, you'll always find a welcome at Danby Farm, Driffield. Anyone in the village will point you in the right direction.' She stood up, staggering a little as the train reduced speed. 'Goodbye, young Joss. You be good for your ma, do you hear me?' She ruffled his curls and picked up her basket. As the train slowed to a halt Gladys tugged at the leather strap to let the window down. She leaned out to unlock the carriage door and climbed stiffly down to the platform. 'Goodbye and good luck, lass. I think you may need it.' She gave Eloise a cheery wave as the train pulled slowly out of the station.

It was dark by the time they arrived at Scarborough station. Both Joss and Beth were sleeping and Eloise had to summon a porter to help her with her luggage. She stepped down onto the platform with Beth hitched over her shoulder and Joss, still half asleep, clinging to her hand. Eloise gasped as the bitterly cold air hit her lungs. The familiar sooty smell of London had been replaced by the bracing tang of salty air blustering in from the North Sea. The porter stood with her battered suitcase in one hand and her valise in the other. 'Is anyone meeting you, ma'am?'

Eloise could hardly speak as her lips were already numbed with cold. The wind seemed to cut straight through her thin woollen mantle and she cuddled the children closer to her. 'I think so.'

The old man eyed her with some sympathy. 'Let me see if there's a carriage waiting for you then, ma'am. You'll want to get the little ones inside out of the cold.' He led the way along the almost deserted platform to a waiting room where a coal fire blazed up the chimney. 'You wait in here while I go and take a look outside.'

Eloise went to sit by the fire, thankful at least that Beth was still sleeping, and she lifted Joss onto the seat beside her, holding him close as his head lolled against her. She was tired, cold and hungry, not having eaten anything since breakfast, and then she had only managed to swallow a couple of mouthfuls of toast. She could still see the tears glistening in her mother's eyes as she tried to make conversation at the breakfast table. It had been a gloomy meal and Papa had barely spoken at all, except to promise to send a telegram to Cribb's Hall, asking them to meet the London train. A spark shot out of the fire and lay glowing on the tiles in the grate. Eloise stared it at until its bright light turned to ash. That was how her life seemed to be right now. She had left everyone she loved in London, and in a few days' time her parents would be on board ship bound for Mombasa. Mama had promised to write every day, but they had both known that letters could take weeks, even months, to reach England, if at all. Papa's mission was at a place with an unpronounceable name which was many miles from the nearest town. Eloise tried hard not to think about the dangers that might beset them. Wild animals, poisonous snakes, disease – the list was terrifying and endless.

She turned with a start as the door opened. It was not the friendly face of the aged porter but another, equally elderly man, with weather-beaten features that seemed to have been knapped from flint. 'Come with me, missis.' Without waiting for her reply, he picked up her luggage and left the waiting room, leaving the door to swing back on its hinges so that she had to wedge it open with the toe of her boot.

Eloise was too overwrought and nervous to complain. With both children clasped in her arms she followed the old man along the dimly lit platform, out through the main booking office onto the station forecourt where a ponderous and old-fashioned carriage was waiting for them. A young lad who had been holding the horses leapt forward to open the door for her while the coachman tossed her luggage onto the box.

'Here lady, let me hold the young 'un while you get in.'

She was hampered by her long skirts and Eloise reluctantly allowed the boy to hold Joss while she climbed the steps and settled herself on the seat. 'Thank you,' she said, as he laid the sleeping Joss on her lap. 'What is your name, boy?'

'Ted, miss. I'm stable boy at Cribb's Hall.'

'Thank you, Ted.' She managed a wan smile as he grinned at her and tipped his cap before closing the carriage door. She leaned back against the squabs that smelt oddly musty with a faint hint of pipe tobacco and Macassar oil lingering in the well-worn leather, but at least it was a few degrees warmer inside than outside. As the coach lurched forward, Eloise clung to her babies for dear life. She could not imagine what lay before them as the vehicle lumbered onwards, plunging into pitch darkness when the street lights came to a sudden end. It was a moonless night and she could see nothing outside the windows except the flashing of the carriage lamps reflected in the snow, as the carriage jolted over ruts and potholes in the road. She drifted into the sleep of sheer exhaustion but was awakened some time later by the sound of voices and a cold blast of air as the carriage door was wrenched open. Feeling dazed and disorientated, Eloise allowed Ted to take Joss while she stepped down onto hard-packed snow. She blinked in the sudden light from the blazing flambeaux that illuminated the imposing and rather awesome frontage of the Gothic mansion. The leaping flames of the torches reflected eerily in the panes of the tall windows, creating the illusion of lighted candles held in unseen hands as if ghosts were performing a stately dance in the empty rooms. Even the red-brick walls seemed to glow as though the whole building was on fire and the snow surrounding the mansion was tinged with crimson, like spilt blood. Eloise suppressed a shudder as she gazed up at the turrets and gargoyles glaring down at her from the roof.

'Go on up, ma'am,' Ted said, handing Joss back to her. 'They're expecting you in the big house.' He tipped his cap and hurried to answer a summons from the irate coachman. Eloise couldn't hear what the man said, but it was enough to make Ted snap into action. The carriage drew away, heading towards the stable block, and she was left standing alone at the foot of the wide sweep of stone steps with her cases on the ground beside her. For a moment she thought that no one had noticed her arrival, but then the double doors of the main entrance were flung open and a woman in a severe black gown stood in the doorway. She held an oil lamp in one hand and she beckoned to Eloise. 'Come on in then, if you're coming. Or do you want to spend the night on the doorstep?'

Shocked by the woman's brusque tone, Eloise carried the children up the steps, pausing at the top to stare at the person who had addressed her in such a rude way. 'I beg your pardon, ma'am. But I thought I was expected here.'

'Of course you are. Come inside and let me close the door.'

'My luggage,' Eloise protested.

'It will be dealt with, never fear.' She looked Eloise up and down as if she were evaluating the cost of her outfit. 'So you are Ronald's widow.'

Eloise swallowed hard. She had thought this woman must be the housekeeper, but she did not appear to be a servant, despite the chatelaine holding a bunch of keys which hung from her waist. 'I am Eloise Cribb, but you have the advantage over me, ma'am.'

'Such a grand lady and yet only a parson's daughter without two pennies to rub together, judging by the clothes she wears. I suppose our Ronald was taken in by a pretty face.'

'I'm sorry, I don't know who you are, but you have no right to speak to me in this manner.'

'So, you're not as soft as you look. You'll need a bit of spirit if you're going to survive in this house. I am Ronald's aunt, Joan Braithwaite.' She turned on her heel, calling over her shoulder. 'My sister is waiting for you in the parlour. Follow me.'

She led the way across the entrance hall, which was as ornate and oppressive as the exterior of the house. Stuffed animal heads and sets of antlers hung from the oak panelling, and the sound of their footsteps on the red, white and black tiled floor came back as an echo from the dark recesses of the upper floors. Eloise glanced upwards, and for a moment she thought she saw a pale face peering at her over the carved oak balustrade. She quickened her pace in order to keep up with Joan and the feeble gleam of the oil lamp. Joss was snivelling softly with his face pressed against her neck and she could feel his small body rigid with fatigue. Only Beth slept on oblivious of their new surroundings.

Joan opened a door on the far side of the hall

and went inside. Eloise followed her into the large, high-ceilinged room lit by paraffin lamps and candles. 'She's come,' Joan said, setting the lamp down on a side table. 'Can't you stop that child crying? It's making my head ache and you've only been in the house for a few minutes.'

An angry retort rose to Eloise's lips, but before she could speak her mother-in-law rose from her chair by the fireside. She shot a quelling glance at her sister. 'That's our little Ronald you're talking about, Joan.'

'You're mistaken, ma'am,' Eloise said, hardly able to believe her ears. 'My son is called Joseph. We call him Joss.'

Hilda drew herself up to her full height. 'He is Ronald's son and heir, and he will be known as Ronald from now on. You are welcome to stay in my house, Eloise, but you are only here on sufferance because you are the mother of my grandchildren.'

'Ronald should have married a Yorkshire lass,' Joan muttered, scowling. 'We have no time for soft southerners here, miss.'

Looking from one hostile face to the other, Eloise felt as though she had walked into a nightmare. No one in all her life had treated her with such open contempt and dislike. She was numbed with fatigue and faint with hunger. If it had not been so cold and dark outside, and if

Cribb's Hall had been closer to town, she would have walked out there and then. Anger roiled in her stomach. 'You have made it obvious that I am unwelcome here, ma'am. If my presence is so odious to you both, I will leave here in the morning and take the train back to London.'

'That's right,' Joan sneered. 'Run away back to your mama. Except that you cannot, because your folks have abandoned you.'

'That's enough, you vinegar-tongued old witch,' Hilda said, turning on her sister with her lips curled in a feral snarl. 'This is my house and you are here under sufferance too, don't you forget it.'

'I won't forget it because you never let me,' Joan hissed.

'No, I won't, because if I hadn't taken you in you would have had to go into service.'

'I am in service, you bitch. Who runs this house? Answer me that. I do, and I do it for nowt. You won't get cheaper than that.'

'And I have to put up with your miserable face every day of my life,' Hilda shot back at her.

Eloise stared at them in disbelief. They were goading each other like two wildcats. If they had fur she was certain that their hackles would be raised. Any minute now she expected them to tear at each other with their claws. She cleared her throat. 'Excuse me, but all I ask is a bed for the night for myself and the little ones.

Tomorrow I'll leave, and you will never be bothered with us again.'

Hilda turned to her, staring as if she had only just realised that she was in the room. 'No need to adopt that high and mighty tone, my girl. You are Ronald's widow and the mother of his children. Where else would you go?' She retired to her chair by the fire. 'Joan, ring for Mabel and ask her to show Eloise to her room. You can take the little ones to the nursery.'

'What?' Eloise backed towards the door, holding the children to her with real fear gripping at her heart. 'No, I won't hear of it. My babies sleep with me. I won't have them shut up in a strange room.'

Joss began to wail in earnest, and awakened by his shrieks so close to her ear, Beth too began to cry.

'Good grief, are we to put up with this?' Joan stormed. 'The sooner you get a girl from the village to act as nursemaid the better, Hilda.'

'My babies sleep with me,' Eloise shouted, close to panic. 'And I will care for them. I won't have them looked after by a stranger.'

'You'll do as you're told when you're under my roof,' Hilda said with narrowed eyes. 'But, for tonight perhaps it's best that you keep them with you.'

'Thank you,' Eloise said weakly. Her nerves were shattered and she was close to collapse. All she wanted to do was to lie down in a warm bed holding her babies in her arms. Tomorrow, she would think about what to do next, but for now sleep was what she craved.

Joan pushed past her to tug at a bell pull. 'The girl will take you to your room.'

'Have you eaten?' Hilda demanded. 'We have our tea at five o'clock on the dot. We keep regular hours here in Cribb's Hall, but if you and the boy need food, Mabel will oblige.'

Inexplicably, this modicum of kindness brought tears to Eloise's eyes. 'Thank you, ma'am.'

'If you're to live here with us, then you shall call me Mother,' Hilda said, inclining her head regally, as if this were a huge honour. 'And I shall call you Ellen, which is a good no-nonsense name.'

'Ellen,' Joan repeated, rolling the name round her mouth with relish, as if it were a sugared almond or a piece of chocolate. 'That's better. I can't be doing with fancy names myself.'

'Call me what you please,' Eloise said tiredly. 'I'm sure I don't mind at all.'

Joan wrenched the door open in answer to a timid knock. 'Mabel, show Mrs Ellen to her room.'

'And fetch her some tea and bread and butter,' Hilda said with a condescending smile. 'Never let it be said that we don't keep a good table at Cribb's Hall.'

As Eloise walked past her, Joan caught hold of her arm, her bony fingers pinching Eloise's flesh. 'You may call me Aunt Joan, though don't think that gives you cause to take liberties, young woman. You are as nothing in this house. Nothing.'

Eloise had no answer for this. Her main concern was for her little ones and she followed the flickering trail of candlelight as Mabel crossed the hall and mounted the stairs. Up and up they went until Eloise lost count of the number of stairs they had climbed. Her room was on the third floor, just below the attic rooms where the servants slept. It was cold and had a damp, fusty smell, as if it had been unused for a long period of time. Heavy, mismatched furniture loomed out of the shadows creating monster shapes, and the sash window rattled as if shaken by unseen hands. Mabel lit the candles on the mantelshelf and on the washstand. 'It's a bit cold in here, but I'll put a match to the fire and it'll soon take the chill off the room.'

'Thank you, Mabel.' Eloise went over to the big brass bedstead and sat down, still clutching the children to her. Beth needed a feed and Joss was so tired that he was merely snivelling in a low moan that went straight to her heart.

Mabel soon had the kindling alight and it sent tongues of flame licking round the coals. She sat back on her haunches and turned to Eloise with a shy smile. 'You'll have a right good blaze in a few minutes.' Scrambling to her feet, she approached the bed. 'I'll fetch you summat to eat, and some tea. Would the little fellow like some hot milk?'

'Thank you, Mabel. That would be just the thing.'

'And I daresay a jug of hot water wouldn't go amiss. They say below stairs that you've come all the way from London on the train. Nasty dirty things them trains are, belching steam and spitting out bits of cinder to fly into your eyes. I've only been on one once, but that were enough. Give me the pony and trap any day.'

Eloise's head was beginning to pound, but she managed a weak smile. 'You're very kind, Mabel. But I wouldn't want you to get into trouble with Miss Braithwaite.'

Mabel tossed her head. 'Oh, her! A right nasty piece of work is Miss Joan. Sour old puss she is, it's no wonder she's an old maid.' She clapped her hand over her mouth. 'I'm sorry, miss. I've said too much. I was forgetting you're family.'

She backed towards the door, bobbed a curtsey and had left the room before Eloise had a chance to answer. Beth's cries could no longer be ignored and Eloise was thankful that she would now be able to suckle her baby in peace. As she sat propped up on pillows, with Beth at her breast and Joss curled up at her side, Eloise closed her eyes, shutting out her surroundings. Outside the house the wind moaned and sighed like a soul in torment. Joss had his thumb plugged firmly in his mouth and his cheeks were tear-stained and grubby. Eloise stroked his damp curls back from his forehead. Ronald, indeed! How dare the hateful woman change her son's name to that of his dead father? How could she even think of shutting two small children up in a nursery far away from their mother? Ronnie would not have stood for such treatment, but then he was not here. She was their only surviving parent and it was up to her to care for them, feed them and protect them from the cruel outside world. She had not been looking forward to placing their lives in the hands of her in-laws, but she could never have imagined the hostility with which she had been greeted.

What would she do? If she left Cribb's Hall, where would she go? Her tired brain could not find an answer. Tomorrow she would think of a way, but one thing was certain, she would not stay in this hateful house a moment longer than was absolutely necessary.

Eloise opened her eyes and was suddenly wide awake. The room was in almost complete darkness, except for the pale outline of the window. She sensed rather than saw a movement at the foot of the bed where Beth lay sleeping in a drawer from the chest. Joss was curled up at her side like a warm puppy, but the sound of breathing was not his, nor was it her own. There was someone else in the room and Eloise snapped upright in the bed. 'Who's there?' Her voice sounded thin and quavery, like that of a frightened child. She sprang from the bed to snatch Beth from her makeshift cradle, and as she did so she felt a waft of ice-cold air rush past her, and the sound of a smothered sigh, or it could have been a muffled giggle. Then there was silence. With Beth in her arms, Eloise tiptoed across the room to close the door, which had been shut when she went to bed but was now wide open. She stood for a moment, listening for sounds of movement in the house, but all was quiet. She had no clear idea of the time, but she tried to rationalise her terrifying experience; perhaps a maidservant had entered the room by mistake? It would be easy enough in the dark. There were no such things as ghosts, she told herself as she closed the door. It must have been a draught which caused it to open, and her overactive imagination had done the rest. With Beth in her arms, she hurried back to bed.

Chapter Three

'I've brought you a cup of tea, miss.'

Eloise opened her eyes, focusing with difficulty. This time it was not a phantom that had awakened her, it was the reassuringly solid and friendly shape of Mabel who stood at her bedside, holding a cup and saucer in one hand and a candle in the other. It was dark outside and Eloise blinked at her, wondering why she had been woken up when it was obviously still the middle of the night. 'What time is it?'

Mabel grinned as she put the cup on the bedside table. 'It's six o'clock, miss. We're early risers here. The master leaves for the factory prompt at seven every day except for Sunday. The mistress has breakfast at ten minutes past seven precisely, so I thought I'd give you time to get up and dressed. She's a stickler for time, as she is in all things.' Mabel bustled over to the fireplace and began clearing the ashes from the grate. 'I'll soon get the fire going. Then I'll fetch you some hot water for washing.'

Eloise sat up in bed and wrapped her shawl around her shoulders. Beth was awake now and hungry. Joss was still sleeping, and Eloise moved carefully so as not to disturb him as she put Beth to her breast. 'Thank you, Mabel,' she said softly. 'You're very kind.'

'Why no, miss. I'm just doing my job.'

Eloise reached out for her tea and took a sip. 'What time do you start work, Mabel?'

'Half past five, miss. Except on Sundays when it's six o'clock. Why do you ask?'

'Oh, nothing. I must have had a nightmare because I thought someone came into my room last night. The door was wide open although I know I closed it before I got into bed.'

'I daresay it were the wind, miss.' Mabel scrambled hastily to her feet. 'That's done. I'll fetch you the hot water now.'

She bobbed a curtsey and had sped from the room before Eloise had a chance to continue the conversation, leaving her even more mystified than before. In her heightened state of emotion, she was quick to notice the subtle change in Mabel's demeanour. Perhaps she was protecting someone? It was just possible that one of the servants walked in their sleep. That would be a commonsense explanation and it might explain Mabel's reluctance to speak.

Joss stirred and opened his eyes. 'Mama?' He clambered to his feet, wrapping his chubby arms round her neck to give her a rather moist kiss on her cheek.

'Hello, sleepyhead.' She brushed the tip of his button nose with her lips. 'Be a good boy for Mama while she sees to Beth, and then we'll get dressed and go down to breakfast.' Eloise kept her tone light, but the thought of facing her mother-in-law and Joan filled her with trepidation. Then there was Ronnie's father. At the wedding he had appeared to be so overshadowed by his domineering wife that he had merged into the background. In fact she could hardly remember him at all. He had seemed nice enough, and had welcomed her to the family, but Hilda Cribb had been tight-lipped with disapproval, even though she had made an obvious effort to be pleasant. Maybe she had wanted to show her best side to her son's new wife and family, or perhaps people changed as soon as they entered the grim portals of Cribb's Hall. If his wife was anything to go by, Harcourt Cribb would probably beat his servants, whip his horses and ill-treat his workers. Eloise hitched Beth over her shoulder and rubbed her back until she emitted a satisfactory burp. Joss was jumping about on the bed with unbounded energy: at least their ordeal of yesterday did not seem to have upset her children. Eloise swung her legs over the side of the bed and laid Beth in her makeshift cradle while she dressed. Her skirt and blouse were sadly creased and crumpled, and felt rather damp, but they would have to do.

She would ask Mabel to iron the rest of her clothes and hang them somewhere warm to air – if there was such a place in this cold, damp house.

Half an hour later, Eloise made her way to the dining room, following Mabel's somewhat vague directions. With Beth on her hip and Joss holding her hand, she counted the doors leading off the entrance hall, which seemed just as forbidding in the early morning as it had done last night. The stuffed deer heads stared glumly down at her and a fox with its tongue hanging out between bared teeth seemed to be smirking at her discomfort. Dark oil paintings of Highland scenes with stags at bay and another depicting dead pheasants, trophies of the shoot, did nothing to lighten her mood. After trying several wrong doors, finding two locked and one that turned out to be a cloakroom, Eloise at last came to the dining room. The aroma of fried bacon, sausages and hot toast assailed her nostrils and she realised that she was ravenously hungry. So was Joss, judging by the way he dashed towards the table and attempted to climb onto the nearest chair.

'Joss, darling. Wait for Mama.' She stopped short as she realised that they were not alone in the wainscoted dining room. Seated at the far end of the vast mahogany dining table was her father-in-law, a small, grey-haired man with side whiskers and a moustache which sat oddly on his round cherubic face, as if someone had stuck them on for a joke. He half rose from his seat, and he was smiling. 'Come and sit down, lass. I'm sorry I wasn't here to welcome you last evening, but I had business in Leeds and didn't get home until past midnight.' He motioned her to take a seat beside him at the table.

'Thank you, Father-in-law.' Eloise lifted Joss and set him down on a chair. She did not immediately take a seat, but paused awkwardly, not quite knowing how to express her condolences to Mr Cribb on the loss of his son. It was hard even to think of Ronnie without breaking down into tears. 'I – I just wanted to say – I mean – Ronnie's death came as such a blow to me, I can only imagine how it must feel to his parents.'

Harcourt stood up, mopping his eyes with a red silk handkerchief. 'Nay, lass. There's no need for you to fret about us. Mother and me have always known the risks that our Ronald took by choosing a life at sea. Don't think we don't feel his loss as keenly as any other parents, but we're private folks and we keep our tears to ourselves.' He held out a chair for her. 'Sit down and have summat to eat. Heaven knows you've no meat on your bones as it is. We don't want you fading away, now do we?' He chuckled deep in his throat and he patted her on the shoulder. 'What can I get you, lass? Bacon and sausage – our own make of course. Scrambled eggs, kippers – we have the lot here. We keep as good a table as any of the gentry round these parts, and I swear by a good breakfast as being the best start to the day.'

'Some scrambled eggs would be lovely, thank you.'

Harcourt hurried off towards the chiffonier, which was positively groaning beneath the weight of silver serving dishes. A maidservant answered the tug of a bell pull and he sent her off to bring a fresh pot of tea and some toast. He returned with a plate piled high with scrambled egg for Eloise and a smaller one for Joss. 'Here,' he said, holding out his arms. 'Let me hold the little lass while you eat. She's a right bonny little thing, isn't she? I'll wager she has blue eyes just like young Ronald here. They take after our Ronnie in that respect.' He cleared his throat and sat down, cradling Beth in his arms.

'I don't want to hold you up,' Eloise murmured, choosing to ignore the fact that Harcourt had called Joss 'young Ronald', but it made her even more determined to have the matter out with her mother-in-law at the first opportunity. She continued to spoon egg into Joss's mouth. He could feed himself but it was a messy business and she didn't think that Hilda would be too pleased if she came down to breakfast and found her grand dining room turned into a pigsty.

'I'm the boss,' Harcourt said blithely. 'I can

afford to come in late if I choose. I don't do it very often because I believe an idle master makes idle servants, but today is an exception. I just wanted to tell you that from now on you must think of Cribb's Hall as your home.'

'Thank you, but I'm not sure Mrs Cribb would agree with you. I think maybe it's too soon after losing Ronnie for her to take kindly to me.'

'Nay, lass. You mustn't think that way. My Hilda can be a bit forthright at times, but she's a fine woman, and I'm sure she meant no harm. Some folks have difficulty in dealing with their loss, and Hilda thought the world of our Ronnie.'

Eloise swallowed a mouthful of egg, wiping her lips on the starched white linen napkin. 'I'm sure you're right, sir.'

'I know I am. Just give her time. I know it will be strange for you at first and you must miss your mother and father, but you'll soon settle in and adjust to our ways.'

Eloise nodded, unable to speak. The mention of her parents had only added to her anguish, bringing the ready tears to her eyes. She struggled to regain her self-control. The last thing she wanted was to disgrace herself in front of this kindly man, who reminded her so much of Ronnie. Not that they looked alike – Ronnie had been tall and broad-shouldered with rugged good looks – but there was something in his father's smile and a light in his blue eyes that was a heartbreaking reminder of his son.

Harcourt took a gold half-hunter watch from his waistcoat pocket. 'My goodness, look at the time. I must be going.' He stood up and laid Beth gently in Eloise's arms. 'Keep your chin up, lass. And don't let Joan bully you. She's not a bad old stick at heart, but you've got to stand up to her.' He bent down to ruffle Joss's curls. 'You be a good lad for your mother, young Ronald. One day, son, all this will be yours, and when you're older I'll teach you everything I know about the pie business. You'll grow up to be one of them kings of industry, young man, or my name isn't Harcourt Cribb.' There was a definite swagger in his step as he left the dining room.

Eloise had listened to him with a leaden feeling in her stomach. So they were all in on the plot to turn Joss into a substitute for his father, even the kindly Harcourt. Ronnie had thwarted his father's plans for him to go into the wretched pie business, and unwittingly, and from no choice of her own, she had placed her young son in the family's power. A frightening glimpse of the future flashed before her eyes. Joss was not yet three, and yet his life was already being mapped out for him. Her hand shook as she held a cup of milk to his lips. The vision of her son being moulded into a pale replica of his grandfather was almost too much to bear. Suddenly her appetite deserted her and she pushed the plate of food away. As she wiped a smear of egg from Joss's face, Eloise grew even more determined to make her stand. No one was going to take her son from her. He was going to grow up to be his own man and she would fight to the death to protect him.

She turned her head with a start as the door opened and Joan stalked into the dining room with an ominous frown on her face. 'The nursery is the correct place for feeding children,' she snapped. 'There'll be greasy fingerprints all over the best silk damask after this, mark my words. That material on the seats was imported especially from abroad and it cost a small fortune. It's not for the backsides and sticky fingers of little tykes like our Ronald. You should have waited in your room until you were told what to do, young lady.'

Eloise rose slowly to her feet, controlling her temper with difficulty. 'What gives you the right to speak to me like this? I've done nothing to offend you, Miss Braithwaite.'

'You took our Ronald from us, that's what you did. He were the apple of his mother's eye and you fair broke her heart.'

'That's just not true. Ronnie left home to join the navy when he was little more than a boy. From what he told me he rarely ventured home, and now I can understand why.'

'Your mother should have washed your mouth

out with soap when you were young. How dare you use that tone to me?'

'You leave my mother out of this. She is a wonderful woman and has never done anything wrong in her whole life.'

Joan folded her arms across her flat chest and tossed her head. 'And she's gone away and left you to live off the charity of others. I don't call that the action of a wonderful mother.'

Eloise put her arm around Joss as he began to whimper. 'You're frightening my boy. Leave us alone.' She pushed past Joan and led a sobbing Joss from the dining room.

'That's right,' Joan called after her. 'Run away when you know you are losing the argument. I know your sort, Eloise Monkham. You don't deserve to bear the name of Cribb.'

With Beth clutched in one arm, Eloise hoisted Joss onto her hip and she hurried across the hall and up the stairs. She was out of breath and very much out of sorts when she reached the relative sanctity of her room. Mabel had been in the process of making the bed and she looked up in alarm. 'Goodness, miss. What's wrong?'

Eloise lowered Joss to the floor and subsided onto a chair by the fireplace, rocking Beth in her arms. Mabel had been generous with the coal and its blaze sent out a comforting warm glow. Outside the window the snow was falling in huge feathery flakes. In the distance, Eloise could see the snow-covered wolds stretching as far as the eye could see. She realised then that she was marooned here in this icy wilderness, and there was no hope of escape, at least until the weather improved.

'Can I do anything, miss? Shall I fetch you a cup of tea, or summat?'

Eloise looked up into Mabel's anxious face and she smiled. 'No, thank you. I'm all right.'

'Let me hold the baby, miss. I know how. I've got six younger brothers and sisters at home and me older brother, Ted, is stable boy here. I daresay you met him last night. He usually goes out with Mr Riley, the coachman, since the old fellow's rheumatics play him up in winter something terrible.' Mabel held out her arms and Eloise allowed her to take Beth. Almost immediately her screams quietened and she gazed up at Mabel with apparent interest.

'She likes you,' Eloise murmured, not knowing whether to be pleased or hurt by the way her baby daughter took to a stranger.

'She's a little flower, that's what she is.'

Joss seemed to sense his mother's distress and he climbed onto her lap. Smiling, Eloise dandled him on her knee, tickling his tummy which always made him chuckle. He obliged her with a deep belly laugh. 'You're such a good boy, Joss. And I won't allow them to shut you up in their horrid old nursery.'

Mabel shifted Beth to her shoulder and rocked her gently, patting the baby's back with a gentle hand. 'They've had the maids scrubbing it from top to bottom, miss. It's not such a bad place really, and I've heard tell that's what the gentry do. Grand ladies give their children over to nursery maids the moment they're born.'

'Well, I'm not a grand lady, and I've no intention of allowing strangers to bring up my children.'

'If you don't mind me saying, miss, you won't have much choice in the matter. If Miss Braithwaite and the mistress want it that way, that's the way it shall be.'

'We'll see,' Eloise said grimly. 'They might be able to bully the servants, but I won't stand for it.'

'You're very brave, miss. I shouldn't like to cross Miss Braithwaite.' Mabel pulled up a stool and sat down at Eloise's side. 'It's common knowledge that she hasn't been the same since she was jilted at the altar. You won't let on that I told you, will you?'

'No, certainly not.'

Mabel glanced over her shoulder as if afraid that someone might overhear her words, and she lowered her voice. 'Well, it weren't exactly at the altar, but as good as. He were a right handsome devil, so our mum said, but it turned out that he already had a wife in Whitby, and they say he had another in York, although I can't say for certain. Miss Joan were a good-looking woman then, according to our mum, and she were all set up to inherit the butcher's shop when their father passed on.'

Momentarily diverted from her own problems, Eloise was intrigued. 'Go on.'

'Well, Miss Joan thought she was too good to work in the shop and so she stayed at home, but her sister, her that's the mistress now, was not so proud. She served in their father's shop alongside Mr Cribb, who was only a butcher's boy then. When old man Braithwaite died of a heart attack all of a sudden like, Mr Cribb took over the business but he married Miss Hilda Braithwaite and not her sister Joan. They lived above the shop and Miss Joan went off sudden-like to stay with her aunt in Bridlington – to mend her broken heart, they say. Anyhow, the master made enough money to buy the shop off Miss Joan, and when she returned from Bridlington a few years later, the master built this fine house and she's been living here ever since.'

The sound of footsteps outside the door made Mabel suddenly alert and she leapt to her feet. 'I'd best get on or I'll be for it.' She laid Beth back in her cradle before going to the door and peeping out. She turned to Eloise with a worried frown. 'I won't be a moment, miss. There's summat I must see to before I finish off in here.'

She slipped out of the room, closing the door behind her.

Eloise waited for a moment, half expecting Joan to erupt into her room and scold her for keeping a servant from her duties, but the sound of footsteps grew fainter and it seemed that Mabel had been called away. Eloise thought no more about it, or of Joan Braithwaite's personal tragedy that had blighted her life. She could feel little sympathy for a woman who had shown her nothing but hostility. Joss jiggled about on her knee, reminding her to play with him, and she obliged, but her mind was racing as she tried desperately to think of a way to escape from Cribb's Hall. She had no relations to whom she could appeal for shelter; both Mama and Papa had been only children and their cousins had either emigrated or were long dead. She had no money of her own, and no qualifications other than that of a reasonably good education.

Gradually, lulled by the rocking movement and the warmth from the fire, Joss fell asleep in her arms. Eloise rose slowly to her feet and laid him in the middle of the bed, with pillows on either side to prevent him from rolling off and hurting himself. There was an old-fashioned escritoire placed beneath the window, and on further investigation she discovered a bottle of ink and a quill pen. She unpacked her leather writing case, which had been a twenty-first birthday present from Ronnie, and she settled down to compose a letter to her mother. The simple act of putting pen to paper brought Mama suddenly so close that Eloise felt her presence almost as if she were in the room. She wrote slowly and chose her words carefully. The harsh truth would only upset her mother and Eloise made light of her trials, omitting entirely the harsh way in which she had been received by her mother-in-law and Joan. She was so intent on her task that she did not hear the door open behind her.

'So, I take it you are writing to your sainted mother.'

The sound of Hilda's strident tones made Eloise jump and a large blot of ink splattered across the sheet of paper. She put the pen down, controlling the urge to snap back at her mother-in-law. Taking a deep breath she rose to her feet, facing Hilda with a defiant lift of her chin. 'Yes, ma'am. I was writing to inform her that we had arrived safely.'

'And to complain of your treatment too, no doubt.'

'No, ma'am. I would not want to distress my parents by telling them that I was an unwelcome guest in your home.'

Hilda inclined her head slightly. 'You have that much backbone at least.' She went to sit in the chair by the fire. 'I admit that I was not best pleased when your father wrote informing us that you and the children would be coming to stay. He might be a man of God, but he assumed a great deal when he foisted you on us in our state of grief.'

'I realise that it is very hard for you, Mother-in-law, as it is for me. I believe that we both loved Ronnie equally, and suffer a great deal from his loss.'

Hilda's tight-lipped expression did not falter. Her eyes were like cold steel as she regarded Eloise with an unflinching stare. 'I'm a plain woman, Ellen. I speak my mind, and I am sure you would not want it any other way. I neither know you, nor do I care about you, but I do care about Ronald's children and I will do my duty by them. Young Ronald and Elizabeth will have the best of care and the finest education that our hard-earned money can buy. As Ronald's widow you have a right to stay in our home, but the children will be raised as we think fit. You may see them as much as you please, providing that you do not spoil them. They will have the upbringing suited to their situation in life.'

Eloise gripped her hands together behind her back so that Hilda would not see how they trembled. She dug her fingernails into her palms to keep the tears of anger and frustration at bay and she controlled her voice with difficulty. 'And what is that, pray?'

'Don't take that hoity-toity tone with me. I know that you and your folk look down on us because we're in trade. Well, we might have made our brass from selling sausages and meat pies, but our fortune was gained through honest toil. Young Ronald and his sister will be looked after by a nanny until they are old enough to be sent away to school. Ronald will learn to be a gentleman as well as a man of business, and the girl will be educated like a proper young lady. You should be grateful to us, Ellen. We could have turned our backs on you, as your parents have done, but I know my duty. So long as you abide by my rules, you will get on well enough in this house. Go against me, and you will find out that Hilda Cribb can be a hard woman.'

'I do not want my babies to be looked after by a nanny,' Eloise said through gritted teeth. 'I will not allow it.'

Hilda rose majestically to her feet. 'You won't allow it? Listen to me, young lady. While you are living under my roof you will do as I say, and I say that the little ones will be raised in the nursery. Of course you will have to be there to feed the girl child, until she is weaned, and they will be brought down for an hour or so at teatime, just like they do in the best of houses. We have come up in the world, Ellen. Harcourt and I are no longer mere butchers, we are the new gentry, and we have standards. If you don't like it, you know where the door is, but Ronald's children stay here. Do I make myself plain?'

It was all too plain, and Eloise soon discovered that she was powerless to prevent her mother-in-law from carrying out her wishes. A girl had been found in the village and next day she was ensconced in the nursery as the nanny, and the children were put into her care. No matter how much Eloise railed against the decision, no one paid her any attention. Even Harcourt brushed aside her complaints when she cornered him after supper that evening. He was not as brutal as his wife, but he put Eloise's anxiety down to nerves and the fact that it was not so long since she had given birth to Beth. He patted her on the arm and with a kindly smile told her that she would soon get used to it, and even enjoy the freedom that she would have with her babies cared for by another.

By way of a slight concession, Eloise was allowed to have her possessions moved to a room adjacent to the nursery, and Hilda only sanctioned this for practical reasons as Beth could not yet go through the night without being fed. 'But,' she had added, having given way just an inch, 'you will not find the room as comfortable as the one you were given in the first place.'

This was patently true, as Eloise found her belongings had been taken to a room half the size of the previous one, situated at the back of the house, overlooking the stable yard and out-buildings. There was a single bedstead with a plain white coverlet, a deal washstand, tallboy and a wheelback chair which would have been better suited to the kitchen than to a lady's bedroom. A rag rug by the bed was the only splash of colour on the brown linoleum which covered the floor. Eloise realised that she might have won the last battle but she was rapidly losing the war. Hilda might have appeared to have given way but in reality had consigned her daughter-in-law to a servant's room. However, that was the least of Eloise's worries. She cared for nothing as long as she was close to her babies, and she made herself as comfortable as possible in the austere surroundings of her new room. The one advantage was that she would be able to hear the children if they cried in the night, which was just as well as it turned out that the new nanny, a hefty country girl with a bovine expression and, Eloise suspected, very little between her ears, was an extremely heavy sleeper.

On the first night away from her children, Eloise had just only just fallen asleep when she was awakened by the sound of Beth's wailing. She leapt out of bed, not stopping to put on her wrap or even to snatch up a shawl, and she hurried into the nursery to find both children awake and sobbing. Nancy Thwaite was sound asleep, lying on her back and snoring. Eloise picked up the children and took them into her room. The fire had gone out and the room was bitterly cold. The curtains barely met in the middle of the window and the sashes rattled as the wind howled round the house, hurling handfuls of sleet at the glass. Eloise scrambled into the bed, holding the children close to her until their sobs quietened. Beth fed hungrily and Joss snuggled up against Eloise's side and was soon asleep.

Eloise had intended to take the children back to the nursery, and she had certainly not meant to fall asleep, but she was awakened suddenly by someone shaking her shoulder. She opened her eyes to find Nancy standing over her holding a lighted candle in her hand which was shaking so much that melted wax was dripping onto the coverlet. 'What's wrong?' Eloise roused herself with a feeling of panic, which subsided as soon as she realised that Beth was sleeping peacefully in the crook of her arm and Joss was breathing softly at her side. 'What's the matter, Nancy?'

'I saw her, mistress. She were leaning over the cots. I thought she'd taken the babes.'

Eloise could barely understand what she was saying, as Nancy's teeth were chattering together and she was shaking from head to foot. Eloise raised herself on her elbow, speaking softly so as not to frighten the children. 'As you see, they were with me. You must have been having a bad dream.'

'Nay, mistress. She had come for them, the ghost of Cribb's Hall. I seen her with me own eyes. She were six foot tall at least and she had eyes like burning torches. I tell you, I seen her, mistress.'

'Nonsense, girl. There are no such things as ghosts. You must have had a nightmare.'

'I were warned about the wandering woman, mistress. They told me below stairs that she roams the house by night. I tell you I seen her just now.'

Eloise chuckled with sheer relief. 'They were teasing you, Nancy. It sounds to me very much like a joke, a rather cruel one, but a joke nevertheless. Go back to bed, like a good girl.'

Nancy shook her head vehemently. 'I'll not sleep in there. I'm scared.'

'Very well, then I'll sleep in the nursery with the children. Hold Beth for me while I get out of bed. You shall sleep in here tonight, Nancy. I will take your bed and I will prove to you that it was just a bad dream.'

Eloise put the children back in their respective cots. Then she went over to the fireplace and, on discovering a few glowing embers, she used the bellows to get the fire going again. With a satisfying blaze warming the room and creating a comforting circle of light, Eloise climbed into the bed that Nancy had recently vacated and she lay down to sleep feeling much happier now that she was in the same room as Joss and Beth. She smiled to herself as she thought of Nancy's vivid imagination and the enormously tall ghost with flaming eyes.

She must have fallen into a deep sleep for when she was awakened by a soft shuffling sound, Eloise sat bolt upright. In the faint glow of the dying fire, she saw something that made her gasp with fright. Leaning over Beth's cot was a tall figure dressed in a flowing white robe. Eloise stuffed her hand in her mouth to stifle a scream.

Chapter Four

Without stopping to think, Eloise took a flying leap off the bed and dived across the floor with the ferocity of a female tiger protecting her young. 'Go away,' she screamed. 'Leave my babies alone.'

With a strangled cry, the woman crumpled to the floor, covering her head with her arms as if to ward off a rain of blows. Eloise stopped short, staring at the cowering figure in a mixture of shock and dismay.

'Don't hurt me, missis.' The muffled voice sounded oddly childlike and the woman was trembling violently.

Eloise laid a tentative hand on her shoulder. 'I won't hurt you. Get up and let me see your face.'

Obediently, the woman rose slowly but she backed away from Eloise, keeping her head bowed. Although the poor creature was head and shoulders taller than she, Eloise was oddly touched by her obvious distress. Now that she knew her children were safe her heart had ceased to thud painfully against her ribs and she was able to think rationally. 'Are you a servant in this house?'

The woman shook her head.

'Then who are you? What are you doing here?'

Staring down at her bare feet, the woman began to weep. 'I did no wrong. Don't punish me.'

'Sit down, please.' Eloise pulled up a chair, hoping that the distressed creature would sit before she collapsed onto the floor. 'Don't be frightened. No one is going to harm you. Won't you at least tell me your name?'

'My baby,' the woman whimpered, burying her face in her hands. 'I came to find my baby. I heard her crying, I know I did.'

Realising that the woman was past reasoning, Eloise approached her cautiously. She took her gently by the hand and led her to the chair. 'I am sorry, but that is my baby, not yours.'

'N-not mine? But I heard a baby crying.'

'The baby you heard is mine. Her name is Elizabeth, but we always call her Beth, and my son Joseph is sleeping in the other cot. We call him Joss and my name is Eloise. What do they call you?'

'Ada, that's what she calls me.'

'And who is that, Ada?'

'Miss Joan. She'll be cross with me and beat me. You won't tell her that you saw me, will you? I just wanted to see my baby, but you say she's not here.'

Eloise slipped her arm round Ada's thin shoulders. 'No, dear. Your baby is not here. I am so sorry.'

'I'll go now,' Ada said, rising unsteadily to her feet. She bent her head to peer into Eloise's face. 'I like you.'

'And I like you too,' Eloise said gently. Even in the dim light she could see that Ada's face was smooth and unlined like that of a young child, although she was clearly an adult and could have been any age from twenty to forty. 'Shall I take you back to your room, Ada?'

'N-no, missis. I'll get a whipping if she finds out I've been wandering again. I'm not supposed to wander. They mustn't see me.'

'Who mustn't see you?'

'The others. The servants and the other people in the house. I have to stay in my room.'

'All right,' Eloise said slowly, not wanting to alarm her further. 'But I still think I should see you safely to your room and make sure you are tucked up in bed. Shall I do that, Ada?'

As trusting as a small child, Ada held out her hand for Eloise to hold. 'My mama used to put me to bed. She's dead, you know; that's why I had to come to live with Miss Joan.' Ada clamped her hand over her mouth. 'I shouldn't have told you that.'

Eloise led her to the door. 'I won't tell a soul.'

Seemingly satisfied with this, Ada allowed

Eloise to accompany her along the corridor and up the staircase to the servants' quarters on the top floor. At the very far end of a long narrow passage, Ada opened a door that led into another and even narrower passage. It was obvious from the musty smell and the mesh of cobwebs dangling from the ceiling that this part of the house was little used. It was so dark that Eloise could only just see the pale glimmer of Ada's white nightgown as she blundered onwards, seemingly oblivious to the claustrophobic atmosphere. When they finally came to a halt, Eloise thought at first that Ada was kept hidden away in some sort of garret, but on entering the room she was amazed to discover a large airy space. Thick pads of snow covered the roof windows, gleaming palely in the light of several oil lamps, and a fire burned in the grate behind a brass nursery fireguard. A large wooden rocking horse stood in the middle of the floor, and the stark white walls were adorned with what appeared to be pages torn from a scrap book. In one corner stood an iron bedstead covered with a bright patchwork quilt, and rag dolls with painted smiles on their faces lay on the rumpled pillow. The bare floorboards were dotted with brightly coloured rugs and littered with children's books.

Ada loped over to the bed and leapt upon it, scooping up an armful of dolls and cuddling them to her flat chest. 'Mine,' she said, smiling for the first time. 'I made them all, as I made the baby that grew in my tummy.' Her face crumpled and tears spilled from her pale eyes. 'They took her away from me. I keep looking for her but I can't find her.'

Touched beyond measure by this simple child-woman, Eloise went to put her arms around Ada and she gave her a hug. 'I am so sorry, my dear. That must have been dreadful for you.'

Ada wiped her nose on the sleeve of her cambric nightgown. 'They say she died, but I don't believe them. My mama died and she was cold and stiff, but my baby was soft and warm and she had blue eyes, like me. I'll find her one day, I will.'

'I'm sure you will, but I think you ought to get into bed now and try to sleep.' Eloise pulled back the coverlet and held it while Ada obligingly snuggled down between the sheets. It was like dealing with Joss, Eloise thought sadly as she bent down to kiss Ada on the forehead. 'Goodnight, my dear. Sleep tight – don't let the bed bugs bite.' It was a silly saying from her earliest memories of childhood, but it seemed appropriate and it drew a responsive chuckle from Ada, who curled up with an armful of dollies and closed her eyes.

Eloise crept out of this strange other world and closed the door softly behind her. It was bitterly cold on the top floor and her thin nightgown felt like ice as it touched her bare skin. She was terrified of losing her way in the dark, but some deep instinct and a desperate need to return to her children guided her feet through the maze of corridors as she hurried back to the nursery. After making certain that Joss and Beth were sleeping peacefully, Eloise crawled into bed, but she could not relax. She was chilled to the bone, and as she lay there shivering her mind was filled with questions. Who was Ada? Why would Joan Braithwaite want to keep her hidden from sight? Obviously the servants had a vague knowledge of Ada's existence, but both Mabel and Nancy seemed to think of her as a ghost rather than as a flesh and blood being. Eloise was intrigued and curious but also saddened to think that such a simple soul could be treated with such callous indifference. There was little she could do about it, but she knew she would not be able to rest until she had discovered the dark secret which kept poor Ada a virtual prisoner. Of one thing she was certain: the person who had all the answers was the formidable Joan.

Next morning Eloise was already up, dressed and had given Beth her morning feed when Mabel arrived with a jug of rapidly cooling water for the washbowl and a scuttle filled with coal for the fire. 'Goodness me, missis. You never slept in here, did you? What will Miss Joan say?'

Eloise patted Beth's tiny back as she lay over her shoulder. 'Miss Joan won't know and I doubt if she would care. Nancy had a bad dream and so I allowed her to sleep in my room. Anyway, I prefer to be in here with my children.'

Mabel put the jug down on the washstand. 'She won't like it, missis. I can tell you that for nowt.' She hefted the scuttle over to the fireplace and went down on her knees, energetically riddling the cinders. 'And I almost forgot, but Miss Joan told me to tell you that breakfast is served and you must go down to the dining room right away.'

'I'd rather take my meals here in the nursery with the children. You can tell her that when you go downstairs, Mabel.' Eloise laid Beth on the bed while she turned her attention to Joss, who was not yet dressed and was toddling around the room exploring his unfamiliar surroundings.

Mabel shook her head. 'I doubt if she'll allow it. She's a right stickler for rules is Miss Joan.'

'And my children come first,' Eloise said firmly. 'If you're too scared to tell her, then I'll do it myself.'

Mabel answered by ducking her head down and sweeping the ash into a dustpan. Eloise resigned herself to another battle with Miss Joan. Leaving Joss and Beth with Nancy, who had finally put in an appearance still slightly bleary-eyed with sleep, Eloise went downstairs to face her mother-in-law and Joan in the dining room.

'You're late,' Hilda snapped. 'I've told Hopkins to take the food back to the kitchen. You'll have to eat in there with the servants if you can't be bothered to keep to proper meal-times.'

Joan looked up from buttering a slice of toast. 'I warned you, young lady. Don't say as how you weren't warned.'

Eloise faced them with her hands clasped firmly in front of her. 'I came to tell you that I would prefer to eat in the nursery with my children.'

'What you would prefer is neither here nor there,' Hilda said grimly. 'Children eat in the nursery and grownups eat in the dining room.'

'Yes,' Joan added with a spiteful sneer. 'If you want to be treated as a member of this family then you will abide by the rules, Ellen.'

'My name is not Ellen. It is Eloise and my son's name is Joseph, not Ronald.' She had not meant to raise her voice, but she was furious with these two hard-faced women who pretended to have loved Ronnie. She doubted if they knew the meaning of the word.

Joan rose to her feet and her cat-like eyes blazed with malice. 'You will be called whatever we choose to call you, lady. And you will learn manners while you are living here under my sister's roof. Your presence will be tolerated even if it isn't welcome, but you will do as you are told.'

'I am not a child, Joan Braithwaite,' Eloise said in a low voice. 'Nor am I a simple-minded soul who can be locked up in an attic room and kept out of sight.'

Joan collapsed back onto her seat and her pale face flushed wine red and then paled to ashen. 'You've been snooping, you little viper.' She turned to her sister. 'You heard how she spoke to me, Hilda. Say summat, for pity's sake.'

Hilda shook her head and her lips twisted into a snarl. 'I told you it would come out sooner or later, Joan.' She rose from the table. 'It's your mess, sister. You clean it up.' She stalked towards the door, but as she passed Eloise she paused and her voice lowered to a hiss. 'And you will mind your manners, Ellen, or you will find yourself turned out on the street without a penny to your name. It's a long walk to Africa.' She slammed out of the dining room.

'You little bitch,' Joan snarled. 'See what you've done. Why did you have to come here and stick your nose into our business?'

'It was not from choice,' Eloise retorted angrily.

'No, I don't doubt that. Ever since you set foot over the threshold, you've made it plain that you consider us to be beneath you. Well, a fine family you come from, I must say. They couldn't wait to be rid of you.'

'That is not how it was. Don't you dare criticise my parents.' Eloise drew a deep breath. Controlling her temper with difficulty, she realised that Joan had skilfully manoeuvred the conversation away from herself. 'But we weren't talking about my family, were we? I'm not surprised that you want to conceal the fact that you have a poor soul locked away upstairs and that you mistreat her.'

Joan rose slowly from the table and she advanced on Eloise with a martial gleam in her eyes. 'You don't know what you're talking about.'

'Then tell me why you have Ada shut away like a lunatic, when she is obviously no danger to anyone.' Eloise held her ground. She was a little scared of Joan, but she was also extremely angry. She met Joan's basilisk stare without blinking, even though inside she was quaking. 'Well? What do you say to that?'

'I say that you are a meddling little busybody who ought to keep out of other folks' business. But I'll tell you this for nowt, Ellen. That creature is my cousin, Ada Braithwaite, who was left orphaned some years ago and who would have been locked up in a madhouse if I and my sister had not taken her in.'

Eloise took a step backwards as Joan leaned so close to her that she could feel her hot breath on her cheek. 'I – I'm sure she is no danger to anyone.'

'So you think, lady. Well, let me tell you I have the scars to prove it, when all I have ever shown her is kindness. Don't be fooled by our Ada. She can be meek and mild as anything one moment, and a raving madwoman the next.'

'She said you beat her.'

'And you would take the word of a lunatic above mine?' Joan tossed her head and her lips curled in a sardonic smile. 'Mind your own business, Ellen. And don't meddle in matters that do not concern you. Now, go to the kitchen and see if Cook has saved you some breakfast. If not, you'll have to go hungry until dinner time, which is served prompt at midday. Anyway, I have better things to do than to stand round wasting my breath on the likes of you.' With that, Joan walked away with a swish of starched petticoats, leaving Eloise standing alone in the dining room, staring after her. Somehow she did not quite believe Joan's story. She could not put her finger on it, but there was something in it that did not ring quite true. That Ada was disturbed was obvious, and that she had the mind of a child was also apparent, but Eloise could not believe that Ada was a violent lunatic.

In the days that followed, life settled into a basic if dull routine. Hilda and Joan remained in ignorance of the fact that Eloise slept in the nursery with her children. Nancy was delighted to have a bedroom all to herself and Mabel had been sworn to secrecy, so the flouting of Hilda's wishes passed unnoticed. Eloise spent her days mainly in the nursery with Joss and Beth, only leaving them for her compulsory meals in the dining room, or occasionally during their nap times when she took the opportunity to venture outside the house in order to get a breath of fresh air.

Joan largely ignored her and if Hilda spoke it was only to deliver some homily, or occasionally to enquire as to 'our Ronald's' health. She still refused to call him Joss, and she showed little interest in Beth, who was merely a girl. Eloise soon learned that she could not win with her mother-in-law. If she said nothing, she was accused of sulking. If she attempted to voice an opinion she was branded a know-all, and if she retaliated when goaded, she was told to hold her tongue and given a lecture on ingratitude.

In the evenings, when Harcourt dined at home, Eloise was grimly amused to note that Hilda and Joan treated her quite differently. On these occasions, Hilda masked her animosity towards Eloise with such skill that an onlooker would have been convinced that she was a concerned and affectionate mother-in-law. Joan was not so hypocritical, but she refrained from making the barbed and bitter comments that were her customary way of speaking to Eloise. Unfortunately business called all too often and Harcourt rarely returned home until long after the evening meal was over, but Eloise was well aware that without his benign influence life at Cribb's Hall would have been intolerable.

As the days turned into weeks, Eloise came to rely more and more on Mabel, who kept her up to date with everything that went on below stairs and amused her with scraps of gossip from the village. As the weather began to improve, Eloise had let slip to Mabel that she would love to take the children out walking, but this was almost impossible, as Joss could not walk very far and Beth was too heavy to be carried for long distances. One sunny morning in late March, Mabel came to the nursery bubbling with suppressed excitement, and she insisted that as it was such a lovely day it would be criminal to stay indoors. With the children well muffled against the biting east wind, Eloise followed Mabel down the servants' stairs and out into the stable yard, where she discovered that Ted was waiting for them grinning from ear to ear. With a flourish that would have done credit to a stage magician, he snatched a piece of sacking from a sturdy wooden pushcart. 'There, ma'am. What do you think to that?'

Mabel nudged Eloise in the ribs. 'It's for the little 'uns,' she whispered. 'Our Ted made it all by himself.'

'I daresay it isn't as grand as them peram-bulators that the rich folk have for their babes,' Ted said, puffing out his chest. 'But it'll save you having to carry the little lass, and Master Joss can have a ride when he gets tired of walking.'

For a moment, Eloise couldn't speak. She had grown hardened to the verbal abuse from Hilda and Joan, but this extraordinary act of kindness made her want to cry.

'Don't you like it, ma'am?' Mabel asked anxiously.

Eloise searched for a handkerchief and found she had none. Her mother's words came back to her, and in her mind's eye she could see the tender smile on her mother's lips as she had passed her a handkerchief, saying that she had never known her to have one when needed. It was these little flashes of memory that were so poignant, but also acted as a painful reminder of their enforced separation. Eloise swallowed hard and dashed the tears from her eyes with the back of her hand. 'It's beautiful, Ted. It's absolutely splendid and you are so kind – I don't know what to say.'

'Steady on, ma'am,' Ted said, blushing to the roots of his hair. 'It's only a cart made out of old crates.'

'And if I fetch a cushion and some blankets, it'll be comfortable enough,' Mabel added hastily.

Lost for words, Eloise hugged Mabel, and to

Ted's obvious embarrassment she took him by the hand and kissed him on the cheek. 'You are the kindest boy I have ever known,' she murmured, smiling through her tears. 'If Mabel will be good enough to get something to sit Beth on, we'll go for a lovely long walk.'

Mabel scurried off into the house and Ted backed away with a sheepish grin. 'Glad to be of service, ma'am. It were only a few bits of wood, after all, and I like working with me hands.' A shout from Riley in the stables made Ted hurry back to work and Mabel came scurrying from the house with a crocheted blanket and an old cushion covered in cat hairs. Eloise made Beth comfortable and they set off for their first proper outing since they arrived in Yorkshire. After that she took the children out as often as the variable weather conditions allowed, and with fresh air and exercise she found that her spirits began to revive.

In the evenings, after the nightly ordeal of a meal with Hilda and Joan in the dining room, Eloise would put the children to bed and sit by the fire in the nursery, writing letters to her mother or reading old copies of *The Young Ladies' Journal*, which she knew that Hilda and Joan studied avidly, although neither of them seemed to have profited from their reading. It was on one of these evenings, when the wind was soughing round the house and rain was lashing at the windows, that Eloise was startled by the sudden opening of the door as Ada erupted into the room, gasping for breath as if she had run all the way from the far corner of the house. She closed the door and stood mutely, shivering in her thin nightgown and clutching a book to her bosom.

Eloise put aside her writing case and smiled, holding out her hand. 'Come and sit down by the fire, Ada. You look perished.'

Ada came slowly towards her, holding out a dog-eared copy of a book of fairy tales. 'My book,' she murmured as she knelt down by Eloise's side. 'Pretty pictures.'

Eloise studied the crumpled illustrations and she nodded her head. 'Very pretty, Ada. Do you like fairy tales?'

'Dunno,' Ada said, staring at her blankly. 'I can't read. My mama used to read to me until she fell asleep and didn't wake up again.'

Eloise reached out tentatively to brush a lock of mouse-brown hair back from Ada's forehead, and her heart swelled with pity for her. 'Would you like me to read to you, dear?'

Ada nodded eagerly and settled down at Eloise's feet to listen to the story of Cinderella with rapt attention. She sobbed broken-heartedly when the Ugly Sisters were cruel to Cinders and she clapped in childlike glee when the glass slipper fitted Cinderella and she married her prince.

After this, Ada brought her books to the nursery every evening and she would sit, warming her bare feet by the fire, listening to Eloise as she read her tales about beautiful princesses and handsome princes. She showed such enthusiasm that Eloise began teaching her to read, and to her surprise, Ada was an apt pupil. Although Eloise could elicit very little more about Ada's childhood, apart from the fact that she had been born and raised in Bridlington, any mention of Joan and their relationship upset her so much that Eloise thought it best to let the matter lie.

Every evening, after Ada had gone back to her room, Eloise would spend an hour or so writing to her mother. The only address she had was of the mission headquarters in Mombasa, but she hoped that they would forward the letters to wherever it was in the depths of Africa that her parents had been sent. It was too much to hope that she would receive news from Mama in the near future, as mail took many weeks to arrive, but it gave her comfort to put pen to paper. She wrote mainly of the little milestones that Joss and Beth had passed. Beth had cut another tooth and Joss had drawn a picture on his slate; it might look like a squiggly line to anyone other than a doting mother, but Eloise could see quite clearly that it was meant to be a puppy just like the one that Mabel had smuggled into the nursery. Joss had fallen totally in love with it and had cried bitterly when the puppy had to be returned to its mother in the kennels where Mr Cribb kept his hunting dogs, but Mabel had promised faithfully to bring it to the nursery whenever possible.

One day, Eloise thought, as she folded the letter and tucked it into an envelope, we will have a home of our own again. Joss and Beth will have a puppy and a kitten too if they want one. She sighed. It was just a dream, but holding on to it was the only thing that kept her from despair. She addressed the envelope and placed it in a drawer out of sight of Nancy's prying eyes. Eloise suspected that Nancy reported everything that was going on to the servants below stairs, but by the same token Eloise knew that she could trust Mabel. Tomorrow she would give the letter into Mabel's hand and she in turn would give it to Ted, who would take it to the post office. He always travelled on the box with Riley when he drove Mrs Cribb on her frequent shopping expeditions to Scarborough, and since Riley was not as agile as he had been, Ted would run errands for Hilda, carrying her purchases or holding the horses' heads while Riley popped into the pub for a beer and Hilda met friends for afternoon tea. Sometimes Joan went on these outings, but Eloise was never invited.

April came, bringing with it skies of a peerless blue as winter gave way to spring, but the weather was capricious and sudden showers could come from nowhere, along with blustering winds that swept across the wolds, bending trees and cutting through outer garments to chill the unwary walker to the marrow. On fine days, Eloise still took the children out into the grounds, but Harcourt was no gardener and he had put all his money into the building of the house. Although trees had been planted in order to form a windbreak, they were still little more than saplings and the rest of the land had been put down to lawn. Sheep grazed on the grass, keeping it short, but this was not the sort of garden that Eloise remembered from her childhood in the gently rolling countryside of Dorset.

As the weather improved, Eloise put the children in Ted's cart and ventured outside the walled perimeter of Cribb's Hall to the open countryside where swathes of yellow daffodils grew wild on the hillsides, and the hedgerows were softened by a haze of green buds. Eloise had discovered a pleasant walk by the river, which was overhung with catkins dangling from willow trees and its banks were studded with primroses. On one of these outings in late April, when the sun shone brightly and there was no hint of rain, Eloise made the bold decision to take Ada with them on their walk. Hilda and Joan had gone off in the carriage to Scarborough for luncheon with friends and a shopping expedition. It would be teatime at least before they returned.

With Mabel's assistance, Eloise managed to get Ada dressed in outdoor clothes borrowed from one of the taller housemaids, who just happened to be one of Mabel's many cousins, and could be trusted not to tell. Mid-afternoon was always a sleepy time in Cribb's Hall, when the maids had a couple of hours' rest before starting up again later with preparations for dinner, lighting fires and turning down beds. It had been relatively easy to smuggle Ada out of the house unnoticed, and Eloise felt a degree of elation and a sense of triumph in her achievement. She could not openly defy her mother-in-law or Joan, but at least she could do something to alleviate the tedium of Ada's dreary existence. As they came to the riverbank, Eloise was rewarded by Ada's sudden outpouring of joy as she began to gambol about as crazily as any of the spring lambs that could be seen in the distant fields. Her ungainly limbs seemed quite out of control as she waved her arms above her head, raising her pale face to soak up the warmth of the sun. Eloise was afraid that Ada might tumble into the fast-flowing river, but she could not help laughing as she watched her antics. Joss ran about too and Beth sat up in the cart chuckling and clapping her hands. It was such a happy scene that Eloise felt her spirits rise. The harsh reality of the winter seemed far behind them at this moment, and she experienced a surge of optimism which was not entirely due to the freedom of being outside Cribb's Hall, or the beautiful spring weather. She pulled the cart over to a tree stump and she sat down to reread the letter from her mother, which had arrived only that morning.

It had been posted in Gibraltar not long after the start of her parents' long journey. It was a determinedly brave missive, filled with love and hope that their enforced separation would be short, but there were water marks where Eloise could only guess that Mama had shed a few tears, as she had herself when she had first read the letter. She read it and reread it, closing her eyes and trying to picture the cabin, which Mama said was dreadfully cramped, and the bunks which were hard and too narrow, but apparently her father was in his element. He held services on board every Sunday and was convinced that he was following his true calling. He could not wait to arrive in Africa and begin his work as a missionary. Eloise folded the letter, raised it to her lips and kissed it before tucking it away beneath her stays, close to her heart.

Joss chose this moment to take a tumble and began to howl, but before Eloise could get to him, Ada had picked him up and was cradling him in her arms. 'Poor boy,' she crooned. 'All better,

Joss. Kiss it better.' She angled her head and kissed his sore knee.

Eloise approached her slowly, not wanting to alarm her, but Ada was teetering very close to the water's edge and in her concern for Joss she was quite unaware that one step backwards would send them both tumbling into the rushing waters of the river. Joss had stopped crying and was smiling up into her face as he tugged at a lock of her long, lank hair.

'Ada, dear,' Eloise said softly, 'bring Joss over here.'

'My baby,' Ada said dreamily. 'Joss is my baby.'

Moving as stealthily as a hunter, Eloise reached her just as Ada swayed backwards and she grabbed her by the arm, dragging them both away from imminent danger. 'Don't be frightened, Ada. You were too near the riverbank, my dear.'

Ada glanced over her shoulder and her lips trembled. 'She pushed me into the sea. The water came over my head.' She thrust Joss into his mother's arms. 'Joan pushed me into the sea.'

Horrified, Eloise cuddled Joss to her breast. 'No, she couldn't have done such a thing, Ada. It must have been an accident.'

Ada shook her head and tears spurted from her eyes. 'No, she wanted me dead. She took my baby and she wanted me to die.'

Beth had begun to cry and clouds had

obscured the sun. The snow melt running off the hills had turned the river water to a milky grey and the willows swayed in the wind. Eloise bundled a protesting Joss into the cart beside Beth and she took Ada by the hand. 'Come, dear. I think it's going to rain. We'd better hurry home.' For a moment she thought Ada was going to rebel, and Eloise realised with a tug of dismay that there would be little she could do if Ada refused to accompany her back to Cribb's Hall. She might have the mind of a child, but she had the body of a fully grown woman and the advantage of height. Eloise gave Ada's hand a comforting squeeze. 'If we go home now I'll get Mabel to bring us cake for tea, and this evening I will read *Alice in Wonderland* to you.'

'I'd like that,' Ada said meekly, and she allowed Eloise to lead her back the way they had come.

By the time they reached Cribb's Hall, dark clouds had obliterated the tops of the hills and the first drops of rain were beginning to fall. They were only halfway along the gravelled carriage sweep when Eloise heard the rumbling of wheels and the pounding of horses' hooves. There was nowhere to hide and even if there had been she was hampered by the cart's small wheels and by Ada, who had been walking slower and slower as they approached the house. She stopped dead, refusing to budge. 'Won't go back to my room. Don't want to.'

'Now, Ada, dear Ada, don't be difficult,' Eloise said breathlessly. The carriage was drawing closer every second. 'We need to go indoors or we'll get wet, and you'd like a slice of chocolate cake, wouldn't you? It's your favourite.' Eloise tugged at Ada's hand, but she had a set stubborn look on her face, and Joss was trying to climb out of the cart, which had set Beth off and she was howling.

The carriage had slowed down as Riley drove it through the great wrought-iron gates, but the pair of matched greys could move much faster than she, and Eloise could only drag Ada out of the way and pull the cart to safety. A screech from Joan confirmed her worst fears – they had been seen. Obeying orders, Riley drew the horses to a halt. Ted leapt from the box to open the carriage door and put down the steps. He cast Eloise an anxious and apologetic glance over his shoulder as he helped Joan alight quickly followed by Hilda.

'I knew it,' Joan shrieked, pointing a trembling finger at Eloise. 'You evil little bitch. What in hell's name do you think you are about?'

Hilda pushed Joan aside. 'You've done it this time, lady. I'll get Mr Cribb to sort you out once and for all, but I'm telling you now, it'll be the workhouse for you. If I have any say in the matter, you will leave Cribb's Hall today and never return.'

'I will go,' Eloise stormed. 'And gladly. I hate this place and I hate both of you. I'll take my children and we'll never ever set foot in this place again.'

Hilda's small eyes glittered with malice. 'Oh, you'll go all right, lady. But our Ronald's children will stay here with us, where they belong.'

Chapter Five

In the small room that her father-in-law called his study, but which Eloise had always suspected was a bolt-hole where he could hide from the women in the house, Harcourt stood with his back to the fire looking distinctly put out. Eloise could not tell whether he was angry or merely embarrassed as she stood before him, waiting for the promised tirade to begin. She knew that the version of events as told by Hilda would be biased against her, and Eloise held herself stiffly erect. She cleared her throat as a nervous tickle made her want to cough. 'There's no need to say anything, Mr Cribb. I know where I'm not welcome and I will be leaving this house first thing in the morning.'

'Nay, lass. I know things haven't been easy for you, but I didn't want it to come to this.' Harcourt held his hand out in a tentative gesture and then let it drop to his side. 'Won't you reconsider? I mean, a few words of apology to Mrs Cribb would go a long way to heal the rift.'

Eloise shook her head. 'You know nothing of what has been going on, sir. I don't want to speak

97

ill of Ronnie's mother, but Mrs Cribb and her sister have made it plain from the start that I am unwelcome here. They want to take Joss away from me and bring him up as a substitute for his father. Well, I won't have it. Joss isn't a carbon copy of Ronnie and I will take him away from this place and bring him up as I see fit.'

'But, lass, how will you live? Where will you go?'

'I have friends in London,' Eloise lied. 'I will find work.'

Harcourt's expression softened. 'Bravely said, but what could a slip of a girl like you do to earn a living?'

'I can teach. I've had a good education and I can pass it on to others.'

'I don't doubt it, lass. But who will care for the little ones while you are working? Why not leave them here with us, at least until you are settled?'

'Never!' Eloise backed towards the doorway. 'I would sooner leave them outside the doors of the Foundling Hospital than leave them to the tender mercies of Mrs Cribb and her sister.' She stopped, biting her lip. 'I'm sorry if I offend you, but if you'd seen the way that poor creature upstairs is treated you would be ashamed, really ashamed. Her mother would be turning in her grave if she saw how Ada was locked away out of sight and beaten for the slightest reason.'

'Nay, I won't have that. It's true Ada has to be

kept away from the rest of the household, but that is for her own safety as much as anything, for who knows what the simpleton would do if she were allowed to wander free.'

'Whatever the reason, I am sure her mother would not want her to be treated in this way. Your hunting dogs are better cared for, Mr Cribb.'

A wry smile curled Harcourt's lips. 'Quite probably, lass. It's said that I have the finest pack of fox hounds and beagles in the county. I may not be gentry, but I enjoy riding with the hunt.' His smile faded and was replaced by a worried frown. 'But that's by the by, and you are misinformed about Ada's mother, she is certainly not dead, and she would not deliberately mistreat her own daughter.'

Jolted out of her anger, Eloise stared at him in surprise. Had she heard him correctly? 'You say her mother is not dead?'

'She were very much alive half an hour ago.' A flicker of humour momentarily lit Harcourt's blue eyes. 'Ada is our Joan's daughter, born out of wedlock more than twenty years ago. It's not something that we like to dwell on, but I'm sure that the servants have told you all about Joan's unfortunate past.'

'They said she was jilted, but no mention was made of a child.'

'That's because it isn't common knowledge. All

families have their secrets and skeletons in their cupboards. When the truth came out about the man she was due to marry, Joan went to live with her Auntie Mary in Bridlington to escape from the gossips. When it turned out that she was in the family way, it was thought best that she stayed on after the child was born. My sister, Mary, had been recently widowed and Ada grew up thinking that she was her mother and not our Joan. Then five years ago Mary died, and there were no one to look after Ada, so we brought her here.'

Eloise could hardly believe her ears. She stared at Harcourt in disbelief. 'Why are you telling me this now?'

'Knowing the truth of the matter might help you to understand our Joan a bit better, and you really should not judge her too harshly. She only did what she thought was best for Ada.'

'Ada says she had a baby and it was taken from her. Is that all a fantasy?'

Harcourt moved slowly round his desk to sit in the padded leather chair. 'Ada has the mind of a child and the body of a woman. Mary was ailing for a long time, and not in the best position to keep an eye on the girl. It's true, Ada did bear a child, but there was no question of her being capable of raising it herself. It were found a good home, and Ada was told that it were stillborn. We thought that were the kindest thing to do in the circumstances.'

'Kind?' Eloise stared at him in disbelief. 'You think that was kind? That poor young woman is constantly looking for her baby; she is broken-hearted and suffers terribly. You weren't being kind, you were just saving face. I thought you were different, but I can see that you are just as bad as Hilda and Joan. You only think of your good name and of making money. Well, I'm ashamed to be related to you, even by marriage, and I can't wait to leave this house for good. And I will be taking my children with me. Neither you nor anyone else is going to stop me.' Choking back angry tears, Eloise raced from the room.

She did not join the family for supper that evening, but Mabel took pity on her and smuggled some food from the kitchen. As Eloise ate hungrily, Mabel stood watching her with tears in her eyes. 'I shall miss you and the little ones. It won't seem the same here without you.'

Eloise swallowed a mouthful of cold ham and pickle. 'I shall miss you too, Mabel.'

'But how will you get on, ma'am?' Mabel asked anxiously. 'How will you even get to the station?'

'I'll walk,' Eloise said firmly. 'I'll put the children in the little cart that Ted made for them and I'll walk every step to Scarborough if I have to. Who knows, we might meet a kind carter or a farmer on the way there who will give us a lift, but go to the station I will.'

Mabel wiped her eyes on her apron. 'Ada will go into a decline, I know she will. She'll be heartbroken, poor thing.'

'I know, and I feel terrible about it, but I cannot take her with me. Even if I could, Miss Joan would never allow it.'

'They say below stairs that Miss Joan is Ada's mother, but it's only servants' gossip. I don't suppose it's true.'

Eloise bit into a hunk of bread and butter which rendered her temporarily speechless and saved her from answering. She might heartily disapprove of the Cribbs' treatment of Ada, but she had to respect their right to keep the sad truth to themselves. 'That was so good,' she said at last. 'Thank you, Mabel. I'll always remember your kindness to me, and Ted's too.'

Impulsively, Mabel rushed over to throw her arms around Eloise's neck. 'I will really, really miss you.' She drew away hastily, and burying her face in her apron she ran from the room.

When she was certain that both children were fast asleep, Eloise went upstairs to see Ada. She had intended to break the news of her departure gently and to assure Ada that she would write to her and send her picture postcards from London. She had known that it was going to be difficult, but she was unprepared for the sight that met her eyes when she entered the room. Ada was lying on the bed with both hands tied to the brass head rail and with her ankles strapped together by a length of cord. Her face was swollen and blotchy from crying and her lips were cracked and bleeding as if she had bitten them. Eloise rushed over to her and began untying the cords that bound her. 'Ada, who did this to you?'

'Miss Joan,' Ada whispered hoarsely. 'She beat me and tied me up so that I couldn't come and find you. She said you were going away and I would never see you again.' She collapsed against Eloise's shoulder, and her whole body was racked with sobs.

Eloise rocked her in her arms and stroked Ada's hair. 'There, there, don't cry, dear. You know I wouldn't go away without telling you.'

'But you are leaving, she said so.'

'I have to go, Ada. I cannot stay here.'

'I want to come too.'

'If it were possible I would take you, but I cannot.'

Ada pulled away from her. 'You don't want me. You're just like her. Miss Joan don't want me neither. No one wants me.'

'Please, Ada, don't think that. You mustn't think that ever. It's just that I've very little money and I don't know how I'm going to manage even with my own children.'

'But you're taking them,' Ada cried fiercely. 'You won't leave them, so why can't you take me? I'm a good girl. I can help you look after Joss and Beth. Take me with you, I'm begging you on my knees. Take me with you, please.'

Eloise crept through the deserted kitchen carrying her suitcase and valise. Ada followed close behind her with Joss clutching her hand and Beth cradled in the crook of her arm. The first grey light of dawn filtered through the windows and Eloise knew they must hurry or the scullery maid would find them when she came downstairs to light the fire in the range. She glanced over her shoulder at Ada, who looked like a walking scarecrow in her odd assortment of clothes. The skirt that she wore over her nightgown must have been made for her many years ago and barely came down to her ankles. Her straw bonnet and cloak were those borrowed from one of the maids and were green-tinged with age but serviceable, and on her feet she wore a pair of boots that had belonged to one of the under-grooms and discarded because they were past repair.

If matters had not been so dire, Eloise might have chuckled at the sight of the gangling young woman in her outlandish garb, but fashion was not uppermost in her mind at this moment. She led them through the scullery and was about to open the door to the stable yard when the sound of footsteps coming from the kitchen made her freeze to the spot. She held her breath, raising her finger to her lips as a warning to Ada to keep the children quiet. But it was Mabel who came hurrying through the door, and in her hands she clutched a package wrapped in brown paper. 'It's only me,' she said breathlessly. 'Norah the scullery maid's been took sick. Cook thinks it might be the measles, and I had to get up extra early to do Norah's chores.' She thrust the parcel into Eloise's hand. 'Here's summat for the journey. It's just a bit of bread and cheese, but it will keep you going for a while.' Without waiting to be thanked, she pushed past Eloise and opened the door to the stable yard. The cobblestones were bathed in the pale green light of early dawn but the shadows were deep and dark as the small party made their way across to the stable block. Eloise stifled a cry of fright as a figure emerged from the doorway but Mabel turned to her with an encouraging smile. 'It's only our Ted. I told him what you planned, ma'am. He's got the cart all ready for you and he'll walk you part of the way.'

Seeing Ted, Joss uttered a cry of pleasure and broke away from Ada's grasp to run to his friend. Ted swung him up in his arms. 'Hello there, young fellow.'

Eloise glanced nervously over her shoulder. The shadows seemed to be filled with menace and she could have sworn she saw a movement out of the corner of her eye, but she told herself it was just an agitation of her nerves, and she was imagining things. 'Ted, I can't thank you and Mabel enough for helping us, but we must get away before we're seen.'

'Too late,' Ted muttered, staring over her shoulder in the direction of the house. 'It's the master.'

Eloise spun round to see Harcourt striding towards them and her heart sank, but she was not about to give in. 'Put Beth in the cart, Ada. We're leaving no matter what Mr Cribb says.'

Harcourt came hurrying towards them. 'Hold on a moment, lass. This is not right. Not right at all.'

'You won't stop us, Mr Cribb. I'm leaving and I'm taking my children with me and Ada too.'

'I'm going with Eloise,' Ada whimpered, cowering behind her. 'Please let me go, mister.'

Harcourt shook his head. 'I cannot allow it, lass. You belong here with your mother.' He seized Ada by the hand, dragging her to his side. 'It's for your own good, Ada.'

'Please let her come with me,' Eloise pleaded. 'I will look after her, I promise.'

'I don't doubt you'd try, but I can't allow it. This is Ada's home and she must stay. I cannot stop you from going, Eloise, nor will I see your children taken from you.' Harcourt took a small leather pouch from his pocket and pressed it into her hand. 'There is enough brass there to keep you and the little ones for a while at least. I won't see my grandchildren starve, but you must realise that if you leave now, you can never return to Cribb's Hall. Our Hilda will take it very much to heart and she'll never forgive you for taking young Joss away from her.'

Eloise took the pouch and tucked it away in her skirt pocket. 'Thank you. I am truly grateful to you, but nothing would induce me to return to this place.'

'Don't leave me,' Ada sobbed. 'Don't go.'

'I must, Ada. I'm so sorry, my dear.' Eloise turned away, hiding her own tears of grief on leaving the poor creature to the mercies of the Cribb family. 'Ted, if you'll put Joss in the cart perhaps I can balance the suitcase on one end, and the valise will hang on the handle. Obviously you cannot come with us, even part of the way.'

Ted cast an anxious glance at Harcourt. 'Can I go with them just a bit of the way, master?'

'I won't hear of it,' Harcourt said grimly. 'Put Jester in harness, Ted, and bring out the dog cart. You must drive them to the station.'

'Thank you,' Eloise murmured, taking Joss from Ted's arms. She watched him disappear into the dim recesses of the stables and then she turned to Harcourt with an attempt at a smile. 'You at least have shown me kindness, Mr Cribb. I won't forget that.'

'Nay, lass. I had a duty to our Ronnie's wife and I fear I have let you both down. It's the least I can do for you.' He hooked his arm around Ada's shoulders. 'Stop struggling, Ada. You cannot go with them and there's an end to it. Come inside and Mabel will take you up to your room.'

Eloise gave Mabel a hug. 'Goodbye, dear Mabel. You have been a true friend to me and I will never forget you.'

'G-goodbye, ma'am,' Mabel said, gulping back tears. 'I shan't forget you either.'

'I'll need you to help me,' Harcourt said, attempting to control the wildly struggling Ada. 'We must get her back indoors before the rest of the household stirs.'

With great difficulty, for Ada was putting up a valiant fight for freedom, they half dragged, half carried her across the yard to the scullery. Beth had begun to cry and Joss was whimpering against Eloise's shoulder and it took her all her time to pacify them. After what seemed like hours, but was only minutes, Ted brought the dog cart out of the stables and he tossed the luggage in the back. As soon as Eloise and the children were settled on the driver's seat, he leapt nimbly up beside them and took the reins. 'To the station then, ma'am?'

'To the station, Ted,' Eloise said, sighing with relief. Inside the house she could hear voices, and bleary-eyed grooms were stumbling out of their sleeping quarters to hold their heads under the pump in the yard. Ted flicked the reins and Jester sprang forward, eager to be off. Eloise could have shouted for joy. She was escaping from Cribb's Hall and she had her children clutched to her breast. Her only sadness was on leaving Ada, but she prayed silently that now Harcourt was fully aware of her plight, he would do something to improve her lot. Eloise might hate her mother-in-law and Joan with a passion, but she had a sneaking liking and a certain amount of respect for her father-in-law. Had things been different, she knew that she could have grown quite fond of Harcourt Cribb.

A blood red sun was slowly edging its way above the horizon and they were heading into its fiery light as Ted expertly handled Jester, driving the dog cart down the drive and out through the wrought-iron gates. To Eloise it was like escaping the mouth of hell and she knew that whatever the future held, it was not going to be quite as awful as the months she had spent in Cribb's Hall.

'Are you all right, ma'am?' Ted asked anxiously.

'I'm perfectly fine,' Eloise replied, smiling. 'I'm just sad that I had to leave poor Ada behind.'

Ted glanced over his shoulder. 'Look round, ma'am. I think Miss Ada had other ideas.'

Eloise twisted in her seat and saw the ungainly figure of Ada with her arms flailing like a windmill and her long legs gangling like those of a newborn colt, racing after them with her bonnet hanging off and her cloak flying out around her.

'Stop, Ted,' Eloise cried, tugging at his arm. 'For pity's sake stop.'

Ted drew Jester to a halt and he sprang down to help Ada, who had fallen headlong and was sprawling lengthwise in the mud. She was limping as he helped her to the vehicle and bundled her somewhat unceremoniously onto the back seat.

'Ada, are you hurt?' Eloise asked anxiously. 'What happened? How did you get away?'

Breathless and muddy, but smiling broadly, Ada brushed the mud off her face. 'I twisted me ankle, but I don't care. I run away, I did. I run away and I'm coming with you, Ellie.'

'Are you sure this is what you really want? Things won't be easy.'

Ada nodded emphatically. 'I'm coming with you. We'll find my baby.'

Eloise exchanged worried glances with Ted as he climbed up beside her. 'Perhaps we ought to take her back.'

He shook his head. 'I wouldn't send my worst enemy to live with the mistress and Miss Joan. The master is all right, but I don't know how he puts up with those old witches.'

'Then drive on, Ted. The sooner we get on the train to London, the better.'

'I'm right sorry, ma'am,' the man in the ticket office said, peering at Eloise through the thick lenses of his spectacles which made his eyes look huge, like those of a goldfish in a glass bowl. 'The London train went half an hour ago and there won't be another until midday.'

Eloise had somehow imagined that the train would be there waiting for them to leap on board, and now she was terrified that Joan and Hilda might come in hot pursuit. 'Is there another train southbound before then?'

'The Hull train is due any moment, ma'am.'

At least Hull was in the right direction and they could wait there in safety for the London train. 'Two single third class tickets for Hull, please.' Eloise glanced over her shoulder to where Ada was standing with Beth in her arms, watching Joss who was bouncing on the suitcase at her feet.

'Third class, ma'am?'

'Third class,' Eloise said firmly. She had not had a chance to count the money in the pouch, but she must save every penny she had. She might have escaped from Cribb's Hall, but she knew that only a complete fool would be complacent. From now on, life was going to be hard and the future was uncertain. She pushed all such thoughts to the back of her mind as she paid for the tickets, thanked the man politely and went over to pick up her luggage, refusing the help of a porter as that would mean sparing some money for a tip.

The platform was crowded and they had to fight their way into an overfull third class compartment. They managed to get seats but these were little more than wooden benches with slatted backs, and had obviously been designed for utility rather than comfort. Ada's odd and dishevelled appearance was drawing curious looks from their fellow passengers and a certain amount of sniggering at her expense, mainly from children. Eloise glared at them, but her attention was soon diverted by concern for Beth, who did not seem to be her usual sunny self. She had been sleepy and uninterested in taking her milk that morning, but Eloise had put this down to their early start and their hasty departure from Cribb's Hall. After sleeping fitfully during the cart ride to the station, Beth was now awake and crotchety; her cheeks were flushed and she was abnormally hot. Eloise recalled Mabel's words with a stab of fear. Norah, the scullery maid, was one of Nancy's sisters, and if she had gone down with the dreaded measles it was just possible that Nancy might have passed it on to Beth, who was obviously running a temperature, and seemed to be getting worse by the minute.

Ada was sitting opposite Eloise, doing her best to keep Joss amused, but even she noticed that something was wrong, and when Beth had a mild convulsion, Ada began to scream. 'Is she going to die? My baby died. Beth is going to die too.'

'Hush,' Eloise cried, close to tears herself. 'You're not helping, Ada.'

A woman who had been sitting on the opposite seat leaned over to feel Beth's forehead. 'She's proper poorly, lass. I know, because I lost three babies to fever. You don't want to take chances.'

By this time, Eloise was completely terrified and close to panicking. 'What should I do?'

'Where are you bound, lass?'

'To Hull and then on to London.'

'I doubt she'll make it if you stay on the train. Driffield is the next station. Get off there and ask the station master to direct you to the doctor's surgery. I wouldn't take risks if I was you.'

By the time the train stopped at Driffield, Ada was hysterical and Joss was sobbing with sheer fright. Helped by some of the other passengers, Eloise managed to get them all onto the platform, as well as her luggage. Clouds of steam enveloped them in a thick, damp mist as the train pulled out of the station and Eloise watched it leave with a heavy heart. She had pinned all her hopes on reaching London by nightfall. In her haste to escape from Cribb's Hall she had formed no definite plans, but she had vaguely thought that she would return to Myrtle Street and seek shelter with the Higgins family for a day or two until she could find lodgings and suitable employment. The chugging sound of the engine and the clatter of its wheels as they ran over the points grew fainter as the train disappeared into the distance. Eloise had never felt so lost and alone in her whole life as she attempted to quieten Joss. Ada was clinging to her mantle like a frightened child and Beth was lying in Eloise's arms, deathly pale now and terrifyingly still.

'Can someone help me?' Eloise cried out in desperation, and to her intense relief the door to the station master's office opened and a gentleman in a frock coat emerged. He placed a top hat on his head and strode towards them. He looked rather fierce but Eloise was too desperate to worry about offending a railway official. 'Please, sir, I need help. My child is ill and we have had to leave the train before we reached our destination.'

His stern expression softened into a look of concern. 'The doctor's house is not far from the station. If you'll wait here for a moment I'll summon a porter to carry your luggage and he will take you there.'

'Thank you,' Eloise murmured. 'You're very kind.'

He tipped his hat, looking slightly embarrassed. He turned away to summon help in a booming voice, and almost immediately an old man wearing a porter's uniform came through the ticket office pushing a trolley. 'Yes, master?'

'This lady has a sick child, Brough. Take her luggage and escort her to the doctor's house.'

'Aye, master. Right away. Follow me, missis.' Brough hefted the cases onto his trolley and shambled off the way he had come.

Murmuring her thanks to the station master, Eloise took Joss by the hand, and with Ada clinging to the hem of her mantle she followed Brough out of the station. He led them to a neat red-brick house set a little way back from the road, surrounded by a well-kept garden which in summer must be a riot of colour, but was now carpeted with golden daffodils filling the air with their fresh scent. Brough set the luggage down outside the front door and he rapped on the knocker. With Ada snivelling at her side, Eloise could not hear what he said to the pleasant-faced woman who stood in the doorway, but she pushed past him and came towards them with her arms outstretched. 'Come in, my dear. Let me take the babe while you look after the little lad.' She glanced at Ada. 'That will be enough of that noise, miss. You are not helping.' Taking Beth from Eloise, she marched into the house. 'Leave the lady's luggage in the hall, Brough.'

Eloise fumbled in her purse to find a coin, but the aged porter laid his gnarled hand on hers. 'No need, ma'am. I'm pleased to help.' He tipped his cap and walked off down the garden path.

'Thank you, Mr Brough,' Eloise called after him and was rewarded by a backward glance and a crooked smile. Lifting Joss over the threshold, Eloise hurried into the house.

'Come into the front parlour. My husband, Dr Robinson, has been called out but he should be back soon.' Mrs Robinson ushered them into her small front room. 'But until he returns, I'll be happy to take a closer look at the baby, if you will allow it, Mrs . . .'

'Mrs Cribb, Eloise Cribb. I fear that Beth is very sick, ma'am. I believe that she has been exposed to measles. She had a convulsion on the train and she is burning up with fever.'

Joss clutched his mother's hand, his blue eyes swimming with tears and his lips trembling. Ada was quieter now, but she still clung to Eloise as if scared to let her go.

'And this young person?' Mrs Robinson stared at Ada with a puzzled frown. 'She seems very distressed, Mrs Cribb.'

'Ada is very sensitive,' Eloise said hastily. 'She suffers with her nerves.'

'I'd advise her to sit down and take a hold of herself. Giving way to hysteria is a sign of weakness.' Mrs Robinson drew Eloise aside. 'Is she quite right in the head?'

'She is a little bit simple but there is no harm in her,' Eloise answered in a low voice. 'She will calm down in a moment, but please, I am so worried about Beth. Is there anything you can do for her until the doctor returns?'

'We will take her to my room, where she can be kept quiet until Steven gets home. I used to be a nurse, so you can trust me to take care of your baby. I suggest you stay here with your son and the simple soul, who seems to need a great deal of comfort.'

'I – I don't want to leave Beth,' Eloise began, but Mrs Robinson raised an imperative hand.

'Not only am I a nurse, but I have had six children of my own. I know what I'm doing. You must not worry.'

Still uncertain, Eloise followed Mrs Robinson out of the parlour. 'What do you think is wrong with her, ma'am? It has come on so suddenly and her little face is flushed, when just now she was white as a sheet.'

'I've seen it many times before, and, unless I am very much mistaken, your baby has definitely contracted measles. Now go to your boy, Mrs Cribb. He might be sickening for it too, so you must see to him.'

Eloise went back to the parlour where she found Ada curled up on the sofa, apparently fast asleep, and Joss sitting on the floor looking dazed and lost. She scooped him up in her arms and held him close. Measles – the dreaded disease that killed so many young children. Eloise felt Joss's forehead, but he was cool with no sign of fever. She was not afraid for herself as she remembered having the disease when she was six or seven, but she sent a silent prayer to her father's unforgiving god in the hope that he might heed her plea to make Beth well again. Beside herself with fear, Eloise smothered a sob. If only her mama were here now. She would know what to do. She always rose to a crisis, and she had seen many of them in her years as a vicar's wife. She had nursed sick children and comforted the bereaved, taken calves' foot jelly to the ailing and food to the needy. Mama had always been so brave and strong, if only she were more like her. Eloise felt her world crumbling about her shoulders. If Beth died it would be all her fault for bringing her to this. She cuddled Joss closer to her and she cast an anxious glance at Ada. Perhaps she had done a foolish thing by taking them away from Cribb's Hall? Maybe they would have been better served if she had abandoned them to the care of Ronnie's family? At least they would have been fed, clothed and well educated. What future could she offer them? She was now a woman on her own – so very much on her own.

She had not heard the footsteps outside in the hall and Eloise jumped as the door opened and a tall man with a pleasant smile entered the room. 'Mrs Cribb, I am Dr Steven Robinson. No, don't get up; you'll only disturb the little lad.'

Eloise realised then that Joss had fallen asleep in her arms. 'My baby. Have you seen her, doctor?'

He closed the door and pulled up a chair. 'I have, and I'm afraid that Hannah was correct in her diagnosis of measles.' He reached out and laid his hand on her arm. 'Don't distress yourself, Mrs Cribb. Beth is an otherwise healthy infant and has every chance of making a full recovery, provided that she has the appropriate care.'

'What am I to do, doctor?' The hoarse voice that came from her own throat sounded strange to Eloise's ears. She seemed to be lost in a maze of terrifying circumstances.

'The first thing is to find lodgings where you can nurse Beth back to health. It's very likely that your boy will succumb to the illness as well, and you certainly cannot continue with your journey. Where was it that you were headed?'

'To London,' Eloise murmured, shaking her head. 'I have friends in London.'

'I'm afraid that is impossible, Mrs Cribb. You cannot travel until the child is well again. I know that it is none of my business, but is there someone you could call on for help? A relative or a close friend? Your husband . . .'

'I am a widow, doctor. My friends and family are all in London. We were visiting relations near Scarborough, but it is not possible for me to return there just now.'

'I am sorry, but I can only advise you as a physician that to move the child now could prove fatal. Do you know anyone in Driffield who might be willing to take you in?'

Eloise was going to say no, and then she remembered the kindly lady whom she had met on the train. She stared down at Joss's face, innocent and defenceless as he slept in her arms. Her acute maternal ear caught the sound of Beth's feverish cries from the room upstairs, and Ada muttered in her sleep. They all depended on her and she must do everything in her power to protect them. She raised her eyes to meet Dr Robinson's sympathetic gaze. 'There is someone. A lady I met on the train when I first travelled to Yorkshire, but I doubt very much if she would want to expose her own children to such a dreadful disease. I hardly think it would be fair to ask it of her. I just don't know what to do.'

Chapter Six

Eloise's first impression of the farmhouse was that it looked like a child's toy that someone had strategically placed in the picturesque setting of the green and pleasant wolds. From the top of the hill she could see a river running like a silver ribbon through a wide valley and stands of trees just springing back to life after the long cold winter. Dr Robinson had to slow his horse as he drove his trap down the hill towards Danby Farm. The spirited little cob snorted and tossed his head as if he could smell spring in the air, but he slowed his pace to a sedate trot.

Eloise was too concerned about Beth to appreciate the full glory of the scenery, and she sat by Dr Robinson's side glancing anxiously down at her baby's flushed face every few seconds, in order to reassure herself that Beth had not taken a turn for the worse. Ada was sitting on the back seat with Joss perched on her knee, and her voice rose in a crescendo of excitement as she drew his attention to cows grazing in the fields and the sheep dotted about on the grassy hillsides. Eloise couldn't help being amused by her enthusiasm, and she was grateful to Ada for keeping Joss occupied with her childish chatter, but her concern for Beth was compounded by anxiety as to their reception at the farm. Both Dr Robinson and his wife, Hannah, had assured her that Gladys Danby was the nicest of women, and could be relied on to keep her word. If Gladys had seen fit to invite them to visit the farm, she was not the sort of person to turn them away in their time of need. Eloise wished that she could be so certain. It was one thing to call in for a cup of tea and a chat, and quite another to foist a sick child, possibly two sick children, as well as Ada, on an unsuspecting farmer and his family.

As they drew closer to the farmhouse Eloise's heart was in her mouth. What would she do if Gladys Danby turned them away? It would be impossible to travel on to London and the only alternative would be to return to Cribb's Hall. It simply did not bear thinking about.

'Here we are,' Dr Robinson said cheerfully as he drove the trap through the farm gates. 'Danby Farm.'

The mellow brick building with its dormer windows glinting in the sunlight like smiling eyes, and the farmyard bustling with chickens pecking at the ground and geese waddling around like sentries, looked so welcoming that Eloise's spirits rose as the trap drew to a halt.

'Wait here, Mrs Cribb,' Dr Robinson said, giving her a reassuring smile as he handed her the reins. 'It's probably best if I speak to Gladys first.' He vaulted down from the trap and waded through the livestock to the front door.

Eloise waited, hardly daring to breathe. Beth was stirring in her sleep and her small body still felt abnormally hot. It was well past midday and Eloise was tired, hungry and close to tears as she waited for someone to open the door. Perhaps they were all out working in the fields, and might not return until nightfall? Dr Robinson rapped on the doorknocker again, and when no one came, he came slowly back to the trap. 'There doesn't seem to be anyone at home,' he said, frowning. 'It's not market day, so Gladys ought to be somewhere about on the farm.'

'Perhaps we ought to go back to the town,' Eloise murmured. 'I could take a room at the inn.'

Dr Robinson opened his mouth to reply but closed it again as his attention was caught by a movement in one of the outbuildings. His brow cleared and he sighed with relief. 'I see someone. Hello there.'

A figure emerged from the henhouse, and Eloise recognised the plump shape of Gladys Danby. She came hurrying over to them with a basket of eggs hooked over her arm. 'Dr Robinson, this is a surprise.' She paused, staring at Eloise and the children, and then a broad smile creased her weather-beaten face. 'Why, it's the lass from the train and the little ones.'

'May I have a word with you, Gladys?' Dr Robinson drew her aside and spoke to her in a low voice.

Eloise strained her ears but she could not hear what was being said, and Beth had awakened now that the swaying motion of the trap had ceased. She began to wail in a high-pitched monotone that was more upsetting than howls of rage. Gladys came hurrying towards the trap and she was not smiling now. Eloise braced herself to accept a refusal, but Gladys held out her arms to take Beth. 'Give her to me, lass. Bring the little lad and the young woman into the house.'

'Are you sure, Mrs Danby?' Eloise said, hesitating. 'I don't want to impose on your kindness.'

'Fiddlesticks! I invited you, didn't I? Gladys Danby is not a woman to give out invites willy-nilly. You are most welcome, and we've all suffered the measles at one time or another, so there's no fear of infection. You look fair done in, you poor soul. Come inside at once. I'll not take no for an answer.'

The interior of the farmhouse was as warm and welcoming as the homely exterior. The front entrance led straight into a large kitchen with a low beamed ceiling hung with bunches of herbs and strings of onions. The fragrant scents of dried mint, marjoram, sage and rosemary mingled with the salty aroma of hams being smoked in the chimney breast above the black-leaded range. A pan of soup simmered on the hob and the appetising aroma made Eloise's stomach rumble with hunger, but she was too concerned for her children to bother about her own needs.

Gladys took a seat in a chair by the fire and began to unwrap the swaddling around Beth's small body. She examined the fine red rash which had spread all over Beth's trunk and she nodded her head. 'It's measles all right.'

Dr Robinson's lips twisted into a wry smile. 'I'm glad you concur with my diagnosis, Gladys.'

She looked up at him and chuckled. 'Well, I daresay as how I've seen just as many cases as you have, doctor, and nursed them back to health too.'

'I know you have, Gladys. And that is why I was certain that you would help this unfortunate young woman. You have a heart of pure gold.'

'Get on with you, doctor,' Gladys said, flushing to the roots of her grey hair. 'Save your flattery for them up at the big house. Any road, you know you can leave everything to me, and if I need you I'll send our Reggie to fetch you.'

'Beth will be all right, won't she, doctor?' Eloise asked anxiously as Dr Robinson made to leave. 'And what about Joss? Do you think he will get it too?'

'It's more than likely, Mrs Cribb. There are no guarantees with this sort of thing, but your children stand as good a chance of recovery as any, in fact more than most. You know where to find me if I'm needed.'

Eloise followed him to the door. 'Your fee, doctor. I must pay you.'

Gladys rose to her feet, cradling Beth in her arms. 'Hold on to your money, lass. There's a basket of eggs in the dairy, doctor. I'm sure that Hannah could find a use for them.'

Dr Robinson set his top hat back on his head and he smiled. 'I'm sure she could. Thank you, Gladys.'

As the door closed on him, Eloise turned to Gladys. 'I really do appreciate this, Mrs Danby.'

'There, there, lass,' Gladys said with a careless shrug of her shoulders. 'What sort of woman would I be if I turned my back on someone in need? Come upstairs with me and we'll make the little one comfortable.'

'Hungry,' Joss murmured, clinging to Ada's skirts.

'Me too,' Ada said, eyeing the pan of soup and licking her lips.

'And we will all have summat to eat just as soon as we've settled the babe. Why don't you take the little lad out into the yard and wash his hands and face at the pump? Do you think you could manage that?' Gladys turned to Eloise. 'What is her name?'

'Ada, Ada Braithwaite. She's travelling with us to London. It's a long story.'

'Braithwaite.' Gladys repeated the name, angling her head as if she were trying to recall some long forgotten fact, then her face brightened. 'I remember now. There was a scandal years ago involving Joan Braithwaite, Hilda Cribb's sister. She went to live with her aunt in Bridlington, unless I'm very much mistaken.'

'You're not mistaken, Mrs Danby,' Eloise said in a low voice. 'It's a long story.'

Gladys acknowledged this with a nod of her head and then turned to Ada with a cheery smile. 'Well now, Ada, will you do that for me?'

Ada nodded her head vehemently as she took Joss by the hand. 'Find the pump and wash Joss's hands and face. I can do that, missis.'

'Good girl,' Gladys said approvingly. 'When you've done, you can come back here and take a seat at the table. We'll be down directly.' She winked at Eloise as she led the way out of the kitchen into a narrow, wainscoted hallway and up a twisting staircase to the first floor. The oak panelling made the long corridor seem very dark, but when Gladys opened a door at the far end, the bedroom was filled with sunlight. A bright patchwork coverlet on the bed, floral-patterned curtains and colourful rag rugs scattered over the polished floorboards emitted a warm and homely first impression, so at odds with the cold splendour of Cribb's Hall.

'There,' Gladys said, dragging a wooden cradle from a far corner and placing it beside the bed. 'Four generations of Danbys have slept in this cradle. The little lass will be all right in here and there's a cot up in the attic for young Joss. I'll get our Reggie to fetch it down later.'

Beth was sleeping fitfully and Eloise laid her in the cradle. She pulled up a chair, intending to sit where she could watch over Beth, but Gladys shook her head. 'Nay, lass. Your need is greater than hers at the moment. You need a little sustenance. You won't do the baby any good if you fall sick yourself. I'll get our Meg to come and sit with the babe while you have your dinner. She'll be in from the dairy directly, and I'll send her straight up.'

Eloise shook her head. 'What if she wakes and finds me gone? She'll be frightened if I'm not here.'

'She'll not wake for a while, love. The fever has her in its grip, and even if she does wake, I doubt if she'll recognise you for a while at least. We must keep her cool and once the fever passes she'll be right as rain, I promise you.'

Reluctantly, Eloise followed Gladys down-stairs. In the kitchen they found Ada and Joss seated obediently at the table with a tall, thin girl standing and staring at them with a frown on her face.

'Who are they, Mum?' the girl demanded suspiciously. 'I found them in the yard and she wouldn't speak to me. Is she not all there or summat?'

'Don't be rude, our Meg,' Gladys said hastily. 'We've got company, so you mind your manners.'

Meg wiped her hands on her apron, pouting. 'I only asked.'

'Well, now you've been told. This is Mrs Cribb and her little lad Joss. The other person is Ada, a friend who was accompanying them to London when Mrs Cribb's baby got took sick. I want you to go upstairs to the back bedroom, Meg. You must keep an eye on the baby, and call us if she wakes. Do you understand me?'

'I want me dinner,' Meg said sulkily.

'And you shall have it as soon as our guests have eaten. Now, off you go, there's a good lass.' Gladys shooed the girl out of the kitchen, flapping her apron as if Meg was an unruly feathered creature that had escaped from the henhouse. 'Right then, sit down, Mrs Cribb, and taste a bowl of my rabbit stew. My sons say it's the best in the East Riding, but then they would, wouldn't they?' Chuckling, Gladys went to the range and ladled out three bowlfuls of piping hot stew. She placed them on the table in front of her guests and went back to the oven to take out a freshly baked loaf of bread, which she proceeded to cut into generous hunks. 'You'll all do a lot better with full bellies,' she said, liberally buttering the bread before handing it round.

The stew was delicious and Eloise ate ravenously. Her appetite had almost deserted her during the last few days in Cribb's Hall and she had forgotten what it was to enjoy a meal. Despite her anxiety about Beth, there was something so comforting and reassuring about Gladys that Eloise found herself relaxing just a little. Ada ate sparingly, but Joss pushed his plate away after the first mouthful and only toyed with a slice of bread and butter. Eloise reached out to feel his forehead and her heart did a back flip inside her chest. 'He feels very hot, Mrs Danby. I think he might be coming down with the sickness.'

'Very probably, love,' Gladys said, mopping up the last of her soup with a hunk of bread. 'Better to get it over and done with in my opinion.' She glanced at Ada and frowned. 'I shouldn't be surprised if that one doesn't go down with it too.' Gladys lowered her voice. 'Just how is she related to the Braithwaites, Mrs Cribb?'

'My name is Eloise, but my family call me Ellie, Mrs Danby.'

'And you can call me Gladys. We don't stand on ceremony up here.' Gladys leaned across the table to give Ada an encouraging smile. 'Now you've finished your dinner, why don't you take the little lad outside into the yard and let him have a run round?'

'All right,' Ada said reluctantly. 'Will you read me a story later, Ellie?'

'Of course I will. We brought one of your favourite books with us, I believe.'

Ada jumped to her feet. 'Yes, we did. I can read a bit of it, missis,' she added, addressing the remark to Gladys. 'Ellie is teaching me to read. Come on, Joss, let's go out and see the chickens.'

When they had gone, Gladys poured tea from a brown china pot which had been brewing beneath a knitted tea cosy, and she passed a cup to Eloise. 'The men will be in for their dinner soon, lass. It might be a good idea if you told me what has been going on with you, and what brought you to this sorry pass. Not that I'm being nosy, mind you, not at all, but I cannot help you if I don't know what has driven you from your in-laws' home. I'm thinking it couldn't have gone too well for you at Cribb's Hall. Am I right?'

It was a relief to unburden her soul to Gladys, and Eloise withheld nothing, even going so far as to tell her about Ada's sad history and her harsh treatment at the hands of her mother, Joan Braithwaite. Gladys listened in silence until

Eloise had finished. 'Eh, lass. What a sorry tale to be sure. You know you're welcome to stay here with us as long as you want.'

'Thank you,' Eloise murmured, blinking back tears. It was almost harder to take the kindness and generosity shown by Gladys than it was to bear the insults that she had endured from her mother-in-law and Joan. 'You're very kind, Gladys. But as soon as Beth recovers I must be on my way. I need to get back to London and find work so that I can support my children.'

'And Ada, what about her? The poor soul is simple, that's plain to see. She would be more of a hindrance to you than a help.'

'I know, but I cannot desert her. It would be like leaving a child to fend for itself.'

Gladys tipped her teacup, swirling the leaves round in the bottom and staring intently at them. 'You say she were born in Bridlington?'

'Yes, and she was raised to think that Joan was her cousin and not her mother. Poor Ada is still searching for her own baby, which was taken from her soon after its birth, although if she lived, the girl would be almost a woman by now. In fact, probably the same age as your daughter, Meg.'

Gladys looked up with a startled expression. 'Oh, Meg's not my daughter, Ellie. When our youngest daughter got wed, I needed someone to help me about the house and in the dairy, and we got Meg from the orphanage. She were about eleven or twelve then, and would either have been sent into service or to work in a mill. There's many an unwanted child that suffers a similar fate. She calls me Mother, and we treat her as one of the family, but goodness knows who her parents were.'

'Well, I think it must have been her lucky day when you took her into your home,' Eloise said, smiling. 'And I must go and relieve her so that she can get her dinner. Perhaps you could send Ada up with Joss when they come indoors. I wouldn't want them to get in the way.'

Gladys put her teacup back on its saucer. 'They'll hardly be noticed. My Frank and the boys will see nothing but the food on their plates when they come in from the fields. You'll meet them later, but for now you go and tend to your babe.'

Eloise rose from the table feeling much stronger and more positive now she had eaten. Acting on instinct, she bent down to drop a kiss on Gladys's wiry grey hair. 'You are so kind, and I am truly grateful to you.'

Later that day, when the men came in for supper, Ada was sent upstairs to keep an eye on Beth while Eloise snatched a bite to eat. With obvious pride, Gladys introduced Eloise to her stalwart husband, Frank, a big, burly man with a kind smile and an easy-going manner. Then there was Reggie, their eldest son, who at thirty was still unmarried and rather bashful, but who exuded the same good humour and kindly nature as his parents. He was, so Gladys told Eloise in confidence, unofficially engaged to Maud Fosdyke, whose father owned the local ironmongery. They had been stepping out together for four years, and Maud was not getting any younger, but Reggie was a slow fellow and wouldn't be hurried. Then there was Jacob, his younger brother by a year, who was in contrast taciturn and disinclined to talk, seemingly more interested in his supper than in being agreeable to an uninvited house guest. Jacob was courting the miller's daughter, Gladys said with a beaming smile, and they would be married before the year was out. Two sons had not survived infancy, she admitted sadly, but her six daughters were all married and living close by. Between them they had already produced twelve children, with another two babies expected soon. Eloise could only envy this large, happy family, but their closeness made the separation from her own mother all the harder to bear, and as soon as she had eaten her meal of bread, cheese and pickles, washed down with farmhouse cider, she retired to her room to put Joss to bed in the cot that Reggie had hefted down from the attic.

Ada was given a small boxroom at the end of

the corridor, but she was scared to sleep alone in a strange house and she dragged her feather mattress and coverlet into Eloise's room, placing it on the floor in front of the hearth. With Joss settled in the cot and Ada lying by the fire, Eloise read them both a fairy story from Ada's favourite book, but after just a few pages she realised that they had both fallen asleep. Having reassured herself that Beth was no worse and that she too was sleeping peacefully, Eloise took her writing case from the valise and climbed into bed. She managed to write a few lines to her mother, but she could hardly keep her eyes open and she lay down to sleep.

She was awakened in the night by a child crying and she sat bolt upright in the bed, staring into the faint glow of the fire as the embers turned into ash. For a moment she couldn't think where she was, or who was crying. Then it all came rushing back to her and she leaned over to examine Beth, but although she was still in the grip of the fever she was not making the noise. Eloise leapt out of bed as she realised that it was Joss who was wailing miserably. She snatched him out of his cot, and her worst fears were realised when she found that his little nightshirt was soaked with sweat and his body was burning up with fever. She lit a candle, and even in its pale light she could see that he was covered in a rash. She bathed his hot body with cool water from the washbowl, and finally she took him into her own bed, but he complained of earache and she spent the rest of the night walking the floor with him in her arms when the pain became too great for him to bear. His sobs eventually awakened Beth but Ada slept on, snoring loudly, while Eloise did her best to console her sick children. When the first light of dawn filtered through the lattice window, Eloise was exhausted and the children had fallen into a fitful sleep. Moving carefully so that she did not wake them, Eloise climbed out of bed. There were sounds of stirring in the house, and activity in the farmyard below. She could hear the clatter of milk pails and the swooshing sound of water being drawn from the pump, the lowing of cows in the milking parlour and the clarion call of the cockerel.

She wrapped her shawl around her shoulders and tiptoed out of the room, leaving the door slightly ajar so that she could hear the little ones if they should start to cry. Her bare feet made soft pattering sounds on the floorboards as she went down the stairs to the kitchen. She had hoped to find Gladys there but she stopped short when she saw Reggie sitting at the table drinking a mug of tea. He jumped to his feet, knocking his chair over in his haste.

'I'm sorry, I didn't mean to startle you,' Eloise said, wrapping her shawl a little tighter around her body. Being seen in just her nightgown by a man who was neither her husband nor her father caused her cheeks to flame with embarrassment, but she could see that Reggie was just as uncomfortable. He righted the chair and stood behind it, staring down at his boots.

'Er, morning, ma'am.'

'I was looking for your mother,' Eloise said hastily. 'My little boy was taken ill in the night. I'm afraid he has the measles, and I wondered if someone could go for the doctor.'

Reggie raised his eyes and his rugged features crumpled with concern. 'I'm right sorry to hear that, ma'am. I'll go for him myself.'

'That's very kind of you, Reggie. I would be so much obliged if you would.'

'I'll go right away.' Smiling shyly, he picked up his cap and jacket and made for the door, but he paused on the threshold. 'Ma's out collecting eggs, but I daresay as how she won't be long. Shall I tell her you want her?'

'No, please don't disturb her. I can manage until the doctor comes.'

He nodded his head briefly. 'Aye, well, there's tea in the pot. Help yourself, lass. I mean, ma'am.'

'No, please. My name is Eloise, but my friends call me Ellie.'

'Ellie. That's a pretty name,' Reggie said, flushing beneath his tan. 'I'd best go.'

As he left the house, a blast of cold air pungent with the smell of the farmyard blew into the kitchen. Eloise poured a cup of tea for herself and one for Ada, which she laced with sugar and then took upstairs to her bedroom.

When Dr Robinson arrived later that morning, he confirmed that Joss had measles, but that in his opinion it was just a mild attack. He examined Beth and to Eloise's intense relief he told her that the crisis was past. Beth was quite poorly, but there was no sign of complications and she should make a complete recovery, although there was no question of their being able to travel for a week at least. The little ones would need careful nursing, rest and nourishing food until they were completely restored to health. Eloise shook his hand warmly and thanked him profusely. Her relief was so great that she had to restrain herself from throwing her arms around his neck and kissing him, but that would be an improper thing to do, and she thanked him once again. Slightly embarrassed, Dr Robinson refused to accept any payment, saying that Gladys had more than made up for his fee with newly laid eggs, a jug of cream and a pound of butter. He left the farm, promising to return in a couple of days' time to check up on his patients.

The ensuing week was a much happier one for Eloise once she was certain that her children were on the road to recovery. Away from the stultifying atmosphere of Cribb's Hall and the constant carping and interference from Hilda and Joan, Eloise began to relax and to feel more like her old self. The open-handed kindness of the Danby family acted like balm to her soul. Frank said little, but when he spoke to Eloise she couldn't help noticing that he lowered his great booming voice to a whisper, bending his shaggy head and smiling gently at her, as if he was dealing with a highly strung thoroughbred filly. Jacob rarely spoke to her at all, but she took his silence for shyness rather than ill temper, and Reggie did everything he could in his clumsy, bumbling way to make her feel at home. Sometimes he brought her little posies of cowslips and sweet cicely, or a juicy apple from their winter store. He unearthed a slightly tatty rocking horse from the attic and carved a wooden boat out of a block of wood, both of which went a long way to keep Joss amused. Eloise wondered what Maud Fosdyke would have thought about all this, but at least she could honestly say that she had given him no encouragement. However, as the days went by Reggie's apparent fondness for her began to be a worry, and she raised the subject during a conversation with Gladys, who laughed and said that Reggie was a big soft-hearted marshmallow and that Maud was not the sort of woman to stand for any nonsense. Maud would sort him out.

In some ways, Gladys reminded Eloise of her own mother, particularly by the way that she had taken them all under her wing like a mother hen with a brood of stray ducklings. In between her chores, Gladys took turns at sitting with the children, who in their convalescence were sometimes crotchety and difficult to amuse, but this allowed Eloise some time to herself. Ada was less clinging now, which also helped. She and Meg had formed an unlikely alliance. Despite the fact that Ada was old enough to be Meg's mother, they got on so well together that they were soon the best of friends. Meg took Ada with her wherever she went on the farm, allowing her to try her hand at milking and she taught her how to skim off the cream and to churn butter. This left Eloise free to take walks in the countryside, breathing in the sparkling clear air that was unpolluted by the stench of the city. Quite often, in fact too often to be written off as pure coincidence, Eloise came across Reggie during these walks. Sometimes he would apparently be walking in the same direction on some errand which was immediately forgotten as he fell into step beside her, and occasionally he would be driving the farm cart and would offer to take her up beside him while he drove to market, or visited the feed merchant. Even after such a short time, Eloise sensed that he was developing a genuine fondness for her. She found it touching and rather sweet, but she gave him no encouragement, hoping that he would forget about her when she had left the farm and return to Maud before she grew tired of waiting for him to pop the question and married someone else.

Joss and Beth were recovering rapidly now, and Eloise planned to continue their journey to London as soon as Dr Robinson agreed that the children were well enough to travel. She knew she would have mixed feelings on leaving the farm, where she had met nothing but kindness, but she would not impose any longer than was absolutely necessary on the Danbys. She must return to London to find work and lodgings until her parents returned from Africa. It was as simple as that.

Eloise was returning from her walk one afternoon with a large bunch of primroses in her hand, which she intended to give Gladys. The sun was shining and the hedgerows were alive with small rodents, insects and nesting birds. The white flowers of the blackthorn shone like tiny stars in the tangle of black branches and twigs. The damp earth, warmed by the spring sunshine, exuded a rich fruity smell and the woods were carpeted with sweetly scented bluebells. As she drew nearer to the farmyard, Eloise could see Dr Robinson's trap with his old cob waiting patiently between the shafts, occasionally pawing the cobblestones as if to remind his master of his presence. She quickened her step and almost bumped into Ada who was lolloping along in her gangly fashion, following Meg who was running on ahead and laughing wildly. For a split second, Eloise saw what appeared to be an incredible likeness, not so much of their features as the ungainly way in which they moved and their peals of childlike laughter. It was, of course, just her fancy and she pushed the thought to the back of her mind as she hurried into the house.

She found Dr Robinson and Gladys sitting at the kitchen table drinking tea and munching on slices of fruit cake. Joss was on the floor playing with a mongrel puppy and Beth was attempting to crawl, but was hindered by her long nightgown. Their swift recovery from what could have been a fatal illness seemed like a miracle to Eloise, and she smiled to see them looking so well and happy.

'Ah, Mrs Cribb, good news,' Dr Robinson said, getting to his feet. 'Both Joss and Beth are doing so well that, in a day or two, you will be able to continue your journey without fear of prejudicing their recovery.'

'That's wonderful,' Eloise said, smiling. 'Thank you so much, Dr Robinson. You've been so kind and I'm truly grateful.'

He made a deprecating noise and shook his head. 'All in the line of duty, Mrs Cribb.'

'Well, I for one am not happy,' Gladys said with a mock frown. 'For it means I shall have to say goodbye to my little ducks, and to Ellie, who has become almost like a daughter to me.'

'I can never thank you enough, Gladys,' Eloise said, taking off her bonnet and shawl and hanging them on a wooden peg behind the door alongside the family's outdoor clothes. 'You have made us feel so much at home. I will miss you very much, but I must return to London.'

'There is someone else who will be more than sorry to see you go, Ellie,' Gladys said with a knowing wink. 'I think our Reggie might have something to say to you, if the great lummox can find the right words, although what poor Maud will make of it, heaven only knows.'

Dr Robinson picked up his top hat and gloves. 'I must be going. Thank you for the tea and cake, Gladys.' He turned to Eloise with a hint of a smile. 'I shan't need to call again, so I'll wish you good fortune and a safe journey back to London.'

'Thank you, doctor. Thank you for everything.' Eloise stood on tiptoe to plant a kiss on his bewhiskered cheek.

He looked slightly taken aback and a genuine smile lit his normally sombre grey eyes. 'You are a brave young woman, Mrs Cribb. It has been a privilege to know you.' As he went out through the door he was almost bowled over by Meg, closely followed by Ada. Both of them were dishevelled and giggling uncontrollably.

Gladys leapt to her feet. 'Good heavens! Just look at the state of you two. What a pair indeed. Go back outside and clean the mud off your boots. You can wash your hands too before you come back in my nice clean kitchen.'

Ada hung her head and her mouth drooped at the corners. 'You won't beat me, will you, missis?'

'Lord, what a thing to say. As if I would do such a thing. Meg, take the poor soul outside and help her to wash. And don't smirk, lass. You're just as bad as she is, and you ought to know better.' Gladys flopped down on her chair and refilled her cup with tea from the pot. 'Those two are a right pair when they get together. You'd think they were sisters, the daft things.'

Eloise scooped Beth up in her arms and hugged her. 'Sisters! Ada is old enough to be Meg's mother.' She stopped short, shocked at the thought that had crossed her mind as she met Gladys's startled gaze. 'No, that's impossible. It couldn't be, could it?'

Gladys took a mouthful of tea and swallowed convulsively. 'By heck, you know it's just possible, Ellie. We took Meg from an orphanage close to Bridlington, and they had no knowledge of her parentage. She were just left on the doorstep like a bundle of washing when she were only a few days old. Sadly, it's quite commonplace.'

'And sadly we'll never know for sure,' Eloise said, nuzzling Beth's curly blonde hair. 'Poor Ada, she's had such a hard life. I just hope I can give her a better one.'

A yelp from Joss made Eloise spin round just in time to see the puppy backing away from him and uttering comical little attempts at barking. Joss held out his hand where a small scratch was oozing tiny droplets of crimson blood. 'Bad puppy,' Joss sobbed. 'Bad boy hurt Joss.'

Laughing, Eloise passed Beth to Gladys and she picked Joss up in her arms. 'I think it might have been a bad boy who pulled Puppy's tail.' She wiped the tiny spots of blood away with her finger. Once again she had no pocket handkerchief and she smiled at the thought of what her mother would say. She kissed the injured spot on Joss's hand. 'Kiss it better, Joss. And beware of puppies with needle-sharp teeth and claws in the future.'

'It's a lesson well learnt,' Gladys said, chuckling. 'He'll not make that mistake again.' Her smile faded and she heaved a great sigh. 'Eh, but I shall miss you and the little ones when you go, Ellie. That's God's honest truth. Won't you reconsider, lass? I mean there's plenty of room in this old house now the girls have upped and married. And I know someone who would more than welcome you to stay on. You might even come to like our Reggie if you got to know him better.'

'I do like Reggie,' Eloise said gently. 'I like him very much, but it's less than a year since my husband died, and I doubt if I could ever love a man as I loved Ronnie. We must leave here, Gladys, and perhaps it would be best if it were sooner rather than later.'

'I see that your mind is made up, Ellie. I won't argue with you, lass.'

That night, when Ada and the children were asleep, Eloise took her suitcase and valise from beneath the bed and began packing their things. She awakened early next morning and went to wake Ada, but she would not be roused. It only took a few seconds for Eloise to realise that Ada was extremely unwell, a fact which Dr Robinson confirmed when he visited later that morning. Ada had contracted measles, and there was no question now of them leaving until she was well again. Measles was a much more serious disease in adults, Dr Robinson said with a worried frown, and Ada's constitution was not robust. Eloise, Gladys and Meg took turns in sitting by Ada's bedside in the small back bedroom where Reggie had carried her on the first day of her illness. Eloise read to Ada from her book of fairy tales, and Meg chattered on about seemingly nothing, but the sound of her voice seemed to soothe Ada even at the height of her fever. Gladys made nourishing broths and milk puddings to tempt the invalid's appetite, but all to no avail.

Eloise was beside herself with worry, and when Dr Robinson came out of the sickroom one morning, shaking his head, she challenged him to tell her the truth.

'I'm afraid that Ada has pneumonia. It is one of the complications of measles, especially in adults such as Ada who were not of a very robust constitution in the first place.'

Shocked and barely able to believe what she heard, Eloise clutched his arm. 'She's – she's not going to die, is she, doctor?'

'It's in God's hands now, my dear Mrs Cribb. I've done everything in my power to save her, but we just have to hope and pray.'

'She won't die,' Eloise said, gritting her teeth. 'I won't let her die. She will get better. She will.'

Chapter Seven

Eloise had been up all the previous night, sitting by Ada's bedside, alternately holding her hand and telling her what they would do, where they would go and the sights they would see in London. When she ran out of things to say, she read out loud the stories that she now knew almost by heart, even though she doubted whether Ada could hear her. She had lapsed into a semi-comatose state, her cheeks were deathly pale and her breathing had become shallow. Dr Robinson had warned them that the end was near and Eloise was already grieving for the child woman who had become her dear friend. Although she was most reluctant to leave Ada's bedside, Gladys had insisted on taking over the vigil at dawn, assuring Eloise that Meg would be only too happy to relieve her when she came in from the dairy.

Eloise went to her room intending only to have a brief rest on her bed, but she must have fallen asleep as she was awakened abruptly by the sound of voices outside her bedroom door. She leapt out of bed, still drugged with sleep, but desperate to speak to Dr Robinson, whose deep tones were now so familiar. She opened her door and found him out on the landing talking to Gladys, who was mopping her eyes on her apron.

'She's not . . .' Eloise couldn't say the dreadful word. 'Doctor?'

'We were going to wake you,' Dr Robinson said gravely. 'I'm afraid it won't be long now.'

Gladys clutched Eloise's arm. 'Meg is with her, lass. Our Reggie is keeping an eye on the little ones downstairs. We'd best go in before it's too late.'

Moving like a sleepwalker, Eloise followed Gladys and Dr Robinson into Ada's tiny room where she lay on the bed looking like a wax doll, with her long limbs stiff and still beneath the white counterpane. Meg was leaning over the bed, holding Ada's hand and speaking to her in a soft crooning voice as she begged her to fight for her life. She raised her tearstained face to cast an agonised look at Eloise and Gladys. 'She's slipping away. I can barely hear her breathing.'

'Oh, Ada,' Eloise murmured, her voice hitching on a sob. 'Don't leave us, dear Ada.'

Gladys gave her arm a comforting squeeze. 'She looks so peaceful.'

Ada's almost transparent eyelids fluttered open and her gaze focused on Meg's face. Eloise held her breath as she saw a flicker of recognition in Ada's pale eyes, followed by a ghost of a smile as a long drawn out sigh escaped from her lips. Her eyes closed and she was still.

Meg uttered a cry of anguish and buried her head in her arms as sobs racked her thin body.

Gladys hugged Eloise, holding her tightly. 'At least she'll be able to find the babe she's been searching for in heaven, Ellie.'

'I think she's already found her,' Eloise whispered. 'I think Ada knew it too, at the very last.'

Although Frank had ridden into Driffield to send a telegraph to Cribb's Hall, advising them of Ada's death and the date and time of the funeral, there had been no reply forthcoming and Eloise was the only family member present as Ada's coffin was lowered into her grave. It was a beautiful sunny day and warm for the beginning of May. The clear blue sky was cloudless and the air was filled with birdsong, which almost drowned out the sound of clods of earth raining on the coffin and Meg's heartbroken keening.

Eloise had no tears left to shed now, and she dropped a small posy of violets onto the scattered earth. 'Goodbye, dear Ada,' she whispered softly.

Gladys bent down to lift Meg from her knees. 'Come along, lass. We must get you home.'

Frank put his cloth cap back on his head. His Sunday best suit was a little too tight for him and the buttons barely met over his portly belly. He looked hot and uncomfortable as he ran his finger round the inside of his starched shirt collar. 'Poor lass,' he murmured.

Eloise was not sure whether he meant Meg or Ada, but she nodded her head in agreement. Jacob and his pretty fiancée, Clara, stood on the far side of the grave with Dr and Mrs Robinson. Apart from Reggie, who was standing close to Eloise, they were the only mourners at the simple service. The vicar murmured a few words of comfort and then walked away with his surplice flapping like the wings of a great white seagull as he returned to the church.

Gladys and Frank led the sobbing Meg down the path to the road where they had left the pony and trap. With his wife on his arm, Dr Robinson came over to speak to Eloise. 'I'm so sorry for your loss, Mrs Cribb.'

'I am too,' Hannah said, adding hastily, 'I mean I only met the young woman once, but it's very sad, my dear.'

'Thank you,' Eloise murmured. 'I shall miss Ada very much.'

Dr Robinson nodded his head. 'You will be returning to London now, I suppose?'

'Yes, there's nothing to keep us here any longer. We will be leaving in the morning.'

As the doctor and his wife moved away, followed closely by Jacob and Clara, who were arm in arm and in a world all of their own, Reggie cleared his throat as if to remind Eloise of his presence. 'Must you go so soon, Ellie?'

'I must, I'm afraid. I have a living to earn, Reggie.'

'Come on, lass,' Frank called from the driver's seat of the trap. 'We should be getting back to the farm.'

'I'm coming.' Eloise waved to him and began walking, giving Reggie no alternative but to keep up with her.

'You could stay here,' Reggie said, covering her hand with his as it rested on his arm. 'You don't have to work, Ellie. I would look after you and the young 'uns. If you'd let me.'

'Don't, Reggie. Please . . .'

He drew her clumsily to a halt. 'I must say it, lass. I can't let you go without telling you that I – I love you, Ellie. Marry me, and I swear I'll make you happy.'

'Oh, Reggie!' Eloise raised her hand to stroke his weathered cheek and her eyes brimmed with tears. 'I know you mean it, and you are the most splendid fellow. But there is someone else who is far more deserving of your love than me.'

'I know you're talking about Maud, but that were never an official engagement. She'll understand.'

Eloise shook her head. 'I don't think she will, Reggie.'

'I'm a patient man, Ellie. I know you still love your husband, but he's dead and gone. I'm here and alive and I love you. Won't you stay just a bit longer and give me a chance to prove myself to you?'

'Hurry up, you two,' Frank shouted impatiently. 'Farm won't run itself.'

'And we shouldn't leave old Ma Baker on her own with the babes for too long,' Gladys added. 'She's a bit forgetful at times.'

Eloise drew her hand away. 'I must go. My children – I'm sorry, Reggie. I just can't . . .' She picked up her skirts and ran down the path to climb into the trap. As Frank flicked the reins and encouraged the old horse to plod onwards, Eloise stared straight ahead of her. She could not bear to look back to see the anguish on Reggie's face. He was a good man, and a kind one, but she did not love him and she was desperate now to return to London where she had been happy once, and would be again. Of that she was certain.

As Eloise stepped off the train onto the platform at Euston, she breathed in the fuggy city air with a sigh of relief. Not for her were the rolling wolds of Yorkshire, the biting east winds and the fruity smell of damp earth, or even the mellow countryside of her childhood Dorset. This bustling, dirty place with its polyglot crowds and frenetic pace of living was her home. Despite their uncertain future, she realised suddenly that she only felt truly alive in London. Her heart and mind were here and the ghosts from the past were comforting rather than frightening. She braced her shoulders and gave Joss an encouraging smile as he clung to her, gazing nervously around, wide-eyed and obviously scared by the bustling populace and the ear-splitting noise of the great iron monsters letting off steam.

Eloise beckoned to a porter who trundled his trolley over to her and tipped his cap. 'Afternoon, ma'am.'

'My luggage is on the rack,' Eloise said, hoisting Beth over her shoulder and gripping Joss firmly by the hand. 'If you would be so kind as to lift it down?'

'Certainly, ma'am. Is someone meeting you, or would you like me to find you a cab?'

Eloise hesitated. She knew to the last farthing how much she had in her purse, and she had carefully calculated how far it would stretch, but she had forgotten things like tipping a porter and the hire of a cab to take her to Myrtle Street. Nonetheless, it was too far to walk and she certainly could not manage suitcases and two small children and so she nodded, saying with confidence, 'A cab, please.'

As she followed the porter and his trolley

along the crowded platform and through the busy main concourse, Eloise felt suddenly daunted and very small and insignificant in the scheme of things. During the past few months she had grown accustomed to the slower pace of life in the countryside, and now she was suddenly nervous. Her plan was to stay with the Higgins family until she had found work. She had had no qualms about arriving unannounced on their doorstep, although now she was actually here, she was not quite so sure of herself. Fanny was her friend and she often took in a lodger or even two to make ends meet. Of course there would be a welcome for them; how could she possibly doubt it?

'There you are, ma'am,' the porter said, having hefted her cases into the cab. He stood there, looking at her expectantly.

Eloise fumbled in her purse and gave him a generous tip. It hurt her to part with the money, but the man probably had a wife and children to support, and his need was as great as her own. He gave her a broken-toothed grin. 'Let me help you, ma'am.' With his hand beneath her elbow, he helped her climb into the cab, and then he tipped his hat again and shambled off pushing his trolley.

'Where to, missis?'

'Myrtle Street, please, cabby. Number fourteen.'

As she settled herself against the leather squabs,

Eloise wrinkled her nose at the smell of stale cigar smoke mixed with the familiar odours of the filthy streets. Beth had fallen asleep on her shoulder but Joss was bouncing up and down on the seat. He had slept for most of the journey and was now refreshed and full of life. Any moment he would start asking for food, and Beth would be hungry too when she woke up. Eloise hoped that Fanny would have a pot of soup simmering on the hob. She had eaten nothing since breakfast, and then had only nibbled a piece of toast. Her parting with the Danbys had been tearful on all sides, and she was already missing them more than she would have thought possible. She had left Fanny's address with them and had promised to write as soon as she was settled. Suddenly the enormity of her undertaking crowded in on her and she shivered. Had she made a terrible mistake by returning to London? Eloise tried hard to be positive. At least she would be here when Mama and Papa finally returned from Africa. Tomorrow, when they were settled at Fanny's house, she would go to the Missionary Society's headquarters and give them her address. They might have news of her parents, and she would give them the letters she had written over the past few weeks to forward to the mission in Kenya. She leaned back, closing her eyes. Everything would come right in the end. Janet always said that, and she was invariably right.

'We're here, missis.'

Eloise opened her eyes with a start. Joss had curled up beside her and it seemed that they had both dozed off. He awakened with a start and was attempting to get out of the cab when the cabby jumped down to help them alight. Oh dear, Eloise thought grimly as she climbed down from the cab, another person who wants a tip. She paid their fare and tipped him, though not too generously. She put her purse away and hesitated for a moment, with Beth in her arms and Joss clinging to her skirts as if he was suddenly afraid. She glanced up and down the once familiar street, but to her surprise she felt like a stranger. The house which had been her home for the three short years of her married life looked identical to the other dwellings in this shabby street. There was nothing about its appearance to mark it out as having once been her home. It had seemed like heaven when she first moved in with Ronnie. She had not noticed the peeling paintwork then, or the run down neighbourhood with lines of washing strung across the street like pennants and the mangy curs fighting over scraps of food, or even the barefoot, lice-ridden children who hung about in doorways. Life had been so exciting in those far off days, and she had looked at everything through the eyes of a young woman very much in love. Now she was viewing things quite differently. She was a woman alone with two tiny children who depended upon her for everything. Once she had had a loving, if unpredictable, husband and her parents had been close at hand. Now she was very much on her own.

'Hungry, Mama,' Joss cried, tugging at her skirts and bringing her abruptly back to the present.

'And you will have something to eat very soon, darling,' Eloise said soothingly. She took a deep breath and knocked on Fanny's door. She listened for the sound of children's voices and the clatter of hobnails on the bare floorboards, but the house was unnaturally silent. She knocked again and this time there was an answering shuffle as someone padded across the floor. The torn and filthy net curtain fluttered and then hung limply. Eloise felt a gnawing fear growling in her belly. Fanny had always kept the house spotlessly clean. She would have died rather than allow her much darned nets to get in that state. The door opened and a complete stranger stood there, glaring at her. 'No hawkers, tinkers or diddicoys wanted.' The woman was about to slam the door in her face, but Eloise was too quick for her and she stuck her booted foot over the doorsill.

'Excuse me, ma'am. But where is Fanny?'

'Fanny who?'

The woman shoved her weight against the

door, but Eloise was not going to give in so easily even though the bones in her foot were being painfully crushed. 'Fanny Higgins. This is her house.'

'Not any more it ain't. Get your bleeding foot out of me door or I'll break every bone in it.'

Joss was crying with fright and that had started Beth off as well. Eloise was in too much pain to argue and she withdrew her foot. The door slammed shut. She stared at it in disbelief. How could things have changed in such a short time? When she had left here in January, the Higgins family had had no thought of moving house. Now there was a complete stranger living in their home. Eloise went to the house next door where old Ma Johnson lived with her two strapping sons, who were employed by the Gaslight and Coke Company.

Ma Johnson opened the door just a crack. 'Who's there?'

'It's me, Mrs Johnson. Eloise Cribb from number sixteen.'

'The snooty bitch moved away in January,' Ma Johnson muttered, squinting myopically at her.

Eloise ignored the insult. It was well known in the street that Ma Johnson was a bit doolally tap. Eloise attempted a smile. 'I've come back, Mrs Johnson. I was looking for Fanny Higgins, but it seems that there is someone else living there now.'

'That's right. She's not there any more. Don't waste my time, whoever you are.'

'Please don't shut the door. It's Eloise; you remember me. Please tell me where Fanny has gone and why she moved away.'

Ma Johnson opened the door a little wider. 'You won't find Fanny here, nor her nippers. Her old man got hisself killed on the railway; fell under a train, the silly bleeder. She's gone to the workhouse – they've all gone there. You won't see them again, and that's for sure. There's only one way out of that place – feet first.' With a shrill cackle of laughter, Ma Johnson slammed the door in Eloise's face.

Eloise stared blankly at the battered door panels and the iron doorknocker hanging by a single screw. She could hardly believe her own ears. Poor Fanny, who had been her staunch friend and ally through the difficult times, and now she was incarcerated in that terrible place, the mere mention of which cast terror into people's hearts. Eloise shuddered. She had not anticipated anything like this, and now she was completely at a loss. She looked round desperately, and was wondering what to do next when she saw one of Ma Johnson's sons strolling down the street towards her. She had always kept well away from Abe and Isaac Johnson, who shared the reputation of drinking too much on a Saturday night and getting into brawls. She attempted to pick up her luggage, but Joss hampered her every movement and the cases were heavy.

'Hold on a moment, ducks.'

Eloise had no alternative but to stay where she was. She was not sure whether it was Abe or Isaac who had quickened his pace and was advancing on her. She half expected him to rant at her for disturbing his mother, but as he drew nearer she saw to her relief that he looked more concerned than angry. 'Hello, Abe.'

He dragged off his cap, grinning. 'It's Isaac, Mrs Cribb. I thought as how you'd moved away from here.'

'I came to see Mrs Higgins, but your mother told me that she's gone to the workhouse.'

'The old girl's got it right for once, although most of the time you can't believe a word she says.'

Beth was howling with all her might now, almost deafening Eloise as she bent down to comfort Joss, who was also getting beside himself with hunger and exhaustion. Her mind had gone completely blank and she could think only of her two sobbing children. All she knew was that she must find them shelter for the night and a hot meal. She cast a wary glance at Isaac who was watching her with interest. 'Mr Johnson, Isaac, I have just returned from the north and I need to find somewhere to stay. Do you know where I can find a respectable lodging house that is not too far from here?'

'I know a place. I'll take you there.'

'That's very kind of you.'

'It's no trouble. The little fellah looks done in and you do too, if you don't mind my saying so.' Isaac scooped Joss up from the ground and set him on his shoulders. 'There, young 'un. Now you're bigger than me, so you can stop piping your eye and enjoy the ride.' With a cheery wink at Eloise, Isaac picked up the two pieces of luggage and set off down the street.

Eloise had no alternative but to follow him through the busy streets. Isaac strode on with Joss bouncing on his shoulders and gurgling with laughter, all his woes forgotten as he enjoyed this new experience. When at last Isaac came to a halt in Nile Street, it was outside a four-storey house in the middle of a late eighteenth-century terrace. Eloise stared up at the soot-encrusted brick façade, which might once have housed a prosperous merchant and his family, but was now looking decidedly shabby and run down. There were several pubs in the street which were quiet at this time of day, but, Eloise thought, would probably prove to be quite rowdy late at night. Dotted amongst them were a few small shops with dilapidated signs hanging above their doors and flies buzzing angrily on the insides of their grimy windows.

Eloise was struck by the stark contrast between the Danbys' homely farmhouse and this grey forbidding place which looked more like a prison than a welcoming refuge. It was just temporary, she told herself as Isaac rapped on the front door. Tomorrow she would find them somewhere to stay in a more salubrious area. Isaac thumped the knocker again, and after a few moments the door was opened by a tiny maid-servant. A white mobcap came so low over her eyebrows that she had to tilt her head back to look up at him, and the print dress she was wearing was several sizes too large for her so that it swamped her small frame. Eloise was almost too tired and distraught to care, but she could see that the girl was probably no more than nine or ten years of age.

'Hello, Annie,' Isaac said, patting her on the head. 'How's my best girl?'

'Leave off, mister,' Annie said, poking out her tongue in response. 'What d'you want?'

'I've brought some new tenants. This lady and her children need a room for the night.'

'This ain't no hotel,' Annie retorted, standing arms akimbo. 'You brung her to the wrong place, cully.'

Isaac's smile was replaced by an ominous scowl. 'That's enough of your sauce, girl. You can let us in for a start and then I want you to fetch Mrs King, d'you hear me?'

Annie took several steps backwards and her pinched features assumed the look of a whipped cur. 'All right, all right. Keep your hair on, mister.' She turned and ran down a long and narrow passageway, calling out for her mistress.

'Step inside,' Isaac said, motioning Eloise to enter the hallway. 'This ain't Buckingham Palace, but Queenie runs a respectable house and it's clean.'

Momentarily forgetting her misgivings, Eloise stared at him in disbelief. 'Queenie King?'

Isaac nodded his head and chuckled deep in his throat. 'Aye, that's the nub of it. Good name, ain't it? And you'll find she's a queen amongst women, as long as you keep on the right side of her.' At the sound of approaching footsteps, Isaac set Joss down on the ground and he hid behind his mother as a large woman bore down on them like a brigantine in full sail. She was tightly corseted and her ample bosom was hung with gold chains and glass beads which clanked together with every step she took in her high-heeled boots. She ignored Eloise but she smiled coquettishly at Isaac. 'Well, now. Isaac, me old cock sparrow, where've you been hiding these past few weeks?'

He moved forward swiftly to grab her round the waist and Eloise could not help noticing that his arms only just stretched round Queenie's great girth in spite of her corsets. He planted a smacking kiss on her cherry-red lips, which Eloise suspected were rouged; as were Queenie's cheeks which were unnaturally rosy for a woman of advancing years. It occurred to her inconsequentially that Papa would have been quite censorious about a woman who painted her face and wore a gown cut low enough to leave very little to the imagination. Eloise put the vision of her father's shocked face out of her mind. What did it matter, after all? She was just here to lodge for a night or two until she found suitable rooms to rent. She managed a smile as Queenie extricated herself from Isaac's arms and surged towards her with a questioning look on her face. 'So, you are a friend of Isaac's, are you, lady?'

Eloise shook her head. 'No, Mrs King, not really. We were neighbours in Myrtle Street and Isaac, I mean Mr Johnson, offered to help me find lodgings.'

Queenie shot Isaac a knowing glance. 'I'm sure he did. Well, as it happens you're in luck, my dear. I have a good room at the back of the house, which was vacated today by a commercial traveller – reluctantly, I may say. My rooms are much in demand, Miss – er – Mrs . . . ?'

'Mrs Cribb,' Eloise said with a proud tilt of her head. 'I am a widow, ma'am.'

'Are you indeed? Well, Mrs Cribb, dear, you follow me, and you, Isaac Johnson, can go to my parlour where we will renew our acquaintance over a glass of blue ruin.' She flashed him a smile and then set off down the passage towards the back of the house.

Eloise held her hand out to Isaac. 'Thank you very much, Mr Johnson. I'm truly grateful for your help.'

He dragged his cap off his head with a bashful smile. 'It weren't nothing, ma'am. Glad to be of help. Goodbye, young Joss. Be a good boy for your ma.'

Joss plugged his thumb in his mouth and reached up to grasp his mother's hand. With a last grateful smile in Isaac's direction, Eloise lifted Beth to a more comfortable position on her hip and she hurried after Queenie.

'There!' Queenie said, throwing a door open with the air of a conjuror pulling a bunch of paper flowers from his coat sleeve. 'Now don't tell me this ain't the best room you've ever seen. I pride myself in keeping a clean house, so no muddy boots allowed.' Queenie eyed Joss severely and he buried his face in his mother's skirts. Eloise entered the room, wrinkling her nose at the smell of boiled fish that was wafting in through the open window. Queenie hurried past her to slam the sash down. 'The kitchen's below, but you'll get used to the smell of cooking. Friday is always fish for supper, not that I'm one of them Jesuits but all denominations are welcome here. I do me best to make everyone feel at home. Will you be taking supper tonight, Mrs Cribb?'

Eloise did not much fancy boiled fish, but she had not eaten since midday when she and Joss had shared a hunk of bread, freshly made that morning by Gladys, and a slice of cheese from the farm's own dairy. She felt suddenly quite homesick for Danby Farm.

'Supper is extra, of course,' Queenie continued without waiting for a reply. 'But you won't get better food in Shoreditch, I can promise you that.'

'Thank you, I will take supper, and breakfast too, if that's possible.'

'Breakfast is served in the dining parlour at eight o'clock on the dot, and supper is at seven. Those who don't sit down on time go without. I have to have rules, Mrs Cribb.'

'Yes, I'm sure.' A wave of tiredness swept over Eloise, but Joss seemed to have found his second wind and he clambered onto the iron bedstead and began rolling around on the coverlet.

'Not with his shoes on, if you please,' Queenie said, frowning. 'I don't hold with nippers running riot, Mrs Cribb. I hope you will keep the young rascal under control.'

'Of course,' Eloise said, setting Beth down on the bed and shaking her head at Joss. 'Don't bounce on the bed, dear. You know Mama doesn't allow it at home.'

Queenie nodded her head. 'Quite right. A firm hand is what is needed from the start. There's just one thing before I leave you to settle in, ma'am. Money!' Queenie held out her hand. 'I charge three shillings a night and that includes breakfast, but supper is extra. However, I'm a generous woman and I won't charge you for the nippers, but you'll have to buy their milk from the dairy on the corner. I don't usually take in children, but I'm making an exception as you're a friend of Isaac's. Money in advance if you please, and an extra shilling for supper. Only the best food is served in my dining parlour.'

Eloise took out her purse and counted out four shilling pieces, but Queenie raised her eyebrows and extended her plump hand a little further in a gesture suggesting that this was not enough. 'You'll be staying more than the one night, I suppose. Cash strictly in advance, Mrs Cribb.'

'Two nights at the most, ma'am,' Eloise said, counting out another four coins. 'I'm obliged to you.'

'I'll have your luggage brought to you. And the privy is in the yard at the back of the house. We have the usual conveniences, and the girl will bring you warm water for washing in the morning. I run this establishment like a high-class hotel, as I am sure you will soon see.'

Just as Queenie was about to leave the room,

Eloise called her back. 'Do you think we could have coal for the fire, ma'am? It still gets a bit chilly at night and my children have only recently recovered from an illness.'

Queenie's pencilled brows shot high up into her coiffed head. 'Nothing catching, I hope?'

'Nothing to worry about, Mrs King.'

'Fires lit in the rooms from October to the end of April only. I cannot make exceptions, Mrs Cribb, or all my lodgers would want the same.' Queenie swept out of the room, closing the door behind her.

Eloise sank down on the bed to cuddle Joss and Beth, rocking them in her arms. 'We'll get through this, my darlings. Mama will make everything better, you'll see.'

Supper was served, as Queenie had promised, promptly at seven o'clock. Eloise took her seat at table, with Beth on her knee and Joss sitting on a pile of cushions at her side. The dining table would have seated ten quite comfortably, but to her relief there were only two of the residents present on this particular evening. One was an elderly gentleman who was obviously extremely deaf, but even with the use of an ear trumpet it was clear that he could barely make out what Annie was saying when she yelled at him. She seemed to be the maid of all work and came tottering in with a large tureen of soup. She served the elderly gentleman first. 'It's oxtail soup, Mr Wallace,' she shouted into his ear trumpet. 'Eat up. Eat up.'

'Eh, what did you say?' Mr Wallace demanded crossly. 'Speak up, girl, don't mumble.'

'Daft old bugger,' Annie muttered, slopping soup into the plate of the bespectacled gentleman sitting at the far end of the table. His starched wing collar and shiny black suit suggested to Eloise that he held some kind of clerical position, but he seemed very reserved and did not speak at all unless spoken to. He did not even complain when Annie spilt some of the soup on his hand; he merely gave her a reproachful look and wiped it off on his table napkin.

'Soup for you, missis?' Annie demanded, hovering at Eloise's side with the tureen.

'Yes, please, and just a little for Joss.'

'You could sop some of it up on a bit of bread for the babe,' Annie said, eyeing Beth with interest. 'I used to feed the little 'uns when I was in the Foundling Hospital. I'm good with babies, I am.'

'I'm sure you are,' Eloise said, smiling at this proud statement. 'How old are you, Annie?'

'I ain't too sure, but I think I might be ten or thereabouts. I was left on the doorstep, I was. Another hour and they said I would have froze to death, but I'm a tough 'un – it would take more than that to kill me. I've had measles, mumps and scarlet fever and I'm still here to tell the tale.'

'Well, you're very lucky then,' Eloise murmured, dipping bread into the soup and feeding it alternately to Joss and Beth. 'You must be tough indeed, and I'm sure you work very hard too.'

'That I do, missis.' Annie pulled out the chair next to Eloise and sat down, warming to her theme. 'I'm up at five and I light the fire in the range. Then I cleans the grate in the fat old cow's parlour, although don't let on that I called her that, or she'll skin me alive. I help Cook with the breakfasts and I clean the men's boots. I'm a real slave, I am. Here, let me feed the baby while you get some food inside you.' Without waiting for an answer, Annie took a chunk of bread and broke off tiny pieces, which she popped into Beth's eager mouth. 'She's a pretty little thing. What's her name?'

'Oy, you, girl.' Mr Wallace waved his ear trumpet at her. 'I want some more soup.'

Annie waved back at him. 'Shut your gob, you silly old goat.' She looked up at Eloise and grinned. 'He's deaf as a post, but so long as I keep smiling and let him pat me bum occasionally, it keeps the old fool sweet.' She blew him a kiss. 'Daft old squit.'

'Annie, please,' Eloise murmured. 'Watch your language in front of Joss; he's just learning to talk.'

Annie wrinkled her snub nose and pulled a

face. 'He'll learn the bad words long afore he learns to speak proper, but I'll try to watch me mouth. I like you, missis. You talk to me like I was a human being and not something what someone scraped off the bottom of their shoe. Not like her, the fat old crow. She beats me black and blue if I don't do just what she says, but I get me own back. I spit in her hot chocolate before I gives it to her, and I put maggots in her mashed taters. She's so blooming greedy that she munches them up without even noticing.'

Eloise swallowed a mouthful of soup with difficulty. She was so hungry that she would have eaten almost anything, but surprisingly the soup was very tasty. 'I hope you didn't . . .'

Annie threw back her head and roared with laughter. 'Not for you, missis. I only does it to them as gets on me wrong side.' She paled and leapt to her feet as the door opened and Queenie entered the room. 'I was just helping feed the baby, missis.'

'That's not part of your job, you idle little slut. Get back to the kitchen and help Cook serve up the boiled haddock or it'll be the worse for you.' Queenie's scowl dissolved into an ingratiating smile as she glanced round the room. 'I hope everything is to your satisfaction, gentlemen and lady?'

'More soup,' roared Mr Wallace. 'I want more soup.'

Queenie clipped Annie round the ear. 'Serve Mr Wallace with more soup, and then go about your duties.' She turned to Eloise. 'And you, Mrs Cribb? I trust you are satisfied.'

'I am, thank you, but I have to say that the girl was just being helpful.'

Queenie's bright smile vanished. 'She isn't paid to be helpful to you; I pay her to do as I say.'

Later that evening, while Joss and Beth slept in the bed at her side, Eloise lay wide awake. She was exhausted, but her mind was racing round in circles and sleep eluded her. Harcourt had given her twenty pounds when she left Cribb's Hall. She had thought it was generous and that it would last her for several months at least, but it was dwindling much faster than she could have imagined possible. She knew that she would not be able to afford Queenie King's prices for very long, and that she would have to look for rooms in a cheaper establishment. She must find work, and she would need someone to mind the children. Eloise lay, looking up at a maze of cracks in the ceiling. Her life seemed like that maze and she was stuck in the middle unable to find the way out.

Chapter Eight

Next morning when she went into the dining parlour, Eloise came face to face with the rest of Queenie's lodgers. Apart from the two gentlemen who had been at supper, there were six more males of varying ages and differing occupations, judging by the way in which they were dressed. They mostly seemed to be commercial travellers or clerks, but there were two who were garbed in more practical attire, suggesting that they were involved in some kind of manual labour. Whatever their occupations, they had one thing in common, and that was the way in which they were applying themselves enthusiastically to their meal of bacon, eggs and a small mountain of toast. The room was filled with the sound of their jaws champing on their food and a certain amount of appreciative lip-smacking. They barely looked up as Eloise took her seat at the table. Apart from asking her to pass the toast or the butter, no one spoke to her and she concentrated on feeding the children. Annie brought in a plate of scrambled eggs especially for Joss and Beth, and when one of the men demanded the same she slapped him on the back of his hand and told him that this was food for the nippers and not for great hulking men who worked on the railways. The man subsided with a scowl and Eloise tried to ignore the black looks he was sending in their direction. She felt very uncomfortable and out of place in this male domain, but Joss was obviously fascinated by the variety of table manners exhibited, from the bird-like pecking of the prim office clerk in the shiny suit, whom Annie addressed as Mr Potter, to the rather disgusting slurping sounds made by a bald man with a shiny pate who did not seem to have any teeth in his head, and who dipped his bread in his tea and then sucked it noisily. Joss was staring open-mouthed at the display, and Eloise was heartily glad when the meal was over and the men filed silently out of the room, leaving them alone with a pile of dirty crockery and cutlery.

Annie came breezing in with a large wooden tray and began clearing the table. 'So, what are you going to do today, then?' she asked cheerfully. 'It's lovely and warm outside. I think summer's come, although I don't see much of it meself and it's bleeding hot working in the kitchen with flies buzzing round your head. You might think they're raisins in the spotted dick, but I tell you, most of them is flies what fell in the mixture. Don't eat nothing with raisins or currants in, that's my advice.'

Eloise tried hard to keep a straight face. 'Thank you, Annie. I'll bear that in mind.'

'I got a bit of time off this afternoon,' Annie said, piling dishes onto her tray. 'I could take little Joss for a walk to the Foundling Hospital if you like. I always goes back there on me afternoon off. There's a nice bit of grass, some big trees, and flowers. It's like I imagine the country might be, though I've never been there, but one day I will. I made up me mind to it, I have. One day I'll ride on a train and go into the countryside and see fields and cows and pigs and such. I've seen pictures of them in some of the magazines the lodgers have in their rooms.' She lifted the tray with difficulty and staggered out of the room, calling over her shoulder, 'I'll see you later then.'

Eloise was left feeling breathless, amused and also rather sad to think that this child who had had such a hard life could have such simple dreams, which for her were almost unattainable. As she wiped Joss's mouth and sticky hands and then turned her attention to cleaning up Beth, who had jam all over her face, Eloise thought of her own pleasant childhood in the Dorset vicarage. They had certainly not lived in luxury. It had been a poor parish, and her father had had no private income to supplement the meagre salary of a country clergyman. It was a well known fact that most of the clergy were younger sons of the landed gentry, but Papa had come from a more humble background and had worked his way through theological college in order to follow his calling. Eloise felt her throat constrict as she thought about her parents. She loved and respected her father, but she had always been a little in awe of him and even a bit frightened of him at times. But if Papa had been a little too overbearing and strict, then Mama had made up for his lack of warmth, and there had always been Janet to pet and spoil her. In the sleepy Dorset village, close to the sea, there had been the village children for her to play with, and if she climbed trees and tore her clothes, Mama would darn them before Papa saw the damage and could seize the chance to complain about the cost of replacing ruined garments. There had been egg rolling competitions at Easter, dancing around the maypole at the May Day celebrations, swimming in the river during the long hot days of summer and bonfires in November; followed by Christmas, with carols sung in church and presents under the tree.

Eloise came back to reality with a start as Joss knocked a glass of water over and it trickled off the table onto Mrs King's best red Turkey carpet. Eloise mopped it up hastily and then took the children back to their room to make them ready for a trip to the vicarage in King's Square. She had given it a lot of thought during her wakeful hours before finally falling asleep from sheer exhaustion. The obvious person to go to for help was a man of the cloth like her father, and who better than the person who had taken over his parish? She hoped the new vicar might be able to help her to find work, or at the very least to advise her on the best way to start looking for a position where she would be allowed to keep her children with her.

The Reverend Martin Collins steepled his fingers and stared solemnly at Eloise over the tips of them as if he were about to pray for her eternal soul. 'My dear Mrs Cribb, it is quite unthinkable for a young woman such as you to enter the workplace. You are a mother and your first consideration must be your children.'

Eloise clenched her hands in her lap. She had already explained the circumstances to this man, but he seemed not to have understood a word she had said. 'I do not want to leave my children, vicar. I want to find a position where I can take them with me.'

He raised a delicate eyebrow. 'My dear young lady, I'm afraid that is highly unlikely. I mean, you could apply for a position as governess to a private family, but they would hardly be willing to take two such small children on as well. You cannot teach in a school for the same reason.'

'Sir, I came here for advice. You are telling me

what I already know, but I have to find work as I have very little money, and, as you are aware, my father and mother have gone to Africa and are not expected to return for at least two years. I need to earn my own living, and I am at a loss as to what to do.'

'I am sorry to hear it, Mrs Cribb. I can only suggest that you swallow your pride and return to your late husband's family in Yorkshire. I am sure that the rift between you could be mended by an appropriate apology, and it must needs come from you. Pride is a sin, you know. Take my advice, my dear, and travel back to Yorkshire forthwith. Make your apologies and wait for your parents to return from their good works in Africa. I think you know that that is the right and proper course to take.'

Eloise rose to her feet and found she was trembling with suppressed anger, but she was determined not to let it show. 'Thank you for seeing me, vicar. I am sorry to have taken up your valuable time.'

Mr Collins looked up at her, and a flicker of what might have been sympathy softened his expression. 'If you do not intend to leave London immediately and would like to leave your address with me, I will contact you should I hear of anything which might suit.' He handed her pen and paper.

When she was outside the vicarage, Eloise

stamped her foot. 'Stupid, pompous idiot of a man,' she cried angrily. Then, seeing that Joss was looking scared and bewildered, she bent down to kiss him on the tip of his nose. 'Mama is not cross with you, poppet. I'm angry with that silly man who told us to return to Yorkshire. Well, I won't do it. I'll take in washing or sewing. I'll make matchboxes or sell bootlaces on the street. I won't go back to Cribb's Hall and that's final.'

Back at the lodging house in Nile Street, Eloise was let in by an excited Annie. 'There's a gent to see you, missis. I never seen him afore, but he's a big giant of a chap who speaks funny. I put him in Mrs King's parlour, seeing as how she's gone to the dressmaker's to be fitted for another new gown. If the old mare gets any fatter she'll have to have her frocks put together by a sailmaker.' Annie scuttled off along the passageway, chortling at her own wit.

Mystified, Eloise followed her. Isaac was the only person in London who knew where she was staying and Annie said it was a stranger who had called. There must be some mistake, or else the poor child was a little touched in the head.

'He's in there,' Annie said, pushing a door open. 'Don't let him keep you for long. She'll be back in an hour or so, and she don't approve of gentlemen callers.' With a saucy wink, Annie strolled off in the direction of the back stairs leading down to the basement kitchen.

Holding Joss firmly by the hand and with Beth balanced on her hip, Eloise peeped round the door of Queenie's private parlour. Standing in the middle of the room, Reggie looked out of place amongst the array of china ornaments and heavy crimson-velvet drapes. His face was flushed and he looked uncomfortable in his Sunday best suit, which was made of heavy tweed, more suited to the colder northern climes than to the heat of London in May.

Smiling with genuine pleasure, Eloise entered the room. 'Reggie. What a lovely surprise. What are you doing here?'

His craggy features relaxed into a shy grin. 'Ellie! I've had a right hard time trying to find you, lass.'

Joss broke free from his mother's hand and ran to Reggie, holding up his chubby arms and chuckling with delight.

Eloise set Beth down on the floor. 'I don't understand, Reggie. How did you find us and why are you here in London?'

He bent down to pick up Joss and chucked him under the chin. 'I've missed you, lad. We've all missed you back on the farm.' He sat down on the nearest chair, scooping Beth up and settling her on his knee beside Joss. 'This is grand,' he said happily. 'Just like old times.'

'It's good to see you again, Reggie,' Eloise said, taking a seat opposite him, 'but you haven't told me why you've come, or how you found us.'

'Well, lass, you gave Mother the address in Myrtle Street and I went there first, thinking I'd find you, but the woman were a right old bitch and she slammed the door in me face. So I went next door and received much the same treatment. I have to say I don't think much of the way southerners behave, but then just as I were leaving, this big fellow comes out of the house and asks what my business is with you. We went to the pub for a pint of ale and a chat, and when he knew why I wanted to see you, he directed me here. And here I am.' After this extraordinarily long speech for him, Reggie paused for breath and sat grinning at Eloise as if he had accomplished something quite splendid.

'But you still haven't said why you've come.' Eloise tried not to sound impatient, but she was beginning to think the worst. Perhaps Gladys had been taken ill, or Meg. Perhaps the farm had been razed to the ground by fire? 'For goodness' sake, Reggie. I only left you yesterday. What could have happened in such a short space of time?'

His smile faded and he set the wriggling children down on the ground. 'Your in-laws turned up at the farm soon after you'd left on the train for London. The old fellow seems a decent enough chap, but his wife and her sister are another matter. My old lady didn't take to them at all. You should have heard her going on at that Miss Braithwaite for not coming to her own daughter's funeral. I almost felt sorry for the old witch.'

'But what did they want, Reggie? Why did they choose that time to come?'

'Happen they didn't know where you were until they got the telegraph about the funeral. It seems they weren't interested in poor Ada, but your mother-in-law has set her heart on having young Joss to bring up as she sees fit. Ma told her it were a bad idea and she couldn't think of taking him away from his mother, but Mrs Cribb wouldn't listen to her. She said as how he were their Ronald's son and he must be brought up as such and be educated like a gentleman, since one day he would take over the business. She made no mention of Beth, but I'm of the opinion she won't rest until she gets her hands on young Joss, or Ronnie as she kept on calling him.'

Eloise stared at him in horror. 'No! No, she has no rights over him. Joss is my son. You didn't tell them where we'd gone, did you?'

'I never, but Meg let it slip you'd gone to London and they know you lived in Myrtle Street. The old woman screamed at Cribb and told him he must travel south to find you. That's why I come down on the night train. I knew I must seek you out and warn you what were afoot.'

'But they would never find me here.'

'I did,' Reggie said simply.

Eloise jumped to her feet. 'I must find somewhere else to stay. We must leave here today.'

'Or you could come back with me, lass.' Reggie stood up, carefully avoiding treading on the children who were clamouring to be picked up again. 'Marry me, Ellie. I know you don't love me, but I love you enough for us both. If you're my wife then I can protect you and the little ones from the likes of the Cribbs. You'd be safe on the farm with us. What do you say, lass?'

In the light of what the Revered Martin Collins had said, Reggie's proposal looked like an easy way out, but tempting as it was she simply could not marry a man for whom she felt nothing more than friendship. Eloise raised her head to look steadily into Reggie's eyes. She knew she was going to hurt him, but far better to do it now than to marry him and make his life miserable in the future. 'You hardly know me, Reggie.'

'I know you well enough, lass. Sometimes it only takes a moment for a man to know he's in love with a lass, and will be for the rest of his life.'

'I'm so sorry, Reggie,' Eloise said gently. 'You are a dear, sweet man, but I cannot marry you.'

He dropped his gaze and bowed his shaggy head. 'I know I'm a great, clumping thing, and not what a lady like you is used to, but I would be true to you, lass. I would be good to you and I would love the little ones just like my own.'

Her heart wrung with pity for him and Eloise put her arms around Reggie and kissed him tenderly on the lips. It was a brief embrace and she drew away immediately, but not before the door had been flung open and Queenie stood on the threshold, breathing heavily. 'What's this? Who is this man, Mrs Cribb? I don't allow followers in my establishment.'

Eloise stepped away from Reggie, hastily composing herself. 'It's not what you think, ma'am. Mr Danby is my cousin from Yorkshire. He is in London on business and called in to pass the time of day.'

'Is that so?' Queenie eyed Reggie suspiciously.

He reached for his cap, clutching it before him like a shield, and looking so sheepish that Eloise had to stifle the desire to giggle. She linked her hand through Reggie's arm. 'He was just leaving, Mrs King. Reggie has a train to catch.'

'Then the sooner he goes the better,' Queenie said, bridling.

Eloise felt Reggie's arm muscles tauten and she could see a pulse beating in his throat. She had never seen him angry before but she sensed that he was about to put Queenie firmly in her place. She squeezed his arm. 'We're still dressed for outdoors, so we'll walk a little way with you, Reggie.'

'If you say so, Ellie,' he muttered between clenched teeth.

'We would like another little walk, wouldn't we, Joss?' Eloise said brightly. 'Perhaps Cousin Reggie would give you a piggy-back?'

Reggie glared at Queenie, and was obviously having difficulty in controlling the desire to tell her a few home truths, but to Eloise's relief he said nothing as he plucked Joss from the floor and set him on his shoulders. Queenie stood by the door with her arms folded in front of her and watched him leave the room with a martial light in her eyes. Eloise was about to hurry past her when Queenie barred her way. 'You only paid for two nights, Mrs Cribb. Your room is taken by one of my regular business gentlemen from tomorrow onwards, so I will have to ask you to find somewhere else to stay.'

'That suits me, Mrs King,' Eloise said with as much dignity as she could muster. 'I wouldn't want to stay on here even if board and lodging was offered free.' She did not believe Queenie for one moment, but she was not going to beg to be allowed to stay in this awful place, and she left the room with her head held high.

When they were outside on the pavement, Reggie gave her a searching look. 'What did the old bat say to you then, Ellie?'

'Nothing of importance.' Eloise slipped her hand through the crook of his arm. 'We'll walk with you as far as the Eagle Tavern in the City Road, and then I really must get back to the lodging house and give the children their dinner.'

Reggie looked deeply into her eyes. 'Won't you change your mind, lass? If you won't have me for your husband, just come back to the farm and live with us as you did afore. I won't press my suit, in fact I'll never mention marriage again.'

'It wouldn't work, Reggie. For one thing I would be too near the Cribbs, and they would never stop harassing me, and for another – I couldn't expect your family to take us in. It wouldn't be fair on them.'

'They love you, Ellie,' Reggie said with a catch in his voice. 'We all love you and the children.'

'Don't make this harder for me, please. I really can't come with you, but I will always remember how kind you all were to me.' Eloise flashed him a smile, even though she felt more like crying, but she forced herself to sound cheerful and confident. 'Anyway, I have a position in mind with comfortable living accommodation included, and an employer who does not object to my taking Joss and Beth with me. We will be all right, Reggie. I promise you.'

'You never mentioned it before,' Reggie said suspiciously.

'You didn't give me a chance,' Eloise replied, hoping that God would forgive her for such a big, black lie, but she knew she must convince Reggie that they would be safe and secure or he would refuse to leave without her. 'The vicar who took over from my father knows of a family who need a governess for their children and they do not mind if I take Joss and Beth with me. We will be all right, Reggie. I promise you.'

They walked on in silence until they came to the Eagle Tavern, which was a well-known rowdy pub and music hall; a place where shameless women flaunted their charms in front of drunken men, or that was what Papa had claimed when Janet had once said she would like to go there to see a show. He had made it plain that it was not a place he would wish his parishioners, let alone members of his family circle to patronise. Eloise had always been curious as to what actually went on in such a venue, but at this particular moment the Eagle was just a landmark, not too far from Euston station. Standing on tiptoe, she kissed Reggie on the cheek. 'This is as far as I go. Goodbye, dear Reggie. Give my love to your ma and pa, and remember me to Jacob and Clara. Tell them I wish them all the happiness in the world and I am just sorry that I cannot see them married.'

'You could,' Reggie said, setting Joss down on the pavement. 'You could always come up for a visit.'

'Maybe I will, if my new employer allows it.'

'And you will let us know your new address?'

'Only if you promise not to let Meg pass it on to the Cribbs,' Eloise said with a teasing smile.

'Oh hell!' Reggie said, pushing his cap to the back of his head in an impatient gesture. 'I almost forgot to give this to you, Ellie.' He pulled an envelope out of his breast pocket. 'Your father-in-law passed it to me when his wife's back was turned. He said it had arrived soon after you left. I think it's come all the way from Africa.'

Eloise gasped with delight as she took it from him. It was her mother's handwriting and the tattered envelope looked as though it had passed through many hands before it had been placed in hers. She clasped it to her breast, moving her lips in an attempt to thank him, but a lump in her throat made it impossible to speak.

'I'd best be on me way, lass.' Reggie ruffled Joss's hair and patted Beth gently on the cheek. 'Goodbye, Ellie,' he said in a choked voice. 'I'll never forget you.'

'Nor I you, Reggie.' Eloise had a struggle to hold back tears as he walked away. If only she could have found it in her heart to love him, but she knew that would never happen and she could but hope that he would put his feeling for her aside and turn to faithful Maud for consolation. She watched Reggie striding off with only a slight hunch of his shoulders to betray his distress, and she fought down the desire to run after him. It was so tempting to take the easy way out, but that would not have been fair on either of them. She tucked her mother's letter safely away in her reticule; she would save it for later when the children were in bed and she could read her mother's words again and again.

Grasping Joss's hand, Eloise turned in the direction of Nile Street. There were more pressing matters on her mind now, and the most important of all was to find another lodging and soon. She would have had to leave anyway, even if Queenie had not said they must. The thought of being discovered by the Cribbs was even more frightening than the threat of being homeless. Eloise hugged Beth, who had grown tired of being carried and wanted to be put down on the ground. 'Mama will get you some milk in a moment, precious.'

'Me too,' Joss clamoured, tugging at her hand.

Eloise gave his fingers a gentle squeeze. 'There's a costermonger's barrow a little further down the street. Mama will buy you a nice juicy orange.' She hurried towards the barrow and was in the process of buying two oranges and a pound of apples when she heard someone speak her name. Momentarily paralysed with fear, Eloise could not move, but as the man repeated her name she realised that it was not Harcourt's voice. She turned her head and was surprised to see the Reverend Martin Collins hurrying towards them, holding his hat on his head as a sudden gust of wind threatened to whirl it up with the rest of the straw and bits of paper that were flying about in the air. 'Mrs Cribb, wait.'

She breathed a sigh of relief. 'This is a coincidence, Mr Collins.'

'Not at all, ma'am. I was on my way to call on you.'

'Really?'

'Although it grieves me to see a young woman like yourself having to go out into the world to earn her own living, I realised on reflection that you were unhappy at the prospect of returning to your in-laws in Yorkshire, and I felt I owed it to your father to come to your aid.'

'You can help me?'

'It's just possible, Mrs Cribb. After you had gone, I remembered a gentleman who used to be a parishioner of mine before I moved to King's Square. He is a respectable man who was once a warder at the House of Detention. He has an invalid wife, and due to his own advancing years he is finding it increasingly hard to cope with just a cook-general. Mr Hubble has been looking for a suitable person to assist in the daily running of their household for some time, and I took the liberty of mentioning your name. The long and the short of it is that I've just come from his house in Clerkenwell Green, and he would very much like to meet you.'

Eloise could hardly believe her ears. 'He wants to see me? When?'

'Now, if it's convenient. I could take you there this minute, if you are agreeable.'

Eloise nodded her head vigorously. This could be the answer to all their problems. 'I would be happy to go now, Mr Collins. Most happy.'

Joss tugged at her hand, pointing to the fruit. 'Mama.'

Beth began to whimper and Eloise was about to ask Mr Collins to wait while she peeled an orange for them when he forestalled her. 'I think your little ones are hungry, ma'am. May I suggest that we find a coffee stall and purchase some hot milk for them and a slice of cake? I believe I could manage a cup of coffee myself, and perhaps I could tempt you?'

For the first time since they had met, Eloise saw a glimmer of humanity in the vicar's grey eyes and she nodded in agreement. 'You're very thoughtful, sir.'

He inclined his head, as if to agree. 'It is quite a long walk to Clerkenwell Green for the little fellow, so we'll stop on the way. Follow me, ma'am.'

They set off, stopping briefly on the way for refreshments at a coffee stall, and having drunk hot milk and shared a slice of cake with Beth Joss was content to trot along at his mother's side, while Beth fell asleep on her shoulder. When they arrived in Clerkenwell Green, Eloise was pleasantly surprised by the village atmosphere. The green was surrounded by late eighteenth-century houses, still elegant but slightly faded like a group of ageing courtesans. The tall spire of St James's church rose above the treetops and there was a market in progress. The smell of boiling hops wafted from Reid's Brewery, mingling with the fragrance of freshly baked bread from the bakery. Stallholders shouted their wares and crowds of shoppers thronged the market place, which was bathed with sunshine. There was a fairground atmosphere, even though the House of Detention loomed above the buildings at the end of St James's Walk, and the House of Correction was a couple of streets away, a fact that Martin Collins was only too pleased to pass on. Eloise was not sure she wanted to hear about this as her spirits had risen considerably in this pleasant, almost festive atmosphere.

'This is the house,' Mr Collins said, stopping outside a four-storey townhouse squashed between a watchmaker's premises and a bank. Without waiting to see Eloise's reaction to his pronouncement he rapped on the front door.

They were admitted by a slatternly-looking woman with a suspicious yellow stain beneath her nose suggestive of an addiction to snuff. She muttered something unintelligible and motioned the vicar towards a narrow staircase, before hobbling off down a long and dark corridor.

'The parlour is on the first floor,' Mr Collins explained as he mounted the staircase. 'Mrs Hubble is unable to climb stairs and her room is on the ground floor at the back of the house. Follow me, Mrs Cribb, and do watch your step. I'm afraid the carpet is a little threadbare in patches.'

Eloise wrinkled her nose at the smell of must and general decay which seemed to seep out of the plasterwork on the walls. The house had a dilapidated, almost derelict feeling to it, quite at odds with its elegant façade. She urged Joss on with an encouraging smile, although the dark stairway sent shivers down her spine. Mr Collins was well ahead of her and he disappeared round a bend in the stairs. She heard the click of a door being opened on the first landing. Hurrying after him, she caught up as he entered a room at the front of the house. Daylight filtered in through three tall, but decidedly grimy windows and the drawing room overlooked the green, but although the view was pleasant the interior of the room was shabby and decidedly gloomy. The crazed plaster on the ceiling was flaking off and falling occasionally with soft plops on the bare floorboards. Ashes spilled from the grate onto the hearth and there was a chill in the room even though it was warm outside. The walls, which badly needed a coat of paint, were unrelieved by paintings or even a framed print, and the curtains which hung limply at the windows were riddled with moth holes. The furniture was an eclectic jumble of items which looked as though they had been picked up in salerooms, or rescued from dust heaps. Seated in a wingback chair by the fireplace, an elderly gentleman with white hair and a florid complexion sat with one heavily bandaged foot resting on a stool. 'So you've come back, vicar. Didn't think you would.'

'I'm a man of my word, Ephraim,' Mr Collins said piously. 'May I introduce Mrs Eloise Cribb, the young widow of whom we spoke earlier?'

'Yes, yes, you have done so, but there's no need to shout. I may suffer from gout but I'm neither deaf nor senile.'

Mr Collins turned to Eloise with a vague smile. 'Mr Hubble has a wonderful sense of humour. I'm sure you two will get along splendidly.'

'I haven't said I'd take her on yet, Collins,' Ephraim snapped, leaning forward to stare at Eloise with piercing green eyes. 'Come here, girl. Let me look at you. And put the baby down on a chair or something. Collins, you take the boy and keep him quiet while I talk to his mother.'

Mr Collins blinked but he did as he was told

and went to sit on a rickety chair, holding out his hand and offering to peel an orange for Joss, who toddled over to him trustingly with a piece of fruit clutched in his small hands.

Eloise had disliked Ephraim Hubble on sight, but she was desperate for work and a place to stay and she could not afford to offend a prospective employer. Reluctantly, she moved closer to the old man. 'How do you do, Mr Hubble?'

'Oh, it's a lady, is it? You didn't tell me that, Collins.'

'I told you that Mrs Cribb's father was my predecessor, Ephraim. Have you forgotten already?'

'I haven't forgotten, you psalm-singing pedant. Nor have I forgotten that you said her father was as poor as a church mouse and had gone off on some tomfool mission to Africa, where he'll probably end up in a stew pot like some of his forerunners.'

'Really, Ephraim, I don't think you ought to talk in that manner,' Mr Collins said, frowning.

'I'll speak as I please in my own house.' Ephraim turned to Eloise, giving her a searching look. 'Now, lady, tell me why you need to take on work as a skivvy? Haven't you got any rich relations you could impose on?'

'I'm a widow, sir. My in-laws live in the north and I do not choose to impose on them, as you put it.'

'Huh! I see you have a bit of spirit in spite of being a parson's daughter. Can't stand mealy-mouthed, prim and proper misses. But you don't look strong enough to do housework.'

'Housework? I thought you wanted a house-keeper.'

Ephraim uttered a mirthless cackle of laughter. 'Call it what you will. I want someone to wash and clean my old woman and feed her when she's hungry, which ain't too often these days.'

'It sounds as though you need a trained nurse, sir.'

'I ain't paying for a nurse. Waste of money. The old girl's not for this world much longer, or so I hope. I should be handing her over to one of Mr Collins's colleagues soon enough and they can bury her and send her nagging soul to heaven or hell. I don't really care where she ends up. But if you're too grand for the job, lady, just speak out now. Don't waste my time.'

Eloise glanced at Joss who was happily suck-ing a segment of orange, and at Beth, who lay rosy-cheeked and sleeping on the horsehair sofa, and she knew she had no choice. 'Very well, I'll do it, as long as you allow me to keep my children with me.'

'They can stay as long as I don't see or hear them. Keep them out of my way while you scrub and clean the floors and you'll not find me a hard taskmaster.'

'Scrubbing and cleaning?' Eloise bit her lip. 'I thought you wanted someone to nurse your wife?'

'That don't take all day. You'll have plenty of time for keeping house when you've poured a bit of laudanum down her throat. She sleeps most of the time as it is. What's the matter, lady? Are you too high and mighty to roll up your sleeves and do a bit of cleaning?'

Mr Collins set Joss on the floor. 'Really, Ephraim, this is most improper talk.'

'If you don't like it, you can leave, vicar. And you can take her with you if she's not of a mind to help out an elderly gent in distress.' Ephraim leaned towards Eloise with his eyes glinting malevolently. 'Forty pounds a year, and free board and lodging. How does that sound, my lady?'

It's only temporary, Eloise told herself. Just until I can find something better. She nodded her head. 'I'll do it.'

'But, Mrs Cribb, are you sure . . .' Mr Collins began, clearing his throat nervously. 'I mean, I truly didn't know that there would be so much expected of you.'

'Ain't you up to it, lady?' Ephraim demanded, obviously enjoying the spectacle of their discomfort. 'Say now, if you ain't.'

Chapter Nine

'I can do it,' Eloise said firmly. Although she was far from certain that this was actually true, she was now desperate. All her instincts were telling her neither to trust nor like Mr Hubble, but if she accepted his offer it would provide a roof over their heads for the time being, and the Cribbs would never think to look for her here. She was not afraid of hard work; she would scrub floors and clean privies if it enabled her to provide for her children. 'When can I start?'

'Mrs Cribb,' Mr Collins said, rising to his feet. 'Perhaps you ought to take time to consider Mr Hubble's offer?'

'Be silent, Reverend,' Ephraim snapped. 'Let the girl make up her own mind.'

Eloise stooped to pick up Beth, and she took Joss by the hand. 'My mind is made up, sir. I will need to collect my belongings from Mrs King's lodging house, but I am free to begin today if you want me to.'

Ephraim let out a low chuckle, which sounded suspiciously like a growl. 'I want you to, young lady. You'll brighten up the old place a treat; just keep them nippers out of my sight. I can't abide children.'

'Is this wise?' Mr Collins asked, keeping his voice low. 'I mean, perhaps you ought to stay on in Nile Street until something more suitable turns up.'

'I came here at your suggestion, vicar.'

'Yes, I know that, and it is for that reason that I would ask you to think again. I might have misjudged the situation.' Mr Collins glanced anxiously over his shoulder at the hunched figure crouching in the chair.

'Stop muttering, vicar,' Ephraim shouted, pointing his walking stick at him. 'If you've something to say, speak up or hold your tongue.'

'I was just offering to assist Mrs Cribb with her luggage, Ephraim.'

'You're a liar, sir, and you a man of the cloth! Shame on you.' Ephraim threw back his head and roared with laughter. Taking a leather purse from his pocket, he took out a coin and held it up between his thumb and forefinger. 'Here, lady. This will pay for a cab from your lodging house. Never let it be said that Ephraim Hubble is a mean man.' He tossed the coin to Mr Collins who caught it deftly in one hand. 'Your job is done, vicar. You'll not see me again until I attend me old lady's funeral. Then the one who'll be singing the loudest will be me.'

Ephraim's coarse laughter followed them as

Eloise hurried down the stairs followed by Mr Collins. He caught her by the arm as they went outside into the street. 'Mrs Cribb, I am not sure . . .'

She gave him a reassuring smile. 'Please don't worry about me, Mr Collins. I am sure I will be well suited here.'

'I hope so, ma'am. I feel a certain amount of responsibility, having introduced you to Mr Hubble.'

'I am sure you don't need to worry, and I am very grateful to you for going to so much trouble on my account. I mustn't keep you any longer from your parish duties.' Eloise turned and started to walk away but he caught up with her.

'I will walk part of the way with you, Mrs Cribb.'

They parted in the City Road and Eloise hurried on to Nile Street. She had hoped to slip away without being noticed, but in the end she had to enlist Annie's help in carrying the luggage out of the house. Annie scuttled off to hail a cab.

'Found one at the end of the street,' Annie gasped breathlessly, having run all the way back to where Eloise waited on the pavement with Joss and Beth. 'He's just turning the thing round, which ain't easy with all the traffic these days.' Annie clasped her hands to her chest. 'Cor blimey, that's took it out of me. I ain't as sprightly as I was when I was younger.'

Eloise laughed in spite of everything. 'You mean when you were eight or nine?'

'It's all due to her wearing me out with hard work. Won't you take me with you, missis? I could help with the nippers.'

'I would if I could, believe me, but I'm afraid it's impossible. I'm not even sure how I'll get on in Clerkenwell Green.'

'I'll come and visit you there on me afternoon off then. I get one every month or so if she's in a good mood.'

Eloise bit her lip. She had not meant to tell anyone where she was going. The cab was rumbling towards them and she had to raise her voice to make herself heard above the clatter of the horse's hooves. 'You won't tell anyone where I've gone, will you, Annie?'

Annie's eyes widened with curiosity. 'Why not?'

'There might be someone enquiring after me and the children. I don't want them to find me. Do you understand?'

Annie nodded emphatically. 'I can keep a secret, but I can come, can't I?'

'Of course you can, dear. Look for the house with the blue door facing the green. You can't miss it.'

'I will,' Annie promised, hefting the two pieces of luggage into the cab. 'And I won't tell no one nothing. Cross me heart and hope to die.'

The cabby set them down outside the house in Clerkenwell Green. Eloise knocked on the door with a feeling of trepidation. Once again she was plunging herself and her children into the unknown. She dared not think too far ahead. Day to day life had whittled down to the bare necessities of having enough food to eat and a bed to sleep in at night. She waited nervously for the sound of approaching footsteps. She knocked again and this time was rewarded by a faint shuffling sound. The door opened and the elderly woman with the snuff-stained face glared at her. 'What d'you want?'

'I am the new housekeeper. Mr Hubble hired me this morning.'

'Housekeeper! That's a laugh. If you're the housekeeper, then I'm Queen Victoria.' She moved away and the door would have swung shut in Eloise's face if she had not shoved her suitcase over the doorsill with her foot. She dragged the valise over the step and edged into the hall, with Beth held firmly in one arm and Joss clinging to her hand. 'Wait a minute,' Eloise called after the fast disappearing woman. 'You will have to show me my room, and I need some help with my cases.'

The woman stopped and glanced over her shoulder, scowling. 'I don't have to do nothing, missis.'

'My name is Mrs Cribb, and I would be obliged if you would show me to my room, Miss – er – Mrs . . .'

'It's Agnes Smith. Miss Smith to you.' Agnes hobbled off down the passageway. 'Follow me then, unless you want to sleep on the doormat.' She led them down the hallway to a room at the back of the house. Thrusting the door open she stood aside to let Eloise pass. 'There you are. Make yourself comfortable, if you can.'

'But I thought this was Mrs Hubble's room,' Eloise said, hesitating. 'Mr Hubble said . . .'

Agnes threw back her head and laughed. 'He says lots of things. Like poor Mrs Hubble is sick. Well, I tells you, lady, she is more than sick. She's been dead this past four months. Dead and buried in St James's churchyard.'

A feeling of nausea swept over Eloise and for a moment she felt quite faint. 'And this was her room?'

Obviously enjoying herself, Agnes grinned. 'She died in that very bed, but it weren't nothing catching, she pegged out peaceful enough. Although there's some what might say a large dose of laudanum helped her on her way, but that's just gossip.'

'There must be some mistake,' Eloise murmured, peering nervously into the depths of the darkened room. 'Mr Hubble said . . .'

'Lord save us, missis. You don't want to pay no

attention to what he says. He'd swear that day was night if it got him what he wanted.'

'But he said I was to help care for his sick wife?'

'He would say that. I'd put it out of me mind if I was you. Take a look inside. It ain't so bad, well it might need a bit of dusting, seeing as how it's been shut up since the old lady breathed her last. Don't stand there gawking, girl. She ain't still in there.'

Joss ran into the room but Eloise still hesitated. 'Why did Mr Hubble say his wife was still alive? Why did he tell an out and out lie to the vicar?'

Agnes pulled a poke of paper from her pocket and took a pinch of snuff. 'He's a crafty old sod, that's what he is. Folks round here know all about old man Hubble and his liking for pretty young women, except that he can't get them so easily nowadays, what with his gout and his lameness.'

The truth was slowly dawning on Eloise as she realised that the Reverend Martin Collins had been tricked into thinking Ephraim needed a house servant, when it appeared that the old man had other things on his mind. She was tempted to walk out of the house there and then, but it was late afternoon and her children were tired and hungry. She was exhausted after the emotionally draining events of the day, and the only other alternative would be to spend some of her fast dwindling money on a night's board in another lodging house or an inn. She stepped into the musty-smelling room and a shiver ran down her spine. The curtains were closed, and when Eloise drew them back she half expected to discover the corpse of Mrs Hubble laid out on the bed. A shaft of sunlight filled with dancing dust motes filtered in through grimy windowpanes, but a quick glance over her shoulder confirmed that the bed was empty. Strangely enough, the room was not as awful as she had first thought. The single bedstead was covered by a white counterpane, which appeared to be reasonably clean. There was a washstand with a jug and basin decorated with violets and primroses, a rocking chair with a faded chintz cushion on its seat, an empty bookcase and a tallboy in one corner. A thick layer of dust covered everything like a sprinkling of sugar on sour fruit, but that could easily be remedied with the use of a duster. If she cleaned the ashes out of the grate and lit a fire, it would soon take the chill off the room and the simple act of opening the window would clear the air. Eloise set Beth down on a rug and went to fling up the sash. A gusty breeze laden with the smell of hops and yeast from the nearby brewery ruffled her hair and made the curtains billow out like ragged sails.

'You're well suited then?' Agnes demanded from the doorway. 'You ain't going to skitter off like a scared cat as the last one did?'

Eloise turned to face her. 'There have been others?'

'Half a dozen at least. They never lasted more than a week. I give you twenty-four hours at the most. Just you wait until he puts his hand up your skirt; you won't look so confident then, lady.'

'I shan't put myself in that position,' Eloise said firmly. 'Thank you for warning me, Miss Smith. I'll be on my guard.'

'Best lock your door tonight then, or you might get a nasty surprise.' Agnes turned to leave but Eloise called her back.

'Miss Smith, what time is supper? And could I have some warm milk and bread and butter for the children?'

Agnes curled her lip. 'I only cook for him upstairs. You'll have to find your own food.'

'Oh!' Taken aback, Eloise stared at her in surprise. 'Well, all right. I have not come prepared, but if you'll tell me where the kitchen is . . .'

'My kitchen is in the basement, but I don't like people interfering with my things. I'll tell you that for nothing.' Agnes stomped off muttering beneath her breath.

Eloise would have followed her, but out of the corner of her eye she saw that Joss was playing with something small and furry. She hurried over to him and bit back a cry of disgust as she saw that his new toy was a dead mouse. She picked it up by the tail and hurled it out of the window. Joss began to cry and she went down on her knees to cuddle him. 'It's all right, sweetheart. Mama will make everything come right for you and Beth.' Eloise held her arm out to Beth who was crawling over to her with a trusting smile on her small face. Eloise hugged them both to her breast. They had all been through so much in such a short space of time; surely things could not get much worse?

'Hungry, Mama,' Joss said, pulling away from her and rubbing his tummy. 'Want a drink.'

Eloise dashed a tear from her eyes and she rose to her feet, lifting Beth in her arms. 'Of course, you must be very hungry and thirsty. Come along, Joss, let's go down to the kitchen and see what we can find to eat.' She took him by the hand and went to look for the back stairs which led down to the basement kitchen. Just let that woman get in my way, Eloise thought with a militant twitch of her shoulders, if she dares say one more word out of place I will show her that I didn't live in Myrtle Street for three years without learning how to stand up for myself. How far away that life seemed now. Eloise made her way down the narrow staircase to the basement. How it would grieve Ronnie if he could see to what depths she had fallen. But sadly, Ronnie was gone forever, and there was no use dwelling on what she had lost.

She entered the kitchen ready to do battle, and found Agnes seated by the range with her feet up on the brass rail, holding a stone bottle to her lips. Judging by the satisfied smile on her face and a certain amount of sighing and lip-smacking, Eloise could only assume that Agnes was drinking something stronger than lemonade. Ignoring her, she set Beth down on the flagstones, which were covered with white sand; or at least it must have once been white but was now mixed with the carapaces of dead cockroaches, half-eaten crusts of bread and scattered vegetable peelings. Joss squatted down and began to trace patterns in it with the tips of his chubby fingers, and Eloise had to snatch a dry crust from Beth's hand as she tried to put it in her mouth.

Whatever it was that Agnes did in this house, cleaning was certainly not her priority. The large, deal table was littered with dirty crockery, a heel of cheese and a loaf of bread that was sprouting a coat of blue mould. A piece of meat was barely recognisable beneath a shifting mass of bluebottles, and an earthenware jug was filled with milk that had curdled and formed a sour-smelling cheese which would not turn out no matter how hard Eloise shook it over the stone sink. The larder was even more of a nightmare, and a large black rat scuttled out as Eloise opened the door. It streaked across the kitchen and disappeared through a hole in the wall that was large enough for a cat to slither through. Eloise felt sick, but she stifled a cry of dismay and continued her search for something edible. The shelves were thick with dust and cobwebs hung from the ceiling of the larder. There was a bag of flour but the resident rodents had gnawed a hole in it, and what they had not managed to consume was spread all over the floor where ants were busy carting away crumbs of bread and swarming over an open jam pot.

'You won't find nothing to eat in there,' Agnes called out in a slurred voice. 'Him above stairs ain't allowed nothing but boiled fish and cabbage – doctor's orders on account of his gout. You'll have to go to the pie shop on the corner if you want food.'

Eloise bit back an angry retort. Why hadn't the wretched woman told her this in the first place? She snatched up Beth who was attempting to gnaw on a chop bone, and she howled miserably when Eloise took it from her. 'Come along, Joss. Mama will take you out for supper.'

'You'll have to go out the back way,' Agnes said, taking another hefty swig from the bottle. 'There's only one key to the front door and he keeps it in his pocket, just like the jailer he always was. Be thankful he don't keep leg irons or manacles in the attic.' She let out a roar of laughter and lay back in the chair, rocking it and closing her eyes. 'Don't disturb me when you come back. I need me sleep.'

Eloise said nothing as she led Joss out through the small scullery which was just as untidy as the kitchen and filled with all manner of rubbish from broken teapots to buckets with missing handles, piles of rotting vegetables and old shoes. The wooden steps leading up from the area were rotted in places and there were gaps where a couple of treads had broken off completely. It was a hazardous ascent and led to a back yard which housed the pump with a stone trough covered in green slime, and a privy which, judging by the noxious smell and the cloud of blowflies buzzing around the door, was in an even more parlous state than the house. Eloise hurried past it and out into the service lane at the back of the terrace.

They ate their supper in the pie shop and on their way home Eloise purchased a china jug from a stallholder, and she stopped off at the dairy to buy a pint of milk. There was a bakery next door and she decided to get up early in the morning to get some fresh rolls for their breakfast. It was patently obvious now that their food was not included in the forty pounds a year, and even if it had been, she would not have wanted to feed her children with anything that came from the kitchens in Ephraim Hubble's house.

It was a balmy night and the trees surrounding

the green were bathed in a soft golden glow from the gaslights. The air smelt much fresher now that the warmth of daytime in early June had dissolved into a hazy, heliotrope dusk. Late shoppers moved in and out of the shadows and the pools of light made by the naphtha flares on the market stalls, which were just beginning to close down after a long day's trading. Out here on the green life seemed normal and the people were cheerful and friendly. Eloise did not want to return to the sombre prison-like house, but she had no choice. Beth was grubby but her cheeks were rosy as she slept against her mother's shoulder, and Joss was hanging on to her hand, stumbling along beside her like a small sleep-walker. She must get them washed and put to bed. There was no alternative but to go back to the room where Ephraim's wife had so recently passed away.

Eloise patted her pocket and felt the reassuring crackle of paper from the envelope containing Mama's letter. She had saved it up for last; a reassuring little slice of home to be savoured in private. She would read it by candlelight when the children were asleep.

Mindful of Agnes's warning, once they were safely inside Eloise locked her bedroom door, and to make doubly certain she wedged a chair beneath the doorknob. It had not been possible to wash the children properly, but she had cleaned them up as best as she could at the pump and they were now sound asleep, curled up in two of the drawers from the chest. A fire burned brightly in the grate, although the chimney obviously needed sweeping and occasional puffs of smoke belched into the room, but the flames threw out a comforting light and had taken the chill and smell of must from the air. Seated on the floor by the fire, Eloise read and reread her mother's letter. It was disappointingly short, but Mama assured her that they were all quite well, although Papa had gone down with a fever almost as soon as they landed in Mombasa, and she had been at his bedside night and day until the crisis had past. He was now on the mend and they were looking forward to travelling inland to the mission. Eloise was not certain that she entirely believed this, but Mama was loyal to the core and even had she hated the place wild horses would not have dragged such an admission from her. Instead, she devoted half a page to descriptions of Mombasa itself, of the mission there and the people who ran it, of the heat and the exotic fauna and flora, and the native population with their colourful dress and wonderful dark skins that varied from burnished bronze to deepest ebony. Mama it seemed had fallen in love with Africa itself, but that was no recompense for the pain of being parted from her daughter and grandchildren, and Eloise detected an understated longing for home as she read between the lines. She reread the last paragraph, with tears trickling down her cheeks.

I must finish now, my dearest daughter, or I will miss the post for England, which must go on the next mail ship out of Mombasa. I have not yet received a letter from you, but I hope to do so before we leave for the hinterland. I hope and pray that you and the children are settling down in Cribb's Hall and that Hilda and Harcourt are treating you as their own, dear daughter, as I know I would if circumstances were reversed. Do write to me soon, dearest, and tell me all about little Joss and Beth. It is so hard to be parted from you all and to know that I am missing all the precious milestones of their childhood. But my thoughts are always with you, Ellie my darling. I count the days until I see you and my dear grandchildren again. I kiss the paper so that you can embrace Joss and Beth and tell them it comes from their loving Grandmama.

Papa sends his love to you all, as I send mine.

Your ever-loving Mama.

PS Janet sends all her love too. Sadly she does not like the heat and I know that she pines for home, but she is too loyal to me to complain.

Eloise folded the letter and put it back carefully in the envelope. She tucked it safely away in her writing case, but she was too exhausted and emotionally drained to pen any words tonight. As she scrambled to her feet, she looked round the shabby room with a shudder. This was not how it was supposed to be. She could never have imagined that they would come to this, and yet it was better than being a virtual prisoner in Cribb's Hall with all that entailed. As she undressed by the fire, she thought of poor Ada who was now at peace, and of Meg, who might be her natural daughter, but would never know the truth of her parentage. She thought of dear, kind Reggie, and his proposal of marriage. If only she could have loved him just a little, but she could not go against her own heart, and she could not do him the disservice of marrying him for security alone. She sincerely hoped that he would rekindle his romance with Maud, and that they would have a long and happy life together. As she slipped her nightgown over her head, she thought longingly of her comfortable room in the farmhouse, of Gladys's motherly kindness and of Frank, who said little, but had been unfailingly kind and patient. As she climbed into bed, she tried not to think about poor Mrs Hubble. What a dreadful life that woman must have had with her husband. It did not bear thinking about, nor the way in which she had died. Eloise lay down convinced that she would not be able to sleep a wink.

She was awakened by the rattling of the door-knob, and she sat bolt upright drawing her knees up to her chest and wrapping her arms around them as she strained her ears to catch the slightest sound. The fire had died away to a few glowing embers and their feeble light sent monstrous shadows shifting and moving in the corners of the room. The events of yesterday came flooding back to her and Eloise sat rigid and frozen with fear. Was it the ghost of the departed Mrs Hubble who had come back to haunt her? The hairs on the back of her neck stood up and she shivered, but then she realised that the scraping and shuffling noises came from the other side of the locked door. It sounded as though someone was trying unsuccessfully to insert a key into the lock, and the key on her side of the door jiggled, but remained firm. The doorknob turned slowly, and Eloise held her breath. Her heart was hammering inside her ribcage and the blood was pounding in her ears. She had no doubt that it was Ephraim who was trying to get into the room, and she willed him to go away. The chair wedged beneath the handle shifted a little, but it held fast, and Eloise could have wept from sheer relief. She had not really believed Agnes, but now she was so glad that she had heeded her warning and had locked and barred the door. The hairs on the back of her neck were standing on end like those of a terrified animal, and she was sweating in spite of the chill of the night. Then, just as suddenly as it had begun, the rattling ceased and she heard shuffling footsteps and the tip-tapping of a cane on the bare floorboards as Ephraim went away. She collapsed back against the pillows, breathing heavily and trembling all over, but then anger overcame fear and she sat up again, clenching her fists. This could not be allowed to go on. If she was to stay here for any length of time, she would have to come to an understanding with Mr Ephraim Hubble.

Sleep evaded her for the rest of the night. How long she lay there, planning what she would say to her employer first thing in the morning, she did not know, but as the first streaks of a grey dawn split the night sky Eloise rose from her bed and dressed herself, fumbling with the laces on her stays. She was all fingers and thumbs this morning, but she was determined to take control of events before they spiralled out of hand. The children were still fast asleep and she took the opportunity to slip out of the room, locking the door behind her. She crept down the back stairs and out into the yard where she had to use the disgusting privy, and then washed as best she could at the pump. She held her head under the cold stream of water, regardless of the fact that it dampened her blouse. Feeling better, she shook the water from her long, dark hair and wrapped it in the scrap of towel she had found on the washstand in the bedroom. She went back to her room to check on Joss and Beth. Poor little things, she thought, as she looked lovingly down at their faces so innocent and vulnerable as they slept. What have I brought you to?

Just looking at them put steel in her spine, and made her even more determined to take matters into her own hands – this was not the time to be faint-hearted. Peering into the cracked mirror over the mantelshelf, she wound her damp hair into a knot and fastened it on top of her head with the few hairpins that came to hand. She did not want to waste time by pinning back the long tendrils that escaped to curl around her temples; she would tidy it up later with the aid of a net and more hairpins, if she could find them at the bottom of her valise. She had packed everything so hastily that clothes, hairbrushes and shoes were all jumbled together. There would be time to sort her things after she returned from a necessary visit to the shops to purchase fresh bread, butter and some jam for the children's breakfast. She picked up the milk jug and once again left the room, locking the door behind her and praying that neither Joss nor Beth awakened before she got back.

Outside on the green, the business of the day was already beginning. Costermongers were wheeling their barrows into position, the lamplighter was on his way home after completing his round, and farmers were already arriving from the countryside with carts laden with fresh produce to sell in the market. There was a pleasant community atmosphere that cheered Eloise as she hurried to the dairy and then on to the bakery. Laden with fresh food, she made her way to the lane at the back of the house and let herself into the scullery. To her relief there was no sign of Agnes, who was probably sleeping off the excess of gin she had consumed last night. Eloise took some crockery from the dresser, dusted it off and took it up to her room together with her purchases. Joss and Beth were just waking up, and they greeted her with eager, smiling faces.

When they were fed and dressed, Eloise was preparing to take them down to the kitchen when she heard movements upstairs: the now familiar sound of Ephraim's cane tap-tapping on the bare boards, and the dragging of a heavily bandaged foot. She braced her shoulders, ready to face her new employer and tell him exactly what was what, but she had no intention of doing so in front of her children. She took them down to the kitchen, where she found Agnes riddling the ashes in the range in a desultory fashion. She looked bleary-eyed and still half asleep, or maybe not quite sober, but definitely grumpy. 'Oh, you're up then,' Agnes muttered. 'This is your job, lady.'

'Never mind that,' Eloise said sternly. 'I want you to keep an eye on my children for five minutes while I go upstairs and speak plainly to Mr Hubble.'

Agnes dropped the poker and straightened up. A knowing look flitted across her sharp features. 'So he did pay you a visit in the night, did he?'

'He did, but thanks to you I had locked the door, and he went away.'

'He'll try again, or he'll catch you unawares in a dark corner. He's not one to give up easily.'

'Well, I'm not going to stand for that sort of treatment and the sooner he knows it the better. Now, I want you to keep my little ones safe for a few minutes.'

'I don't know about that . . .'

'I'm not asking you,' Eloise snapped. 'I'm telling you, Agnes.' Seeing a stubborn, mulish look on Agnes's face, Eloise moderated her tone. 'And if you do, I'll clean the kitchen and the scullery, and I won't say anything about you drinking yourself stupid on gin.'

'Bitch,' Agnes murmured, slumping down in her chair. 'I take it for me nerves. You will too when you've been here as long as I have.'

Eloise ignored this remark and she set Beth down on the floor. 'Joss, darling, look after Baby for Mama just for a little while. See she doesn't eat anything off the floor.' Eloise hurried from the kitchen and made her way to the parlour upstairs. Outside the door, she took a deep breath, holding on to her anger. She was not a normally fiery person, but she was both frightened and furious, and ready to take on an army if necessary. She burst into the room without knocking.

Ephraim was seated in his usual chair with his bandaged foot resting on a stool. He glared at her. 'What d'you want, girl? Where's your manners?'

Eloise went to stand before him, arms akimbo. 'And where were yours last night, Mr Hubble? You tried to get into my room.'

His expression changed subtly and he licked his lips. 'What if I did? It's my house, ain't it?'

'It is, but that doesn't give you the right to take liberties with me. Did you really think I would let you in last night? I am a respectable widow, sir. I agreed to work for you, but even servants have their rights.'

'I do like a woman with spirit. Come closer, dearie, and let me look at you.' His parted lips exposed a row of broken and blackened teeth and Eloise could smell his foul breath from several paces away.

'For what? So that you can treat me like a common whore?' Eloise felt a small surge of triumph at the look of astonishment on his face. She angled her head. 'I may not have lived in the East End all my life, but I've been here long enough to know what goes on every day in the streets. Until now I had the protection of my father and then my husband, but even though they are both gone I'm quite capable of looking after myself and my children. I warn you, if you come near me again, or try to touch me in an inappropriate manner, I will report you to the police and to the governor of the House of Detention, where I believe you used to work. I expect they thought highly of you there and you wouldn't want your precious reputation to be sullied by scandal, now would you?'

Ephraim scowled at her. 'Don't try to blackmail me, girl. I'm a hardened old screw and I don't take orders from the likes of you.'

'Maybe not, but I wonder how a prison warder can afford to live in a big house like this, even if you have let it go to rack and ruin?' Eloise's pulses were racing and it was difficult to breathe, but she was fighting for survival. 'Could it be that you were not such an honest and upright citizen when you worked at the prison?'

'I'm a sight more honest than them that I locked up, and if they paid me for services rendered that's nobody's business but mine. You may think you're smart, but you won't get one over Ephraim Hubble. Cleverer ones than you have tried and failed, so be warned. Now do what you're paid for and fetch me my breakfast. Tell that old hag downstairs that I want bacon and sausage with a couple of fried eggs. I'm sick of gruel and dry toast.' Ephraim waved his stick at her. 'Are you deaf or stupid? Remember who pays your wages, or you'll end up on the streets with your two little bastards.'

In the face of this tirade, there was nothing Eloise could say. Holding on to her last scrap of self-esteem, she left the room. It would have been so satisfying to slam the door behind her, but she did not dare. Ephraim might be a hateful old man, but the thought of being thrown out with nowhere to go was frankly too terrifying to contemplate. At least she had said her piece and he might think twice before trying to take liberties with her in the future. She hurried back to the kitchen and found to her intense relief that Joss and Beth had come to no real harm, although they were both extremely dirty from rolling around on the sandy floor, which had seemingly kept them amused but had left them looking like filthy street urchins. Eloise picked up Beth and prised a piece of rotten apple out of her fingers before dusting her off. 'Ugh, dirty! You don't want to eat that, sweetheart.'

'What a fuss over nothing,' Agnes remarked into her mug of tea. 'There's plenty of nippers as would be grateful for a nice bit of apple.'

'This place is a midden,' Eloise said with a shudder. 'How can you live like this?'

'Very well until you come along with your airs

and graces, missis. If you don't like it, then you get to work and clean it up.'

'I will, because I can't live like a sewer rat, even if you can. Oh, and by the way, Mr Hubble says he wants bacon, sausage and fried eggs for his breakfast. That's your job, Miss Smith.'

Agnes slurped her tea, smacking her lips. 'The old devil can wait. He's getting gruel, like it or not, and you can take it up to him. That's your job, Mrs Cribb.'

A bell on a board above the door jangled suddenly, making Eloise jump. Joss leapt to his feet pointing at it and laughing. 'Ding dong bell, Mama.'

'He's getting impatient,' Agnes said with a throaty chuckle. 'Best take his gruel up or he'll fly into one of his rages.'

Reluctantly, Eloise filled a bowl with thin gruel from the blackened saucepan on the range. It looked and smelt unappetising and she was barely surprised when Ephraim hurled it at the wall with an exclamation of disgust and fury. The china bowl smashed and the grey glutinous mass trickled slowly down the cracked plaster to settle in a pool on the floor. 'I said I want a proper breakfast, not that disgusting muck.' Beads of perspiration stood out on his forehead and he shook his fist at her. 'Do as I say or you can take your brats and leave my house. And don't expect me to pay you for your time, neither.'

'Miss Smith said it was doctor's orders, sir.'

'Bugger the doctor and bugger you too, lady. Now get down them stairs and bring me some proper food.'

At the end of a long day Eloise crawled into her bed stiff and sore from doing the sort of house-work that was normally done by a skivvy. She had scrubbed floors, washed shelves in the larder and thrown out all the rotten food, and, worst of all, she had had to clean the festering privy in the back yard. Her hands were red and raw, her back ached miserably, and she had been too exhausted even to eat the bread and cheese she had bought for their supper. She had used her last scrap of energy to lock and barricade her bedroom door before she lay down on her bed. If Ephraim paid her a nocturnal visit, she was unaware of it as she fell at once into a deep sleep.

It would have taken an army of servants to get the house into good order, but Eloise did her best, and although she had thought she could not stand more than one day of being harried by Agnes and bullied by Ephraim, she managed somehow to survive for a whole week. It was on the seventh day in the early afternoon, when she was holystoning the front step, that the sound of a familiar voice made her stop and look up. She scrambled to her feet with a cry of pleasure. 'Annie. How nice to see you.'

Annie bounded up to her but she was not smiling. 'Missis, thank the Lord I found you. I'm afeared I got bad news for you.'

Chapter Ten

Eloise took Annie indoors and led the way to her own room where Beth and Joss were having their afternoon nap. Annie tiptoed in after her and her worried frown dissolved into a smile at the sight of the sleeping infants. 'Bless their little hearts.'

Eloise motioned her to take a seat on the one and only chair. 'Sit down, Annie, you look fit to drop. What's happened to upset you so much?'

'I had to come straight away to find you, Ellie.' Annie collapsed onto the chair. 'There's been a strange-looking cove come round asking questions about you. Shifty-looking he was – I didn't like the cut of his jib one bit and that's the truth.'

Eloise felt as if the air had been sucked out of her lungs and she clutched her hand to her throat. 'Are you certain, Annie? Are you sure he was looking for me?'

Annie nodded emphatically. 'I had me ear glued to the keyhole and I heard every word. He said he was a private investigator and had been hired by a lady in Yorkshire to trace her grandson who had been took away from his rightful home. He said the boy was to be made a ward of court and then the police would be searching for him. He said it would be better for the young woman who took him to give the little lad up, or she would go to jail, and I think he meant you, Ellie.'

Eloise's breath hitched in her throat. 'A ward of court! I can't believe that she would do something so wicked, or that the law would take a child away from his own mother.'

'Well, true or not, he took old Queenie in right enough. She couldn't wait to tell him that you'd been staying with us and she had to send you packing. She said you wasn't the sort of person she wanted in her respectable lodging house.' Annie stopped for breath and gazed round the room with a disapproving pout. 'This ain't much of a place you've come to neither. You deserve better than this.'

'Never mind that now, Annie. This is only temporary until I find something better.' Eloise reached for the jug that she had filled with water from the pump that morning. Pouring some into a glass, she handed it to Annie. 'Take a sip and calm yourself. Tell me what else Mrs King said to the man?'

'Nothing much. She didn't know where you'd gone and I wouldn't have told her for the world. Wild horses wouldn't drag it from me. They could put me on the rack in the Tower of London and I . . .'

Eloise laid her hand on Annie's sleeve. 'I know you wouldn't, Annie. I trust you implicitly.'

'Do you?' Annie gulped some more water and she grinned. 'I dunno what that means, but it sounds good to me.'

'It means that I know you wouldn't peach on us. The woman in Yorkshire is my mother-in-law and she wants to take Joss away from me, but I won't have it. He's my son and he belongs with me.'

'I should say he does. No one should have to grow up without their real ma to care for them. Ain't I the best example of that? I daresay she had her reasons, but my ma left me on the steps of the Foundling Hospital like I was a bit of rubbish.'

'I expect it broke her heart to abandon you like that, but perhaps she thought she was doing her best for you.'

'If that was her best, I shouldn't like to have suffered her worst, but she'll be sorry one day and I know she'll come back for me.' With a heavy sigh, Annie put the glass down. She stood up, adjusting her mobcap which had tilted slightly over one eye. 'Anyway, none of that matters now and I got to get back, or the old cow will tan my hide. I was only supposed to go to the chemist's shop and buy a penn'orth of laudanum for her headache. Serve her right if her blooming head falls off.'

'Yes, you must make haste. I wouldn't want you to get into trouble on my account, and I do appreciate your coming here to warn me, Annie.'

'Just look out for a short, skinny cove who looks like he could do with a good wash. He had enough dirt under his fingernails to grow taters.'

In spite of everything, Eloise had to suppress a smile. The picture that Annie conjured up was not an attractive one. 'I'll be on the lookout for such a person.'

'I made sure he didn't follow me. I kept looking over me shoulder and dodging into doorways if I thought I saw someone acting odd like.'

Eloise patted her on the shoulder. 'You've done very well, Annie. I can't thank you enough.'

'I thought as how I might come again on Sunday, that's my afternoon off. Maybe we could go for a walk or something. I mean, you don't want to spend too much time in this place. It gives me the shivers.' Annie glanced round the room, shuddering dramatically.

'That would be nice, and the children would love to see you, Annie.' Eloise opened the door and peeped outside to make sure no one was about, and then she beckoned to Annie. 'When you come on Sunday, go round to the back of the house. I'll be waiting for you in the kitchen. I think it will be safer if you're not seen coming in by the front entrance.'

Annie chuckled mischievously. 'Like in a game.'

'Exactly,' Eloise said, kissing her on the cheek. 'Just like a game.' She was smiling as she let Annie out of the house, but inwardly her stomach was curdling with fear. If Hilda really had hired a detective to look for them it would only be a matter of time before they were discovered. When Ephraim paid her at the end of the first quarter, as he had promised, she would start looking for another position in a different part of London. Although, if what Annie had said was correct, the sooner she left Clerkenwell Green the better. If she could persuade him to give her an advance on her wages she could advertise for another position. Waving to the fast disappearing figure of Annie who was racing pell-mell across the green, Eloise went down on her knees to finish holystoning the doorstep while her mind grappled with the problem of finding them a safer place to live. If she wanted to get that money she would have to be nice to the old man, which was not going to be easy. So far she had evaded his grasping hands when she gave him his food or plumped up his cushions, but she had seen the naked lust in his eyes when he looked at her. The mere thought of physical contact brought the bitter taste of bile to her lips, but suffering a little temporary embarrassment and humiliation was nothing compared to losing her precious son to the Cribbs.

They had been at the house in Clerkenwell Green for three weeks. It was Joss's third birthday and it was also Agnes's day off. She had left early that morning to visit her sister in Wapping, and was not expected back until evening. The thought of having the kitchen all to herself was so pleasant that Eloise had raised no objection to being left on her own to prepare Ephraim's supper. She would have a day of relative peace and quiet with her children and maybe give them a special birthday tea. She had no present to give Joss, but she would make up for that when she received her wages from Ephraim. Over the past few days a plan had been forming in her mind, and she decided to make him the sort of meal for which he craved, but that the doctor had forbidden. So what if it brought on an attack of gout? That would be Ephraim's problem and not hers, but she needed to put him in a good mood so that she could ask for an advance on her wages.

Later that morning, armed with some of the housekeeping money which Agnes kept in a pewter tankard on the mantelshelf, Eloise took the children to the shops. She stopped first at the butcher's where she purchased a large piece of rump steak, two fat kidneys and a thick slice of gammon. She went on to her bakery where she bought a loaf of bread and some iced buns. Seeing Joss's eager expression, she broke one of the buns in half and shared it between him and Beth. Joss, of course, ate most of the cake, but Beth's little hand shot out for more as she relished the sweet taste of the pink icing. Eloise smiled at their eager enjoyment of such a simple pleasure. 'When Mama has a good position in a nice house, you shall have cake every day, my darlings,' she said, wiping Joss's face on her apron. 'It won't be long, I promise you that.'

Later, having given Joss and Beth their tea and played games with them until they were exhausted, Eloise put them to bed, and then she began preparing supper for Ephraim. She had often watched Janet in the kitchen at the vicarage, but had rarely been allowed to do anything more than to stir a pudding or lick cake mixture off the wooden spoon. When she married Ronnie it was another matter, and she had struggled at first, making dreadful mistakes and ruining many meals before she became a competent cook. Now, she put all that experience into practice as she prepared to impress her employer and cajole him into a good mood.

'About bloody time,' Ephraim snapped as she entered his room carrying a tray of food. 'What hour d'you call this to bring a man his supper?'

'I'm sorry, sir,' Eloise said mildly. 'It's Agnes's day off and I had to manage on my own.' She put the tray down on a table at the side of his chair and stood back, waiting for his reaction.

Ephraim's nostrils quivered. He sniffed the air like an animal scenting its prey and a dribble of saliva ran down his chin. 'My God, woman. This looks like a proper man's meal.' He grabbed his knife and fork and cut off a chunk of steak, shoving it greedily into his mouth and slapping his lips as he chewed. 'Now this is what I call proper food. You done well, sweetheart. Come here and give me a kiss.'

She had to curb the desire to slap his grinning face or to turn and run. Eloise stood where she was, folding her hands primly in front of her. 'I'm glad it meets with your approval, Mr Hubble.'

'More than that,' Ephraim muttered with his mouth full of fried gammon. 'I haven't eaten like this since me old woman turned up her toes. Poor old soul, she were a fine cook but she had no spirit.'

'I'm sorry for your loss, sir.'

'No you ain't.' Ephraim shoved a whole kidney in his mouth. 'You couldn't care bloody less about me and my wives.'

'Wives?'

'Three at the last count, though I've a mind to take another quite soon.' Ephraim took a swig of porter from the glass on his tray and he gave her a saucy wink. 'How about it, my little strawberry? D'you want to make an old man's last years the happiest in his life?'

Eloise tried to smile. 'That's a good joke, sir. Very amusing.'

'Joking, was I?' Ephraim wiped his lips on his greasy sleeve and his expression hardened. 'I don't make jokes, girlie. How about it? I'm too old to go through all that courtship nonsense. I want someone to warm me bed and cook me food like this. You won't get a better offer, so how about it?'

Stunned, shocked and totally nauseated, Eloise shook her head as she backed towards the doorway. 'I'll fetch your pudding, sir.'

'Playing hard to get. I like a bit of a game,' Ephraim called after her as she fled from the room.

Downstairs in the kitchen, Eloise put out cakes, bread and cheese with trembling hands. Ephraim was a hateful old man. How could he suggest such a thing? The mere thought of intimacy between them made her rush to the stone sink in the scullery and retch, but her stomach was empty and she only brought up bile, which left a disgusting taste in her mouth. She hurried out into the yard and washed her face in cool water from the pump. It took her a few minutes to compose herself, but Eloise knew that she must keep on with the charade for a little while longer or else she would never be able to escape from this awful house. Any moment now Agnes would return and she would be beside herself with rage when she discovered that money was missing from her hoard. Eloise knew that Agnes often dipped into the housekeeping money in order to keep herself supplied with gin and snuff, and she would not take kindly to the fact that her employer had been treated to such a slap-up meal, even though it had been purchased with his own money.

Reluctantly, Eloise returned to the upstairs parlour with the tray of food.

'So you've come back then? I thought you'd run off to fetch your friend the vicar so that he could marry us tonight.' Ephraim leered at her as he reached out to grab a cake from the tray. 'Iced buns. You really do know the way to a fellow's heart, my duck.'

Eloise put the tray down and took a deep breath. 'I'm very honoured, Mr Hubble. But I need time to consider your proposal.'

'It weren't no proposal, dearie. It were an order. You will marry me or you can get out of my house and take your brats with you.'

Her knees were trembling and she felt faint, but Eloise was not going to be browbeaten. She stood her ground. 'You can't do that, Mr Hubble. I've given you no cause to sack me.'

He licked his lips. 'I don't need a reason. I'm your employer and I can do as I please in my own home.' His eyes narrowed to slits. 'At least I mean to make an honest woman of you, you silly creature. You won't do better.'

'I'm sure I won't, and I do appreciate it, but as I said, I need time to think. You've taken me by surprise.'

'Come and sit on my knee. We'll talk about it some more.'

'I – I don't think that would be proper, sir. I mean . . .'

Ephraim pitched the tray onto the floor, slapping his hand on his knees. 'I said sit on my knee. I won't bite. Well, I might nibble you a bit, but I won't eat you.'

'I – think I hear one of the children crying. Or was that Agnes calling out? I'd best go and see.' Eloise ran from the room and did not stop until she reached the kitchen, where she skidded to a halt as she came face to face with Agnes.

'What have you been up to then, Mrs Cribb? No good by the looks of you? Got him to propose to you yet? He does that with every new girl, and when he's had his way with them he breaks off the engagement and there's nothing they can do about it. He's got through more servants that way than I can count.'

'It's none of your business,' Eloise said breathlessly. 'He's a disgusting old man, and I can't imagine anyone wanting to marry him.'

'He's buried three wives. Mind out you ain't

the fourth.' Agnes reached for the pewter tankard. 'I need a drop of blue ruin if I'm to get any sleep tonight.' She tipped the coins into the palm of her hand and her expression hardened. 'You've been thieving my housekeeping money. Give it back or I'll tell him what you done.'

'I didn't steal it. I used the money to buy supper for Mr Hubble. I didn't keep a penny for myself.'

Agnes counted out the coins. 'What did you give the old bugger? Champagne and lobster? I could have fed him for a month on what you've spent.' She tipped the coins back into the tankard and returned it to the shelf. 'You'll pay the money back out of your wages. Every last penny of it, d'you hear me?'

'Go to hell!' Eloise shouted, her nerve snapping. 'Leave me alone.' She slammed out of the kitchen and went to her room, locking and barring the door. It had gone horribly wrong. She was worse off now than she had been before she attempted to get on the right side of Ephraim. She checked on the children and then lay down on her bed fully clothed. She had not eaten all day, but hunger was the least of her problems. Eloise closed her eyes as tears flowed freely down her cheeks. She was determined not to give way to despair, but she was tired and hungry and she longed to hear her mother's gentle voice whispering words of reassurance in her ear. She would say that things would look better in the morning and each new dawn brought with it a fresh opportunity to come to terms with life's problems. Eloise pictured her mother's smiling face, and she could smell the sweet scent of lavender that always clung to her clothes. If she concentrated hard she could almost feel the soft touch of Mama's hand stroking her forehead, as she had done when Eloise was a child and lay sick in bed. Mama would be brave. She was probably facing up to all manner of dangers and discomforts in Africa. One day, in the not too distant future, they would all be reunited and this phase in her life would fade into a memory like a bad dream. 'Take courage, Ellie, dear.' Eloise could hear the words as clearly as if Mama were sitting at her bedside. 'Be brave, my darling girl, and all will come right in the end.'

Next morning, Eloise had to force herself to take the breakfast tray upstairs to Ephraim's room. She felt sick at the thought of facing him after last night, but she had no alternative. Joss and Beth were in the kitchen with Agnes and she dared not leave them alone with her for long. She took a deep breath as she entered the parlour and could have sobbed with relief when she found it empty. The mess of broken china and remnants of his supper lay on the floor where he had pitched the tray in his sudden outburst of rage, but clearing that up was as nothing compared to the thought of putting up with his salacious looks and remarks. Perhaps he had worn himself out last night, or maybe he was suffering a further attack of gout after the rich food? Eloise hoped that he was racked with pain, although she knew that Papa would castigate her for such wicked thoughts. However, she had never pretended to be a saint and the image of Ephraim doubled up in agony was a satisfying one after everything he had put her through since he had taken her into his employ. She had just finished picking up the pieces when she heard the thumping of his cane against the wall. His bedroom was next to the parlour, and he must have heard her moving about. She was not yet in a position to throw up her job, and so she went to see what he wanted.

As she had thought, Ephraim lay in his great four-poster bed and his face was ashen. Deep lines of suffering were etched from his nose to his chin and he looked small and shrunken beneath the canopied tester. 'Fetch the doctor, girl. I'm in agony.'

Eloise bobbed a curtsey, keeping her head bowed in case he saw the gleam of satisfaction in her eyes. 'Yes, sir.'

'No, wait. I'll take a dose of laudanum before you go. It's there on my side table. A few drops in a glass of water will help with the pain.'

'Yes, sir.' Eloise went to the table and was carefully measuring the drops when he roared at her to hurry.

'I'm suffering torments. It's all your fault, you scheming little bitch. You fed me red meat and rich fancies. You did it on purpose. I shan't marry you now. You're just as bad as all the rest. Money-grabbing, immoral harlots the lot of you.'

Eloise handed him the glass. 'I'll go for the doctor, sir.'

'Lift me up then, you stupid whore. I'm crippled I tell you. I can't drink lying down.'

Reluctantly, Eloise lifted his head just a little and tilted the glass so that he could sip the medicine. He drank it down in one greedy gulp, and before she could move away his hand shot out to cup her breast. She tried to struggle free, but his fingers pinched savagely into her tender flesh. 'Undo your blouse,' Ephraim murmured, his eyes glazing with desire. 'Let me see your titties, girl.'

Eloise dropped the glass on the floor and she slapped his hand with all her might, but he only tightened his grip. 'I will not, you disgusting old creature. Let go of me.' She felt the buttons on her blouse fly off in all directions as he tightened his hold.

'I'm suffering. I need a little comfort,' Ephraim whined, grabbing the top of her stays and pulling her towards him. He pressed his face against the swell of her breasts and she could feel his hot breath searing her skin. Revolted and panicked, Eloise dug her fingernails into his hands, scraping at his thin skin so that blood oozed out in long scratches. He released her with a yelp of pain. 'Wildcat. Bitch. I'll have you for that.'

Eloise did not wait to hear the rest of his impassioned volley of threats. She ran from the room sobbing with anger and humiliation and did not stop until she was inside her own room and had locked the door. Trembling violently, she sank down on the bed, struggling to regain her composure. She must not give in to hysteria. She must not let the children see her in this state, and she must gather her scattered wits so that she could think more clearly. Eloise took a deep breath. The children – she must be strong for them and she must be sensible. The desire to leave this awful house immediately had to be curbed, as without money they would have nowhere to go; she had not even enough to pay for a room in the meanest of lodging houses. Then there was the private detective hired by Hilda. He could be lurking outside on the green at this very moment.

Despite the fact that she was trembling from head to foot, Eloise managed to change her blouse and tidy her hair, but it took all her willpower to remain calm and self-possessed.

When she was satisfied that nothing in her outward appearance would give her away, she braced herself to go down to the kitchen and face Agnes as if nothing had happened.

'You took your time,' Agnes said crossly. 'I ain't paid to act as nursemaid to your brats. What was you doing up there? Or need I ask?'

Resisting the temptation to slap the sly grin off Agnes's face, Eloise shrugged her shoulders. 'He's ill in bed. He wants me to fetch the doctor.'

'Worn him out have you?' Agnes cackled with laughter. 'At least the old bugger will die with a smile on his face.'

Eloise picked up Beth and held her hand out to Joss. 'Let's go for a walk on the green, poppet. Mama has an errand to do for Mr Hubble.'

'Mama has an errand to do,' Agnes echoed in a mocking imitation of Eloise's voice. 'You'll get your comeuppance, lady. He'll soon tire of your niminy-piminy ways and send you packing. One day it'll be just him and me again, you'll see.'

The doctor came down to the kitchen to give them a stern lecture on keeping to the appropriate diet for a gentleman suffering from gout. He stressed the necessity for an even stricter regime to repair the damage done by an excess of rich food, and the need to keep the patient quiet and sedated with laudanum. He eyed Eloise with a baleful glare and said that Mr Hubble was not to be excited in any way. She felt her cheeks burning with embarrassment at the inference that she had been responsible for his present condition, and she opened her mouth to protest, but Agnes spoke up first. 'I think that Mr Hubble should have a proper nurse to look after him, doctor,' she said, casting a malicious look in Eloise's direction. 'Someone who would not take advantage of a sick old gent laid up in his bed.'

'Quite so. An admirable idea, if Mr Hubble could be persuaded that it was necessary.'

'And I have the exact person in mind,' Agnes added slyly. 'A good friend of mine, Mrs Jarvis, who is an experienced nurse.'

'Then I'll leave it to you to make the necessary arrangements, Miss Smith. I'll call again tomorrow.' The doctor turned to Eloise, frowning. 'I think it best if you keep away from the sickroom, ma'am. Mr Hubble must not be excited in any way.'

Eloise bit back a sharp retort. Let him think what he liked and let Agnes have her moment of triumph. She seemed to be labouring under the delusion that Eloise had ambitions to be the fourth Mrs Hubble, and that by introducing her friend, Nurse Jarvis, she was thwarting her plans. If Agnes knew that nothing could be further from the truth, she would be laughing on the other side of her face. She was not to know that her intervention had given Eloise a breathing space and time to think. But it was only a reprieve. Eloise was only too well aware that when Ephraim recovered the problem would reassert itself. He was not a man to give in easily.

Mrs Jarvis duly moved in and Eloise could only guess at Ephraim's reaction to this giant of a woman, who was almost as broad as she was tall. It would be a brave man who took liberties with this Amazon-like creature. When she was not in the sickroom, Mrs Jarvis settled down in the kitchen with Agnes. They made it quite plain that Eloise was not welcome in their midst, which suited her very well since they spent their evenings taking snuff, drinking blue ruin and laughing uproariously. In the morning they were both red-eyed and crotchety until they had drunk copious cups of tea and several glasses of seltzer.

On Sunday afternoon, three days after Mrs Jarvis had moved into the house, Eloise was in the kitchen with the children safe in the knowledge that Agnes and her friend had ensconced themselves in Ephraim's parlour and had taken a bottle of his best brandy with them. They would not reappear until it was time for supper, and Eloise could only guess that Ephraim had been given a larger dose of laudanum than usual to keep him quiet. Annie had promised to come, and Eloise was looking forward to having her company and taking the children out for a walk, something she had avoided recently for fear that the detective might be lurking outside. It was quite irrational, she told herself, as there was nothing to lead him to the house in Clerkenwell Green, but all the same she was apprehensive. She had not even dared to write to Gladys informing her of their new address, just in case the information somehow filtered through to the Cribbs.

A rapping noise on the window made Eloise start and Joss jumped up and down with excitement, pointing to the face peering at them through the dirt-encrusted windowpane. 'Annie, Mama. Annie's come.'

Eloise snatched her bonnet off its peg and she hoisted Beth onto her hip. Joss ran on ahead of her, out through the scullery and into the area, where Annie swung him up in her arms. 'Hello, Joss, me boy. How are you today?'

'Annie. Annie.' Joss tugged at her Sunday best bonnet and she tickled him until he let go and collapsed against her shoulder in a fit of giggles.

'I thought you weren't coming,'

'She made me work late, the old bitch,' Annie said, hoisting Joss onto her shoulders and heading up the area steps. 'But I'm here now and I weren't followed. I've kept an eye out for the shifty cove, but I ain't seen him again, so perhaps he's given up and gone back to Yorkshire.'

'I hope so,' Eloise said, following her up the

steps. 'I do hope so. I've hardly dared walk out with the children since you told me about him, and they're growing tired of being forever shut up in one small room.'

'I know exactly the place to go to on such a hot day,' Annie said enthusiastically. 'There's a lovely garden at the back of the Foundling Hospital. I go there on me days off and just sit and look at the trees and flowers. Anyway, I have to be there in case me mum comes looking for me. I think I'd know her if ever I saw her, and I'm sure she'd know me.'

Eloise crossed the yard and opened the gate, holding it to allow Annie and Joss to pass. 'Doesn't it make you sad, Annie?'

'Sometimes it does, but most of the time I'm hopeful. I think if I sits there for long enough, one day she's sure to come along. It's not too far from here.'

The streets were quiet at this time on a Sunday afternoon. The businesses and shops were all closed and it seemed that the city was drowsing in the warmth of the early summer sunshine. The pavements shimmered with a heat haze and the cobblestones were as hot as coals underfoot, but the early heat wave had brought out flies in great swarms. They descended in black clouds, covering the piles of horse dung and rotting rubbish littering the streets in a moving, buzzing mantle of blue-green. The air was thick and still with barely a breeze to take away the stench from the drains and overflowing privies. Eloise experienced a sudden longing for the fresh greenery and clean air of the country, but they were surrounded by an army of tall grey buildings, stained with soot and streaked with bird droppings.

Annie seemed oblivious to all this. She was a child of the city, Eloise thought. She quickened her pace to keep up as Annie danced along ahead with Joss shrieking with delight as he bounced up and down on her thin shoulders. She seemed to know the area well, and she led Eloise through a maze of back streets until at last they came to Guildford Street and the Foundling Hospital. It was a surprisingly pleasant-looking group of buildings surrounded by London plane trees with their summer foliage rustling and whispering in the breeze. Annie led them into the rose-filled garden where families dressed in their Sunday best were strolling or simply sitting on the grass and enjoying the sunshine.

Annie found a shady spot beneath a plane tree and she set Joss down on the grass. He began to race about madly, chasing butterflies and shouting with delight at his newfound freedom. Beth waved her arms, crowing excitedly as Eloise put her down on the grass beside Annie.

'Ain't this a pleasant spot?' Annie said, taking Beth onto her lap. 'Sit down and take the weight off your feet, Ellie.'

Her serviceable black serge skirt billowed out round her as Eloise lowered herself carefully onto the grass. Looking round at the well-dressed merchants and their wives, she felt suddenly dowdy and out of place. Her good clothes were still packed away and she had not thought to change out of her workaday garments. Now she wished that she had, and this made her smile inwardly. She could hear Papa's stern voice telling her that vanity was a sin. Poor Papa, she had never quite managed to live up to his ideal of womanhood. If she had been more like Mama then perhaps he would have been able to love her more, although Eloise had always suspected that, if the truth were told, he had always wanted a son. She had been a disappointment from the start.

'Penny for 'em,' Annie said, nudging her in the ribs. 'You was miles away, Ellie.'

'I was just thinking what a pleasant place this appears to be, at least on the outside. What was it like for you living here?'

'It's just a place,' Annie said, shrugging her thin shoulders. 'We was looked after and treated all right so long as we behaved ourselves. They trained us girls to do housework so that we could go into service, and the boys was brought up to go into the Navy or the army. We was used to the life so we didn't know no different, but I always thought me mum would come one day and take me away. If I close me eyes now I can picture her face. It's round like one of them angel's faces in the scripture books, and she has lots of curly golden hair, and she smells nice, like wallflowers in springtime. She has soft hands, not like mine.' Annie held up her work-worn, calloused hands and chuckled. 'I got hands like a washerwoman, and hair the colour of a rat's arse. No blooming angel am I, but she is, and I'll know her when I see her – the rotten cow, leaving me like that.'

Eloise patted Annie's hand, but Beth chose that moment to escape and launched herself onto the grass, crawling as fast as she could towards Joss. He was so intent on chasing a cabbage white butterfly that he did not notice her and he ran across the path in front of a tall gentleman in a black frock coat and top hat, who was walking with a little girl by his side.

Eloise scrambled to her feet and raced across the grass to pick up Beth before she was trodden underfoot. She caught her just before she reached the path and lifted her, protesting loudly, out of harm's way. Eloise laid a protective hand on Joss's small shoulder and she flashed an apologetic smile at the stern-faced gentleman. 'I beg your pardon, sir. My little boy was not looking where he was going.'

'I suggest you keep him under firmer control, ma'am.' With a brief nod of his head, he walked on. The little girl hesitated, regarding Eloise with a curious expression on her pretty face.

'Come, Maria.'

The child gave Eloise a sweet smile and then skipped off to join the man, who Eloise assumed must be her father or her guardian. She stared after him with a mixture of curiosity and resentment. It had been the briefest of meetings but she was left with the impression of a coldly handsome man, whose features might have been carved by an Italian renaissance sculptor from a block of Carrara marble. His thick, dark hair waved slightly as it flopped over a high forehead, and in startling contrast his deep-set eyes were a clear periwinkle blue. Eloise turned away and began to walk slowly back to where Annie was sitting beneath the tree, but she could not resist taking a quick peek over her shoulder at the man who had virtually ignored her. He, however, did not look back, and she was both irritated and piqued by his apparent lack of interest in her. She might be shabbily dressed, but that did not make her any less of a person. Eloise was unused to men passing her by without a second glance, and if she were to tell the truth, her pride was hurt. 'What a rude man,' she said angrily. 'Who does he think he is?'

Chapter Eleven

'That's Mr Barton Caine,' Annie said in an awed tone. 'He's the governor of the Foundling Hospital. A very important man.'

'A self-important man,' Eloise corrected. 'I don't think I've ever met such an arrogant, unmannerly person.'

'He's handsome, though,' Annie said, taking an increasingly fractious Beth from Eloise's arms and giving her a cuddle. 'I'd say he was the best-looking cove I've ever seen, even if he is old.'

This statement drew a reluctant smile from Eloise. 'To someone your age, anyone over the age of twenty is old. I'd hazard a guess that your Mr Caine is not a day over thirty. If he weren't so full of himself and he was not so haughty, I daresay he might be quite presentable, but I haven't any patience with a man of his standing who considers himself to be so much better than anyone else that he cannot be civil.' Eloise beckoned to Joss who was now playing with a slightly older child who had a puppy on a leash, and all three were gambolling about on the grass. 'Joss, come here, darling.'

'Let him be,' Annie said, chuckling at their antics. 'He can't come to no harm while we're watching and it looks as if Mr Caine has gone home. He lives in a big house in the hospital grounds.'

'Well, I hope he is more pleasant when he is at home. I feel sorry for his poor wife.'

'She died,' Annie said simply. 'Five years ago, when Maria was born. The poor lady did not survive the birth. I was only a little nipper then, but I remember how sad it made everyone in the hospital. She was a kind lady, his poor wife. She used to play the pianoforte and sing to us sometimes after supper. She was beautiful too, a bit like I imagined my mum would be, with golden curls and a lovely smile.'

'If that's so, I am truly sorry for him,' Eloise said sincerely. 'But that still doesn't give him the right to be discourteous. I lost my husband less than a year ago but I don't take my grief out on others.'

'I'd put him out of me mind, if I was you,' Annie said with a sagacious nod of her head. 'You ain't likely to run across him again, so why worry?'

'You're right, of course, and I'm very glad of it too. I shall be quite happy never to cross his path again.' Eloise shaded her eyes with her hand as a commotion in the gardens caught her attention. 'What's going on over there, Annie?'

'It's the hokey-pokey man,' Annie cried, rising to her feet and jumping up and down with excitement. 'It's the Eyetie ice cream man. I'd give anything for a penny lick.'

Eloise put her hand in her pocket. She had very little left of the money that Harcourt had given her, but she could not deny the children this small treat. She took out three pennies and jingled the coins, smiling. 'Go and fetch Joss, and you shall each have an ice cream.'

While the children were busily occupied in the serious business of licking ice cream from small glass pots, Eloise sat on the grass leaning her back against the trunk of the plane tree. If she closed her eyes she could almost imagine she was back in the Dorset countryside, sitting on the village green with the joyful sounds of the May Day celebrations going on about her. She could visualise Mama wearing her white muslin gown and her favourite straw bonnet with blue ribbons and pink silk roses beneath the brim. She would be smiling as she handed out cakes and buns to the children, while Janet poured homemade lemonade into pot mugs, and the men lingered in the refreshment tent drinking ale and cider. Eloise could almost hear the lively music played by the village band on their fiddles, a battered old cello and a slightly out of tune concertina; in her mind's eye she could see the energetic movements of the young men and women as they danced a jig or performed the intricate movements of Gathering Peascods, and Goddesses. It was all a far cry from the harsh realities of steamy London and the uncertainty of her present situation, but in her heart she knew that it was just a pleasant dream; a way of escaping to a safer, kinder world, which might exist only in her imagination.

Someone tugged at her hair and Eloise opened her eyes to see Joss beaming into her face. 'Wake up, Mama.' He waved the licked clean glass pot in her face. 'More, please.'

She gave him a hug. 'Not today, darling. One day you will have all the ice cream you can eat, but not now.' She took the tiny glass pot from his hand and passed it to Annie to return to the hokey-pokey man.

The garden was gradually clearing of people as the shadows lengthened and they began to leave for home. Eloise rose to her feet and shook out her skirts. 'We'd best be on our way too, Annie. You don't want to get into trouble for being late back.'

Annie pulled a face. 'I don't want to go back at all, but I got no choice.' She stretched her arms up towards the sky as if she were reaching up to touch one of the fluffy white clouds that had suddenly drifted across the wide expanse of cerulean blue. 'One day I'll be waiting here and me mum will walk through them gates. She'll come straight to me, no messing about, and she'll take me by the hand. She'll say, "Sorry I kept you waiting, girl, but I'm here now, and I'm going to take you home with me." We'll get on a bus and it'll take us to one of them leafy suburbs what the commercial travellers talk about. I'll never have to scrub another floor nor clean out another privy.'

Eloise laid her hand on Annie's thin shoulder. 'I'm sure she will, dear. You keep your dreams, Annie. Sometimes they're the only thing that keeps us going.'

Annie rubbed her knuckles into her eyes as if she were blotting out the impossible vision of happiness. 'We can come here again on me next afternoon off, can't we, Ellie?'

'Well, I'm not sure . . .'

A grin wiped away the sad look on Annie's cheeky face. 'You ain't likely to bump into the governor again, and if you do you can always cut him dead. That would take him down a peg or two.'

In spite of everything, Eloise managed a smile. 'I'm sure it would, but our paths are extremely unlikely to cross again.'

When they arrived back in Clerkenwell Green, Eloise bade a fond goodbye to Annie and Joss clung to her, giving her a smacking kiss on the cheek. Promising to come again soon, Annie bounded off in the direction of Nile Street and

Eloise took the children round to the back of the house to enter by the yard. She could hear the raised voices of Agnes and Mrs Jarvis even before she opened the kitchen door. Their slurred speech and flushed faces indicated that they had consumed a large amount of Ephraim's brandy, and they appeared to be intent on going out to the nearest pub to consume even more strong liquor.

'You'll see to his supper,' Agnes said, laughing drunkenly as though she had just said something extremely funny. 'You can spoon-feed the old goat with his boiled fish and cabbage. I feel sick at the thought of it.'

'Yes,' Mrs Jarvis added, swaying on her feet. 'And see you do it proper like. I'm his nurse and I say – see you do it proper, or you'll have me to answer to.' She moved towards the door, rocking dangerously from side to side like a badly loaded wagon. 'Come on, Aggie. I fancy a drop more tiddley and a meat pie for me supper.'

Joss clung to his mother's hand and Eloise could feel him trembling with fright at the sight of the two extremely tipsy old women as they blundered out of the kitchen and up the back stairs to the entrance hall. She could still hear their raucous laughter as they made their way to the front door, staggering and bouncing off the walls as they went. Then there was silence and Eloise heaved a sigh of relief. It occurred to her that Agnes must have taken the front door key from Hubble's pocket, but she put the thought out of her mind. It was none of her business.

She fed the children with bread and milk before washing them and tucking them up in their beds. Then she went back to the kitchen to prepare Ephraim's meal. She was tempted to leave him to go hungry, but she could not afford to anger the person who would eventually pay her wages. She cooked a piece of haddock in some milk and cut thin slices off a loaf, which she buttered sparingly. She made a pot of tea and having arranged everything on a tray, she took it upstairs to his bedroom. She had to brace herself to enter, but she felt a little safer knowing that Mrs Jarvis would have given him a fairly hefty dose of laudanum.

The room was in almost complete darkness. The bed curtains were half drawn and Eloise could only just make out the shape of Ephraim's head on his pillow. She tiptoed across the floor, intending to leave the tray on his bedside table and then make a hasty retreat. She had no intention of waking him. She put the tray down as silently as possible and was about to move away when a hand shot out and gripped her by the wrist. Ephraim snapped upright in bed with a triumphant cry. 'Gotcha.'

'Let me go,' Eloise cried, struggling to free herself from his grasp, but his fingers tightened, digging into her flesh until she yelped with pain. 'I'll teach you, lady,' he snarled. 'No one makes a fool of Ephraim Hubble, least of all a chit of a girl who puts on airs and graces.'

He was surprisingly strong for someone who was supposed to be an invalid. He dragged her onto the bed, tearing at the thin material of her blouse. Driven by fear and revulsion, Eloise kicked and struggled, but she was no match for him. In desperation she clawed her fingers and lashed out, catching him across the cheek. He let out a howl of rage and slapped her repeatedly about the face and head. The pain was excruciating and with a last desperate effort to free herself, she sank her teeth into his hand. With a yelp of pain, he gave her a mighty shove which sent her tumbling off the bed onto the floor. Eloise scrambled to her feet, clutching her torn blouse to cover her exposed flesh. 'You wicked, wicked man. I'll . . .' Her voice broke on a sob.

'You'll do what?' Ephraim growled. 'I'll tell you what you'll do, girl. You'll keep your mouth shut and you'll go and fetch me something decent to eat. Now get out of here and make yourself tidy. You look like a trollop off the streets.'

'I'll have the law on you,' Eloise hissed, too angry now to be frightened of him. 'I'll tell the magistrate what you did to me. I won't let you get away with it.'

Ephraim eyed her through narrowed lids and he was not smiling now. 'You'll do no such thing, and who'd believe you if you did. It would be your word against mine, and I'm a respected person with a lifetime of public service behind me. You're a woman of no account.'

'You are an evil old man.' Eloise gripped the bedpost for support. Her legs were trembling so violently that she could barely stand, but she was filled with hatred for the man who had so violently attacked her. 'I will speak to the vicar. He'll believe me.'

Ephraim sat up slowly, rising from the pillows like a leviathan from the deep. 'You won't tell no one, girlie. You got away from me because I'm half drugged with laudanum for me pain, but next time you won't be so lucky. You put yourself in my hands, and you'll do my will or you'll be out on the street with your little bastards.'

'I won't do it. You can't make me.' Eloise glared at him with a defiant lift of her chin. 'You offered me marriage, Mr Hubble. I'll sue you for breach of promise.'

Ephraim's coarse laughter echoed round the dark room. 'Who'd believe a slut like you? Besides which, dearie, I know something about you that will keep you here as long as I care to shelter you and your brats.'

'You're just saying that to scare me,' Eloise said with a catch in her voice. Fear was replacing anger now and the triumphant look in Ephraim's eyes scared her more than all his ranting. 'I – I won't listen to you.'

'Then you don't mind if I tell my friend Mr Pike that you and your kids are living under my roof?'

Eloise tightened her grasp on the bedpost, clinging on to consciousness as a wave of dizziness almost took her feet from under her. 'Wh-who is he?'

'Pike and I were warders at Newgate long before I went to work at the House of Detention. He left to become a private investigator and he came to call on me this afternoon, but it weren't for old times' sake.' Ephraim paused, chuckling deep in his throat. 'I can see you get my drift, girlie. Can you guess why Mr Pike knocked on my door?'

Eloise could not speak, and she shook her head, although she already knew what her tormentor was going to say.

Ephraim's eyes glittered with malice. 'My friend Pike followed that little skivvy from the lodging house in Nile Street. He had a notion that she knew more than she was telling him. We had a cup of tea and a chat about old times, but more important, my lady, he told me that there's a price on your head. Your in-laws up north have offered a reward for anyone turning you and the brats in to them. If you don't give up the boy, they'll make him a ward of court and he'll be taken from you all legal and proper.'

Eloise licked her dry lips. 'And you told him I was here?'

'No, but I will if you don't do exactly what I want. One false move from you, girlie, and I'll hand you over to Pike. Do you understand me?'

'You can't do this. I'll tell Agnes and Mrs Jarvis. They're women too; they must be on my side.'

'Agnes knows all about it. She's been with me long enough to understand that she's secure just as long as I'm happy. If I'm not, then I can turn her out on the streets any time I like, and who would take on an old harpy like Agnes Smith?' He uttered a mirthless laugh. 'Don't stare at me like I'm a piece of shit. I'm your master, girlie, and don't you forget it. I'll have you whenever I feel like it and you'll be nice to me or you know what will happen.'

Eloise sprang to her feet. 'I would rather die. If you touch me again, I'll kill you.'

The sound of his laughter followed her as she tore from the bedroom, and it echoed through the empty house, mocking her as she fled to her own room and barricaded herself inside. She collapsed back onto the bed, shivering violently and stifling the sobs that racked her whole body. No man had ever treated her in such a way. Her whole body was sore and her arms were covered in bruises. Her left eye felt swollen and she could taste the blood from her split lip. She lay in the dark, huddled up on top of the bed, staring into the blackness all round her. The only comfort she had was the soft sounds that Joss and Beth made in their sleep. She longed to take them up in her arms and hold them to her bosom, but she resisted the temptation. She must allow them to sleep and she must clear her mind; forget the pain and humiliation of this evening's events, and she must face the fact that the only course left open to her was to leave this dreadful house tonight. The crime-ridden streets of East London held less terror for her than staying here at the mercy of a man like Ephraim Hubble. As the fog of pain and despair cleared from her mind, she realised that it would be only a matter of time before Pike, the private investigator, discovered her whereabouts. If he continued to watch Annie's movements, it was inevitable that she would eventually lead him once again to Clerkenwell Green and then all would be lost. The Cribbs would invoke the power of the law and her children would be made wards of court and taken from her. Eloise knew that she had no choice. She must wait until everyone in the house was asleep, and then she would take the children and escape from the purgatory into which she had been flung.

When her limbs had stopped shaking and she

could cry no more, she climbed stiffly off the bed and lit a candle. She would have to make a swift getaway and she must travel light. With the utmost reluctance, she abandoned the suitcase containing her good clothes, and she packed just a few necessities for the children and herself in her valise. There was one thing, however, that she was not going to leave behind and that was her writing case. During the past few months her lifeline had been writing to her mother, even if it was only a few lines every day. In the last letter which she had posted just before she left Yorkshire, she had asked Mama to send any future correspondence to the Missionary Society in London. There might even be letters there now, awaiting collection. The thought shone like a candle in the darkness of Eloise's deep despair. She had no idea where she would go when she left Clerkenwell Green, or how she would live with just a few shillings left in her purse, but leave she must and soon, before her resolve wavered.

When she had finished packing, Eloise felt strangely calm. She sat on the edge of her bed straining her ears for sounds of Agnes and Mrs Jarvis returning from the pub. All her thoughts now were focused on escape, and she was oblivious to the physical pain caused by Ephraim's brutal attack. At last she heard the front door open and close and the sound of muffled, drunken voices as Agnes and Mrs Jarvis said goodnight to each other. The stairs creaked beneath their weight as they made their way to their rooms and then there was silence. There had been no sound at all from Ephraim, although she had half expected him to follow her downstairs and repeat his demand for a freshly cooked meal, or worse. But he had not made any attempt to follow her and for that she was supremely grateful. Perhaps he had fallen asleep after his exertions? She hoped his dreams were anything but sweet. Just thinking about him made Eloise shudder and she sipped a glass of water in an attempt to wash the bitter taste from her mouth.

She waited, trembling with nervous tension, until she heard the clock on the church tower strike midnight, and then she roused Joss first and dressed him in his outdoor clothes. His head was heavy against her shoulder as he sat on her lap, still half asleep. She kissed the nape of his neck and breathed in the scent of his curly hair. 'My poor baby,' she whispered. 'No one will ever take you from me, I promise.' She laid him down on the bed while she attended to Beth who awakened with a drowsy smile and fell asleep again as soon as Eloise finished dressing her. At nine months, Beth was no longer the tiny baby she had been when Eloise first travelled to Yorkshire, and she hitched the sleepy infant over her shoulder. If only she had been able to keep the perambulator or the little cart that Ted had made for the children, but she had neither, and, smothering a sigh, Eloise picked up her valise. She told Joss in whispers that they were playing a game and he must hold tight to the handle of the case and not let go. They were going out into the darkness for a big adventure.

As she stepped outside into the chill of the night, Eloise was not so certain about the greatness of their adventure. She was frankly terrified, and if the alternative had not been so dire, she would have gone back into the house and hidden away until morning. Bats were zooming crazily above the dark silhouettes of the trees and somewhere in the distance a dog howled. There was unseen menace in the deep shadows, but the soft saffron glow of the gaslights pooled on the cobblestones forming little islands of light in the darkness. There were more people about than Eloise had expected there to be this late at night, but they seemed to be mainly stragglers making their way back home from the various pubs, or street women on the lookout for a likely punter.

Dew was already forming on the grass and the air was damp and heavy with the lingering smell of soot and chimney smoke. Eloise had to temper her desire to get as far away as possible with the need to find shelter. The only place she could think of where they might spend the rest of the night unnoticed was a busy railway station. King's Cross seemed to be the nearest, and she remembered that there was a ladies only waiting room in the station concourse. It was a long walk, but there was little traffic in Farringdon Road, apart from the odd hansom cab and a few private carriages with tired coachmen huddled beneath their caped greatcoats. The grey buildings that housed banks and businesses were closed and shuttered, and Eloise knew that the financial heart of the City would lie dormant until morning, when the cleaners would bustle into the offices to do their work before the clerical staff arrived to begin the day's trading. The only people she saw were unfortunates sleeping rough in doorways. There but for the grace of God, she thought, hurrying past them with Joss dragging his heels.

'Want to go to bed, Mama,' he whimpered.

'I know, darling. It's not too far now,' Eloise said with as much conviction as she could muster. They had just passed a small family huddled beneath the portico of a merchant bank. The mother was heavily pregnant and she had an infant cuddled in her arms and another child wrapped in her tattered shawl. They were all incredibly dirty, with matted hair and running sores on their hands and faces. The woman's bare feet protruded from the frayed hemline of her skirt, and they were calloused and bleeding, as if the poor soul had walked for many miles before she collapsed from sheer exhaustion. For a moment Eloise thought she was seeing a vision of herself in the future and she shuddered, ignoring Joss's feeble protests and quickening her pace.

It was half past one in the morning when she trudged into King's Cross station. Somehow she had managed to get Joss onto her back and his small arms were clamped around her neck in a stranglehold. The fingers of her left hand were curled into what felt like a permanent claw around the handle of the valise, and she had lost all feeling in the arm in which she carried Beth. The station was deserted, except for a few porters loading the mail train. The huge iron engine belched clouds of steam as it waited like a restless metal beast eager to thunder off along the tracks to its distant destinations. In eerie silence, engines and rolling stock stood alongside platforms like sleeping giants. There was a stale smell in the air and a cold wind hurtled along the platform, almost whipping Eloise's bonnet off her head. She made for the ladies only waiting room and to her dismay she discovered that it was locked. She stood mutely staring at the door. It had not occurred to her that she might not be able to gain access, and tears of exhaustion trickled from her eyes.

She was barely aware of the trundling sound

behind her as a porter pushed his trolley towards the mail train. He stopped by her side. 'You shouldn't have them nippers out at this time of night, ducks.'

His voice was gruff but kindly and Eloise dashed her hand across her eyes, wincing at the pain as she touched the bruised skin. 'It's locked,' she said helplessly.

The porter produced a bunch of keys from a chain hanging at his side. 'I shouldn't do this, ducks, but I can't let a young woman sleep rough.' He unlocked the door and ushered them into the waiting room, which smelt strongly of disinfectant. 'It ain't exactly home from home, but you'll be safe enough in here until morning.'

'Thank you,' Eloise murmured tiredly. She put the valise down and flexed her fingers painfully. 'You're very kind.'

'I got daughters of me own. I wouldn't want them to be roaming the streets at this time of night, especially with their nippers.' He eyed her shrewdly. 'Your old man give you that shiner, did he?'

Eloise lifted her hand to touch her left eye and winced with pain. She had not had time to think about her appearance, but now as she glanced in the mirror above the empty grate she saw a white face with black shadows around her eyes and lips that were cut and swollen. She nodded vaguely but was saved from answering by Joss, who was attempting to scramble onto one of the wooden benches.

'Here, let me.' The porter lifted Joss onto the seat and patted him on the head. 'There you are, boy. You be a good little chap for your ma. She looks fair done in.'

Joss eyed him warily, sucked his thumb and curled up on the bench, closing his eyes.

'Thank you again,' Eloise murmured, sinking down on the seat beside Joss and cradling the sleeping Beth in her arms. 'I'm very grateful.'

'I'll have to lock you in for your own safety, ducks. But I'll unlock the door when me shift finishes at half past five, and you'll have to leave then before the cleaners come in to do their work.'

'Yes, I understand.'

He hesitated in the doorway. 'You should go back to him, love. Even if he knocks you about a bit, you should go back to your hubby. I daresay he'll be sorry for what he done when he sobers up a bit. It's a sad fact, but a bloke often uses his fists when he's had a drop too much to drink. But you won't get far on your own, and that's for certain.' He tipped his cap to her as he left the room, closing the door behind him.

Eloise heard the key grate in the lock and she uttered a sigh of relief. They were safe, at least for the next few hours. She leaned against the wall, rocking Beth gently in her arms. The lights from the station shone through the frosted glass panels on the door, making criss-cross patterns on the tiled floor, and outside she could hear the muted sounds of doors slamming, trolley wheels rumbling along the platform and the piercing blast of the guard's whistle. The engine of the mail train roared into life and she heard its wheels grinding on the rails as it pulled out of the station.

Eloise tried to keep awake by staring at the gaily coloured posters advertising seaside resorts and spa towns that hung on the walls, but gradually her eyelids became heavier and heavier and she began to drift off to sleep.

She was awakened by the grating of the key in the lock and a blast of cold air as the door opened.

'Sorry, love, but me shift's over. I got to ask you to move on.' The porter stood in the doorway, looking apologetic.

Eloise stared at him for a moment, uncertain whether she was waking or dreaming, and then the reality of the situation hit her as Beth began to cry and Joss woke up with a start.

'Here,' the porter said, shuffling into the waiting room. 'I thought you could do with a cup of tea, and there's some milk for the little 'uns.' He placed two mugs on the table. 'I can't stop, ducks, but you ain't got long afore the cleaning woman comes in.'

'Thank you,' Eloise murmured, reaching out for the cup of milk with a grateful smile. 'You've been really kind to us. I won't forget it in a hurry.'

'And you'll go back to your old man?'

'I'll do what's right,' Eloise said tactfully.

'Just so.' He backed out of the waiting room. 'I'll be off then. Good luck, love.'

In between giving Beth and Joss sips of the milk, Eloise drank her tea. She could hear sounds of the station coming back to life after its night's respite, and she knew that she must make a move. The hot, sweet tea was more than welcome, but she was stiff and sore and a quick glance in the mirror revealed a horrifying array of bruises on her face, so much so that she hardly recognised her own reflection. Joss was eyeing her oddly too, and she tried to make light of her injuries by telling him that she fell over and bumped her head. This explanation seemed to satisfy him, but he was now hungry and demanding food. Beth was gnawing at her fist and Eloise was feeling quite faint from hunger. Her first priority must be to get them something to eat, and then she would start looking for cheap lodgings.

As they left the shelter of the waiting room, Eloise saw from the white face of the station clock that it was just half past five. She found a coffee stall that was just setting up and purchased a ham sandwich and a slice of fruit cake, which she shared out between them. The children ate ravenously and Eloise took only a small amount of food for herself. Her split lip made eating difficult and the bread stuck in her throat when she attempted to swallow, but Joss and Beth had no trouble consuming their share of sandwich and cake. Outside the station, Eloise paused on the pavement, wondering which way to go. Even at this early hour the streets were beginning to fill with people on their way to their various places of employment. She kept looking over her shoulder, glancing anxiously at the faces of the men who strode towards her. Any one of them could be the man called Pike, who was intent on finding them. He must have an idea of what she looked like, but in that he had the advantage of her. Too scared to walk the main streets, Eloise went instinctively away from the city centre, heading north towards Maiden Lane. The streets were narrow and clogged with carts containing rubbish and night soil as the carters headed for the dust yard. The air was almost too thick to breathe and the sunrise was partially obliterated by a cloud of dust, so that the sun itself looked like a blood orange lurking behind a veil of gauze. Eloise had no idea where she was going, but she was afraid to turn back. She hesitated, looking round at the unfamiliar surroundings. The stench of the dust yard was appalling and made her want to retch. The noise from beyond the high wall was almost deafening, and she was about to cross the road when a horse-drawn vehicle appeared seemingly out of nowhere.

'Whoa. Look out there, you bloody fool.' The carter's warning shout came almost too late as the carthorse reared in its shafts, and the sudden braking of the huge iron-rimmed wheels caused sparks to fly up from the cobblestones. Clutching Beth to her bosom, Eloise dragged Joss off his feet as she staggered and fell against the brick wall of the dust yard, hitting her head and seeing nothing except the metallic gleam of hooves rising above her head.

Chapter Twelve

'Hey there, you clumsy great oaf. Don't you never look where you're going?'

Eloise struggled back to full consciousness to see a wild-looking woman standing in the road, shaking her fist at the carter. She was covered from the top of her battered black bonnet to her booted feet in grit and coal dust, and a pair of fierce brown eyes glared at the man through a mask of dirt. 'You great booby, you nearly run down this poor soul and her nippers.'

The carter responded with a volley of invective, emphasising each word with a crack of the whip above the poor horse's ears as he steered it through the open gates into the yard. 'I'll have words to say to you later on, Peg Tranter.'

The woman he called Peg stuck out her tongue. 'You can bugger off, Mick. I got nothing more to say to you now or later.' She turned her back on him, giving her attention to Joss who was wailing with fright and pain from a scraped knee. She took off a red scarf that was knotted around her throat and tied it round the injured limb. 'There's a brave little soldier. All better now?'

Despite a bump on the head and a badly bruised shoulder, Eloise's first concern was for Beth who was sobbing in her arms. A quick examination reassured her that the baby was unhurt by their fall, and a kiss and a cuddle soon comforted her. Eloise glanced anxiously at Joss, but he seemed happy enough having the full attention of the strange-looking woman, and he was tracing a pattern in the dirt on her cheek with one small finger. Eloise scrambled to her feet. 'Thank you, ma'am. I think the brute would have run us down if you had not stopped him.'

'Nah, he wouldn't. Mick is just a bag of hot air. Got a temper on him, but he wouldn't harm a fly.'

Eloise tried to smile, but her split lip began to bleed again and she raised her hand to her mouth. 'Thank you, anyway.'

'Well, I dunno what you're doing here at this hour of the morning, and with two nippers in tow, but judging by the looks of you, you already come off the worse from some bloke's fist.' Peg stood back, arms akimbo as she took in Eloise's bruised and dishevelled appearance. 'Jealous sort, is he? Caught you with another fellah, did he?'

Eloise shook her head. 'No. It wasn't like that. Really, I must be getting on . . .' She swayed dizzily and Peg rushed forward to snatch Beth from her arms.

'Why, you're half dead on your feet. You ain't going nowhere for a while. What you need is a nice hot cup of tea and a sit down.' Ignoring Eloise's feeble protests, Peg took Joss by the hand and strode off, leading the way to a narrow alley at the back of the dust yard. Separated from the workings by a high brick wall, a row of dilapidated single-storey cottages lay in the menacing shadow of the dust heap, which towered above them like a foul-smelling black mountain. Eloise paused to catch her breath, staring at the strange monochrome landscape that was unlike anything she had ever seen before. Fine particles floated down from the skies like dry rain, obliterating the cobblestones and smothering the cottages in a grey mantle. The air was thick with the dust, making it difficult to breathe, and Eloise covered her mouth and nose with her hands, but Peg seemed oblivious to it all and she marched up to the first cottage, opened the door and disappeared inside taking the children with her. Eloise had no option but to follow them and she paused in the doorway, blinking as her eyes grew accustomed to the dim light.

It was the most humble dwelling that Eloise had ever set foot in, but the flagstone floor was spotlessly clean, and embers of a fire glowed in a blackleaded grate. Strings of onions and dried herbs hung from the low beamed ceiling, and the plain deal kitchen table had been scrubbed to the whiteness of bleached bone. The room was sparsely furnished with items that looked as though they had been rescued from the rubbish heap and crudely mended with slats of wood from orange boxes and rusty iron nails.

Peg set Beth down on a three-legged wooden stool, and Joss scrambled onto a bentwood chair at the table. 'I expect you could all do with something to eat,' Peg said, reaching out to take a loaf from the crock on the dresser. She hacked off three generous slices. 'This here bread is a bit stale and there ain't no butter until the dairy opens, but there might be a bit of jam left in the pot if the nippers ain't scoffed the lot last night.' She took a jam jar from a shelf and scraped some jam onto the bread. 'That'll keep them quiet for a bit,' she said, turning to Eloise with a broad grin. 'Sit down afore you fall down, and I'll make us that cup of tea.'

Grateful that Peg did not bombard her with questions, Eloise sank down on a chair at the table. She nibbled her slice of bread and jam, smiling at the sight of Joss and Beth tucking into their food. She was grateful for the moment of respite, but she reminded herself that they would have to move on soon. She had a nagging suspicion that when their hasty departure was discovered, Ephraim would act out of sheer spite and set Pike on their trail.

Peg went to the fireplace to riddle the embers.

She threw on a few lumps of coal and as the flames took hold she hung a blackened kettle on a hook over the fire. 'There, that shouldn't take too long,' she said, taking off her leather apron and hanging it on a peg. She turned to Eloise, angling her head. 'I ain't one to pry, but it would help if I knowed your name. I'm Peg, as you might have guessed from that big-mouthed bloke Mick Fowler, who pesters me day and night to marry him.'

'I didn't realise . . .'

Peg chuckled deep down in her throat and she took off her bonnet, sending a shower of dust onto the floor. She shook out her long, luxuriant chestnut hair, which fell in waves around her shoulders, and wiped some of the dirt from her face with a piece of rag, revealing a face that was not only much younger than Eloise had supposed, but she could see now that beneath the thick layer of dirt Peg was very pretty.

Peg gave her a knowing look. 'Yes, there is a girl under all this muck. And I do like him, a bit anyway, though I'd never let on to Mick. I have to keep him in his place or he'd take liberties, if you know what I mean. I have to be firm with my boy, but I intend to marry him one day, though he don't know it yet and I shan't let on until I'm good and ready.'

'You're very sure of yourself.'

'I am so. I have a good job as a sifter on the dust

heap and I can earn upwards of a shilling a day when the weather is fine. Me dad was the hill man, that's foreman of the heap to you, but he died a year or two back of lung fever, and now me brother Cyril is the hill man. Ma is a sifter like me, and me brother Jimmy is a filler-in and young Danny is a loader. Cora and Daisy are too young to help out, but when Cora is six she'll carry the bones, rags and bits of metal to the various heaps.'

'So the whole family is employed on the dust heap?'

'That's how it is. There are several more families who work the yard. We like to keep it that way.'

'It must be very hard work, and dirty too.'

Peg took a chipped brown china teapot with only half a handle from the dresser and a battered tin tea caddy from the mantelshelf. She warmed the pot and measured out the tea leaves. 'It's hard, but it's a living,' she said, pouring boiling water into the pot. 'There, we'll let that brew and then we'll have a nice cup of tea, while you tell me your story. And don't give me the one about walking into a door. I've heard it all before.'

As she sipped the hot, sweet tea, Eloise found herself telling Peg everything, from the tragic news of Ronnie's untimely death to the shameful way in which Ephraim had taken advantage of her. Peg listened, round-eyed and suitably impressed. 'Well, I never did. And you a vicar's daughter too.'

'I didn't mean to burden you with my troubles, Peg. Thank you for the food and tea, but I think it's time we were on our way.' Eloise went to stand up, but a wave of dizziness made her sink back onto the hard wooden seat of the chair. 'Perhaps another five minutes' rest will set me right.'

Peg shook her head. 'You can't go nowhere in that state. What if you fell into a dead faint and there was no one to look after the nippers? No, you'd best stay here until you're fit enough to go on.' She raised her hand as Eloise opened her mouth to argue. 'Ma will be up in a little while and she'll agree with me. She'll say it was lucky I done the night shift and it were fate that made Mick almost run you down outside the dust yard. Ma believes in all that stuff. You sit right where you are. I'm going out to the dairy to fetch milk and butter, and then I'm going to the bakery to get the bread. When Ma comes in, you tell her I said you're to stay.' Peg crammed her bonnet back on her head, picked up a wicker basket and breezed out of the cottage. Eloise stared dumbly after her. It did not seem possible that Peg had already done a night shift in that horrible place and still had the energy to go out for provisions. She heard movement in the next room, and she braced herself to face Mrs Tranter with an explanation as to their presence in her home.

But when the interior door opened it was two small girls who tumbled into the room, still wearing their calico nightgowns and with their hair tied up in rags. They stared at Joss and Beth. 'Who are you?' demanded the elder girl, who could not have been more than four or five. 'What are you doing here?'

The younger child put out her hand to touch Joss's blond curls. 'Hello, boy.'

Joss gave her a shove that caught her by surprise and she sat down with a painful thud and began to cry. A small, thin woman rushed into the room, stopping short when she saw Eloise. 'What's going on?'

She was so like Peg that there was no mistaking her for anyone other than Mrs Tranter and Eloise rose a little unsteadily to her feet. 'I'm sorry, Mrs Tranter. Peg said you wouldn't mind if we rested here for a little while.' She caught Joss by the shoulders and turned him towards the small girl. 'Say you're sorry, Joss.'

He took on the stubborn, mulish look that always reminded Eloise forcibly of Ronnie and he shook his head. 'Shan't.'

Mrs Tranter's lined face cracked into a smile. 'I wish I had a penny for every time I've heard that word.' She bent down to pick up her wailing daughter. 'You're not hurt, Daisy. Rub it in.' She rubbed the child's backside with her hand and then set her down on the ground. 'Cora, take Daisy into the bedroom and get her dressed. Go and wake the boys up or they'll be late for work and they'll have their pay docked. You tell them that.' She shooed the small girls into the back room and then turned to fix Eloise with a curious stare. 'So, what's your story then, love?'

By the time Peg returned with fresh bread, milk and butter, Eloise had retold her story, and Mrs Tranter had listened with knowing nods of her head and sympathetic murmurs. 'Your poor dad would turn in his grave if he knew what had happened to you, ducks.'

A cold shiver ran down Eloise's spine. 'My father isn't dead, Mrs Tranter.'

'Heavens above, did I say dead? I meant to say departed – not in the way of being deceased, you understand. I meant that he weren't here to protect you and the nippers. That's what I meant.'

Mrs Tranter and Peg exchanged worried glances which did nothing to comfort Eloise.

'It was a slip of the tongue,' Peg said hastily. 'It ain't true what they say about Ma having second sight. That's just a load of old nonsense.'

'It could be just the sickness,' Mrs Tranter murmured. 'Mortal bad sickness.'

Before Eloise had a chance to question her, the door to the bedroom burst open and two young boys tumbled into the tiny living room, followed by a young man of eighteen or nineteen.

'Boys, where's your manners?' Mrs Tranter demanded, cuffing the one nearest to her round the head. She tempered her action with a proud smile. 'These are my boys, Ellie. This is Jimmy and the young one is Danny, and the big fellah who ought to know better than to chase his brothers is my Cyril. He took over as hill man when my hubby passed away two years since.' She held her hand out to Cora and Daisy. 'And these are my babies. I lost three, but I thank the Lord for the survival of the rest.'

Eloise lifted Beth onto her lap, fearing that someone might accidentally tread on her. 'It's nice to meet you all,' she murmured. The boys were staring openly at her disfigured face, making her feel extremely uncomfortable. 'But you'll want to have your breakfast, Mrs Tranter. I'm afraid that we're in the way.'

'Sit down, ducks,' Mrs Tranter said, taking the loaf from Peg's basket. She took a knife from a drawer in the table and cut thick doorsteps of bread, scraping them with butter. 'And me name is Gertie. No one stands on ceremony in Magpie Alley.' She gave the largest slice of bread to Cyril, who muttered something unintelligible, rammed his cap on his head and hurried from the house, followed by the two younger boys who were cramming bread into their mouths as they went.

It seemed little enough food to keep them going all day, and Eloise thought guiltily of the breakfasts she had taken so much for granted at home. The white damask tablecloth set with bone-handled cutlery and Mama's prized willow-pattern china. The bowls of porridge laced with cream and sugar, the crisp bacon and glossy fried eggs that Janet served sometimes with sausages and at others with tender kidneys and fried bread; the hot buttered toast and home-made marmalade or raspberry jam. She had taken it all for granted and had sent back platefuls of uneaten food, simply because she was not hungry. Papa had frowned and scolded her for wasting good food. She could hear him now as he had stood at the head of the table, wagging his finger at her. 'There are thousands of people in this world who are starving and would be grateful to have a meal like that.' She had felt guilty then, but she could never have imagined what it was like to be really hungry – until now. If she ever had a chance to live well again she would not waste a single crumb, and when they said grace before a meal she would recite the words with feeling.

'Have a slice of bread and butter, ducks,' Gertie said, spearing a piece of bread on the tip of the knife and waving it in front of Eloise's nose. 'You look as though you could do with a good meal.'

'Thank you, but Peg gave me some earlier,'

Eloise said, eyeing the bread hungrily but she could not in all conscience take any more of the hard-earned food. 'You're very kind, Mrs Tranter. I mean, Gertie.'

'We all have to look out for each other in these parts, love. If you stay here for any length of time, you'll come to know that for a fact.'

'No, really. I mean, I'm truly grateful for breakfast, but I cannot stay. We have to move on.'

'And where will you go?' Peg demanded, taking a seat opposite Eloise at the table. 'You're done in and you won't get far in that state. You can stay here until you're fit enough to travel. Ain't that so, Ma?'

Gertie pulled on a bonnet similar to the one Peg had just discarded. She tied the tattered ribbons beneath her chin and reached for her leather apron. 'If you don't mind sleeping on the floor in here, then you can stay as long as you like, girl. That bloke Pike won't think to look for you in a dust yard, and I daresay as how Cyril will find you work when you're strong enough, so you can earn a bit of money to see you on your way. We look after our own here. You'll learn that afore long, Ellie.'

When Gertie had left for the dust yard, Peg showed Eloise where they fetched water from a communal pump at the rear of the cottages. There was a stone trough where they washed clothes and dishes and did their ablutions, and two outside privies set side by side in wooden huts which also served the whole community. Peg explained that the women took it in turns to keep them clean and the night soil collector came round every day to empty them. Eloise helped Peg to wash the dishes and to stack them neatly on the dresser. After tidying the kitchen, Peg went into the back room to sleep. Eloise had noted their sleeping arrangements as she went through to the back yard, and she was even more impressed with the strength and fortitude of the family who slept top to toe on straw-filled palliasses, which in the morning were rolled neatly away. How they managed to keep so cheerful in such harsh conditions, Eloise did not know, but she was filled with admiration.

Eloise sat in the rocking chair by the fireplace, but no matter how hard she tried to keep awake so that she could watch over the children, her eyelids were heavy and she kept drifting off into a fitful sleep. She would never normally have left a five-year-old in charge of Joss and Beth, but Cora seemed old for her years and was obviously used to looking after Daisy. Every time she dragged herself back to consciousness, Eloise discovered that Cora was completely in charge. She was stricter with Joss than any adult nanny and she bossed him about shamelessly, which he took in good part. She marshalled the younger children with the skill of a small general and she even included Beth in her games. Eventually Eloise relaxed enough to slip into a deep sleep and awakened to find Peg riddling the ashes in the grate and preparing to relight the fire.

'I'm sorry,' Eloise murmured, rubbing her eyes. 'I didn't mean to let the fire go out.'

'Don't worry about it,' Peg said, grinning. 'I've only just got up meself. I'll make a pot of tea and then we'll see about supper. Ma and the boys will be home in half an hour or so, and they'll be starving as usual.'

Eloise watched Peg's deft movements as she urged the fire back into life. 'I don't know how you keep so cheerful, Peg. I mean, you have to work so hard in that awful place.'

'It's just the way things are. I'm used to it and I don't know no different. If I'd been born a lady who works in a shop up West, or a clever person with book learning who had worked in an office, then I might not be content. As it is, we've got enough to eat and a roof over our heads. We got each other and we got the other families who work in the dust yard as friends. It ain't so bad once you get used to the smell, the flies, rats and dirt. I can think of worse jobs.'

Eloise did not answer this. She could barely think of anything more awful than to work in such a place, but she did not want to hurt Peg's feelings. She held her arms out to Beth, who had tired of being bossed by Cora and was crawling over to the safety of her mother's lap. Eloise picked her up, giving her a loving hug.

Peg sat back on her haunches. 'So what are you going to do, Ellie? You know you can stay here as long as you want.'

Eloise rubbed her cheek against Beth's hair, holding her close. 'I need to find work, and cheap lodgings.'

'And you need to steer clear of that Pike fellow.'

'Yes, that most of all.'

'Well, it's up to you, of course, but I suggest you ask Cyril for work on the dust heap. You need to keep out of sight until your face goes back to normal. It's a dead giveaway, if you don't mind me saying. If your old master lets on to Pike that you got two black eyes and a split lip, it's going to make it that much easier for him to find you. And I daresay you ain't got much money left, so you haven't got a lot of choices.'

Eloise nodded her head. What Peg said was quite true. 'If your mother doesn't mind, then I will stay, and I'm not afraid of hard work.'

'Good. We'll make a sifter of you yet, Ellie.'

If Eloise had admired the Tranters before she started work in the dust yard, her respect for them quadrupled after a day of backbreaking toil in conditions that were like something out of a dreadful nightmare. Cyril had given her a job as sifter, working alongside Peg, her mother and half a dozen other women and girls at the base of a huge dust heap. Jimmy shovelled dust into the women's sieves and they worked in a constant fog of fine particles, almost as thick as a pea-souper, and even smellier. Within minutes their hands and faces were blackened, making them look like chimney sweeps. The grit found its way into Eloise's eyes and mouth; it clogged her nose and she kept scraping her knuckles and making them bleed, but there was no time to stop and the blood congealed in dark red scabs. Her back ached and the muscles in her legs went into painful cramps as she bent over her work. The other women kept up a cheerful stream of banter and lewd jokes that made Eloise blush, but at least it took her mind off her physical discomfort. They were rough, tough women but they had accepted her good-naturedly, and teased her mercilessly, although none of it was malicious. They were sympathetic in their own way and they made no comment when she had to keep stopping for a rest.

By midday, Eloise was exhausted and in pain, her lungs were clogged with dust and her mouth was filled with grit, but somehow she kept working. She had no intention of letting the Tranters down, and she was desperate to earn money. The noise in the dust yard was constant and deafening. Carts filled with rubbish clattered into the yard to unload and afterwards to be reloaded with breeze or cinders which were taken to the brickworks, together with the fine dust for brick making. Rags, bones and old metal went to marine store dealers; old boots and shoes were sold to the Prussian blue manufactories. Old iron and tin had their place in the scheme of things, as did broken bricks and oyster shells which went to be used in road making or foundations of new buildings. In the midst of this hive of activity, chickens and geese roamed the site, pecking at the ground for scraps of food. Large black rats made off with anything edible, risking attack from the feral cats that stalked them or lay in wait behind heaps of rubbish.

Somehow, after surviving the first day, the second was not nearly so bad, but if it had not been for the kindness of the Tranter family, Eloise would have thought that she had landed up in hell. Their open-hearted acceptance of her acted as a balm to her spirit after her recent harsh experiences and she did not even mind sleeping on the flagstone floor every night. Peg gave her an old palliasse that had definitely seen better days. The straw stuffing was matted and thin, but Eloise was so tired that she fell asleep without any difficulty and barely noticed the discomfort or the cold seeping up through the flagstones.

At first, Eloise was anxious about leaving Joss

and Beth in the care of someone as young as Cora, but there were many such children amongst the families who worked the dust heaps, and none of them seemed to come to any harm. They played together in the dirt outside the cottages and soon Joss and Beth were as grubby as the rest of those who were too young to be put to work. The elder children looked after the little ones, but this was small comfort to Eloise when she heard their shrieks and shouts as they played and she worked. It was almost impossible to tell whether the screams were of excitement or agony, and she had to steel herself to keep on sieving even though her maternal instincts urged her to rush outside the yard to make sure her children were unharmed.

At the end of the first week, Eloise queued up with the rest of the workers to receive her wages. It was the first time in her life that she had earned any money and she pocketed the six shillings with a feeling of pride and achievement. That evening she was able to give Gertie Tranter money to pay for their food and lodging, and the remainder she put in her purse. Grateful as she was to the Tranters, Eloise was determined to move away as soon as possible. This was not the sort of life she had envisaged for herself or her children, and the tiny cottage was already crammed to capacity without adding three extra persons, even if two of them were very small. Not that they were in the house very much, except to eat and sleep. As the summer progressed, the warm evenings found the inhabitants of Magpie Alley sitting on their doorsteps, neighbour chatting to neighbour, while the children played in the street. The men mostly took themselves off to the local pub, coming home late at night having washed the grit from their throats with several pints of beer. Although Peg denied tender feelings for Mick Fowler, and she spent most of her time arguing with him, she did not often refuse him when he lumbered into the cottage and asked her to go for a walk, or offered to take her to some form of public entertainment. Peg loved the theatre and music halls. Her favourite outing was to visit the Pavilion or the City of London Theatre and watch a melodrama from the dizzy heights of the gallery. On these evenings she was always in a good mood with Mick and when he walked her home there was a good deal of scuffling and giggling as they said goodbye outside the front door.

After living with the Tranters for some time, Eloise had discovered that what Peg said about Mick was true. He had a ferocious temper, when roused, but in general his loud voice, fierce manner and bad language were just a cover to hide his good nature from those who might take advantage of him. In contrast to his great height and bulk, Peg was tiny, but she had him well and truly under her thumb. One quelling look from her, or a sharp rebuke, would turn poor Mick into a quivering wreck, but he was still her devoted slave. Eloise marvelled at their relationship and sometimes she was even a little envious. Now that the initial horror of Ephraim's assault on her had faded along with the bruises, Eloise experienced a vague longing and a sense of loneliness, even though she was surrounded by people. It was not for Ronnie that she yearned, and that also disturbed her. Their few short years together were now fading to a precious memory, stored like a wedding gown wrapped in tissue paper and locked away in a wooden chest. Sometimes she even had difficulty in visualising his face and it seemed as though he was gradually dissolving into the misty past. But she was still young, she told herself, not yet twenty-four, and although she felt she ought to be ashamed to have what Papa had called carnal thoughts, she missed the tender loving relationship that exists between a man and a woman. She could not imagine giving herself willingly to another man, and yet . . . Her life seemed to stretch ahead of her in a long and lonely path.

On a particularly hot evening in July, when Joss and Beth were snuggled up asleep with Cora and Daisy in the back room, Eloise was alone in the kitchen, sitting at the table and attempting to write to her mother, but her mind kept wandering from the subject. Outside she could hear the older children playing and the sound of the women's voices as they sat in the evening sunshine, chatting about the events of the day. Eloise stared at the few lines that she had written and frowned. It was so difficult to think of anything positive to tell Mama, especially when she had not received any correspondence for several weeks. For fear of being spotted by Pike, Eloise had not dared to venture into the part of town where the Missionary Society had their offices to collect her mail. She could only hope that by now he would have reported back to Cribb's Hall, informing Hilda that his quarry had disappeared without trace, and that he had given up his search. Eloise stroked her cheek with the feathery tip of the quill pen and decided that the time had come to be brave. After all, she could not hide forever and she was desperate for news of her parents. Tomorrow she would venture into town.

She folded the unfinished letter and put it back inside her writing case. Then she took out a fresh sheet and penned a note to Annie, telling her that she would be in the gardens at the Foundling Hospital on the following Sunday afternoon, and suggesting that they might meet. With a new sense of purpose, Eloise put the letter in an envelope and sealed it. She could not and would not hide away any longer. She must take charge of her own life.

Next day, Eloise put on her only clean change of clothing and she set off for the post office and Missionary Society office with a spring in her step. To her great delight there were two letters from her mother, and she could hardly wait to tear open the envelopes and devour their contents. Tucking them safely in her reticule, she set off along Gray's Inn Road, walking briskly until she came to the gardens of the Foundling Hospital. At this time of day they were quite deserted, and she sat down in the shade of a plane tree and tore open the first envelope with trembling fingers. It was not a very long letter and some of the news was disturbing. The missionary post was in a village deep in the bush, and a long way from what her parents considered to be civilisation. Their home was little more than a windowless mud hut with a dirt floor and a thatched roof. It was set in a compound surrounded by a hedge of tall, thick-stemmed grasses to keep out the wild beasts, but that had not prevented a spitting cobra from nesting in the roof of the privy and a green python inhabited the flame tree which grew just outside the hut. It was little better inside, according to Mama's account of the frightening, but harmless, praying mantis which climbed up the walls at night to catch flies and insects, or the huge hunting spiders that lurked in the corners ready to scuttle out to eat a cockroach or even a small rodent. Mama said that no matter how hot it was, she and Janet never took off their high button boots until they climbed into their camp beds at night to huddle beneath mosquito nets. Their water was carried from the river daily and every drop had to be boiled before use. They were living mainly off dried and tinned food prepared by their Kikuyu cook, and a few fresh vegetables they had managed to grow in the small kitchen garden. Papa was in his element, she wrote, and he felt that at last he was fulfilling his vocation, although he was often laid extremely low by bouts of malaria and had to take to his bed. Janet was not happy living in what she termed 'this godforsaken place', but although she grumbled she was a tower of strength and Mama repeated several times that she would have been lost without her.

The second letter went on in much the same vein, and Eloise was left feeling rather disturbed. Papa might be in his element, but reading between the lines she sensed that the reality of the African bush was harder for women to bear than for men. She read and reread the two letters, biting back tears of worry and frustration. Of course Papa was a good man, but their lives would have been so much more comfortable if he had not had such high ideals. She was just putting the letters back in their envelopes when the sound of small footsteps on the gravel caused her to look up. A little girl in a white muslin dress was skipping towards her, rolling a large hoop along the ground with the aid of a short stick. It hit a stone and careered off the path to land at Eloise's feet. She leaned over to retrieve it and handed it back to its small owner.

'Thank you, but you shouldn't be in the gardens. The public are only allowed in on Sundays.' The child's voice and manner were so grown up that Eloise had to hide a smile.

'I'm sorry,' she said, getting to her feet and brushing bits of grass off her skirt. 'I didn't know.'

'Well, you do now.'

'Maria!'

At the sound of a man's deep voice, the little girl turned with a guilty start. 'Yes, Papa.'

The man, whom Eloise recognised instantly as Barton Caine, the governor of the Foundling Hospital, came striding along the pathway towards them. 'You are not supposed to be out here, Maria. Miss Trinder has been looking everywhere for you.' He seemed to realise then that his daughter was not alone and he stared at Eloise with raised eyebrows. 'And who might you be, ma'am?'

From the tone of his voice he might have been speaking to a servant. Eloise was suddenly conscious of her shabby attire and the shadows of grime that no amount of carbolic soap would quite wash away from her face and hands. She must look like a skivvy, but there was no need for him to take that tone. She drew herself up to her full height. 'I beg your pardon, sir. I was not aware that I was trespassing. I thought the gardens were open to the public.' Without giving him a chance to reply, she marched off along the path towards the main road, holding her head high, but inside she was seething with anger and embarrassment.

She was still fuming when she arrived back in Magpie Alley, but her anger was replaced by alarm when she saw people milling about in the lane. It was not dinnertime at the dust heap, and anyway most of the workers ate their bread and dripping in the yard. She knew instinctively that something was wrong and she ran towards Peg, who was speaking to Cora in an agitated manner and gesticulating wildly.

'What's the matter? What's happened?' Eloise demanded breathlessly.

'It's young Joss,' Peg said, biting her lip. 'He's gone missing, Ellie. Some of the men are out searching for him, but he's been gone a good hour. Cora said he was playing with young Jimmy Bragg one minute and gone the next.'

All Eloise's worst fears were suddenly realised and one word came into her head. 'Pike.'

Chapter Thirteen

Her heart missed several beats and Eloise swayed on her feet, overcome by a wave of dizziness. Peg took her by the elbows, giving her a shake. 'Don't you dare swoon, Ellie. That won't help to find young Joss. Anyway, Mick and the boys have gone looking for him and they know this area better than anyone.'

Gertie bustled up to them. 'Have a heart, Peg. We're not all as tough as you, me girl.' She took Eloise by the arm. 'Come inside, ducks. I'll make you a nice hot cup of tea.'

Frantic with worry, Eloise snatched her arm free. 'Tea! Is that all you can think about when my boy has been taken by that man?'

'You don't know that for certain,' Gertie said, frowning. 'He's probably just wandered off and got lost. The men will find him.'

Peg linked her hand through Eloise's other arm. 'Come on, Ellie. Ma's right. You wouldn't know where to start looking and you should stay here with Beth.'

Eloise nodded mutely. In her panic she had not given a thought to Beth, who was attempting to take her first shaky steps but was not yet toddling. She allowed herself to be led into the cottage where Beth was sitting on the floor watching the next door neighbour's youngest daughter playing with a cup and ball.

'Thank you, Flossie,' Gertie said, patting the child on the head. 'You can go home now, ducks.'

Flossie skipped off, still attempting to catch the small wooden ball in the crudely carved cup, and Eloise lifted Beth up in her arms to give her a cuddle. At least one of her children was safe, but as the minutes ticked by she became more and more convinced that Pike had somehow discovered their whereabouts and had abducted Joss. He might even now be on a train heading north to Yorkshire and Cribb's Hall. She sank down on a chair, holding on to Beth as though she would never let her go.

'That's better,' Gertie said, taking the bubbling kettle off the fire. 'We'll have a nice cup of tea and wait here for the men to get back.'

'I'm going out looking too,' Peg said. 'We'll find him, Ellie.' She disappeared out into the bright sunshine.

'What if Pike has got him?' Eloise whispered. 'I'll never get him back, Gertie.'

Busying herself making the tea, Gertie gave her a reassuring smile. 'You mustn't think like that, ducks. Your Mr Pike would have to be a clever

301

fellow indeed to trace you here. I'm sure there's a simple explanation and you'll have him back in no time at all.'

'I'll never leave him again. If he comes home safe, I swear I'll keep him close to me forever.'

By mid-afternoon, Eloise was convinced that she would never see Joss again and close to despair. With Beth in her arms she paced up and down the lane outside the cottages, listening for the sound of the searchers returning as they did every half-hour or so to check that the child had not been found, before setting off again and widening their search area. Eloise was frantic. If Pike had not snatched Joss, any manner of accidents could have befallen him. He might have fallen into the canal and drowned. He could have been trampled by a carthorse or run over by a train. By teatime she was even more desperate, and every time someone entered the lane she ran outside demanding to know if they had any news of Joss.

One by one the searchers returned, shaking their heads apologetically.

'We've searched everywhere we can think of,' Mick said, taking off his battered bowler hat and scratching his head. 'I'm sorry, ducks, but there's no sign of the little fellow.'

Peg was at his side and she laid her hand on Eloise's arm. 'It's true, Ellie. We've looked everywhere.'

Eloise thrust Beth into Peg's arms. 'Take my baby. I'm going to look for Joss myself.'

Mick caught her by the hand. 'Don't, girl. You'll only get yourself lost into the bargain.'

'I will go. I can't just stay at home while my boy is out there all alone and frightened.' Eloise struggled to get free but Mick was much stronger than she and he held her in an iron grip, shaking his head.

'Listen to him, Ellie,' Peg urged.

'No,' Eloise screamed, kicking out with her feet. 'Let me go.'

'Hello, there.'

Eloise stopped struggling and turned her head to look at the man striding towards them from the far end of the terrace. In his arms he carried a bundle and her heart was in her throat as she recognised the curly blond head resting against his shoulder. 'Joss.' His name was wrenched from her lips in a cry of sheer joy as she raced towards the man and snatched her son from his arms. 'Joss, my baby.' Eloise clutched him to her breast, sobbing with relief. 'Oh, Joss, you're safe.'

Peg hurried over to her with Beth in her arms. 'Is he all right, Ellie?'

Joss opened his blue eyes and gave them a sleepy smile. 'Mama.'

Ellie buried her face in his curls, unable to speak, and Peg patted her on the shoulder. 'Bring him into the house. I'll bet he's hungry and thirsty.'

Eloise nodded her head and she flashed a watery smile at the man who had found Joss. 'It's Mr Tully, isn't it?'

He tipped his cap. 'Yes, ma'am.'

'Thank you,' Eloise breathed, unable to find the words to express her innermost feelings. Suddenly a heavy weight had lifted from her shoulders and she felt light-headed with relief. 'Thank you, so much.'

Mick held out his hand. 'Good work, mate. Where did you find him?'

'Curled up asleep on me bed. Must've been there all day and I never thought to check the back room until just now. My old lady had left the door open and the little chap must have wandered in.'

Mick slapped him on the shoulder. 'Well, Tully, thank God for that. We'd almost given him up for dead.'

Tully grinned sheepishly. 'He'd have been there until nightfall if I hadn't gone to look for me baccy pouch. But that's kids for you. Anyway, no harm done.'

Eloise could not quite agree with his last statement as she carried Joss into the cottage. No harm had come to Joss, but that was down to good luck. The truth was that someone as young as Cora could not be relied upon to keep an eye on even younger children. Every time Eloise left Joss and Beth to go to work in the dust yard she was exposing them to danger, and it was only now that she realised just how much potential peril there was all around them. Then there was Pike, who might not have given up his search. Although she had tried to convince herself otherwise, Eloise suspected that Hilda had paid him generously for his services and would continue to do so until she had what she wanted. Hilda Cribb was not a woman to give up easily.

That night, as she lay on her palliasse in front of the fire, Eloise knew that their days here were numbered. It would soon be time to move on. Next day very early, before her shift at the dust yard was due to start, she walked to the station and bought a newspaper. She scanned the Situations Vacant columns but there was nothing remotely suitable. All the living-in domestic jobs required single women and she was not trained for any type of office work or even to teach. This left her with little choice other than serving in a shop or doing manual labour in a factory, neither of which would help her to care for Joss and Beth. Each day she spent some of her precious hoard of coins on a newspaper, but it was no use. There did not seem to be anything on offer which would suit her purpose, and it seemed that she would have to stay on at the Tranters' cottage and work in the dust yard for a very long time.

But Joss's escapade had terrified her, and Eloise was no longer content to leave him and Beth with Cora.

The long, hot summer days were taking their toll on everyone in Magpie Alley and those who worked in the dust yard. The carters who brought in the loads of rubbish and night soil were even more grumpy and belligerent than before, and the stench of the heaps was over-powering. It was gruelling work at the best of times, but with the sun hot on her back, and her throat, nose and eyes permanently clogged with dust, Eloise was suffering miserably. Her hands, which had once been soft and white, were now calloused, and the dirt was so ingrained that no amount of soap and water seemed to wash it away.

On the following Sunday, Eloise took the children to the Foundling Hospital gardens. After her last brush with the governor, it was the last place that she would have chosen, but she had promised to meet Annie there and she was not going to allow Mr Barton Caine to deflect her from her purpose. She sat on the grass while Joss and Beth played, and then, getting tired of sitting, Eloise took them for a walk along the gravelled paths between the beds of red, pink, white and yellow roses. Their scent was heady, but it did not disguise the stench coming from the fly-infested dung on the streets outside the gardens. After an hour, Eloise began to think that Annie was not coming. Perhaps Queenie had not given her the time off, or maybe she hadn't received her letter? The children were hot and thirsty and she bought them some ice cream from the hokey-pokey man, but by this time Eloise's head was beginning to ache. The sun bore down mercilessly and when the ice cream had gone Joss began to get crotchety. His mood seemed to rub off on normally sunny-natured Beth, who also began to snivel. Eloise decided then that Annie was definitely not coming and it was time to begin making their way back to Magpie Alley. She picked up Beth, who protested loudly, and she took Joss by the hand. They had just walked out of the gates when a shabbily dressed man barred their way. 'You are Mrs Eloise Cribb?' It was more a statement than a question.

Eloise held her breath. The man who confronted her simply had to be Pike. There was a touch of arrogance in his manner, and a sly look in his narrowed eyes that immediately put her on her guard, but she was not going to give him the satisfaction of seeing that she had guessed his identity. She met his gaze with a hard stare. 'Who are you, sir?'

'My name is Pike, missis. I think you know that well enough. You've led me a merry dance these past few weeks, but I'm on to you now.'

'I don't know what you're talking about, sir. Please allow me to pass.' Her heart was hammering against her rib cage and Eloise could hardly breathe, but she was not going to let this man intimidate her.

He planted his feet wide apart and leaned against the gatepost, pushing his face close to hers so that she was almost choked by the odour of bad breath mixed with stale sweat. 'I am ordered to take the boy back to his grandparents in Yorkshire. You will give him up to me without a fuss, or my client will go through legal channels and have the child made a ward of court.'

'You have the wrong person,' Eloise cried in desperation. 'I am not who you think I am. Allow me to pass, or I'll call a constable.'

'Oh, I don't think you'll do that, lady,' Pike sneered, thrusting his hand into his jacket pocket. He pulled out a tattered piece of paper and waved it under Eloise's nose. 'I knew you'd make a mistake one of these days, and that's just what you did when you sent this letter to the little skivvy in Nile Street. Mrs King intercepted it and passed it on to me.'

Eloise bit her lip. 'That is against the law.'

'I am the law, dearie, or a branch of it anyway.' Pike's wolfish smile was replaced by a snarl. 'Don't try to play games with me. I want the boy and I want him now.'

'You shan't have him. Leave us alone.' Eloise tried to push past him, but Pike barred her way.

'Run for it if you will, but I know now where you've been hiding. There's only two types of work in London where the dirt won't wash off the skin, and I don't think you've been working as a sweep's boy, so you must have been living close to a dust yard. Oh, yes, you was clever enough not to mention that detail to young Annie, but I'm paid to be observant. Even if you get away from me now, it won't take me long to find which yard you're at. You won't get the better of me, ducks, so you might as well hand the boy over now.'

'Never. You'll never take my son from me.' Eloise kicked him hard on the shin, catching him by surprise. Pike howled with pain and hopped on one leg, rubbing his bruised flesh. 'You bitch.'

Eloise didn't wait to hear the rest of her character assassination. Joss was crying from sheer fright and Beth was clinging round her neck. Eloise snatched Joss up under her arm and ran blindly along the pavement, neither knowing nor caring which way she was heading in her desperation to escape from Pike. She could hear him hurling abuse at her and the sound of his booted feet on the paving stones was getting closer all the time. Carrying both children slowed her down and she knew that Pike could outpace her. She looked round desperately for somewhere to hide; a narrow alley that she could dodge down or an open doorway where she could shelter, but there was nothing. As she rounded the corner into Guildford Street she cannoned headfirst into the arms of a tall man whose black frock coat and top hat were somehow. familiar. Momentarily winded, she stared down at his highly polished black patent shoes as she fought to catch her breath.

'Good God, woman. What do you think you're doing? You could have hurt yourself and these infants.'

Gasping for air, Eloise looked up into the coldly handsome face of Barton Caine. 'I – I . . .'

Joss and Beth were howling with fright and their wails reached a crescendo as Pike came flying round the corner and skidded to a halt. When he saw that Eloise was not alone, his expression changed subtly and he tugged off his bowler hat. 'Excuse me, sir. Is this woman bothering you?'

Barton gave Pike a disdainful look. 'And who might you be? Why were you pursuing this young woman?'

'It's no matter,' Eloise said, backing away. 'It was a misunderstanding.'

'No you don't,' Pike snarled, reaching out to catch her by the arm. 'Not so fast, lady. You're coming with me.'

'It seems that the lady doesn't want to go with

you,' Barton said icily. 'I suggest you go about your business, my good man.'

Pike bristled visibly, but he let go of Eloise's arm. 'It's a private matter, sir. A family argument you might say.'

'Then I suggest you continue your argument in private, but only after you've had time to calm down.' Caine turned his back on Pike to address Eloise in a stern voice. 'And you, madam, would do better to take your children home and leave your man to reflect on his duty as a husband.'

Eloise could not look him in the face. The utter humiliation of being taken for Pike's woman had momentarily cancelled out her fear, but now she saw her chance to escape and she took it. Without saying another word, she carried the screaming children down the street, leaving the governor of the Foundling Hospital to castigate Pike for his belligerent behaviour. When their raised voices faded into the distance she stopped to comfort the children, whose hysterical cries had quietened to dull sobs as they clung to her, soaking her blouse with their tears. Eloise found a quiet alley between shuttered business premises which led to a small court surrounded by warehouses. She sat down in the dust, rocking and cuddling the children until they were calm. Wiping their dirty faces on her sleeve, she kissed their tear-stained cheeks. 'There, there, my pets. It's all over now; we're safe from that nasty man.'

'Nasty man,' Joss murmured. 'Bad man.'

'Yes, darling,' Eloise agreed. 'A very bad man, but he won't find us again. Mama will see to that.' But even as the words left her mouth, she knew that she could not return to Magpie Alley. Although there were many dust yards in east London, she was certain it would not take Pike long to discover where she had been working, and that would inevitably lead him to the Tranters' cottage. The realisation that they were again homeless hit her with a sudden shock. They had only the clothes that they were wearing. Luckily she had brought her purse with her, but the rest of her possessions were in Magpie Alley and it would be madness to try to return there for a while. Gertie and Peg would no doubt be frantic with worry, but there was nothing she could do about that for the present.

Eloise fingered her purse and was reassured by the weight of the coins she had so carefully saved. Her main priority now must be to find cheap accommodation for the next few nights, or until she found a suitable living-in position. With a determined twitch of her shoulders, she set off again, keeping to the back streets. This was not a part of London that Eloise knew, but she was desperate to be far away from Clerkenwell and King's Cross and more especially from Pike's prying eyes. It was late afternoon, judging by the position of the sun in the sky, and the children were tired and hungry. With a few words of encouragement and the promise of something to eat soon she walked on, moderating her pace so that Joss could keep up with her, but she kept looking over her shoulder fearing that Pike might by some chance have followed them.

With no clear idea of where she was going, Eloise was relieved to see the familiar landmark of the British Museum, which she had once visited with her father. The sight of it brought back memories of a happy outing, but also a twinge of sadness as she remembered a life that had been so different and now seemed so far away. She realised that their dishevelled appearance was attracting curious glances from the well-dressed citizens of Bloomsbury who were out for a Sunday afternoon promenade, and she hastily moved on. Having reached New Oxford Street, she hesitated, uncertain which way to go. If she went east, she would be back in the area where Pike was probably still searching for them. There was no point in going towards the expensive West End, and north would lead her back towards King's Cross and imminent danger of discovery. She crossed the busy road, threading her way between hansom cabs, hackney carriages and horse-drawn omnibuses, and hurrying south she found herself in an area that was both foreign to her and frightening.

Even though it was Sunday, groups of slatternly, drunken old women stood about on street corners, smoking clay pipes and drinking out of stone bottles. Gangs of ragged children roamed the streets like packs of wild wolf cubs, looking no doubt for a pocket to pick or a purse to snatch. Avoiding a particularly ferocious-looking band of youths, Eloise dodged into Hampshire Hog Yard, but a burly man wearing corduroy breeches and gaiters staggered towards her. He was obviously under the influence of alcohol or even opium, and she fled, dragging a protesting Joss behind her. Beth joined in with his miserable caterwauling and in desperation Eloise turned into a road that bore the reassuring name of Church Lane.

She could still hear the thunder of traffic from New Oxford Street, but Church Lane might have been another world. It was narrow and cobbled and presented an odd sight indeed. Eloise paused for a moment to catch her breath and to stare. Suspended from the windows of the three-storey terraced houses were wooden rods festooned with wet washing. The garments, which hung limply in the still air, were worn and shabby, some of them patched and others little more than rags and tatters. There were several shops, closed for the holy day, and a pub which, despite its being a holy day, was obviously doing a brisk trade. The doors were open and men hung about outside with pint pots in their hands and clay pipes stuck in their mouths. Groups of women stood outside their houses, enjoying the late afternoon sunshine that filtered through the gaps in the tall buildings, and barefoot children played in the road, the girls skipping or whipping tops and the boys play-fighting. Although the area was poor and run down, Eloise did not feel threatened when a tawdrily dressed young woman sauntered over to her. 'Are you looking for someone, love?'

Eloise was wary. The woman was obviously the sort that Ronnie would have scathingly referred to as a dollymop, but her smile seemed genuine enough, and surely it was wrong to judge a person because they dyed their hair and rouged their lips? Eloise shook her head. 'No, but we do need cheap lodgings. Do you know of anywhere near here? My little boy is too tired to walk much further.'

'Poor little sod,' the woman said, ruffling Joss's hair. 'He looks done in and so do you. I reckon I could find you a bed for the night. Old Mother Hilton keeps the cleanest kip-shop in the street. C'mon on, it's not far.' Without a by-your-leave, she bent down and lifted Joss off his feet. 'You be a good boy for Auntie Poll and stop that bawling. You're giving me a headache.'

Joss was obviously taken by surprise at this sudden turn of events and he stopped crying, but he sent a mute appeal for help to his mother as Poll carted him off down the road. Eloise hurried after them. 'Don't worry, Joss, I'm coming.'

Poll stopped outside a house at the far end of the street and she opened the door and went inside. Eloise followed her down a passage whose walls did not appear to have had a lick of paint since the day the house was built. There was no covering on the floorboards other than a sprinkling of white sand, but at least the premises seemed clean and the pervading smell was of carbolic soap. Poll carried Joss down a narrow staircase to the basement kitchen where a fire burned in the range and a large boiler on either side of it bubbled with hot water. A fat woman wearing a faded cotton-print frock and white mobcap sat by the range with her feet up on a stool.

'Mother Hilton, I found this woman and her nippers wandering the street. Any chance of a night's lodgings?'

'Let's see your money,' Mother Hilton said, eyeing Eloise suspiciously. 'I got a room if you've got the cash, but you'll have to share.'

Eloise put Beth down on the floor and she took a few tottering steps before going down on her hands and knees to crawl over to Joss, who had been set down on a stool by Poll and was sitting quite still, staring wide-eyed at the strange surroundings. Eloise flexed her stiff fingers and took out her purse. 'How much do you charge for one night?'

'One and fourpence, take it or leave it. Food is extra.'

'That's a lot for a shared room,' Eloise protested.

'You'd pay three shillings in the City, and three times that in one of them posh hotels up West. This is a clean and respectable establishment.'

Poll snorted with laughter. 'Pull the other one, Mother. Your lodgers are magsmen, coiners and prostitutes.'

'Shut your trap, Poll. I don't care what trade or profession my clients follow, just so long as they don't cause no trouble and they pays up on the nail.' Mother Hilton heaved her large frame from the chair and she glared ominously at Joss and Beth. 'And I don't like nippers. They make a noise and they make a mess.'

'Perhaps I'd better go elsewhere,' Eloise said hastily.

Mother Hilton put her hands on her hips and mimicked Eloise's voice. 'Perhaps I'd better go elsewhere.' Her mocking smile darkened to a scowl. 'Perhaps you had, my lady. I dunno who or what you're running from, but I don't want no trouble from irate husbands or the law.'

'Oh, calm down, you old cow,' Poll said, snatching the purse from Eloise's fingers and shaking it so that the coins jingled. 'She can pay, so what's the fuss about?'

'Two nights in advance then,' Mother Hilton said, holding out her hand. 'And two nights in advance after that, if you're still here.'

Eloise glanced down at her exhausted children huddled together on the stool, and she nodded her head. 'All right, two and eight it is, but I'll be looking for alternative accommodation.'

'I hear they're all booked up at the Hotel Cecil,' Mother Hilton said, chuckling. 'Show her where to go, Poll. I'm going to put me feet up afore the rest of them comes in demanding supper, which is one shilling extra.'

'Come on, love,' Poll said, heading for a door at the back of the kitchen. 'I'll show you your room. It ain't Buckingham Palace, but I'll say this for the old bitch, she keeps a clean house.'

With Beth in her arms and Joss toddling on behind Poll, Eloise followed wearily, forcing her tired limbs into motion. Poll led them through an area that seemed to be used purely as a store-room, where sacks of potatoes, flour and dried peas were stacked along the walls together with cans of paraffin and boxes of candles. At the far end was another door and this led into a room about eleven feet square with a small window that looked out onto the area. It felt damp and the light was poor, but Eloise could just make out the shape of four lumpy mattresses lined up side by side. There was nothing else in the room, not even a table or a chair.

'This can't be right,' Eloise said in despair. 'I'm not paying one and four a night to sleep in a room like this, cheek by jowl with strangers.'

Poll folded her arms across her chest, shaking her head. 'Look, love. I can see that you ain't used to this sort of thing, but let me give you a word of advice. Take it! That's what I say. At least Mother Hilton's beds are reasonably clean. You won't find no bed bugs here and she ain't mean with the victuals. You could get similar in any one of the lodging houses round Seven Dials, but you'd pay more and you never know who's sleeping in the next bed. At least I can tell you that only two of these cots is took, one by old Aggie who falls into a drunken stupor every night and don't wake up till noon, and the other by Ivy who was a maidservant in a big house until she fell pregnant by the butler and then she got thrown out on the street. She lost her baby but without a reference she can't go back into service and so she does the next best thing.'

Eloise laid Beth down on one of the mattresses. 'And what's that?'

'She's a woman of the town, like me.' Poll raised her eyebrows and chuckled. 'I see you don't understand me. Young Ivy is a prostitute.'

'Oh!' Eloise sank down onto the bed beside Beth and Joss. 'I see.'

'When it comes to it, love, there ain't many

ways that women like us can earn enough to pay for their food and lodgings.'

'But there must be other things you could do.' Eloise stopped short and bit her lip. Poll had been kind and the last thing she wanted to do was upset her. She tried again. 'I mean, there's factory work and serving in shops.'

Poll chuckled. 'You have to speak proper and dress right to work in a shop. And as to factory work, well, there's phossy jaw for them what makes matches and lung rot for them that works in the flour mills, just to mention a couple of things that can kill you slow and painful like. To be honest, love, I'd rather do what I do and risk the pox or the occasional beating than waste me life working ten or twelve hours a day for nuppence and a nasty disease at the end of it.'

'But surely there must be honest work a woman can do?' Eloise said desperately. 'I'll be straight with you, Poll. I have to support my children and I must find work.'

Poll took a baccy pouch and a box of matches from her skirt pocket. She proceeded to roll a cigarette, staring thoughtfully at Eloise and the children. 'I'm sorry, ducks, but you got no chance, at least not with them two nippers in tow. Ain't you got no one who would take them in?'

'No, I haven't. And I'll never let my children go. They're all I've got.'

'Widow woman are you? Or wasn't you married to their dad?'

Eloise felt the colour rush to her cheeks. 'I'm a respectable widow. My father is a missionary in Africa and my wretched in-laws are trying to steal my son from me.' Her voice broke on a sob and she wrapped her arms around Joss and Beth, who were strangely and unnaturally silent as they took in their new surroundings.

'That's hard, love. But we've all had it rough. My old man used to knock us kids about something terrible. Battered me brother's brains out, he did, and ended up with a noose round his neck. Ma drank herself to death and the rest of us were left to fend for ourselves on the streets, so don't give me no hard luck story, because I ain't interested.' Poll lit her cigarette and drew in a lungful of smoke, then she seemed to relent and she grinned. 'Don't look so tragic. You got your health and strength so all you got to do is learn to live in the real world. You can earn good money at our trade, if you know what you're about. I'm saving me cash and as soon as I got enough I'm going to move to the country and set up in a sweet shop, where I can eat peppermint creams and chocolate all day if I wants to. That's me plan anyway, and a plan is what you need, girl.' Poll took another drag on her cigarette and offered her pouch to Eloise.

'No, thank you. I don't smoke.'

Poll chuckled. 'You will, love. And you'll be glad of a drop of tiddley on a Saturday night too when you've been here as long as I have.' She made for the door and paused with her hand on the latch. 'Let me know if you change your mind about coming out with me and Ivy. We'll see you right.'

Eloise managed a weak smile. 'You're very kind, Poll. But I won't be changing my mind.'

'Supper is at six. I'll bet them nippers is starving and the old witch ain't a bad cook. Her boiled cabbage and pig's head is one of the best suppers in St Giles.' With that parting piece of information, Poll went from the room leaving a trail of cigarette smoke in her wake.

Eloise sat very still, cuddling Joss and Beth. She murmured words of comfort to them as she rocked them in her arms. Their sleepy heads were heavy against her shoulders and their drooping eyelids were translucent with fatigue as they fought against sleep. A chill rose through the stone floor and the walls that were beneath ground level were oozing with damp. The smell of fungus and mould hung heavy in the air and Eloise struggled to hold back tears of exhaustion and desperation. What had they come to? And where would they go from here? Despite Poll's earthy kindness, Eloise felt that they had left purgatory and ended up in hell.

Chapter Fourteen

Despite all her concerted efforts, Eloise could not find work. She had answered advertisements in shop windows, and in the Situations Vacant columns of newspapers which had been discarded by other lodgers, but as soon as a prospective employer saw Joss and Beth, the door was closed in her face. She had walked miles in her search for employment, knocking on doors in the better areas of Bloomsbury and even venturing into the fashionable streets of the West End. This had proved to be a big mistake and she had suffered both humiliation and embarrassment when she was turned away from the tradesmen's entrances as if she were a gypsy or a vagrant begging for food. She had been forced to pawn her wedding ring in order to buy second-hand clothes from a dolly shop in Seven Dials for both herself and the children, and she had purchased a very old and extremely battered perambulator from a pawnbroker in George Street for Beth, who was only just beginning to take her first unaided steps and was now too heavy for Eloise to carry any great distance.

When Joss grew tired, Eloise sat him in the perambulator next to Beth, and continued her increasingly desperate quest to find a job.

At Mother Hilton's lodging house, Eloise's first two days turned into four, then six, and at the end of a fortnight she still had not found work, and her money was all but gone. In this time she had learned that Mother Hilton had a heart of stone when it came to money, and if a tenant could not pay they were evicted no matter how much they pleaded their case. In just two weeks Eloise had seen things in this part of London which both shocked and appalled her. She was used to living in the East End, but in St Giles the old rookeries, which had been the haunts of thieves and criminals of all classes, might have been demolished, but it was still a savage place where only the toughest survived. She had seen barefoot and half-starved street urchins clad in rags begging on street corners and prostitutes as young as eleven. Some of these children had been left to care for their infant siblings, most of whom would succumb to starvation and disease before they reached their first birthday. There were men and women of all ages who were ravaged by hideous diseases, all vying with feral dogs and cats for scraps of food tossed out with the rubbish that littered the streets. Prostitutes, thieves, drunks and drug addicts inhabited this twilight existence, and Eloise knew that she only remained unmolested because the people of the underworld judged by her down-at-heel appearance that she was one of them. What hope did a poor woman have of raising herself from the gutter? It seemed to her that once a person had sunk this far it was almost impos-sible to claw their way back into decent society. Not for the first time, she wondered why her papa had thought it necessary to take his missionary zeal to Africa, when there were people living just a few miles from his old parish whose bodies and souls were in desperate need of being saved.

Her plight was becoming increasingly desperate and the conditions under which they were living were too awful to put down on paper. Eloise had not written to her mother since they came to Mother Hilton's lodging house. It would break Mama's heart if she knew how low her daughter had sunk, and Eloise could not lie to her. She was living from day to day, not daring to think what the future might hold, but her money was dwindling faster than she could have imagined possible, and the time was approaching when she would have to leave this dire place and face an even worse life on the streets. In order to save money, she had stopped taking the evening meal provided by Mother Hilton, and she bought just enough food each day to feed the children. She ate whatever they left, but it was barely enough to survive on and she went to bed hungry every night.

At the beginning of September the oppressive heat of summer had given way to more mellow temperatures with hazy golden days and cooler nights. The evenings were drawing in fast. Soon autumn would turn into winter and Eloise had only pennies left in her purse. She had not eaten at all that day, having given the children the last of the bread soaked in a little milk, and she had waited until Mother Hilton had gone off to meet her cronies in the pub and the kitchen was empty. Making certain that no one was about, Eloise took Joss and Beth into the kitchen and sat them on the floor at a safe distance from the range, but close enough to enjoy its warmth. The chill in their basement sleeping quarters rose through the flagstone floor and the walls seeped with foul-smelling water from overflowing privies and slops thrown into the street. Eloise was terrified that Joss and Beth might sicken from cholera or typhus, and Beth already had a cough and a runny nose. This was not a healthy place for adults, let alone small children.

She took a small screw of paper from her pocket. It contained a teaspoon of tea leaves which had been used several times and carefully dried. The resultant brew would be weak and barely recognisable as tea, but it was better than drinking plain water and safer too. Eloise went to lift the teapot from the shelf and suddenly the kitchen began to spin around her. The next thing she knew, she was lying on her back on the floor in the midst of shards of broken china. Joss and Beth were screaming hysterically and someone was bending over her. Something cold and wet splashed her face and she attempted to sit up.

'What was you doing, you silly bitch?'

Poll's face hovered above her and Eloise sank back onto the hard tiles. 'I don't know. Everything went dark.'

'You're all right, girl. It was just a fainting fit. Ups-a-daisy.' Poll heaved Eloise to her feet and guided her to a chair. 'There, sit down and I'll clear up the broken china before the old cow gets back from the pub. We'll say that old Martin, the French polisher, broke it. She don't like him much anyway and she's always complaining that he stinks of meths and shellac, so she'll be happy to give him the elbow.'

Joss had run to his mother and was peering anxiously up into her face, and Beth was about to crawl over the broken china when Poll saw the danger and swooped upon her. She dropped Beth unceremoniously on Eloise's lap. 'Here, take your kid before she cuts herself to bits, while I clear up the evidence.'

'Thank you, Poll,' Eloise murmured, watching her whisk a besom round the floor and then sweep the broken pieces of the teapot into a shovel. She disappeared from the room, returning seconds later with a satisfied grin on her face.

'That's that. Now I'll do what I come to do in the first place and that was to make meself a cup of tea and some toast. You look as though you could do with some too.'

'I've got my own tea,' Eloise began, stopping as she realised that she had spilt her precious tea leaves in her fall. Tears spurted from her eyes and she buried her face in Beth's soft curls.

'There, there,' Poll said brusquely. 'Don't take on so. It's just a bit of spilt tea.'

Giving Beth a reassuring hug, Eloise wiped her eyes on her sleeve. 'It's all I had left.'

Poll took another teapot from the dresser and she produced a poke of tea from her pocket, spooning the richly scented dark leaves into the warmed pot. 'And when did you last eat, my girl?'

'I had something last night.'

'Liar!' Poll said dispassionately. 'Just take a look at yourself, Ellie. You're a mass of skin and bone. I bet you ain't had a proper meal since you gave up eating supper with us. My guess is that you're broke.'

Eloise nodded mutely.

'And you can't find work with two nippers hanging round your neck.'

It was a statement rather than a question and Eloise shrugged her shoulders. It was too painful to admit the truth.

Poll handed her a cup of tea generously laced with sugar. 'Get that inside you and I'll make some toast. Come here, Joss. You can hold on to the toasting fork and if you're a good boy I'll give you some when it's done.'

She handed Joss a long brass toasting fork and allowed him to brandish it while she took a loaf of bread from the crock and cut several slices. 'There's a good chap. You watch Poll and see how it's done.'

Eloise hesitated as the words stuck in her throat. It pained her to admit the truth, but then, she thought with a wry smile, it was just her pride that was injured. Papa would have given her a lecture on the sin of false pride. For once she was glad that her parents were far away so that they could not see the depths to which she had plummeted. 'I can't pay you for the bread or the tea, Poll.'

'Shut up!' Poll said, stabbing a slice of bread on the toasting fork and directing Joss to hold it close to the glowing embers behind the bars of the range. 'Don't insult me, girl. I can spare a slice of bread for a friend in need, can't I?' She turned to Eloise with a stern look on her face. 'And you've got to pull yourself together unless you want to end up living in the workhouse across the way, because that's what will happen if you don't start earning some money.'

'I know,' Eloise said miserably. 'I've tried so

hard, Poll. I've worn holes in my boots from tramping the streets in search of work, but no one will take me on.'

'What did you expect? I warned you from the start that no one would want you and the nippers.' Poll shook her head in exasperation and she bent down to turn the slice of bread on the toasting fork. She patted Joss on the shoulder. 'You're doing well, boy. The first slice will be for you and the baby. I'll butter it and you can eat it while I do one for your ma.'

Joss gave her a cherubic smile and puffed out his small chest. 'I'm a good boy.'

'You're all right down one side,' Poll conceded. She picked him up and sat him at the table while she buttered the toast and cut it into soldiers, which she divided between him and Beth. While they were busy eating, she toasted another slice for Eloise. 'You could still come out with Ivy and me,' she said, shooting a sideways glance at Eloise. 'You could earn enough in one night to pay old Mother Hilton's rent for a week. Ivy and me don't do knee-tremblers for the roughs who hang around these parts. We go up West and hang about outside the theatres. There's always a few toffs with a bob or two to spare on the lookout for a good time. How about it, ducks?'

Eloise opened her mouth to refuse, and then she looked down at Beth's innocent face smeared with butter as she chewed on a finger of toast, and at Joss who was busily demolishing soldiers with obvious enjoyment. Their well-being and even their lives hung in the balance, for without money she had no hope of supporting them. The threat of the workhouse loomed over them in a great, dark shadow. The thought of selling her body to strange men was appalling, but a small voice in her head reasoned that it could be no worse than the pain and indignity that she had suffered at the hands of Ephraim Hubble.

Poll shoved a thick slice of toast, dripping with butter, into Eloise's hand. 'Get this inside you, and think about what I just said.'

'I'll do it,' Eloise whispered. She took a large bite of buttered toast, chewed and swallowed. 'I'll do it, Poll. I won't let my babies die of starvation. I'll come with you tonight.'

Late that evening, when the children were asleep in their bed, Eloise crept out of the basement room to join Poll and Ivy in the kitchen. The heat hit her as she entered the room. The mixed odours of burning paraffin from the oil lamps and the greasy smell of boiled mutton that had been the lodgers' supper hit her already nervous stomach, making her retch. Poll and Ivy were sitting on a bench at the table, smoking and drinking gin. Mother Hilton was sprawled in her chair by the fire with her many chins resting on her chest, which rose and fell in rhythmic snores.

Her mobcap sat askew on her iron-grey hair, giving her a harmless and comical look in slumber that she did not possess when awake.

Poll stubbed out her cigarette and exhaled a plume of blue smoke which floated up to the nicotine-stained ceiling. She rose to her feet and drew Eloise into the circle of lamplight, shaking her head and tut-tutting. 'You won't do like that, ducks. You look like a servant girl on her day off.'

Ivy studied Eloise's appearance with a practised eye. 'I could lend you me second best bonnet with the scarlet feathers that would perk you up a bit, love.'

Poll took a small pot of rouge from her pocket, opened it and proceeded to smear it on Eloise's cheeks and lips. 'I got a red satin blouse that would do a treat. You can take off that cotton thing for a start, Ellie. Go and fetch it for me, Ivy, together with your bonnet. We'll soon have her looking like one of us.'

Chuckling, Ivy jumped to her feet and hurried from the room. Eloise could feel her cheeks flaming and it wasn't just the rouge that was making them red. 'No. I mean, can't I go out like this? After all, it will be dark . . .'

'Not where we're going, ducks. Shaftesbury Avenue is lit up like a Christmas tree. We look out for the stage-door Johnnies and mashers who haven't managed to get off with chorus girls or high-class tarts. They're the best payers.' Poll hesitated, peering into Eloise's face. 'Are you all right, girl? You ain't going to swoon again, are you?'

'N-no. I'll be all right. Let's get it over with.'

But she was far from all right. As they made their way towards Shaftesbury Avenue, Eloise felt as though she had entered another world. The costermongers, shopkeepers, carters and street sweepers who plied their trades by day had gone home to their beds and the streets were now crowded with revellers intent on partying until dawn. Lurking in the shadows were thieves, pickpockets, card sharps, runners who lured young men into hidden-away opium dens, and pimps who offered young women and even children to those who were willing to pay handsomely for their services.

As she walked between Poll and Ivy, Eloise's stomach churned with fear and revulsion at the thought of what they were about to do. Wearing Poll's red satin blouse, which was cut so low that it revealed the swell of her breasts and only just covered the top of her stays, and Ivy's gaudy bonnet adorned with scarlet ostrich feathers, Eloise felt like an actress about to go out on the stage. It was only that which kept her from running away. It was not she who was walking the streets like one of Papa's cherished fallen women, about whom he spoke with such passion; it was another woman who set off to earn her living in the oldest profession on earth. With difficulty, she managed to detach herself from the barrage of lewd remarks they received from the men who hung around outside the public houses and brothels. Poll and Ivy fended off prospective but unsuitable clients with practised good humour, and Eloise huddled between them wishing she was dead.

They reached Shaftesbury Avenue just as the theatre crowds were spilling out on the street. Poll and Ivy knew exactly where to position themselves so that they did not offend the respectable matrons who emerged from the theatre on the arms of their husbands. They waited in the shadows until they spotted a likely customer and Ivy was the first to sway into action. A man wearing evening dress, an opera cloak and a shiny black top hat came towards them, weaving slightly as if he had had too much to drink, but this did not deter Ivy. She approached him with a seductive smile and it seemed to Eloise that the drunken gentleman knew her, as they went off down an alley straight away.

'That'll be five bob in her pocket,' Poll said, nodding with approval. 'Maybe ten bob if she's lucky.'

'I – I don't think I can do it,' Eloise murmured, swallowing hard. 'I wouldn't know what to say to a man.'

'Lord love us, ducks. You don't have to say nothing, except ta when they hand over the cash. They ain't interested in what goes on in your head. It's your drawers they want to get into. Just smile and think of Mother Hilton's boiled beef and carrots, pease pudding and spotted dick. Think of chocolate and violet creams. That's what I do, and it works every time.'

Eloise ducked into a doorway as a gentleman well past the first flush of youth staggered towards them with his satin-lined opera cloak billowing out like the wings of a large, black raven. Eloise prayed silently that Poll would not push her forward, but her hopes were in vain.

'There you are, girl,' Poll said, dragging her out of the doorway. 'He's a bit on the elderly side, but that's all to the good. It'll be over all the quicker and he's not short of a bob or two, judging by them shoes. I always judge a man by his footwear, and I'd say they come from one of the best shoemakers in St James's.' She gave Eloise a hefty push. 'Go on. Do your stuff, Ellie. Remember what I taught you.'

Eloise stumbled straight into the man's path and they collided. 'Excuse me, m'dear.' The gentleman's voice was slurred but he spoke in a cultured tone. He hesitated for a second, eyeing her through a monocle, and then he chuckled. 'Why, that was no accident, was it?'

Paralysed with fright and sick with nerves,

Eloise managed to nod her head. Out of the corner of her eye she could see Poll making encouraging gestures with her hand. 'N-no, sir.'

'Well, by gad. You're not the usual sort of street woman one would expect to come across.' The gentleman chucked her under the chin, allowing his finger to wander down her throat to the hollow at the base of her neck. 'Most interesting. What say we find somewhere a little more private, m'dear?'

The temptation to slap his hand away was almost too great for her and Eloise's stomach heaved. Her skin crawled at the touch of his bony fingers as he slid them down to caress her left breast. He licked his lips as saliva dribbled from the corner of his mouth. 'I know of a room nearby,' he said in a thick voice. 'Come, hurry. I have not much time to spare.' He seized her by the arm and hurried her towards the open doors of a public house. 'The landlord is a most amenable chap, as I'm sure you know.'

The strong smell of beer, raw spirits and tobacco smoke, laced with the sweat of bodies packed together in a crowded taproom, hit the back of Eloise's throat, making her cough, and she thought she was going to be sick. The gas-lights flickered and the babble of voices together with raucous laughter rose to a deafening crescendo as they neared the doorway. Someone was thumping a melody on an out of tune piano and drunken voices were singing a bawdy song. 'Come on, you little beauty,' the gentleman urged, slipping his arm around her waist. 'You can show me what you can do upstairs in the private salon.'

'No!' The word was wrenched from her lips in a scream. She could not go through with it, even for the sake of her children. Their faces flashed before her eyes and Eloise broke free, gasping for air as if she had just awakened from a terrible nightmare. Whatever the consequences she could not give herself to a complete stranger. She would rather die than allow this man to violate her body.

He was staring at her with an incredulous look on his face. 'Why, you little tease . . .'

She did not wait to hear the rest. Eloise picked up her skirts and ran. She darted past Poll, avoiding her outstretched hand, and she barged through the crowded streets, pushing people out of the way if they attempted to molest her. Half blinded by tears and with her breath coming in ragged sobs, Eloise headed back the way they had come. She found her way more by instinct than anything else and she let herself into the house, closing the door behind her and leaning against it as if she feared that her disappointed client might have followed her home. It was unlikely, as it would have been impossible for a gentleman of his age and in his condition to run all the way from Shaftesbury Avenue to Church Lane, but Eloise was not thinking clearly. She managed to get as far as the basement kitchen before her legs gave way beneath her and she sank down onto one of the forms at the deal table, laying her head on her arms as she fought to regain control over her breathing.

'Gawd above, look at the state of you.'

Mother Hilton's strident voice made Eloise sit bolt upright, blinking as the beam of light from an oil lamp held close to her face momentarily dazzled her. She held her hand to her eyes. 'I – I didn't hear you come in.'

Mother Hilton raised the lamp higher, staring down at Eloise with a scornful expression on her face. 'You look like something the cat dragged in.'

Eloise rose unsteadily to her feet. 'I'm going to bed.'

'No, not yet you ain't.' Mother Hilton held out her hand. 'You owe me two days' rent.'

'I'll give it to you in the morning,' Eloise said with as much dignity as she could muster. She knew she must look a sight, but she was not going to let Mother Hilton crow over her distress and her all too apparent failure to earn any money.

'You'd better, or it's the street for you and your brats. I'm not running a charity, missis. You pay up or you get out. It's as simple as that.'

'Yes, in the morning,' Eloise said wearily. 'You shall have your money first thing.'

'It's my last warning,' Mother Hilton called after her as Eloise left the kitchen. 'I want it in full.'

Eloise could hear her going on even as she crossed the storeroom and lifted the latch on the door that led into her sleeping quarters. Ivy's bed was empty, but Old Aggie was lying flat on her back, snoring loudly and exhaling gin fumes. Fortunately, Joss and Beth were blissfully oblivious to everything as they slept, curled up together. Eloise bent down to cover them with the thin woollen blanket which was the only bedding that Mother Hilton supplied. She took off Ivy's bonnet and Poll's satin blouse and laid them on the floor by her palliasse; then, without disrobing further, Eloise lay down beside her children and wrapped her arms around them. Through the cracked panes of the area window, she could hear the tramp of booted feet and the sound of drunken laughter. Somewhere, in the distance, she could hear a woman screaming. No doubt she was receiving a beating from her husband or a jealous lover, but her cries would be ignored by the rest of the street. Tomorrow she might be bruised and have broken limbs, or she could even be dead. The police rarely ventured into this area at night; crimes went undetected and murders were rarely investigated.

Eloise slid her hand beneath the palliasse until her fingers came in contact with the two envelopes containing her mother's letters. She eased them out carefully so that the crackle of paper did not disturb Joss and Beth, and she clutched the precious correspondence to her breast, closing her eyes and conjuring up a vision of Mama's beautiful face and her gentle smile. 'Be brave, Ellie, darling.' Eloise heard the words as clearly as if her mother was sitting by her side. She could smell the sweet scent of lavender that always clung to Mama's clothes and hair. Even though they were separated by thousands of miles, the bond between them could not be broken, and Eloise was very glad that her mother was not here to see her in this parlous state.

She was awakened early next morning by the shuffling and grumbling of Old Aggie whose bed was closest to the wall. Ivy's bed looked as though it had not been slept in, and Eloise could only guess that she had met a punter who would pay for a whole night of passion. The older woman crawled off her mattress and pulled on her boots. Although very few words had passed between them, Eloise knew that she rose early in order to get to Covent Garden market where she scavenged for the broken blooms and made them into nosegays to sell on street corners. When at last she stumbled out of the room, Eloise sat up carefully so as not to disturb Joss, but Beth was moaning softly in her sleep and Eloise was alarmed to discover that her small body was unnaturally hot and it seemed that she was running a low fever. It might be nothing more than cutting another tooth or the onset of a cold, but Eloise was even more determined to beg Mother Hilton on her bended knees to give her more time to find the money for the rent. When Joss woke up some minutes later, she examined both children for spots or rashes and was only slightly comforted by the fact that their skin remained unblemished. Eloise dressed them in their day clothes, which were sadly worn and not very clean, and she sighed, thinking of the washhouse in the vicarage yard where, every Monday morning without fail, Janet would light the fire below the copper and do the family wash. The steamy air would be fragrant with the smell of Sunlight soap and filled with the musical sounds of washday: the bubbling of water boiling in the copper, Janet's energetic cranking of the mangle and the squishing sound as water was squeezed from the wet clothes and sheets. Sometimes, if she was in the right mood, Janet would allow Eloise to turn the handle and feed the washing through the giant rollers. It had been hard work, but a companionable activity, and was followed by the never varying Monday luncheon of cold meat and mashed potatoes, served with pickled beetroot and piccalilli. The homely memories brought tears to Eloise's eyes and she dashed them away quickly, before Joss could see them. This was not the time to be sentimental. Their very lives depended on how she handled Mother Hilton.

Eloise waited until the time when the lodgers who worked by day had gone about their business, and the night people like Poll and Ivy would still be in their beds or someone else's, and then she went to look for Mother Hilton. She found her in the kitchen, sitting in her chair and shouting instructions to Minnie, her maid of all work, as she prepared vegetables to put in with the two large oxtails which would cook slowly all day on the range.

'Well?' Mother Hilton said, raising her eyebrows so that they disappeared into her mobcap. 'Have you got the money?'

'Not exactly,' Eloise murmured, setting Beth down on the floor and watching her crawl away towards Minnie, who was little more than a child herself and often gave the children a carrot or a piece of parsnip if her employer was not looking.

'What d'you mean, not exactly?' Mother Hilton demanded, scowling ominously. 'You either have or you ain't. You know what will happen if I don't get the cash on the nail, now.'

'A few more days,' Eloise said, wringing her hands. 'I assure you that I will find work, and I will pay you in full.'

'You wasn't much cop last night, according to what I've heard. Run away like a scared cat and the old geezer hadn't even put his hand up your skirt, so Poll said.'

Eloise cast an anxious glance at Joss, but he was more interested in nibbling a piece of carrot that Minnie had surreptitiously passed to him than in listening to their conversation. 'I couldn't do it,' Eloise said in a low voice. 'You're a woman; you must understand.'

'Oh, I understand all right. But according to what I heard yesterday in the pub, you wasn't so fussy when it come to a certain gent what lives in Clerkenwell Green.'

Eloise caught her breath. 'Wh-what did you say?'

'Don't look so innocent, lady. My friend Mrs Jarvis is a nurse, and we was enjoying a couple of drinks in the pub last night when she happened to tell me about a young woman who was took on to care for an old gent by the name of Hubble. I know all about you, missis. And I know that there's a private detective looking for you, and possibly a reward for them as turns you in.'

Eloise felt her knees give way beneath her and she sat down heavily on the bench at the table. 'It's not me. It's someone else.'

'Don't give me that, ducks. I ain't stupid and I see all sorts coming through my front door. I

343

knowed there was something odd about you the moment I set eyes on you, and I was right.'

'You don't understand . . .'

'I understand that I'll be out of pocket if I let you stay any longer. You can't pay so you have to go, but I'm a fair woman, and I won't send Minnie round to Clerkenwell Green with a message for Mr Hubble until she's finished peeling the taters. If you leave now you'll have a head start over the detective chap, but you've left me out of pocket and I'm out to get that reward so you'd better run fast, Mrs Cribb.'

With a sinking heart, Eloise met Mother Hilton's steely gaze, and she knew that this was no idle threat. It was an appalling coincidence that the old harridan knew Nurse Jarvis, but Eloise had always known that Pike was not the sort of man to give up on the case. She also knew that, whether or not Mother Hilton chose to disclose their whereabouts, it was just a matter of time before he discovered them for himself. Eloise rose shakily to her feet. 'Just give me time to collect my things and we'll go.'

Mother Hilton chuckled deep in her throat. 'A head start – that's fair. Run, you little hare – the hounds will soon be after you.'

Eloise had never moved so quickly in her whole life. She threw their few belongings into her valise and she put Beth, who seemed to have recovered a little, in the old perambulator with

Joss, and they were out of the house in less than ten minutes. She had no plan and no idea where to go, so she headed northwards to the more familiar streets of Bloomsbury. The children were hungry and so was she, and Eloise stopped to count out the pennies in her purse. With just fivepence left in the whole world, she spent three precious pennies on bread, butter and milk, most of which she fed to the children. It had begun to rain, soft steady drizzle that would soak them to the skin within a short space of time, and she headed for the British Museum as the only place she could think of where they could enter free and gain shelter.

She walked the great halls for the rest of the day, showing a largely uninterested Joss the Elgin marbles, the Rosetta stone and the wonders of the Assyrian galleries. Finally, at dusk, when the museum closed, Eloise was forced to leave, not knowing where to go or how they would survive the night without shelter. She stood on the steps of the museum as the door closed behind them. The rain had stopped but the streets were wet and carriage wheels sent up great sprays of water from deep puddles in the road. With two tired, hungry and increasingly fractious children, Eloise was at her wits' end. She had just tuppence in her purse and it would soon be dark. She started walking blindly, and when she came to the gardens in Russell Square she sat down on a bench under a large tree that was just beginning to shed its leaves. The lamplighter was on his rounds, and one by one the gas lamps fizzed and popped with their flickering flames trapped inside glass globes like agitated fireflies. Through the windows of the elegant houses Eloise witnessed scenes of domesticity and opulence that made her present homeless state even harder to bear. She could see maidservants bustling around inside the luxuriously appointed rooms, turning down beds and drawing curtains. She caught the occasional glimpse of the inhabitants and their guests, dressed for dinner and socialising with a drink before going in to dine. It was a different world and one which was as far away from her as the stars. Eloise cuddled her children, rocking them in her arms and murmuring words of comfort which she knew were just words – empty and baseless. How could she tell them that everything would be all right when she could not give them food and shelter for the night? She was lying to her own children, and she had brought them to this state. She was their mother and their lives depended upon her. She had let them down horribly, and she simply did not know what to do next.

Eventually, worn out by hunger and tiredness, Joss and Beth fell into a fitful sleep and Eloise laid them side by side in the perambulator. She was about to stretch out on the bench when a constable on his beat came towards her with a measured tread and a stern look on his face. He told her that she must move on, and advised her to go home to her husband, as if she was an erring wife. There was no point in arguing and Eloise left the shelter of the square, trudging on and barely able to put one foot in front of the other, until she found herself once again in Guildford Street, outside the Foundling Hospital. It was comfortingly familiar and she pushed the perambulator into the deserted gardens, where she slumped down on a bed of fallen leaves beneath the tree under which she had last sat with Annie. It was not so long ago, but it seemed like another lifetime. She slept fitfully, waking at the slightest noise, the snap of a twig or the fall of a leaf. She could hear the sound of horse-drawn traffic in Guildford Street, and the lights in the Foundling Hospital windows went out one by one until the whole place was shrouded in darkness.

In the early hours of the morning it began to rain again, and water dripped through the branches onto her head and face. Soon her skirts were clinging damply to her legs and she was stiff with cold. Eloise peeped beneath the hood of the perambulator and saw to her dismay that the rain had penetrated through cracks in the canvas. Beth's cheeks were flushed and she felt hot to the touch. Joss also seemed to be running a fever and Eloise's blood ran cold. She glanced up at the forbidding walls of the institution with a sinking heart. The very lives of her children were in danger. Without dry clothing, warm beds and adequate nourishment, they would almost certainly die. At this moment, she would gladly have sold her body to any man who was willing to pay for her services, but it was too late for that now.

Eloise rose unsteadily to her feet, barely able to move her cramped limbs. She walked the pathways between the flower beds where the last roses of summer were bowing their heads under the weight of last night's heavy rainfall. The rusty wheels of the perambulator squealed in protest and the gravel crunched beneath her feet. It was only a matter of time before Pike found them and snatched Joss from her arms. It would almost be better to allow the Cribbs to have him than to allow him to die of want on the streets of London. They would take Beth, too, even though they did not really want her. Was that the life she wanted for her children? When it came down to it, Eloise was forced to face the fact that they were now destitute.

She walked in circles, pushing the perambulator before her as she wrestled with her maternal desire to keep her babies with her at all costs, and the small but insistent voice of common sense that told her that there was only one course of action open to her in this dire emergency. There was just one place where she could safely leave them in the certain knowledge that they would be taken in and cared for. She must let them go in order to save their young lives. What happened to her was immaterial. Her fingers were cramped with cold and trembling as she took their tiny garments from her valise and Eloise buried her face in their folds, drawing strength for what she was about to do from the knowledge that they would soon be safe.

It was still dark, but the first signs of dawn were appearing in the east. Moving like an automaton, she pushed the perambulator towards the hospital entrance. She bent down to drop a tender kiss on Beth's hot cheek and another on Joss's forehead. With tears streaming from her eyes, Eloise lifted her hand and tugged at the doorbell. Its strident peal echoed through the whole building. She waited until she heard the tip-tap of leather-soled boots on a tiled floor, and then she backed away, struggling to control the sobs that racked her body. Hiding behind one of the pillars outside the gatehouse, Eloise waited for the great, iron-studded door to open.

Chapter Fifteen

Silhouetted against the sulphurous glow of gaslight, Eloise could just make out the shape of a tall woman dressed in black. In her fevered mind, it was the angel of death who dragged the perambulator and its tiny occupants through the portals of the institution. Eloise stifled a low moan of pain and she fell to her knees on the wet pavement, burying her face in her hands.

How long she knelt there on the cold paving stones she did not know. She seemed to have entered a nether world; a strange place where nothing was real. Her cramped limbs, hunger and thirst were as nothing compared to the agony of having given her babies into the hands of strangers. There was a painful void where her heart had once been and she wrapped her arms about herself, rocking to and fro in her despair. A chill mist had crept in from the river without Eloise even noticing it, and the sky had lightened to a grey dawn. The measured tread of booted feet caused her to look up, and through eyes blurred with tears she found herself looking into the stern face of a police constable. 'Move along now, miss, or I'll arrest you for being drunk and disorderly.'

Automatically, her hand flew to her dishevelled hair. She had lost her bonnet somewhere along the way and her long tresses had come loose from the chignon at the back of her neck. She brushed a stray lock from her eyes and scrambled to her feet, but she had lost all feeling in her lower limbs and she stumbled against the wall of the gatehouse. The constable was eyeing her with undisguised contempt and she realised then just what a sight she must present. 'All right, officer,' she murmured. 'I'm going.'

'Go home, miss.'

Eloise nodded and turned away. She could not bear to see herself mirrored in the eyes of this complete stranger. A small vestige of pride made her hold her head high and she limped away in the direction of Doughty Street, but she turned off at the corner of Mecklenburgh Square and she waited there until the constable had continued on his beat. By this time she knew what she had to do. She was not going to be parted from her children for a moment longer than was necessary. Stopping a passing costermonger who was pushing his barrow along the street, Eloise enquired as to the whereabouts of the nearest public bathhouse. Having thanked him for his help, she set off to follow his directions. It was just six o'clock in the morning, according to the clock on the wall of the bathhouse, but it was already open for business and Eloise went inside, checking the prices carefully before purchasing a ticket. She could not afford first class, but a warm bath in the second class section would cost her tuppence. It was an agonising decision, but she must appear to be clean and decent if she was to seek work at the Foundling Hospital.

As she soaked in the tub filled with warm water Eloise washed her hair and scrubbed her whole body with the tablet of harsh carbolic soap. She lay back and watched the thick scum float to the surface, taking with it the worst of the ingrained grime from the dust yard. At home she had always taken cleanness for granted, barely understanding why Papa bothered to mention the need for bodily as well as spiritual cleanliness in his sermons. Now she felt so much older and wiser. Although she had rebelled against her father's strict moral code and rigid rules, she felt that she understood him a little better now that she had experienced the harsh realities of life first hand. She had been such a green girl before her marriage, sheltered by her parents and pampered by those who loved her. Even after she had married Ronnie, she had still been protected from the grim spectres of poverty and disease. What a spoilt little simpleton she had been in those far off days, she thought, as she wallowed in the rapidly cooling water. She might have helped to raise money for good causes at church fetes and musical evenings, but she had not truly understood the desperate wants of the poor and needy. As she dried herself on a coarse huckaback towel, Eloise felt ashamed of the person she had once been: a silly girl who thought only of herself. She had thought that Papa had been both unkind and unfair in his treatment of her, but now she could understand his reasons for sending her to live in Yorkshire with the Cribbs. He had done what he considered to be right, and he had known just how difficult life could be for a young widow without the means to support herself and her children.

Eloise scrubbed at her skin until it glowed pink. She glanced down at her slender body, which was now too thin to be considered beautiful in the artistic sense. Her breasts, which had been full and voluptuous when she was feeding her babies, were now small, and her waist so tiny that she had no need for stays, which was just as well since hers were frayed and the whalebones broken or had come out completely. She sighed as she put on her only change of clothing, a calico blouse and a navy-blue serge skirt, both of which were patched and darned, but were reasonably clean, and she slipped her bare feet into her down-at-heel boots. Having towelled her hair until it was dry enough to twist into a knot at the base of her neck, she secured it with some hairpins which she had found scattered about on the floor. Then, with renewed strength and purpose, Eloise left the bathhouse and set off at a brisk pace towards the Foundling Hospital.

She marched up to the entrance with a determined lift of her chin and her head held high. She rang the bell and waited. Her pulses were racing and her hands were damp with sweat, but at last she heard footsteps and the door opened. A young maidservant eyed her suspiciously. 'Yes? What d'you want?'

'I've come about the position advertised in the newspaper.' The lie tripped off her tongue in a manner which would have shocked Papa, but Eloise did not feel guilty. She was going to get into the building even if she had to break a window or batter down a door.

'I dunno nothing about that,' the maid said, shaking her head. 'You'd best write to the matron.'

She was about to close the door when Eloise pushed past her. 'I would like to see the matron now, this minute.'

'They're all at breakfast.'

'Then I'll wait here.' Eloise moved to a wooden bench and sat down. They would have to carry her out; she was not going to budge until she had seen someone in authority.

Muttering beneath her breath, the young maid scuttled off down the echoing corridor and then there was an eerie silence. Eloise was desperate to find Joss and Beth, but somehow she managed to control the impulse. She clasped her hands tightly in her lap as she took in her surroundings. The high vaulted ceiling was supported by marble columns, and a wide stone staircase rose majestically from the black and white tiled floor. A stained-glass window on the mezzanine imbued the vast entrance hall with a solemn church-like atmosphere. It was hardly home from home, and Eloise felt for the poor little foundlings who grew up in this impressive but austere place. She thought of Annie and hoped that she would not think that she had deserted her, but most of all her thoughts were with her babies who were somewhere in this building, confused, frightened and wondering where their mama had gone. Eloise heard someone coming and she rose to her feet. As the woman approached her, Eloise was certain it was the same person who had taken the perambulator into the building. Her heart leapt inside her breast, but one look at the woman's hard features and Eloise's optimism took a tumble. This was no kindly mother figure. The woman's face was thin and lined with deep clefts between her eyebrows creating a permanent frown. 'What can I do for you?' she demanded in clipped tones.

Her shrewd eyes reminded Eloise of green glass beads and they seemed to bore into her soul. 'I came in answer to the advertisement in the newspaper.'

'That's impossible. We haven't advertised for months.'

'It might have been slightly out of date, but you required a teacher.'

'You are mistaken. I must ask you to leave.'

Eloise stood her ground. 'If you do not need a teacher, perhaps you require an assistant or a nurse. I am quite capable of turning my hand to anything.'

'No. We need no one. Please go, or must I summon the porter to have you thrown out?'

'But you must need some help. Please won't you give me work, Miss . . .'

'Miss Marchant. I am the matron of this hospital and I can assure you that I don't employ women of your sort.'

'How dare you!' Eloise felt as though something had snapped in her head and she quite literally saw a flash of red before her eyes. 'Don't speak to me like that, Miss Marchant. Everyone, no matter how humble, deserves to be treated with respect.'

'What on earth is going on here?'

An angry voice from the doorway made both women start and turn round to face Barton Caine, who had just entered the building and was standing quite still, staring at Eloise with a look of puzzlement. 'Do I know you, young woman?'

Eloise bobbed a curtsey and bowed her head, unable to meet his gaze. 'No, sir.'

'Then who are you and why are you creating a disturbance here?'

Miss Marchant moved forward to place herself between Eloise and the governor. 'She forced her way in, sir. I was telling her to leave just before you arrived.'

Caine walked slowly towards them and came to a halt in front of Eloise. 'What can I do for you, ma'am?'

Quick to detect a softening in his tone, Eloise raised her head to meet his eyes and was once again struck by their intense shade of blue, and despite his stern expression she sensed that this was a man of intelligence and reason. 'I need work, sir.'

'You need work.' His tone was measured. 'Is that all?'

'Allow me to deal with this, Mr Caine,' Miss Marchant said stiffly. 'This woman is obviously a beggar or a woman of the streets. Let me ring for the porter and he will send her on her way.'

Caine eyed her coolly. 'I'm sure that you have pressing duties elsewhere, Matron. Go about your business and I will deal with this.'

Miss Marchant bristled visibly, but she nodded

her head and sailed off with an offended hunch of her thin shoulders. Eloise breathed a sigh of relief, but a wave of dizziness washed over her and she swayed on her feet. She must not faint, she told herself severely. She would not faint . . .

'Sit down, please.'

Caine had placed his hand beneath her elbow and guided her back to the bench, where Eloise sat down more suddenly than she would have wished. This was not going as she had hoped. 'I'm all right, thank you, sir. It was just a little dizzy spell.'

'What is your name?'

She hesitated. She had not given it much thought, but it occurred to her suddenly that it would be foolish to give her own name. 'Ellen, sir. Ellen Monk.'

'Well, Miss Monk, tell me why you want to work here so badly?'

'I just need work, sir.' Caine was silent for a moment and Eloise could feel his eyes upon her as if he was trying to read her thoughts. She glanced up and met his cold scrutiny with an attempt at a smile. 'I was a servant, unfairly dismissed without a character, and I have no money.'

'And no family?'

'I am an orphan, sir.'

'And for what offence were you dismissed?'

'I was innocent, sir. Falsely accused of – of . . .'

Eloise hesitated. If she said she had been accused of theft that would leave some doubts as to her honesty in the governor's mind. She thought quickly. 'It was said that I was on intimate terms with the butler, but it was not the case. I was dismissed instantly and he was not.'

'And where did this incident occur? Who was your employer?'

'I was lady's maid to the wife of a prominent gentleman who would not thank me for bandying his family's name in public.'

'I admire your loyalty, even in such dire circumstances, or I would if I believed this tara-diddle. I think that you are a liar, Ellen Monk.'

It was true, of course, but Eloise was acting a part and she was angry for the sake of the wronged servant girl, Ellen Monk. She leapt to her feet. 'It's true, sir. Every word is true.'

'You are no servant girl. You speak like an educated young woman, Miss Monk. Would you care to tell me the truth?'

'I need work, sir. You can think what you like of me, but I am begging you to give me a chance. I'll scrub floors if necessary. I don't mind what I do.'

Caine angled his head, staring at her thought-fully. 'Let me see your hands.'

Startled, Eloise held her hands out for him to examine. His fingers were long and lean, but sur-prisingly gentle as they turned her hands palm upwards. Despite her attempts to scrub them clean, there were still traces of dirt beneath her chipped fingernails and small blue scars where cuts and blisters had healed, trapping coal dust beneath the skin. A slight twitch of his winged eyebrows betrayed his surprise and he gave her a long, calculating look. 'These are not the hands of a lady; nor, I would imagine, those of a lady's maid.'

'I am a hard worker, sir.'

'And you are willing to be a maid of all work?'

'As I said, I will scrub floors if necessary.'

'Very well then, but I must warn you that the work is hard and the hours are long. You will live with the servants, obey Matron at all times, and your wages will be six pounds a year, paid quarterly. Do you still want the position?'

Eloise nodded emphatically. 'When do I start?'

'Come with me. I'll take you to Miss Marchant and she will assign you to your duties.'

Miss Marchant was in the refectory supervising the older children as they filed off to begin the day's lessons. The girls, as Caine explained in a low voice, were going to classes that would equip them for life in service and the boys were being educated for careers in the armed services, but mainly the Navy. Eloise stood behind Caine, watching the children as they marched out of the hall silently and in single file. Her heart ached for the orphans and abandoned children who had never known the love of a parent, but even so she had to admit that they looked healthy and were probably quite happy in their ignorance of any other kind of existence. Caine waited until they had gone before informing Miss Marchant of his decision. It was obvious from her tight-lipped expression that she did not approve, but it was equally plain that she dared not go against the governor's wishes. 'Very well, sir. I'll take Monk to the kitchens myself and introduce her to her duties.'

'Thank you, Matron.' Caine acknowledged her compliance with a nod of his head. 'And now I must return home. Maria is unwell and I must be there when the doctor calls.'

'Nothing serious, I hope, sir?'

'I think it's just a chill, but one cannot be too careful.' Caine turned on his heel and strode away.

Eloise was hardly interested in his domestic arrangements. All she could think about was finding Joss and Beth and being able to reassure them that Mama was not far away. She would tell them that they were playing a game in which she was not Mama, but merely Ellen, the maidservant, although she knew they would not understand. Beth was still little more than a baby and only just beginning to say a few words, but Joss, who had mastered quite a large vocabulary, might prove to be a problem. Still, she comforted herself with the knowledge that very young children were adaptable, and once they were assured that she had not deserted them they would be content. As soon as she had saved enough money, she would take them away from this place, but that was in the distant future. Now she must convince the disapproving Miss Marchant that she was a good and reliable worker.

'Follow me,' Miss Marchant said coldly. 'I want you to know that I disapprove heartily of how you wheedled your way into this venerable institution. I will be keeping my eye on you, and at the slightest transgression, you will be sacked. Do you understand me, Monk?'

Eloise bobbed a curtsey. 'Yes'm.'

'Yes, Matron.' Miss Marchant waited until Eloise had repeated the correct form of address and then she stalked off, leading the way through a maze of corridors to the back stairs and down to the basement kitchens. Eloise's first impression was of steam, heat and noise. Women wearing white mobcaps and starched aprons worked at long trestle tables, chopping up gristly cuts of meat, preparing vegetables or shredding suet for the inevitable puddings. The babble of voices ceased on the instant they saw Miss Marchant and they bowed their heads over their work. One woman, obviously the head cook, strode forward to meet them wiping her floury hands on a towel. 'Good morning, Matron. And who is this?'

'This is Monk. Mr Caine has seen fit to employ another skivvy, although I told him that we were fully staffed.' Miss Marchant's expression was hostile as she turned to glare at Eloise. 'You will do exactly as Mrs Cater says, and she will report daily to me, so don't think you can get away with anything, Monk.' She swept up the staircase with a rustle of starched moreen petticoats and the jingling sound of the keys which hung from a chatelaine at her waist.

Mrs Cater peered at Eloise through the thick pebble lenses of her spectacles. 'You don't look much like a scullery maid. Don't think you can get away with airs and graces in my kitchen, girl. I'm a fair woman but I expect people to do their work properly.'

'Yes'm,' Eloise murmured, wondering how soon she could slip away from the kitchens to look for Joss and Beth. 'I'll work hard.'

'Tibbie!' Mrs Cater shrieked at the top of her voice. 'Come here.'

A small face which was almost drowned by an oversized mobcap peered round the corner of a door at the far end of the kitchen. 'Yes, Cook.'

'This here is Monk, the new scullery maid. Show her what to do, and bring me some clean pans. I dunno what you've been doing all this time.'

Tibbie scuttled out of the scullery like a small crab, beckoned to Eloise and then disappeared back into a cloud of steam, which smelt strongly of grease mixed with washing soda and carbolic soap. Eloise followed her, very much aware that the rest of the women were eyeing her surreptitiously, whispering and giggling. She braced her shoulders and rolled up her sleeves as she entered the fog-like atmosphere of the scullery.

Red-faced and sweating, Tibbie was searching through a pile of clean dishes and saucepans for the cooking pots that Mrs Cater had demanded. 'They got to be in here somewhere,' she muttered.

'Here, let me help you,' Eloise said, catching a plate as it was about to fall to the floor.

'Oh, would you?' Tibbie wiped her small hand across her brow, pushing back her mobcap and exposing a head covered with matted mouse-coloured hair.

Eloise realised then that the scullery maid was little more than a child and the poor little creature seemed half demented in her frantic search. Eloise laid her hand on her stick-thin arm. 'Look, behind the big mixing bowl at the back of the draining board.'

Tibbie stood on tiptoe, and with a shout of glee she reached across to seize the pans by their handles. 'Oh, ta. I couldn't see for looking.' She darted out of the scullery with them and returned seconds later clutching her ear. 'The old cow boxed me ears for nothing. That's what she's like, though I doubt if she'll hit you.'

Eloise took a cloth and began methodically to wipe the crockery, setting it neatly on a side table. 'Why do you say that, Tibbie?'

'You're not like the rest of us.'

'Oh, yes I am. I am just like you, and I'll need you to show me what to do so that I don't upset Cook.'

Tibbie's pinched features cracked into a wide, gap-toothed grin. 'Me? Help you? That's a laugh, but I'll do me level best, Miss Monk.'

'It's Ellie, and I'll be very grateful. Perhaps when we've finished you could show me round the building, just so that I know where everything is.'

Tibbie plunged her arms into the stone sink, which was filled with grey, greasy water. 'I can do that all right. I growed up here, so I knows the place like the back of me hand.'

At the end of a long and extremely gruelling day, Eloise was fit to drop, but even more desperate to find Joss and Beth. They had never been parted for more than an hour or two and now it was more than twelve hours since she had seen them. She had spent the best part of the day in the scullery, helping Tibbie with the mountains of dirty plates, pots and pans, until the skin was peeling off her hands, her back ached and her feet were swollen from standing for so many hours on the flagstone floor. It was not until the last piece of crockery from the supper tables in the refectory had been washed, dried and put away, the sink scoured clean with a mixture of sand and soda, and the floors scrubbed, that they were allowed to finish work. Tibbie, who Eloise had discovered was just thirteen and had been working in the kitchen for more than a year, had introduced her to the other servants and had made sure that Eloise had a seat at the table in the servants' hall at mealtimes. Now that they were done for the day, Tibbie took a candle and led Eloise up the back staircase to their sleeping quarters in the attics. There were three narrow iron bedsteads in the room that she was to share with Tibbie and an older girl called Becky who worked in the laundry. A small window beneath the eaves looked down onto Guildford Street, and the roughly plastered walls were bare of any form of decoration. There was brown oilcloth on the floor and a pine chest of drawers which they had to share.

'You can have the bottom drawer,' Tibbie said, slumping down on her bed. 'We don't have nowhere to hang our clothes. They don't seem to think that us common girls need cupboards or wardrobes.'

Eloise set her valise down on the floor with a sigh. 'That won't worry me, Tibbie. What I've got won't take up much space.'

'I don't understand how a person like you wants to live and work with the likes of us?' Tibbie eyed Eloise with her head on one side like an inquisitive sparrow. 'You don't talk like the rest of us, Ellen. How come you're here?'

'It's a long story,' Eloise said, smiling. 'One day I'll tell you, but now you promised to show me round the hospital.'

'I'm tired out. Won't it wait until the morning?'

Eloise lifted Tibbie to her feet. 'No, it will not. A promise is a promise.'

Reluctantly, Tibbie led the way back down the stairs and along the corridors in between the dormitories where the children had already gone to bed. It was strangely silent, but Tibbie explained in whispers that Matron walked the corridors at night and woe betide any children who were caught out of bed or talking when they should be sleeping. At the very far end of the building they came to the night nurseries for the babies and toddlers. Eloise could hardly breathe as they tiptoed up to the large room where Tibbie said the newcomers were isolated until the doctor was certain that they were not incubating one of the dreaded childhood diseases that could quickly turn into an epidemic.

'You don't want to go in there,' Tibbie said, standing nervously outside the door. 'Suppose one of the night nurses should hear you, you'd be in trouble then.'

'I just want to see the little ones,' Eloise said, containing her excitement with difficulty and making a huge effort to appear calm and casual. 'Just a few minutes, Tibbie. If you like you can leave me here. I can find my own way back to the room.'

Tibbie yawned. 'I suppose it'll be all right, but if you gets caught, don't tell 'em it were me what brought you here.'

'Cross my heart,' Eloise whispered, lifting the latch and letting herself into a long, dark room. Holding the candle high, she moved silently between the rows of high-sided cots. Her heart was beating so fast that she was certain it could be heard from the corridor outside, and she held her breath as she bent over the two cots at the far end of the room. She clamped her hand over her mouth to stifle a sob of pure joy as she gazed down at her sleeping children. Joss's blond curls were sticking damply to his forehead and his lips were parted, but as she laid her hand gently on his forehead, Eloise was relieved to find that he was quite cool. His slight snuffling reassured her that he had caught a cold and nothing worse. She leaned over to kiss him softly on his round cheek. Beth stirred in her sleep and Eloise moved to her cot and felt her brow, which again was cool to the touch. Her nose was runny and she too was breathing through her mouth. Eloise took the corner of her apron and wiped Beth's nose, leaning down again to kiss her on the cheek. Her arms ached to hold them both and she longed to be able to snatch them from their cots, but she knew that would be fatal. At least they were safe here in the Foundling Hospital. They would be well cared for and she would find some excuse to come to the nursery every day. She sank down on her knees, content just to be close to her babies for even a short while. It was almost too tempting to wake Joss and to reassure him that Mama was close by, but he would undoubtedly cry and that would awaken the whole nursery, bringing the night nurse rushing in to see what had disturbed them. Eloise had to content herself with just being with them, and it was only when she heard the sound of approaching footsteps that she scrambled to her feet and hid behind the door. A uniformed night nurse holding a lantern in her hand progressed along the line of cots. Eloise crept out of the door unseen and made her way back to the attic room where she found Tibbie and Becky sound asleep in their beds. Eloise slipped off her outer clothes, folding them neatly on the end of her bed. It creaked as she climbed in, but the sound did not disturb her companions who were sleeping so soundly that nothing short of a trumpet call would have woken them. As she huddled beneath the coverlet, Eloise could think of nothing but her children, and how they would feel when they awakened next morning amongst strangers. As she drifted off into sleep she vowed to be there when they opened their eyes. They must be reassured that their mama was close by and would never leave them.

She woke up with a start. At first she could not remember where she was, or why she was lying in a narrow iron bed beneath the sloping roof of an attic room. She blinked and rubbed the sleep from her eyes, and then she snapped upright.

'Best get dressed quick,' Tibbie said, struggling on with her boots. 'Cook will tan our hides if we're late.' She went to shake Becky who was still curled up in a ball and fast asleep. 'Get up, you lazy mare. You've been late twice this week already and you'll be out on your ear if you do it again.'

'Eh? What's the matter?' Becky sat up in bed, her ginger hair standing out around her head like a dandelion clock.

'You'd best get down to the laundry or you'll be for it.' Tibbie lifted the latch on the door and hurried from the room, calling over her shoulder, 'Hurry up, Ellen, do.'

Becky scrambled out of bed, almost knocking Eloise down in her haste. 'You heard Tibbie,' Becky said, pulling on her cotton dress and ramming her curls into a mobcap. 'They're sticklers for punctuality here, and there's morning prayers to attend later. Best run, Ellen, or you really will be in trouble.' With her boots in her hand, Becky raced from the room and her bare feet made soft pattering sounds on the floorboards as she sped along the corridor.

Eloise followed them more slowly, cursing herself for oversleeping. She had so wanted to be there when Joss and Beth woke up, and now she might have to wait all day before she had a chance to go to the nursery. When she reached the kitchen, she found that she was already in Cook's black books for being five minutes late on duty. She tried her best, but she could not concentrate on the task in hand, and then, to make matters worse, she dropped a pile of plates right in front of Cook, who swiped her round the head with her hand.

'That'll come out of your wages, Monk.'

'I'm sorry. It was an accident, Cook.'

'Don't give me none of your lip, girl. Clear up that mess and then you can start filling the sink in the scullery with hot water. I've got my eye on you, Monk.' Cook went back to kneading bread dough, punching it with her fists as if it had done her some terrible wrong.

Eloise carried pan after pan of boiling water from the range in the kitchen to the scullery. The large stone sink never seemed to get any fuller, and the water cooled so rapidly that topping it up seemed like an endless task. Eloise tried hard, but her thoughts were with Joss and Beth and she simply could not give her full attention to her work. Her hands seemed to be unconnected to her brain and she spilled boiling water on the kitchen floor, which had to be mopped up quickly before it caused an accident. Then she dropped a pan of porridge just as she was taking it into the servants' hall for their breakfast. Tibbie rushed to help her clear up the glutinous grey mess, but there was a general outcry from the hungry women, who would now have to make do with bread and margarine. There was such an uproar that Cook threatened to expel Eloise from the kitchen if she did anything else wrong. This gave her an idea. If she proved herself to be totally inept she might be put to work scrubbing floors or cleaning the wards.

After a breakfast of bread and scrape, which she ate alone and in disgrace at a small table in the corner of the servants' hall, Eloise waited for a suitable moment to put her plan into action. She helped Tibbie wash and dry the dishes, and she was in the china cupboard stacking the clean crockery away when Cook ordered her to leave what she was doing and fill the hod with fuel for the range. As she shovelled at the pile of coke in the yard, Eloise knew exactly what she would do. It was going to be a considerable risk, as she might equally be given the sack, but she was desperate. She hefted the hod into the kitchen and was about to tip some onto the fire when she pretended to slip, sending a shower of coke cascading onto the floor. Her timing was perfect and Cook, who had come in from the cold larder carrying a plate piled high with offal, trod on a lump of coke, staggered and fell. The plate flew into the air, splattering its bloody contents over Mrs Cater and two of the women who were up to their elbows in making pastry, and finally landing on the floor to mingle in a gory mess with shards of china and lumps of coke.

'That's it!' Mrs Cater roared, scrambling to her feet, red-faced and fuming. 'Get out of my kitchen, girl. Get out and don't ever come back.'

'I'm very sorry, ma'am,' Eloise said humbly. 'It was an accident.'

Mrs Cater shook her fist at her. 'Accident! You're an accident. You're a disaster. I'm going to tell Matron to send you packing.'

Chapter Sixteen

Miss Marchant was in her office. She did not look too pleased at the interruption when Mrs Cater dragged Eloise into the room, after a perfunctory tap on the door.

'What is it, Cook?' Miss Marchant shifted her angry gaze from Mrs Cater to Eloise and her lips pursed as if she had just sucked a very sour lemon. 'I might have guessed you would be at the bottom of this, Monk.'

Eloise opened her mouth to argue, but Mrs Cater pushed her aside. She leaned over the desk, shoving her flushed face close to Miss Marchant's. 'This person is causing mayhem in my kitchen, Matron. I won't have it, I tell you.'

Miss Marchant sat back in her chair, steepling her fingers and frowning. 'I knew that taking you on was a mistake, Monk. I felt it in my bones, and now you have proved my instincts to be correct. You can pack up your bags and leave this institution right now.'

'That's not fair, Matron,' Eloise protested, desperate to save the situation. 'You have not heard my side of things.'

Mrs Cater gave Eloise a spiteful dig in the ribs with her elbow. 'You heard what Matron said. You're not wanted here. Now get out.'

'I will not go without a fair hearing,' Eloise cried angrily. 'What happened downstairs was an accident. I'm not used to kitchen work.'

Miss Marchant rose to her feet. 'Enough of this, Monk. You told Mr Caine that you were willing to do anything. Now I find that you cannot be trusted to do the simplest things that any of our older girls could do with their eyes shut.'

'Ho! That explains it, ma'am,' Mrs Cater said with a derisive chuckle. 'Monk must have had her eyes shut and that's why she nearly wrecked my kitchen. Throw her out, Matron. She's nothing but trouble.'

'May I ask what is going on?' Caine strode into the room. 'I could hear raised voices from my office at the end of the corridor.'

A dark flush suffused Miss Marchant's normally pale features and her eyes glittered with malice. 'It is as I warned you, sir. This woman has caused trouble from the moment you employed her.'

'What have you to say for yourself, Miss Monk?' Caine's expression remained as impassive as ever. Eloise wondered what it would take to crack his cast-iron countenance into a smile or even a scowl.

'I admit that I have been clumsy, sir, but

everything that happened was an accident.'
Eloise spoke boldly. She guessed that Caine was
not a man who suffered fools gladly, nor one
who would accept lame excuses. 'I am sorry,' she
added, shooting a sideways glance at Mrs Cater.
'I will try to do better.'

'Not in my kitchen, you won't,' Mrs Cater
snarled. 'I wouldn't give you another chance not
if you was to go down on your bended knees.'

'Thank you, Cook,' Miss Marchant said, raising
her hand for silence. 'That will do. You may go
back to your work. I'll deal with this matter.'

'Yes, Matron.' Cook inclined her head and
stamped out of the office with an air of affronted
dignity.

'You see what this person has done, Mr Caine,'
Miss Marchant said, folding her hands primly in
front of her. 'Have I your permission to dismiss
her without a character?'

Eloise sent him a mute plea for clemency. She
held her breath, waiting for his decision, and he
met her anxious gaze with a long, cool look. She
had the uncomfortable feeling that he could see
into her soul and she looked away, biting her lip.
If only he would say something. She crossed her
fingers behind her back and willed him to speak
up for her.

'Well, sir?' Miss Marchant prompted, fingering
the chatelaine at her waist so that the keys jingled
impatiently on their chains.

'Miss Monk has apologised, Matron,' Caine said slowly. 'She has admitted being clumsy and unfitted for kitchen work. However, I think we can afford to give her a second chance, although I suggest that you find her work that keeps her out of Cook's way.'

Miss Marchant's expression betrayed her anger and frustration, but she managed a tight-lipped grimace and a nod of her head. 'Very well, sir. If you say so.'

'I do say so, Matron.' Caine moved towards the doorway, pausing to address Eloise in a stern voice. 'Don't let me down, Miss Monk.'

Eloise could have cried with relief and she had to suppress the desire to throw her arms around him out of sheer gratitude, but she lowered her gaze and bobbed a curtsey. 'I won't, sir. Thank you, Mr Caine.'

He nodded brusquely and left the room.

'You might have fooled the governor,' Miss Marchant hissed. 'But I have your measure, madam. You will scrub the floors from the attics to the basement, and if I find a speck of dirt at the end of the day, you will be out on your ear. Just because Mr Caine has seen fit to champion your cause doesn't put you above the rest of my staff. Do you understand me, Monk?'

'Yes, Matron.'

'Then get about your business. You will find everything you need in the sluice, and your first job tomorrow morning will be to empty the night soil from the chamber pots in the dormitories and to scour them out thoroughly. We'll see how long you last here, Monk, but I'll wager it won't be very long.'

'Yes, Matron,' Eloise murmured. 'Thank you, Matron.'

Despite Miss Marchant's threat that Eloise must scrub and clean the whole hospital on her own, she was relieved to find that there were two other women who came in daily to do the cleaning. They eyed her suspiciously, as if they thought that she was going to do them out of a job, and reluctantly they showed her where to find the mops, buckets and scrubbing brushes. Eloise could hardly believe her luck when the more vociferous of the two told her to begin on the floor where the nurseries were situated. Judging by the way they were smirking, they thought they had done her a disservice, but Eloise could have crowed with delight.

Garbed in a large white apron and with her hair tucked into a mobcap, she hefted a pail of water up two flights of stairs to the nursery floor and began to scrub the floorboards, working her way as swiftly as she could to the room where she had found Joss and Beth. It was unnaturally quiet in the corridor, but a friendly young nurse-maid informed Eloise that it was the children's nap time. Their routine was strict and involved naps both morning and afternoon. It was good for the nippers, she said, grinning, and good for the staff because it gave them time for a cup of tea and a chat. Eloise worked on, getting nearer and nearer to her children, and then the silence was broken by a loud wail followed by heart-breaking sobs. She knew instantly that it was Joss, and without thinking she leapt to her feet and raced down the corridor to fling the door open. Standing up in his cot with his small hands clutching the bars, Joss was almost hysterical.

A nurse was attempting to pacify him, but every time she tried to pick him up he kicked out with his feet and screamed. She was alone in the room, and the other infants had been awakened by the noise and were starting to cry. She glanced over her shoulder at Eloise. 'Who are you?'

'Just the cleaner,' Eloise murmured. She had to stop herself from rushing across the floor and snatching Joss from his cot. She must not make a false move now, or she would give herself away. She clasped her hands together so tightly that her knuckles cracked. By this time, Joss had thrown himself face down on the mattress and was in the throes of a tantrum.

'Shut up, for Gawd's sake, you little horror,' the nurse said angrily. 'Be quiet, boy. You're waking the whole bloody lot of them.'

Eloise could stand it no longer. 'He's only a

baby,' she said, controlling her voice with difficulty. 'Here, let me have a try.'

'He's a wild one,' the nurse said, backing away from the cot. 'I reckon he's not right in the head. He'll end up in the loony bin.'

Eloise lifted Joss from the cot, hugging him to her breast. 'Don't say things like that. He's just upset.'

At the sound of her voice, Joss immediately began to quieten. His loud wailing calmed down to great heaving sobs, and he turned his head to stare up into her face wide-eyed but seemingly without recognition. Frightened by his vacant expression, Eloise wiped his tears away with the tips of her fingers. 'There, there, it's all right, my pet.'

His eyes searched her face but still he did not seem to know her. It was only then that Eloise realised the full horror of what she had done to a helpless child. It was as though he had awakened from a nightmare but could not drag himself back to reality. She rocked him in her arms, stroking his damp curls back from his forehead. 'Oh, my baby,' she whispered. 'What have I done to you?'

'That's shut him up,' the nurse said, grinning. 'You got a way with nippers. What's your name?'

'Ellen. What's yours?'

'Phoebe. I'm ain't been here long, but they go

and put me in charge of these wild things. Gawd knows where they come from or what they might have wrong with them. Some of them comes in with their heads full of lice and we has to shave their hair off, and others is covered with scabs and sores. At least that one is fairly clean, and so is the little one who come with him. Matron reckons they're brother and sister, but the boy is dumb. He don't say a word.'

'Dumb!' Eloise stared at her in dismay. 'He was making enough noise just now.'

'Oh, he's got a temper all right. Needs a good smack round the lughole if you asks me, but we ain't allowed to hit them. More's the pity I say. They needs discipline from a young age, or that's what my mum says, and she never spared the rod. I got ridges on me backside to prove it.'

Beth sneezed and began to whimper. With Joss clinging to her like a small limpet, Eloise reached over to lift Beth from her cot. Glancing over her shoulder she saw that Phoebe was fully occupied, attempting to restore a semblance of order to the nursery, and Eloise cuddled her children, whispering words of comfort and assuring them that she was not far away and would come and see them every day. Beth snuggled up to her and smiled, but Eloise could not tell whether Joss had understood, and this was more distressing than all his tears and tantrums.

Phoebe had managed at last to soothe most of the infants, and she bustled up to Eloise with a new air of confidence. 'Well, don't that beat all? That's the first time I've managed all on me own, with a bit of help from you, of course, Ellen.' She held her arms out. 'Let me take the boy and I'll sort his wet bum out. Perhaps that will put him in a better temper.'

Joss recoiled visibly at the sight of her, and Eloise clutched him even tighter. 'Let me do it, Phoebe.'

'I dunno about that,' Phoebe said, shaking her head. 'Matron will chew me ears off if she finds out that I let a charwoman do me job.'

'I got six younger brothers and sisters at home. I bet I've changed more wet bums than you have, and I like babies.' The lies came tripping off her tongue, but Eloise did not care if she died and went to hell; nothing could be worse than being separated from her children and this was her chance to give Joss some loving care and attention. It broke her heart to realise that he had withdrawn into a world of his own where she could not reach him.

'Oh, all right then. I suppose it won't hurt just this once, but you'll get into trouble if Matron finds out you've not done the cleaning.'

'I was nearly finished anyway, and I'll work twice as fast when I've settled these two little moppets.' Eloise settled Beth back in her cot while she saw to Joss, and he allowed her to change him without a protest.

Phoebe cocked her head on one side and she ran to the door, opening it a crack and peering out. 'Hurry up, Ellen. Matron is doing her rounds. You'd best get out of here or we'll both be in trouble.'

With a final kiss on their cheeks, Eloise had to drag herself away from her children. With the utmost reluctance, she slipped out of the nursery unseen by Matron, who had stopped to speak to another nurse just a little way along the corridor. With renewed vigour, Eloise set about scrubbing the floorboards. Her joy on being reunited with her babies was tempered by concern for Joss. Beth was too young to be fully aware of what had happened to them, but Joss was obviously in a state of shock and his inability or unwillingness to speak was more frightening than a hundred screaming fits. She must visit them as many times a day as she could manage, but she must also take care not to antagonise Matron any further. It was going to be difficult, but where her children were concerned anything was possible, and no risk too great.

The rest of the morning passed uneventfully and even Matron could find no fault with the quality of Eloise's work. The other two char-women eyed her warily and made it plain that they did not appreciate someone who worked too hard, but Eloise was unrepentant. She was, however, a little anxious as to her reception from the rest of the staff when she went down to the dining room for their main meal, which was served after the children had eaten at midday. Having spilt and spoilt their breakfast porridge and caused Cook to have an accident, Eloise was certain that she would be the most unpopular person in the whole hospital. It was hunger that finally forced her to enter the dining room, which she did with a determined lift of her chin, ready to parry any barbed comments she might receive. It came as a surprise to find that, far from being a pariah, she was welcomed with smiles and pats on the back.

Tibbie had saved a place for her at the main table and she waved and beckoned to Eloise, smiling broadly. 'You done it on purpose, didn't you? You tipped the coke on the floor just so that the old cow would fall flat on her backside.'

Becky had come to join them and she slapped Eloise on the shoulder. 'I heard what you done, Ellen. Good for you. The old bitch had it coming.'

Around her, everyone was smiling and winking as though she was a heroine, and Eloise was dazed by the sudden turn of events. She acknowledged their unspoken approval with a nod and a smile, and then she bent her head over her plate of food, not wanting to draw any more attention to herself. She had already made an enemy of Mrs Cater and Miss Marchant; she could not afford to offend them further.

Late that afternoon, when Matron was busy supervising the children's teatime meal, Eloise managed to slip upstairs to the nursery where she found that Phoebe was still on duty. She was sitting in a low chair giving one of the babies its bottle. 'You just can't keep away, can you, Ellen?'

'I always wanted to be a nursemaid,' Eloise said glibly. 'I thought if I got a bit of practice in, I might be able to apply for a position in a big house or even here.'

'Dunno why anyone would want to work with nippers,' Phoebe replied, shrugging. 'I wanted to be a proper nurse but they don't take on girls like me. I'm too common to train in one of them schools of nursing, so I ended up here, wiping dirty bums and clearing up baby sick.'

'There are worse jobs,' Eloise said, craning her neck to catch a glimpse of Joss and Beth.

'That's as maybe, but I'm not going to stay here any longer than I have to. I'm stepping out with a chap who works on the docks. We're going to get hitched when we've saved up enough, or if I happen to get in the family way, whichever comes first. Not that I particularly want nippers, not after putting up with this lot.'

Eloise edged closer to the cots where Joss and Beth lay behind bars like tiny prisoners. Although Beth slept peacefully enough, apart from the occasional sneeze, Joss was wide awake, lying on his back and staring at the ceiling.

'He won't eat,' Phoebe said, shaking her head. 'Won't touch nothing, but his little sister she took her bottle all right at dinnertime in spite of her nose being all blocked up, and she even managed a bit of mashed tater and gravy. In fact, she ain't no trouble, but him, he's a difficult one.'

Eloise lifted Joss from his cot, and as she held his small body in her arms a frisson of fear ran through her veins. His limbs were stiff and his cheeks were pale. He rested his head against her shoulder but he neither spoke nor gave any obvious sign that he knew her. In the middle of the room a table was set with tea, and those who were big enough to sit unaided and feed themselves were seated in high chairs eating bread and butter. Eloise carried Joss to the table and she tried to tempt him with a thin slice, but he turned his head away. She poured milk into a cup and held it to his lips. At first he shook his head, but she persevered gently and finally he took a sip. 'Good boy, Joss,' Eloise whispered in his ear. 'Try a little more, darling.'

Studying her face as if he was trying to place her, Joss took another mouthful, and then seemed to realise that he was thirsty and finished the whole cupful. Eloise could have cried with relief, but she schooled her features into a smile of approval. 'Now, how about a little bit of bupper?'

The familiar baby name for his favourite tea-time food seemed to register with Joss and he opened his mouth. Eloise broke off a morsel and popped it between his lips, followed by another and another until he had eaten the whole slice.

'Well, I said it afore and I'll say it again,' Phoebe said, hitching the baby over her shoulder and patting its back. 'You got a way with nippers, Ellen. You can come in any time I'm on duty and look after young master awkward there. I can't do nothing with the little perisher.'

Eloise bit back a sharp retort and she hugged Joss a little closer. 'Maybe if you knew his name you might get more out of him.'

'I told you, he's not all there. He probably don't know his own name, even if he could speak, which he can't.'

'Maybe he'll speak to me,' Eloise said casually. 'I'll whisper in his ear and make out we're playing a game.'

'Suit yourself, but you'll be wasting your time. He's a mute if ever I saw one.'

Eloise placed her lips close to Joss's ear and whispered the question. As she had feared, he did not respond, but she forced her cold lips into a smile and raised her voice so that Phoebe could hear. 'Now you whisper to me, my boy. What is your name?' She put her ear close to his face, but Joss remained silent. She turned again to Phoebe. 'He says his name is Joss.'

'Well I never! Are you sure?'

'I heard him quite clearly. I think the poor child is just too frightened to speak, but he whispered his name in my ear.'

Phoebe rose to her feet and placed the baby back in its cot. She hurried to the table to scold a child who had spilt his milk. 'Naughty boy. You shan't have any cake for that.'

'Oh, come now, Phoebe,' Eloise protested. 'That's not fair. It was an accident.'

'Yes, and you'd know all about accidents. I heard what went on in the kitchen. You was lucky that Matron didn't give you the sack, but maybe she quite liked the idea of Cook sprawling flat on her back like an upturned beetle. Wish I'd seen it.'

Eloise gave Joss a last loving hug and set him back in his cot. 'Mama will come again later, sweetheart,' she whispered, and then as Beth was stirring she picked her up in her arms. 'Would you like me to see to this one, Phoebe?'

'You can have her for all I care,' Phoebe replied crossly. She made a tut-tutting sound as one of the small girls spat a lump of half-chewed bread and butter onto the table. 'I dunno! Bloody little animals.'

'Mama!' Beth said in a loud clear voice. 'Mama.' She wrapped her small arms around Eloise's neck and gave her a rather moist kiss on the cheek.

'She thinks you're her ma,' Phoebe said scornfully. 'Both of them are soft in the head if you ask me, but they seem to have taken to you. Why don't you ask her what her name is?'

Eloise held a cup of milk to Beth's lips and watched her drink with an inward sigh of relief. 'I think she's a bit young to tell me that, but maybe Joss knows.'

'Go on then, you ask him.'

Eloise went through the same routine as before, leaning over Joss in his cot and speaking to him in whispers. She straightened up, settling Beth on her hip as she went to fetch some bread and butter from the table. 'He says she is called Beth. He is quite sensible, Phoebe. You just have to treat him right.'

'I got twelve little buggers to care for, mostly single-handed. I ain't got the time to pander to their carryings on.' Phoebe snatched up a child who had fallen off her seat and was bawling loudly. 'There, there, Dora. Rub it in. That's what my mum always says to us.' She turned to glance at the white-faced clock on the wall. 'Just look at the time. You'd best get going, Ellen. It's almost time for Matron's ward round. She inspects every morning and every afternoon at teatime. She'd better not find you here.'

Reluctantly, Eloise sat Beth in a high chair and gave her some bread and butter. Although Beth was full of cold and finding it difficult to eat and

389

breathe at the same time, she was obviously hungry and that was a good sign. Eloise hesitated, watching her daughter's attempts at eating with an aching heart as she recalled happier times in the days before Ronnie was lost at sea. She thought of teatime at her little house in Myrtle Street, sitting round the fire in winter with Joss kneeling at her side as she impaled slices of bread on the toasting fork and held them close to the glowing coals. She could almost smell the appetising aroma of hot toast which they ate dripping with butter and jam or honey. Beth was a tiny baby then, sleeping peacefully in her cradle, and it had never occurred to Eloise that life could change so drastically, and so much for the worse.

'For Gawd's sake stop daydreaming, Ellen,' Phoebe said pushing her towards the door. 'She'll be here any minute and we'll both be in real trouble.'

Eloise came back to reality with a start. 'Yes, I'll go now. But I'll come again tomorrow.'

'Good, but be careful. You don't want to get on the wrong side of Miss Marchant.'

In the middle of the night, Eloise awakened from a deep sleep with the feeling that something was terribly wrong. She sat up in her narrow bed, grimacing as the iron bedstead groaned in protest, but Tibbie and Becky were fast asleep and did not stir even when the floorboards creaked or the latch on the door made a loud click. Barefoot and wearing nothing but her shift, Eloise crept downstairs to the nursery. Even before she reached the door, she could hear loud wailing and she knew that it was Joss. The keening noise was more like that of an animal in distress than a small child and Eloise burst into the room, not caring if she roused the whole hospital as she ran to snatch her son from his cot. His anguished sobs had awakened most of the other infants and they had added their cries to the cacophony of sound. Eloise rocked Joss in her arms, pacing the floor and praying silently that whoever was on night duty would not come rushing into the nursery and discover her presence. She began to sing a lullaby that she had sung to Joss when he was a tiny baby, and gradually he began to quieten. His small fingers were entwined in her long hair, and his body shook even though his sobbing had ceased. Eloise went through her whole repertoire of lullabies and the crying gradually ceased as small faces turned towards her. She moved from cot to cot, smiling and wiping away tears with a clean napkin. One by one, the infants closed their eyes and drifted off to sleep, and feeling Joss's head heavy against her neck and hearing his soft, rhythmic breathing, Eloise realised that he too had succumbed, and she laid him gently in his cot. She went round the nursery covering the ones who had kicked off their blankets, and finally checking again on Joss and Beth. As she leaned over the cot rails to kiss them, the hairs on the back of her neck prickled and Eloise knew that she was being watched.

Slowly, hardly daring to breathe, she straightened up and turned round to face the door. There, standing in the shadows, was a tall figure dressed in black. She could not see his face but she knew instinctively that it was Caine. He beckoned silently and she moved towards him like a sleepwalker. He held the door open and she went past him into the corridor, anticipating the full force of his wrath.

He closed the door softly. 'This is not the place to talk, Miss Monk. Be so good as to come to my office.' Caine took a lighted oil lamp from a side table and walked off along the corridor to a room at the far end.

She was certain that this time she would be dismissed, but she had no option other than to follow him. In her agitated state Eloise had almost forgotten that she was naked beneath her shift, but as he ushered her into the room she realised what a sight she must look. The skimpy material of the garment left very little to the imagination as it skimmed the curve of her breasts and clung to her narrow hips, outlining her thighs and stopping just above her ankles.

She flicked her long hair over her shoulders in an attempt to cover her modesty and she wished the floor would open up and swallow her.

Caine set the lamp down on his desk and turned to give her a cursory glance. 'You're shivering,' he said, taking off his frock coat and slipping it around her shoulders. 'Take a seat by the fire, Miss Monk.'

Eloise had expected an angry tirade but this chivalrous treatment left her confused and even more embarrassed. 'It's not what you think,' she began tentatively.

'What do I think? Tell me. I would like to know.'

'You're playing with words, Mr Caine.'

'I find you in the nursery, in the middle of the night when those who are not on duty are asleep in their beds. What am I to think?'

'I couldn't sleep and I heard a baby crying. No one seemed to take any notice of the poor little thing and so I went to see what was wrong.'

'It was none of your business. If anything you should have reported the lapse to me or to Matron.'

Eloise tossed her head. 'I wasn't to know that you were about, sir. It seems that I am not the only one who cannot sleep.'

'I do not need much sleep, Miss Monk. I catch up on my paperwork at a time when I can usually be certain of working without any interruptions.'

Eloise huddled beneath the satin lining of his frock coat and a shiver ran down her spine. Wearing a man's garment that was still warm from his body and had the scent of him in every fibre was oddly disconcerting and too personal for comfort.

'You are still cold,' Caine said, frowning. 'Please go and sit by the fire.'

This time, Eloise did as she was told, and she went to sit in a wingback chair at the side of the carved oak fireplace, watching silently as Caine moved to a side table and poured something from a cut crystal decanter into two glasses. He crossed the floor to hand one to her and a wry smile curved his lips. 'It seems that we have been here before, Miss Monk. Am I always to find you in a state of distress?'

She eyed Caine warily and was surprised to see how much more human and approachable he looked in his shirtsleeves. Seeming to sense her scrutiny he met her gaze with a questioning look, and for a brief moment it felt as though they were equals and she was not afraid. If he had been really angry, surely he would have dismissed her on the spot?

Caine stood with his back to the fireplace, cupping his hands around the bowl of the glass. 'Well, Miss Monk. You are unusually silent. Would you like to tell me why you were in the nursery in the middle of the night?'

'As I said, sir, I heard a child crying. There did not seem to be anyone about and so I went into the nursery to comfort him.'

'To comfort him? You recognised the boy's cry?'

Realising her mistake, Eloise shook her head emphatically. 'No, sir. What I meant to say was that I discovered a boy who was very upset, and I – I . . .'

'And you went into the nursery to comfort him?'

The brandy was making her feel slightly muzzy in the head and Eloise suspected that he was trying to catch her out. 'I was looking for the night nurse, sir.'

'But you've already said there was no one about, Miss Monk. Would you like to begin again and tell me why you were wandering about the hospital at this hour? You couldn't possibly have heard a child crying from the staff quarters in the attic.'

'I – I must have been sleepwalking. I found myself in the corridor outside the nursery and that's when I heard the child crying.'

Caine took a seat in the chair on the opposite side of the fireplace. 'Do you really expect me to believe such a ridiculous story?'

Stung by his attitude, Eloise took refuge in anger. 'Are you calling me a liar, sir?'

'Miss Monk, the aim of this hospital is not only

to save the lives of abandoned children, but also to reclaim their mothers from a life of poverty and degradation. We try, if at all possible, to reunite mother and child. Women who have been driven to leave their children on our doorstep do occasionally return, either to reclaim them or, more often than not, just to reassure themselves that their offspring are being looked after properly.'

Despite the warming effect of the brandy and her proximity to the roaring fire, Eloise shivered beneath the folds of Caine's coat. He was so close to the truth that it had taken her breath away and she did not know how to respond. He leaned towards her and his piercing blue eyes challenged her to tell the truth. 'You do not have anything to say, Miss Monk? I find that strange since you have not been so reticent before.'

'I have nothing to say because there is nothing to say,' Eloise countered. 'I am sorry for the women of whom you speak, but I am not one of them.'

'And yet you have been seen going in and out of the nursery as if you could not keep away.'

'I like children, Mr Caine. I feel sorry for the foundlings.' Eloise rose rather shakily to her feet. 'Sir, if you are going to dismiss me, please do it now. Don't keep me in suspense. I cannot stand it.'

Chapter Seventeen

Caine rose from his seat and took the glass from her trembling fingers. 'You may have broken some of Matron's cast-iron regulations, but I am not going to dismiss you. As far as I can see you have done no harm, but I would advise you to abide by the rules in future.'

'Yes, sir. I will. May I go now?'

He turned away to set the glasses back on the side table. 'Yes, go back to bed and get some sleep.'

'Good night, sir.' Eloise shrugged off his coat and was struck by a sudden chill. It was like slipping off someone's skin and she felt suddenly vulnerable. She hung the garment tidily over the back of a chair and was about to leave the room when he called her back.

'Miss Monk.'

'Yes, sir.'

'It's nothing. You may go.' He walked round his desk and sat down, bending his head over a sheaf of papers.

Eloise needed no second bidding. She hurried from the office, closing the door behind her. She paused for a moment, leaning against the wall in an attempt to control her erratic heartbeats. She had had a reprieve, but it was a close call and she must be more careful in future. The sound of movement inside the office galvanised her frozen limbs into action and Eloise raced along the dark corridor as if the devil himself was on her heels. When she reached the safety of her room, she crept in without disturbing Tibbie and Becky and she climbed into bed, but sleep eluded her as she lay shivering beneath the coverlet. Her conversation with Caine had been disturbing. He was not a likeable man, she decided. His manner was harsh and he was arrogant, but he was not the sort of person who could be easily fooled. She knew that he did not believe her story, although he could prove nothing. She decided that she must be more careful in future. If she lost this job she would be separated from Joss and Beth for the foreseeable future, and that was unthinkable. Eloise closed her eyes. If she worked hard and avoided getting into more trouble, perhaps she could persuade Matron that she was a suitable person to work in the nursery. She must try harder. She would try harder.

After her confrontation with the governor, Eloise was extra vigilant when she crept down to the nursery every night. She had discovered the night nurses' routine and she knew that just after midnight they congregated in a room on the first floor to chat and drink cocoa. She waited until she could smell the fragrance of hot chocolate, mixed with the faint waft of illicit tobacco smoke, before creeping silently to the nursery. Joss was never asleep. It was almost as if he knew that she was coming and he forced himself to stay awake so that he could see her. She was certain now that he recognised her, but he still did not speak. The day staff had written him off as a mute, but no one seemed unduly worried about his condition. Perhaps they were relieved to have a silent child on their hands, as it made life easier for them.

When she entered the nursery, Eloise always went straight to Joss, lifting him from his cot and talking to him in a low whisper. He listened attentively, never taking his eyes off her face, and his small hand would reach up to touch her lips or her cheek, which made her want to cry, but she held back the tears. She must never allow him to see that she was upset or that might distress him even more. Beth was always asleep when Eloise arrived in the nursery but the sound of her mother's voice seemed to penetrate her dreams and she too would wake up, out-stretching her arms in a plea to be picked up and cuddled. These moments alone with her children were more precious to Eloise than the snatched minutes she spent with them during the day. She had organised her routine so that she reached the nursery at dinnertime when she knew that Phoebe would be glad of some help, and again at teatime. She had to be careful not to pay too much attention to her own children, and this was a form of torture in itself, but her clash with the governor had made her even more wary of discovery.

As the weeks went by, Eloise lived in two worlds. In the daytime, she was just Ellen, the charwoman with ambitions to be a nursery nurse, but at night she was able to give Joss and Beth all the love that was denied to them by day. The other infants usually slept, and if they awakened and began to cry, she would sing lullabies until they fell back to sleep. She dared not linger for too long and risk being caught again, but the pain of leaving her children never seemed to ease. Each time she left the nursery it felt as though she left a piece of her heart clutched in their tiny hands. Soon she would have none left, and perhaps the agony would go away. Eloise had never believed that a heart could physically break – now she was not so certain.

After her nocturnal visits, Eloise was in the habit of looking up and down the corridor to make sure that the coast was clear, and every night she saw a faint pencil line of light beneath Caine's office door. She could almost feel pity for such a tortured soul who never seemed to sleep, and she began to wonder what it was that had turned a comparatively young man into a block of ice. She had even gone so far as to question Tibbie, who was an inveterate gossip and had been only too delighted to pass on what little she knew about the governor. His wife, she said, had been almost too beautiful for words. Not that Tibbie had ever seen her; she was just telling Eloise what she had heard, and there was a portrait of Rosamund Caine hanging in the drawing room of the governor's house. It was said that little Maria was the image of her blonde and blue-eyed mother, and just as lively. Rosamund had been a talented musician; she had played the pianoforte and had the singing voice of an angel. The older members of staff waxed lyrical when they spoke of how Mrs Caine had played and sung for them at their Christmas party. They said how light she was on her feet when she danced with the governor, and how devastated he had been when she had died in childbirth. He had never got over it, so Tibbie said, wiping a tear from her eye. Some said that he used to be a charming fellow, with a ready wit and a smile for everyone. His heart was broken, and that was a fact. It was well known that he worked all night. Perhaps he never slept at all. Tibbie was not certain about that, but what she did know was that he spoiled his little daughter something rotten, and little Maria Caine had had so many nannies that everyone had lost count. Miss Maria's tantrums were something to behold. If she was thwarted in anything her screams would even drown the sound of traffic in Guildford Street. What she needed, in Tibbie's opinion, was a firm hand. 'Matron would sort the young lady out good and proper,' Tibbie said, nodding wisely. 'Spare the rod and spoil the child is what she always says, and I think she's right.'

Eloise listened to this diatribe with interest, although privately she thought that Miss Maria would gain little from corporal punishment. Her mother would be just the person to deal with a child such as Maria Caine. If only Mama were here now. Eloise had gone straight away to her room and taken the writing case from its hiding place beneath her mattress, and she had begun the first letter to her mother that she had attempted to write since she left Ephraim Hubble's house in Clerkenwell Green. At least now she could say that she had a respectable position in the Foundling Hospital, although she omitted to add that her children were institutionalised and that she was merely a charwoman. She made no mention of all the traumas they had suffered in the intervening weeks, and she said nothing about working in the dust yard or her failed attempt at earning her living as a prostitute. If she lived to be a hundred, she would never tell either of her parents how low she had sunk during that long, hot summer.

She thanked Mama for her letters and said she hoped that Janet was now settling in more happily at the mission, and that Papa had not suffered a recurrence of the fever which had laid him so low. It was just a short letter, but Eloise was satisfied that it would set her mother's mind at rest after so many weeks of silence. On her afternoon off, Eloise went to the post office in Holborn and sent her letter on its way to Africa. As it was a fine late September afternoon with mellow sunshine and a degree of warmth, she decided to walk as far as the Missionary Society offices to see if there was any correspondence awaiting her. To her delight there was a letter addressed to her with the envelope written in her mother's neat hand, but there was another which bore a Yorkshire postmark. Eloise did not recognise the handwriting and her heart skipped a beat at the thought that it might have come from Cribb's Hall. With her imagination running riot, she hurried out into the street and made her way to Lincoln's Inn Fields where she found a bench beneath the trees. She sat for a moment, staring at the envelope which had come from the north, hardly daring to open it. Suppose the Cribbs had gone through with their threat to make Joss and Beth wards of court? If they knew that she collected mail from the Missionary Society, it would be easy for Pike to lie in wait for her there and follow her back to the Foundling Hospital. All would be lost then. Mr Caine would be forced to dismiss her, and her children would be wrenched from her arms. She could see it all in her mind's eye and she sat trembling, hardly daring to open the letter. Dry leaves drifted from the trees, floating to the ground where they lay in heaps of golden brown, like mounds of fools' gold. She took a deep breath and ripped the envelope, exposing the letter inside. She hardly dared to unfold the paper, but when she eventually plucked up courage to read it, she uttered a sigh of relief.

Danby Farm
Driffield
Yorkshire
1 September 1879
Dear Ellie,

I hope this letter finds you, as it leaves me, well and in good health. We have missed you and the dear children since you left the farm, but I hope that you have found yourself a good position and that you are settled back in London.

The reason I am writing to you, my dear, and it do not come easy to a woman like me, is to tell you that Reggie is engaged to be married to Maud Fosdyke. He was courting her for several years before you came to stay with us, although, as you know, there was no formal contract between them. Reggie told me all about his asking you to marry him and I cannot say I was surprised that you had turned him down. I could wish it was different, but I know it was not to be. You must not be surprised or hurt at the way he has acted, which might seem to be fickle, but I think he knew all along that you were above his reach. I am sure that Reggie will always hold you dear in his big, soft heart, but the time has come for him to settle down and Maud is a good and homely young woman who will adapt well to life on the farm.

There have not been any more visits from those people, you know who I mean, but I put flowers on poor Ada's grave every time I visit the church.

Do write to me if you have the time, my dear. I always think of you warmly and remember with pleasure the time you spent with us.

Your very good friend,
Gladys Danby.

Eloise read and reread the letter to make certain there was no mention of further visits from the Cribbs. She smiled ruefully at the idea that she might be upset by Reggie's apparent fickleness. In fact she could understand his sudden decision to marry his old sweetheart and she sincerely wished him well. It was a relief to think that she might have bruised his male pride by rejecting his proposal of marriage, but that he had recovered sufficiently to honour his previous commitment to Maud, who was either extremely good-natured or rather desperate to catch a husband, if she was prepared to be second best. Eloise folded the letter and put it back in its envelope. Second best would not suit her. She could never marry a man whose heart belonged to another, or one whose heart was buried in the grave. She snapped back to the present with a jolt. What could have put that thought in her head? She had a fleeting vision of Barton Caine walking in the sunlit gardens of the Foundling Hospital with his young daughter, and her first impression of him as a cold and haughty man. Nothing had happened to change her mind, so why had thoughts of him suddenly come into her head, and in such a context? He was the last man on earth whom she could ever think of as a prospective husband. Shocked by her own thoughts, Eloise applied herself to reading the letter from her mother. It had been written in response to the first of Eloise's letters to reach the mission house, in which she described the grandeur of her new surroundings in Cribb's Hall. With her customary insight, Mama had sensed that all was not right with her daughter, even though Eloise had been at pains not to mention the bullying tactics of Hilda and Joan. As she read her mother's words, Eloise thought grimly that what had happened in

Cribb's Hall was as nothing compared to the dire consequences of her return to London. She would never be able to tell Mama even half of what she had suffered.

She read on, and despite her mother's attempts to remain positive, it seemed that life in the bush was fraught with hardship and danger. Whether it was poisonous snakes, lions prowling round outside the compound and crocodiles lurking in the undergrowth on the riverbank, or the various diseases that threatened their health, it was certainly not a vision of paradise. Both Papa and Janet suffered recurrent bouts of malaria, although by some strange quirk of fate Mama seemed to have escaped the scourge. Janet was having difficulty in coping with the heat and discomfort, but Mama put a brave face on matters, saying that the mission was thriving and she had started up a school for the village children who were such dears and so responsive to her. Papa, she said, was working hard, and even though his ill health was making life difficult, he really seemed to have found his true vocation and he loved his flock with a deep and burning passion. Eloise read the brave words but she was not fooled by them. It was obvious that both her mother and Janet were suffering. She struggled with the unworthy thought that her father was a selfish man whose vaingloriousness had brought misery to the women who loved and depended upon him. She sighed as she folded the letter and put it back in its envelope. Her parents seemed even further away, and reading about their strange existence in the wilds of the African bush only widened the gulf between them.

As she set off in the direction of Guildford Street, Eloise felt more alone than she had for a long time. But it was a glorious autumn day, and it was hard to be sad when the sun was shining and the rain which had come in the night had done much to wash the grime from the streets and dilute the stench of horse dung and overfull sewers. Soon the November gales would strip the leaves from the trees and there would be fog and frost to contend with. Life in the Foundling Hospital was far from ideal, but at least they were warm, well fed and safe from the prying eyes of Pike and the machinations of Hilda Cribb. If her arithmetic was correct, her parents were due home on leave in less than eighteen months, and there would be a joyful reunion. If Papa felt that he had done his duty, maybe he could be persuaded to accept a country parish and then Mama would be able to see her grandchildren growing up and Janet would be able to spoil them as she had spoiled Eloise.

She was smiling at the thought and without realising it she had quickened her pace arriving back at the Foundling Hospital much earlier than she had intended. It was an hour until the children's teatime, and now it was an established routine that she went to help Phoebe when her day's work was done. Whether or not the governor had had words with Miss Marchant on the subject, Eloise did not know, but if Matron knew about it, she turned a blind eye. As she entered through the gates, Eloise glanced automatically up at the windows of the governor's house, and she thought she saw a small child peering out. She smiled and waved but the little girl merely stared at her and then turned her head, as if someone in the room had summoned her away from the window. It occurred to Eloise at that moment that Maria Caine must be a lonely child. She had no mother to care for her and no siblings to play with. Her father was preoccupied with his job and she had had a succession of nannies who could not cope with her bad behaviour. A wave of sympathy washed over Eloise and she found herself wishing that she could do something to help the spoilt but unhappy little girl. She stopped to admire a deep crimson rose with petals that looked as though they were made of velvet. Just as she bent her head to inhale its sweet scent, she caught a movement out of the corner of her eye and turned her head to see Annie standing in the middle of the lawn with her arms outstretched and a look of delight transforming her plain features.

'Mum,' Annie shrieked. 'You've come. It's me, your Annie.'

Eloise looked round and realised with a shock that they were alone in the gardens and Annie was racing towards her with an expression of pure joy on her face, which was wiped away as she drew close and replaced by a look of puzzlement. 'Ellie! Is it really you? I thought – I mean, the sun was behind you and in me eyes – I thought for a moment that she had come for me.'

'Oh, my dear Annie. I am so sorry, it's just me.' Eloise held out her arms and Annie ran into them, hugging her round the waist and then she pulled away, wiping her eyes on her sleeve.

'Silly me. I dunno what come over me. But it's good to see you, Ellie. Where've you been all this time?'

Eloise slipped her arm around Annie's thin shoulders. 'It's a long story, but I am so happy to see you again. Come and sit down and I'll explain, and you must tell me what has been happening to you at Mrs King's.'

'Oh, her!' Annie said, wrinkling her snub nose. 'She never changes. She's still a mean old cow and I hates her. If me mum don't come and find me soon I think I'll run away from Nile Street and take me chances somewhere else. I might even go on one of them big ships to Canada or Australia. I'll bet there's plenty of work there for girls like me.'

Acting on a sudden whim, Eloise plucked the damask rose and gave it to Annie. She grinned with pleasure and buried her face in the soft petals. 'That smells so good. It's how I imagine me mum will smell when she comes to find me. I'm sure she will come one day, and perhaps we'll get on that ship together.'

'That's a happy thought,' Eloise said, not wanting to spoil Annie's impossible dream.

'She will come for me. I know she will.'

Eloise smiled. 'I hope so, Annie. Let's sit down for a while and you can tell me what's been happening to you.'

'Never mind me. I'm dying to know what's been going on. And where are the little 'uns? I ain't going until you've told me everything.'

They sat on a bench in the sunshine and Eloise talked while Annie listened in wide-eyed silence. When Eloise had finished, Annie blew her nose noisily on a corner of her pinafore. 'Well I never did. And now you're living in here,' she jerked her head towards the hospital building, 'just like I did, and no one knows that the nippers belong to you. Why, it's my story all over again.'

'It is, almost, and you must never give up hope, Annie. Sometimes it's all we have to keep us going.' Eloise paused at the sound of childish laughter and her attention was diverted by the sight of Maria Caine skipping towards them along the path. Caine strode along behind her and he called out to Maria, but she ignored him and ran up to Eloise, stopping in front of her with her hands clasped behind her back.

'I saw you from the window,' she said conversationally. 'And you smiled at me. You looked nice and I wanted to speak to you, so I made Papa bring me out into the gardens.'

Eloise rose to her feet, meeting Caine's stern gaze with an apologetic smile. 'I'm sorry, sir. I didn't mean to distract your daughter from her lessons.'

Caine tipped his hat. 'That would not be difficult, since Maria has just sent her latest governess into a fit of hysterics. I think we will find that Miss Trinder has her notice written out by the time we return to the house.'

Maria looked up at him with a mischievous grin. 'But I don't like her, Papa. And she makes me sit still and stitch my sampler all afternoon when I want to come out and play.'

'It is all part of your education, young lady,' Caine said with a reluctant smile. 'And I have work to do.'

Eloise stared at him, fascinated by the change that a smile wrought in his set countenance. 'I still have half an hour left, sir. I would be happy to look after Maria until teatime. Perhaps she could come to the nursery and take tea with us. She could help to feed the babies if she wishes.'

Maria jumped up and down, clapping her

hands. 'Oh, Papa. May I? That sounds so much more fun than practising embroidery stitches. I hate sewing and I hate Miss Trinder.'

Caine's smile turned into a frown, and the lines between his eyes deepened. 'I have an important meeting, which I left at Miss Trinder's request, Maria. I am not sure that you deserve to be let off your lessons.'

Maria clutched his hand and held it to her cheek. 'Please, Papa. I promise to be good if you will only let me stay with this person.' She turned to Eloise, angling her blonde head. 'I don't know who you are.'

'I am Ellen. I work in the Foundling Hospital, and this is my friend, Annie.'

Maria gave Annie a cursory glance and did not look impressed. She reached out to grasp Eloise's hand. 'You will look after me, won't you, Ellen? Then Papa can get back to his silly old meeting and I can help look after the babies. I'm never allowed into the hospital to play with the children, but I can see them from my window and I can hear them laughing when they are allowed out to play.'

'I will look after her, sir,' Eloise promised, squeezing Maria's hand.

'Very well,' Caine said reluctantly. 'I must get back to the meeting, but I'll have words with you later, Maria. And you be good, or Miss Monk will tell me and you will be punished.'

Annie nudged Maria with her elbow. 'I'd be good if I was you, young 'un. He looks like he means business.'

Eloise cast a nervous glance at Caine, thinking that he might take offence at Annie's careless remark, but she saw to her surprise that his lips twitched, although he managed to keep a straight face as he regarded Annie. 'Is that rose from this garden, young woman?'

Annie whipped it behind her back. 'I never took it, guv. It weren't me. I don't steal.'

'It's all right, Annie,' Eloise said, patting her on the shoulder. 'It was me, Mr Caine. I couldn't resist picking it and I gave it to Annie.'

'Do you like roses, Miss Monk?'

Eloise nodded. 'Who doesn't? They are everything that anyone could wish for in a flower.'

'Quite so.' Caine cleared his throat and turned his attention to Maria. 'I will allow you to stay with Miss Monk, but only on condition that you behave yourself, young lady.'

'I will, Papa. I promise.' Maria threw herself at him and he patted her on the head, as if she were an over-boisterous puppy, then he turned on his heel and strode away along the path and out of the gardens.

'He didn't remember me,' Annie said with a note of disappointment in her voice. 'But then why would he? I was just one of the many, as I am now. No one notices a foundling child.'

'Well, that's just not true,' Eloise said firmly. 'I noticed you from the start, Annie. You have a personality all of your own and when you are grown up you will be a very striking young woman. You are brave and you are loyal, and I am proud to have you as a friend.'

Annie's small face crumpled up and she covered her face with her pinafore. 'No one's never said nothing so nice to me before.'

'Why are you crying, girl?' Maria demanded. 'Are you a bit simple?'

'Hush, Maria,' Eloise said, shaking her head. 'Of course Annie isn't simple. She has not had your advantages in life, that is all. Now you wanted to play in the gardens, so you'd better enjoy it while you can. It will soon be time to go indoors.'

Maria skipped off, running round the gardens like a small white butterfly.

'I ain't simple,' Annie sniffed. 'I ain't.'

'Of course not,' Eloise said, giving her a hug. 'Maria is just six years old. She doesn't know what she's saying.'

'She needs a spanking,' Annie muttered.

Now where have I heard that before? Eloise thought wryly. Perhaps she does need a firm hand, but maybe she just needs an outward display of affection, and that seems to be something sadly lacking in her father.

As the shadows began to lengthen, Annie

departed for Nile Street, promising to return again on her next afternoon off, and Eloise took Maria into the hospital. They went straight to the nursery where Phoebe was at first aghast to think that the governor's daughter was going to join them for tea, and then when she grew accustomed to the idea, she admitted grudgingly that perhaps it wouldn't do any harm. The older infants seemed delighted to have Maria's attention and Joss in particular appeared to have taken quite a fancy to her. As Eloise watched them playing together, she wished that Mr Caine could see the change in his daughter, from spoilt brat to happy, well-behaved child.

Eloise was helping Phoebe to clear the table and Maria was organising the toddlers into a game of her own making when the door opened and Caine strolled in. He paused, taking in the scene with a look of astonishment on his face. Maria was so busy that she had not noticed her father's arrival. Phoebe snapped to attention, but Eloise continued to stack the dirty crockery onto a tray ready to take back to the kitchen. Beth had been allowed to join in the game, although she was still finding her feet and could only take a few steps before losing her balance. She chose this moment to take a tumble and began to howl dismally. Maria was at her side in an instant and she went down on her knees to give Beth a cuddle.

'Maria. It's time to come home,' Caine said in a stern voice.

'Not now, Papa. I'm busy.'

Eloise bit her lip to prevent herself from laughing out loud. Phoebe sucked in her breath, eyeing Caine nervously, but he seemed unperturbed.

'Now, Maria. Mrs Dean has your tea ready on the table.'

'I've had tea with the babies, Papa. Now we're playing a game and must not be disturbed.' Maria turned her back on her father and she took Joss by the hand. 'Come along, boy. I am your mother and we are going to the market to buy some apples.'

Eloise could see that this was going to turn into a contest between father and daughter and would inevitably end in tears. She hitched Beth onto her hip and stepped in between Maria and Joss. 'I think that the market will be closed now, Maria. Say goodnight to Joss and perhaps your father will allow you to come and play with him tomorrow.'

Maria stared up at her, pouting ominously, with her fair eyebrows drawn into a scowl so like her father's that again Eloise wanted to laugh, but she managed to control the impulse and she met Maria's angry gaze with a calm smile. 'I'm afraid he won't allow it if you disobey him, Maria. And Joss would be disappointed if you could not continue the game tomorrow afternoon.'

Caine made a move towards his daughter, but Eloise turned to him with a slight shake of her head and he hesitated. For a moment it seemed that Maria was going to argue, but then she held her hand out to her father with a beguiling smile. 'May I come here tomorrow, Papa? I have been a good help, haven't I, Ellen?'

'You have indeed,' Eloise said solemnly. 'I don't know how Phoebe and I would have managed without you.'

'You see, Papa,' Maria said, beaming. 'I am a good girl sometimes.'

Caine took her hand and he smiled down at her. 'I am very glad to hear it, and if you continue to be good you may come here providing that it doesn't upset the running of the nursery.'

Maria turned to Eloise. 'It won't, will it, Ellie? Tell him I may come again.'

'I wouldn't dream of telling Mr Caine anything,' Eloise said, smiling. 'But I'm sure that Phoebe and I would be very pleased to have Maria's help. Wouldn't we, Phoebe?'

Phoebe blushed scarlet and bobbed a curtsey. 'I'd be honoured, sir.'

'I can see that I'm outnumbered,' Caine said with a reluctant smile. His eyes flickered to Eloise and then he looked away. 'Come along, Maria. It's getting late.'

'Phew!' Phoebe said, breathing a sigh of relief

as they left the room. 'I thought we was going to be for it then.'

Eloise said nothing. She had seen another side of Governor Caine that day and it had left her feeling confused and even a little sorry for him. He obviously cared deeply for his daughter, but he neither knew how to show his affection for her nor how to handle a small, wilful girl.

'Tell you what, Ellen,' Phoebe said, fanning herself with her hand. 'I could do with a break. Will you stay and get the nippers ready for bed while I take the dirty crockery back to the kitchen and get meself a cup of tea?'

'Yes, I'll be glad to,' Eloise said, jumping at the chance of a few minutes alone with Joss and Beth.

'You're a glutton for punishment, that's all I can say.' Phoebe picked up the tray and Eloise ran to open the door for her.

Having had time to play with her children, and having taken care to include the other toddlers in their game, Eloise wiped their sticky hands and faces and began changing the infants into their nightgowns. She was just laying Beth in her cot when the door opened and Miss Marchant strode into the room. 'So, you're here, Monk. I was told that you would be.'

Eloise straightened up. 'It's my afternoon off, Matron. I was helping Phoebe.'

'You were seen in the gardens earlier. I saw

you talking with Mr Caine and you brought little Maria into the hospital without my permission.'

'I – I'm sorry, Matron. Mr Caine agreed to it and I thought . . .'

'That's just it, Monk. You did not think at all. The reason we keep these new additions isolated here in the nursery is for the protection of all the children in the hospital. You might have exposed little Maria Caine to any one of a number of fatal childhood diseases.'

'But Mr Caine . . .'

Miss Marchant drew her neck back and her green eyes glittered with malice. 'You will not advance yourself by sucking up to Mr Caine. He might have singled you out for special notice, but don't think that makes you important in my eyes, Monk.'

'I have not gone out of my way to be noticed, Matron. If Mr Caine has shown me any kindness, it is just his way.'

'You presume to know your employer better than I do? You are impertinent, Monk. You put on airs above your station and I will not stand for it.'

'If the governor speaks to me I can hardly ignore him,' Eloise protested, stung by the unfairness of Miss Marchant's accusations. She had not gone out of her way to be noticed, and she had taken pity on Maria simply because she was a motherless child.

With an angry hiss, Miss Marchant raised her hand and struck Eloise on the face, causing her neck to snap backwards with the force of the blow. 'One more word out of you and you can pack your bags and leave this establishment. I won't have you speaking to me as if you were an equal, and I will not stand by and watch you making sheep's eyes at the governor.'

Joss had witnessed the slap, and that, together with the sound of raised voices, made him utter a loud howl of fright, and the rest of the children began to snivel in sympathy. Miss Marchant covered her ears with her hands and slammed out of the nursery. It took Eloise some time to calm them all and despite her sore face she managed to sing lullaby after lullaby until each one of them succumbed to sleep. It was dark outside and as she lit the night lights she wondered what had kept Phoebe so long, or perhaps she had simply taken the opportunity to finish early that evening, and who could blame her? With one last check on the sleeping infants, Eloise leaned over the cot rails to kiss Beth and Joss, and then she crept out of the nursery, closing the door softly behind her.

The corridor was unlit and the long shadows seemed to shift about, creating eerie pools of darkness as Eloise made her way towards the staircase. A door that had not been secured properly swung on its hinges in the draught and the sound of it closing made her jump. She was not normally nervous of the dark, or of walking the deserted corridors alone at night, and she could only think that Miss Marchant's tirade and physical assault must have upset her more than she had thought possible. It might have been some primitive instinct that warned her of danger or perhaps a slight movement in the shadows, but as Eloise was about to pass the sluice, she realised too late that someone was lurking in the doorway. A figure leapt out at her, grabbing her by the arms and pinning them behind her back with a triumphant cackle of laughter. Eloise could smell the sour stench of a woman's unwashed body and she fought to free herself, but her attacker had the advantage over her, and no matter how hard she struggled Eloise could not prevent herself from being dragged bodily into the sluice. 'Who are you?' she gasped, wincing with pain as the pressure on her arms increased. 'Let me go.'

'We got our orders and it'll be a pleasure to take you down a peg or two, missis. I got her, Maud. Come and do your stuff.'

Eloise recognised the voice – it was Flo, one of the charwomen who had taken against her from the start. 'I don't understand. Why are you doing this to me?'

'Shut up, you.' Maud emerged from the back of the room brandishing a pair of scissors. The silver blades flashed in a shaft of moonlight as she advanced on Eloise, eyeing her with contempt. 'You took work from us, you stuck-up bitch, and you've upset the matron good and proper this time.'

'Get on with it, Maudie. She's kicking me shins to bits.'

'Hold her tight, Flo. Let's see if the governor fancies her without them long tresses she's so proud of. Don't struggle, missis, or you'll be saying hello to the sharp points of these here scissors, and it would be a shame to spoil that pretty face with an ugly scar.'

Chapter Eighteen

Eloise lashed out with her feet but Flo was surprisingly strong, and with each movement she tightened her grip, twisting Eloise's arms until she felt that her bones would snap. Maud reached out to grab a lock of her hair but as Eloise jerked her head sideways in an attempt to avoid the snapping blades, one of them gashed her cheek and she yelped with pain.

'You bloody fool, Monk,' Maud shouted. 'That was your fault. Keep still or I'll lop your ear off this time.'

More furious than frightened, Eloise dug her heels into the ground and with a mighty effort she pushed backwards, catching Flo off guard so that she stumbled against the door with a resounding thud. Momentarily shocked by the force of colliding with solid wood, Flo loosened her grip and Eloise pulled free. She clapped her hand to her cheek and felt warm, sticky blood trickling through her fingers. She was desperate to escape from the sluice, but Flo was barring her way and Maud was preparing for another strike. Just when it seemed that there was no way out, someone rattled the doorknob. 'What's going on in there?'

'Phoebe!' Eloise recognised her voice with a sob of relief. 'Help me.'

'Let me in,' Phoebe cried, pounding on the door. 'Open up or I'll fetch Matron.'

Flo shuffled away from the door, muttering beneath her breath, and Phoebe burst into the room. She stopped, staring aghast at Eloise. 'What the bleeding hell has been going on in here?'

'Mind your own business,' Maud said, pushing past her. 'Get out of me way or I'll spoil your face too.'

'You did this to her, you vicious bitch. I know where you live, Maud Riley, and you too, Flo Brown. Lay a finger on me and me dad will be round your place with his fists flying.'

'Keep out of this, Phoebe. It ain't got nothing to do with you. No need to say nothing of this to no one.' With a menacing scowl, Flo squeezed out through the door, leaving Maud to face a furious Phoebe on her own.

'I'll report you to Matron for this,' Phoebe said, advancing on Maud with her hands fisted.

Maud backed towards the doorway. 'It was Matron who told us to teach the silly cow a lesson,' she snarled. 'Anyway, it was Monk's fault. All I meant to do was snip a bit off her hair.'

'It's all right, Phoebe. Let her go.' Eloise leaned

against the sink as a wave of dizziness threatened to take her feet from under her.

Phoebe gave Maud a shove that sent her tottering into the corridor. 'Get out. And you'd best leave Ellen alone in the future, or you'll have me to deal with, and all me brothers too.'

Closing the door and shutting out the sound of Maud and Flo muttering to each other, Phoebe pulled up a chair. 'Here, sit down before you fall down and let me look at that cut.' Eloise sank down onto the hard wooden seat and reluctantly took her hand away from the wound, allowing Phoebe to examine her cheek in the light of a single candle. 'It's just a nick, luckily for you, but it's bleeding a lot. I should send for a proper nurse to see to it for you, Ellen.'

'No, no, it will be all right. Can you just clean it up for me?'

'I'll do me best, but I ain't no Florence Nightingale.'

Word of the assault spread rapidly round the hospital and by morning it seemed to Eloise that everyone knew what had happened in the sluice. People were sympathetic but wary. It also appeared that Matron's part in the affair was either known or suspected and she was not the sort of person who took kindly to gossip, especially when she herself was involved. Eloise tried to pass the incident off lightly but a swollen cheek and an angry-looking gash were impossible to hide. She kept out of the way as much as possible, spending the morning cleaning the privies in the back yard and emptying night soil from the chamber pots, which she then took to the sluice on the ground floor to be washed. She was in the middle of doing this when Matron entered the room with a forbidding look on her gaunt features. 'I hear that you had a slight accident last evening, Monk.'

'Yes, Matron.'

'You should be more careful in future.'

'Yes, Matron.'

Miss Marchant's lips curled in a spiteful smile. 'You will have a scar which will mar your good looks.'

'Yes, Matron.'

Having failed to induce a reaction from Eloise, Miss Marchant tossed her head impatiently. 'You will spend the rest of the day in the nursery. We don't want any idle talk in the hospital, and you will tell your friend Phoebe that if her silly tongue runs away with her she will find herself dismissed without a character. Do you understand me, Monk?'

Eloise bit back a sharp retort. 'Yes, Matron.'

'Then finish up here and go directly to the nursery. You will work there and take your meals in the nursery until your face heals. I do not want you flaunting yourself around the hospital. Do I make myself absolutely clear?'

'Yes, Matron.'

'Good.' Miss Marchant whisked out of the room, slamming the door behind her as if to prove a point.

So, she doesn't want the governor to know her part in the business, Eloise thought grimly. Matron need not have worried. Barton Caine was the last person that Eloise wanted to see with her face disfigured by an ugly red gash. Not that she cared if her looks were spoiled; that would be pure vanity, and Papa had included that in his sermons, merging it with pride as being one of the seven deadly sins. Eloise peered into the small mirror that the nurses kept on a shelf so that they could make certain their caps were on straight and there were no smudges of dirt on their noses. The light in the sluice was not good, but she was relieved to see that the livid streak of congealed blood was less than an inch in length and it was on the side of her face. If she kept her head turned a certain way, no one would even know that she had received such an injury. She set about washing the rest of the utensils before making her way to the nursery.

Phoebe greeted her with a hug. 'You poor thing. Just look at your face.'

'That doesn't fill me with confidence, Phoebe,' Eloise said, with a gurgle of laughter. 'Anyway, one good thing has come of it – Matron insists that I work in here until my face heals, which couldn't please me more.'

'Well, I wouldn't find it a laughing matter, I can tell you that for nothing. I'd want them two harpies sacked on the spot.'

'They won't dare to touch me again, and I think Miss Marchant has had a bit of a fright too. She wasn't expecting it to go so far, or to get round the hospital so quickly. I think she would be in trouble if her part in it was discovered.'

'I've a good mind to tell Mr Caine, just to spite the old cow.'

'No, Phoebe, please don't. There's been enough trouble. I just want to forget it ever happened.' Eloise went over to Beth, who was holding her arms out and calling for her mama. Joss looked up from the floor where he was playing with some wooden bricks, and she thought she saw a glimmer of recognition in his blue eyes, but his dogged refusal to speak was still a constant worry. She picked Beth up in her arms and she knelt down beside Joss, passing him a brick that was just beyond his reach.

'That Beth really thinks you are her mum,' Phoebe observed. 'It's a pity that the boy isn't as bright as his sister. He's a simpleton, if you ask me.'

'That he is not,' Eloise said hotly. 'He spoke to me, if you recall. He told me his name and his sister's name. I'm sure he'll find his tongue one of these days.'

'Well, I hope you're right for his sake, or he'll end up in a school for imbecile children.' Phoebe turned away to pick up a toddler who had fallen over and was crying.

Eloise felt her blood curdle at the prospect of Joss's being taken away to a special school. This was a possibility that had not occurred to her before Phoebe pointed it out, but now she saw that it might just happen and she was frightened. It would be better to give Joss to the Cribbs than have him suffer that appalling fate. She ruffled his golden curls and Joss looked up with a seraphic smile, but his blue eyes clouded with sympathy when he saw the wound on her cheek. He touched it gently with the tip of his forefinger and, for a moment, Eloise thought his lips formed the word Mama, but she could not be certain. Almost instantly, he turned away to play with the bricks and Beth struggled free from her mother's arms to join in the game. Eloise swallowed hard as a lump in her throat threatened to engulf her in tears. Beth was too young to understand everything that was going on around her, but Joss had chosen this silent world as the only way in which he could protest at being separated from her. His suffering only made her all the more determined to find a way out of their present situation. One day they would have a home of their own again and Joss would find his voice.

The morning passed quickly, almost too quickly as far as Eloise was concerned. It was ironic that in instigating the attack on her, Matron had actually done her a favour. It was worth a cut on the cheek if it meant that Eloise could spend all day with her children, and Phoebe was delighted to have an extra pair of hands to help her cope with her charges. In the middle of the afternoon, when the babies and toddlers were having their nap, Phoebe had gone off to the kitchens to get a cup of tea and Eloise was left in sole charge of the nursery. She was busy tidying up the wooden bricks that had been left scattered on the floor when the door opened and Maria Caine skipped into the room followed by a sour-faced Miss Trinder.

'I've come to play with the babies again,' Maria announced with a bright smile. 'May I wake them up, Ellen?'

Eloise laid her finger to her lips, shaking her head. 'Not yet, Maria, but you can help me pick up all these bricks.'

'She is to stay here for the rest of the afternoon,' Miss Trinder said icily. 'And good luck to you, I say. That little madam has made my life a misery since the first day, and I am glad to be going.'

'You're leaving?'

Miss Trinder's eyes narrowed as she glared at

Maria, who was unconcernedly scrambling about the floor picking up bricks. 'I am leaving this wretched place as soon as I have packed my portmanteau and I shall be on the next train for Chelmsford, where my family reside. I thought I would enjoy working in London, but I was horribly mistaken and I will seek another position in the country where, hopefully, I will find a better child to instruct. Good day to you, Miss Monk. And good luck.' Without waiting for a response, Miss Trinder whisked out of the nursery, leaving a trail of cheap cologne in her wake.

'She's gone,' Maria said, grinning. 'I'm glad.'

'What happened?' Eloise knelt on the floor beside Maria as she laid the bricks neatly in a wooden box. 'What did you do to poor Miss Trinder?'

'Nothing. I promise you.' A roguish smile dimpled Maria's round cheeks and her blue eyes twinkled with mischief.

Eloise couldn't resist giving her a hug, although she didn't believe the innocent act for a moment. 'I think you are a very bad girl, Maria.'

'I'll be good for you, Ellen.' Maria leapt to her feet in a flurry of lace-trimmed petticoats. 'Now may I wake up Joss and play with him?'

It was early evening when Caine came to the nursery to collect Maria. The babies had all been fed and laid down to sleep, including Beth who had been playing with Maria all afternoon and had gone down without a murmur. Maria was helping Eloise to wash the hands and faces of the toddlers before their bedtime and Phoebe was attempting to settle a particularly fractious child who objected to being put to bed.

'I was unavoidably delayed,' Caine said brusquely. 'I hope Maria has behaved herself, Miss Monk.'

'Perfectly, sir.' Eloise put Joss in his cot, taking care to keep her face averted so that Caine could not see her injury. Joss lay silently staring up at her. Without thinking, Eloise leaned over the cot rail to kiss him goodnight and he stroked her cheek with an oddly adult expression in his eyes. She straightened up quickly, fearing that she had betrayed herself, but Caine seemed to be pre-occupied with his daughter, who skipped across the floor to hold his hand.

'I have been a great help, Papa. Now Miss Trinder has gone I can come again tomorrow and the day after that.'

Eloise stole a sideway glance at Caine and was surprised to see a smile transforming his features, but he was looking in her direction and not at his daughter. 'I think that Miss Monk and Phoebe have enough to do without looking after you, Maria.'

Phoebe looked up with an anxious frown. 'I would find it difficult, sir.'

'Ellen will look after me,' Maria said confidently.

'Miss Monk has other work to do.'

Eloise heard the constrained note in Caine's voice, but she said nothing. It was better if he remained in ignorance of her clash with Matron.

'Ellen has to stay here until her face gets better,' Maria said, running over to Eloise and tugging at her skirt. 'Tell Papa, Ellen. Tell him that you have to stay here because they cut your face with a pair of scissors.'

'Hush, Maria. You don't know what you're saying.' Eloise covered Joss with a blanket and she moved away from the cot so that her face was in shadow.

'What's this?' Caine's voice was harsh as he moved towards her, taking the oil lamp from the table and holding it high above her head. 'Look at me, Ellen.'

It was the first time he had ever called her by that name and she raised her head to meet his piercing gaze. 'Maria is mistaken, sir. I – I had a slight accident.'

'With a pair of scissors.' Phoebe crossed the floor to stand by Eloise. 'Tell him, Ellen. If you don't then I will.'

Caine stared at the livid gash on Eloise's cheek and his eyes glittered angrily. 'Who did this to you? Tell me.'

'It was Matron's fault,' Maria interrupted

gleefully. 'I heard Miss Trinder talking to Cook about it. She said that Matron put them up to it because she was jealous of . . .' Maria stopped, clapping her hand to her mouth as she realised that she had gone too far. 'Really, Papa. I did hear her say it. I'm not making it up.'

'My God!' Caine gazed at his daughter in dismay. 'You've been spending too much time listening to servants' gossip, Maria. I should have dismissed Trinder months ago, but she's the only one who's stayed for more than a fortnight. Go and sit quietly by the fire with Phoebe. I want to speak privately to Miss Monk.'

'You called her Ellen just now, Papa.'

One look at Caine's thunderous expression and Phoebe lifted Maria bodily and set her down in a chair by the fire. 'You sit there and mind your manners, miss.'

Maria opened her mouth as if to argue and then shut it again, eyeing Phoebe with new respect.

Caine drew Eloise aside. 'Now tell me exactly what has been going on. Who attacked you and why?'

'I believe it was meant to be a joke, sir,' Eloise improvised. 'The women meant to cut my hair but the scissors slipped.'

'The scissors slipped!' Caine repeated. 'You don't expect me to believe that, do you?'

'It was an accident, sir. I have nothing more to say.'

'You may not, but I have. I won't allow this sort of savage bullying. It must be stopped and I will speak to Miss Marchant right away.' He made as if to leave the room but Eloise ran after him and caught hold of his sleeve.

'Please don't, Mr Caine. Please let the matter drop.'

Caine hesitated, staring at the wound on her face with anger in his eyes. 'This is a serious matter. I cannot allow it to go unpunished.'

'It was my fault, sir. I managed to upset them somehow, and they meant no harm. It really was an accident.'

'So you keep saying, but it would not be the first time you have told me an untruth, Ellen. I will get to the bottom of this, that much I promise you.' Caine turned away from her to summon Maria. 'It's time you were in bed, young lady.'

Maria slithered off the chair and ran to him. 'But I may come again tomorrow, mayn't I, Papa?'

'We'll see.'

That night, Eloise hardly slept. She knew that if Caine challenged Miss Marchant there would be repercussions that might make it impossible for her to stay on at the Foundling Hospital. She would be forced to leave without Joss and Beth, or else she would have to claim them as her own children and face a life on the streets or worse.

436

Her options were strictly limited. If she admitted defeat and handed them over to the Cribbs, she might never see them again, and it was no use writing to Papa and begging him for help. He had been adamant that it was Ronnie's parents who ought to take responsibility for the welfare of their grandchildren, and he was so intent on following his vocation that nothing would dissuade him from the course that he had chosen. It was a bitter pill to swallow, but he may have been right in saying that she would never be able to support her own children and that their best interests would be served by being sent up to Yorkshire, but Eloise was not prepared to give in just yet.

Next morning she awaited the inevitable summons from Matron, and was hardly surprised when it came. Facing Miss Marchant in her office, Eloise waited to hear the worst.

Miss Marchant sat behind her desk with her hands clasped tightly in front of her. Her eyes were agate chips set in a pale face, and her tone was icy. 'I warned you to keep silent about your accident.'

'I told no one, Matron.'

'And yet the whole hospital knew of it, and Mr Caine came to see me last night demanding to be told the facts.'

'I said nothing.'

'No, that at least is true. Mr Caine said that you

437

had stubbornly refused to give an explanation. If it were otherwise you would be leaving this institution right now. However, Mr Caine has once again saved you.'

'I don't understand, Matron.'

Miss Marchant leaned across the desk and her face contorted with spite. 'You have such an innocent face, Monk. But you don't fool me. I recognise you for a scheming little minx, even if you have managed to wheedle your way into Mr Caine's good books. We have discussed the matter and you are to be excused cleaning duties. In Miss Trinder's absence, Mr Caine has decided that Maria should take lessons in the schoolroom every morning. For some reason best known to himself, he has decided to entrust his daughter into your care in the afternoons.'

Eloise could hardly believe her ears. 'I am to look after Maria?'

'The child is spoilt beyond hope, but this is your last chance. Don't think you are getting off lightly, though. In the mornings you will help Phoebe in the nursery and you will do some night duties there also. You will earn your keep, Monk. Believe me, you will earn it.'

It was a reprieve that had come out of the blue, and Eloise could have cried with relief. The sudden change in her circumstances meant that not only were they secure for the foreseeable future, but she would be able to spend more time with her children. It seemed too good to be true.

That afternoon, when she had finished helping Phoebe feed the little ones, Eloise went across the yard to the governor's house. A young maid-servant showed her into the square, white-painted entrance hall, where a flight of stairs rose opposite the main entrance. The polished mahogany banisters glowed warmly red in the sunlight streaming through the fanlight above the front door, and the feeling of warmth was echoed in the rich red carpet on the floor and stairs. On either side of the hall there were two doors and the maid opened one, ushering Eloise into the drawing room where Maria was sitting at a pianoforte, idly prodding the keys. She jumped off the stool as Eloise entered the room. 'You've come. I was afraid you wouldn't.'

Eloise took off her bonnet and shawl. 'Of course I came. Your papa has asked me to look after you in the afternoons, after you have finished your lessons in the schoolroom.'

'You won't stay long,' Maria said, shaking her head. 'No one does. They say I am a spoilt brat and then they leave.'

Eloise smothered a chuckle, keeping her face straight with difficulty. 'Perhaps I have more staying power than the rest.'

'I don't know what that is,' Maria admitted. 'But I am wayward and my papa spoils me because he can't be bothered to say no. He is too busy to take much notice of me, and he misses my mama. That's her portrait over the fireplace. Everyone says that I look just like her, but it was my fault that she died.'

Shocked, Eloise could hardly believe what she was hearing. She glanced at the portrait of the lovely young woman who smiled down at them with self-assured charm, and she shook her head. 'That is just not true, Maria. You were not to blame for your mother's death. It was just one of those sad and unfortunate circumstances, but it was not your fault. As to your father being too busy to notice you, that may be true in part, but I know he loves you and he wants the best for you.'

'Oh, well, perhaps he does,' Maria said, shrugging her shoulders.

'Of course he does.'

'And he likes you too, Ellen.'

It was said artlessly enough, but Eloise felt the blood rush to her cheeks. 'I hope I won't disappoint him. You and I will work well together and that will make him happy.'

Maria angled her head. 'I don't like sewing and I hate practising scales. I get very cross when people make me do either hateful thing.'

'Then I suggest we do something else. Perhaps you would like to visit the British Museum?'

'Do you mean that we can go out for a walk?'

Eloise smiled. 'Of course.'

Maria grabbed her by the hand, dragging her towards the doorway. 'Come to my room and I'll show you where my clothes are kept. I have a new bonnet and a coat with a cape on it and a matching muff trimmed with fur.'

Eloise allowed herself to be led upstairs to the first floor landing. Maria scampered along ahead of her pointing to the doors as she ran past them. 'That is my papa's bedroom, and that is his study. My room overlooks the hospital gardens, which is where I first saw you. The servants have rooms up on the top floor. Miss Trinder's room is empty now. Perhaps you could have it and then you'd be here all the time. I shall ask Papa when he comes home this evening.'

'No, that won't be necessary,' Eloise said hastily. 'I have to do night duty in the nursery, but it was a kind thought, Maria.'

'Well, I might need you in the night,' Maria said, pouting and stamping her foot. 'I have bad dreams sometimes and I wake up crying. I want you to live here with us.'

'I shan't stay at all if you behave like this.'

Maria blinked and stared at Eloise. It was quite obvious that she was unused to being challenged, and Eloise met her angry gaze without flinching.

'You won't leave me?' Maria's voice quavered and her lips trembled.

'Not if you behave like the nice little girl that I know you to be.'

'I will try to be good, but it's not easy.'

'No, but I'm sure you can do it if you try.' Eloise smiled sympathetically. There was something about Maria that touched her to the core, putting her in mind of herself when she had been of a similar age. What a difficult and wayward child she must have been to have earned the severe reprimands that she had received from her father. Mama had been so patient and understanding, but Papa had always been quick to point out her failings, and Eloise had spent many hours locked in her bedroom where she was supposed to contemplate her sins. She smiled as Maria put on her new hat and admired her reflection in the mirror. 'That looks delightful. If you find that smart coat you were telling me about, we'll go to the museum.'

After an uneventful afternoon, when Maria was quite obviously on her best behaviour and out to impress Eloise, they arrived back at the governor's house in time for tea. Jessie, the maidservant, had set the meal out in the morning parlour and Maria sat demurely eating bread and butter, while she kept an eye on the plate of small fancy cakes which Mrs Dean had baked. She stuffed the last morsel of bread into her mouth and her small hand shot out for the cakes; then she hesitated. 'I've eaten my bread and butter, Ellen. Now may I have a cake?'

Eloise nodded her assent.

'And you will tell Papa that I have been a very good girl?'

'Of course.'

'I believe I heard the front door open,' Maria cried, dropping the cake on her plate. 'You can tell him now, Ellen.' Without waiting for permission to leave the table, she jumped up and ran to the door. 'Papa, come here.'

Caine strode into the room, but as Eloise made to rise to her feet he motioned her to sit down. 'Don't get up.' He lifted Maria off the ground, kissed her on the forehead and then set her back on her feet. 'Go and ask Mrs Dean to send in a fresh pot of tea and another cup for me, please, Maria.'

'Why not ring the bell for Jessie, Papa?' Maria demanded with an impudent smile.

He gave her a gentle push towards the door. 'Because I want a few words with Miss Monk in private. Now do as you're told, poppet.'

Maria flounced out of the room and Caine took a seat opposite Eloise. She caught her breath, wondering what he could have to say that could not be said in front of his daughter. Perhaps Miss Marchant had been causing mischief again?

'Don't look so alarmed, Ellen. I just wanted to know how you got on with Maria this afternoon.'

Eloise breathed a sigh of relief, and she smiled. 'Perfectly well, sir. She was on her best behaviour.'

'Jessie tells me that you took her to the museum.'

'Yes, sir.'

He said nothing for a moment and then he rose from his seat and walked over to the fireplace, resting one hand on the mantelshelf and staring down into the flames. 'Ellen, you are something of a mystery. I know almost nothing of your background.'

'There is not much to tell, sir.'

He turned his head to give her a piercing look. 'If I am to entrust my daughter to your care, I must know a little more about you. For instance, it bothers me that an educated young woman like yourself should be in such a dire situation that she is prepared to undertake almost any kind of work merely to put a roof over her head.'

'Circumstances change, sir.'

'Damn it, woman. Will you never give me a straight answer?'

Eloise rose to her feet, facing him angrily. 'I don't think my personal life is any of your concern, sir. As long as I do my work well and my behaviour does not give rise to concern, then quite frankly I don't see that my past has anything to do with you.'

'It has everything to do with me if I am to pay your wages. I might even be giving shelter to a felon.'

'I've done nothing wrong. Now, if you don't

444

mind, it's time for me to return to the nursery or I will be in trouble with Matron.' She turned to leave the parlour, but Caine caught her by the wrist.

'You have fobbed me off with half-truths for long enough. Who are you really, Ellen Monk? Is that your real name, or is that a lie too?'

Eloise stared down at his fingers banding her wrist in a grip of steel and she felt her anger replaced by a mixture of conflicting emotions. She raised her eyes to his face and the expression in his eyes compelled her to tell him the truth, in part at least. 'I am a seafarer's widow, Mr Caine. My husband was lost at sea and I have no alternative but to earn my own living.'

'Have you no family or friends to whom you could turn?'

'No, sir.'

'I'm truly sorry to hear it, but why couldn't you tell me that in the first place? What else are you hiding? You can trust me, Ellen. I might even be able to help you.'

Eloise turned her head away. The desire to confide in him was almost overwhelming, but she simply dared not put her trust in this man. She had a sneaking suspicion that once he knew the true facts he might agree with her father, and in common with most men in a position of authority, he would be convinced that his opinion was the right one. She could not take the risk that he might think that Joss would benefit from the kind of upbringing that the Cribbs could give him. What did a mere man know about a mother's love for her children? Caine might have doted on his beautiful young wife, and have a deep affection for his only child, but he would always follow his head and not his heart.

Eloise met his searching gaze with a stubborn stare. 'Absolutely nothing, Mr Caine. I am not hiding anything.'

He released her wrist as if the touch of her flesh had burnt his fingers. 'I don't believe you, Ellen.'

'I'm sorry, sir.'

'I am sorry too. Trust is the most important factor in any relationship, whether it is personal or professional. If you can't trust me enough to tell me the truth about yourself, I'm afraid I can't continue to employ you in this institution where there are vulnerable young children, to say nothing of my own daughter.'

'I have nothing more to say, sir.'

'Then I have no alternative other than to terminate your employment. You will leave here first thing in the morning.'

Chapter Nineteen

Eloise rubbed her wrist as if trying to smooth away the imprint of his fingers, but the warmth of his touch still lingered on her flesh, and it was oddly disturbing. She stared at him dazedly for a moment, as the full impact of his words hit her with a physical force taking the breath from her lungs. Despite his angry stance, there was a puzzled look in his eyes and a flicker of something that she could not quite understand. It felt as though he was silently urging her to confess everything, but she could not. She dared not. She turned away and walked slowly towards the door. Each step was difficult, like wading knee-deep in water. Tomorrow morning she would have to leave the security of the Foundling Hospital, and no matter what, she would be taking Joss and Beth with her. But, as she realised with a deep sense of foreboding, it was not just the possibility of being homeless again that was distressing her. She had lost the good opinion of the man who had come to her aid when all had seemed lost, and whose approbation meant more than almost anything to her.

'Ellen. Wait.' Caine moved swiftly to her side. 'I spoke in anger and that was wrong of me. I don't pretend to understand why you have built this barrier around yourself, but I must respect your right to privacy.'

She hesitated, not trusting herself to speak.

'I want you to stay. I need you to stay. You have established a rapport with Maria where others have failed miserably. You work hard and whatever your reasons for keeping silent, I have no right to pry into your personal affairs.'

'I must get back to the nursery, sir.' Eloise went to pass him, but he barred her way. Reluctantly she raised her head to look him in the eyes. 'I have my reasons for keeping silent, but I promise you that no harm will come to any of the children in my care, least of all Maria.'

He opened his mouth to reply but a loud clattering outside the door made them both jump, effectively putting an end to the conversation as Maria clamoured to be admitted. Caine reached past Eloise to open the door and she was acutely aware of the heat emanating from his body and the scent of him filled her nostrils: cinnamon, cloves and sandalwood mixed with the heady aroma of a young and virile man. She was dizzy from the intoxicating smell and it stirred old longings that she thought were buried in the past.

Apparently oblivious to the confusion he had

caused, Caine moved forward to take the tea tray from Maria. 'Well done, Maria, but you should have asked Jessie to carry it for you.'

'I knew I could do it, Papa. I wanted to show you that I could.' Maria danced into the room, glancing up at Eloise with a knowing look. 'What's the matter, Ellen? Has my papa been nasty to you?'

Eloise forced her dry lips into a smile. 'No, certainly not. Mr Caine has been most kind and understanding. Now I really must go.'

'You must stay and take tea with Papa,' Maria ordered. 'I say so.'

Caine set the tray on the table and his harsh expression melted into a smile that went straight to Eloise's heart. 'Won't you stay and have a cup of tea, Ellen? I'm sure Phoebe can manage on her own for a little longer.'

The clock on the mantelshelf struck six, bringing Eloise back to the present with a start. Phoebe would be putting the babies down to sleep and Eloise could not bear the thought of Beth lying in her cot without her mother to give her a goodnight kiss. She shook her head. 'I wish I could stay for tea, but I can't let Phoebe down. I will be here again tomorrow afternoon, Maria. That's a promise.'

Later that evening, when Eloise had climbed the last flight of stairs to the top floor of the hospital, she was bone weary and mentally exhausted. As she opened the door to the room she shared with Tibbie and Becky, a cloud of tobacco smoke caught her in the back of her throat causing her to cough. They were wearing their nightgowns and sitting cross-legged on their narrow beds, smoking hand-rolled cigarettes.

'Shut the door,' Becky cried, exhaling a cloud of blue smoke into the rafters. 'Matron will kill us if she finds out we're smoking.'

Tibbie held out a tobacco tin. 'Want to make one, Ellen? You look as though you could do with a smoke. It clears your head and it don't stain like snuff.'

'No, thank you,' Eloise went to sit on her bed and began unbuttoning her boots. 'I'm really tired and all I want is to sleep.'

'So how did you get on with the guv?' Tibbie demanded.

'I hardly saw him. I was with Maria all afternoon. We went to the British Museum.'

'Hmm. It's all right for some.' Becky flicked ash from her cigarette into the chamber pot. 'But you must have seen Mr Caine. He's got his eye on you, girl. Play your cards right and you could end up sitting pretty.'

'Lying flat on her back pretty, you mean,' Tibbie added, chuckling.

Eloise turned her head away to hide her blushes. 'I don't know what you're talking about.'

'Aw, come on, ducks,' Becky said, reaching across the narrow gap between the beds to nudge Eloise in the ribs. 'Why else would the guv pick you out above all the rest of us, if he didn't fancy you something rotten? The poor bloke's been on his own for six years and he's only human, or so I hear tell.' She dissolved in a fit of the giggles.

Tibbie ground out the remains of her cigarette in the tobacco-tin lid. 'Don't take no notice of her, Ellen. She's a vulgar cow. But she's got a point, ducks. Our Mr Caine has been a widower for a long time and so far as we know, and there ain't much that goes unnoticed round here, he's not had a lady friend since his wife died.'

'Well, I wouldn't kick him out of me bed,' Becky said, sliding beneath the covers and folding her arms behind her head. 'He's a good-looking bloke and he can't be a day older than thirty. Next thing you know, Ellen, he'll have you moving into the spare room in his house. Then he'll be paying you a visit in the middle of the night. Lucky cow.'

'Shut up and go to sleep, Becky.' Tibbie leaned over the side of her bed to blow out the candle. 'If he offers, you take it, Ellen. Girls like us don't get chances like that every day of the week.'

'Nor once a year in your case,' Becky sniggered.

Tibbie tossed a shoe at her, but it missed its

target and hit the wall. On the other side some-one thumped the thin partition with a few choice expletives, and then there was silence.

Eloise lay on her back, staring into the dark-ness and listening to the gradual onset of slow breathing as Tibbie and Becky drifted off to sleep. Their ribald remarks had disturbed her almost as much as the realisation that she was deeply attracted to her employer. Her initial dislike of him had changed so subtly that she had not even noticed the warning signs. She might find him aloof and autocratic, but she had also seen a hint of tenderness and humour lurking beneath the frosty façade. He was undoubtedly a complicated man, but she had also sensed a loneliness of spirit in him that was so akin to her own that it was frightening. The physical attraction must have been there all along, but she had been in denial. She had thought that Ronnie was the love of her life and that she could never feel the same way about another man. Hadn't she said as much to Reggie when she spurned his offer of marriage? She had believed it then, but she knew now that it was untrue. Barton Caine had stirred up emotions and longings that she had thought were a thing of the past, and that made him a dangerous person to be near. He had shown her a degree of partiality, but that did not mean that he harboured tender feelings for her. Perhaps what the girls said was nearer the mark.

Caine was a man who had lost the wife he adored six years ago, and he was either looking for a surrogate mother for Maria, or a willing woman who would warm his bed and expect nothing in return. She, Eloise Monkham-Cribb, was neither of those things and her first priority was, and always would be, her children. Her heart and mind might cry out for love and the companionship of a man, but she was also painfully aware that she had a duty to her parents. Mama would probably understand, but her father would never speak to her again if she lived with Caine as his mistress. When they returned to England she wanted to meet both her parents with her head held high and her reputation intact.

The next day, after her work in the nursery was done, Eloise waited until Phoebe's back was turned before she gave Joss and Beth a last cuddle and a whispered promise that she would return later that day. Despite his continued silence, she knew that Joss understood what she was saying and she kissed him on the tip of his button nose, just as she had always done, and was rewarded by a sunny smile. 'Be a good boy, sweetheart, and look after Beth while Mama is away.' She thought that Joss nodded but Phoebe had turned to ask her a question and Eloise moved hastily away from their cots.

Having assured Phoebe that she would be back

in time to help settle the babies for the night, Eloise put on her bonnet and shawl ready for the short walk to the governor's house. A calm September had given way to a cool and blustery October, and the wind whipped strands of hair from beneath the brim of her bonnet. She could feel her cheeks glowing with colour as she rapped on the door knocker and waited for someone to answer her summons. When the door opened it was Caine himself who greeted her. It was just a coincidence, of course, but it almost seemed as though he had been awaiting her arrival. He thrust a single red rose into her hand. 'A peace offering, Ellen. I was too harsh with you yesterday, and I remembered how you love roses.'

It might have been a theatrical gesture, but his embarrassed and almost shy smile made him look ridiculously young and quite unlike the austere, self-contained man whom she had first met. Eloise felt the blood rush to her cheeks and she bent her head to sniff the fragrance, but the perfect flower was unscented. 'Thank you, sir,' she murmured. 'It was kind of you.'

'It was nothing. I had business near Covent Garden and I saw these in the market.' He stood aside to allow her to pass. 'I'm afraid that hot-house blooms have no scent. They are beautiful but they haven't the honesty and fragrance of a garden flower.' His tone was dismissive as he led the way to the drawing room, holding the door open for her. 'They have that in common with some people.'

There was a bitter note in his voice and as Eloise followed his gaze she realised with a sense of shock that he was staring at the portrait of his late wife. 'She was a beautiful woman, sir. You must miss her terribly.'

He turned his head to give her a piercing look. 'Do you still mourn for your husband, Ellen?'

'He has been dead less than a year, but I try to remember the happy times we shared.'

'That sounds as though you have unhappy memories also.'

'Nothing is perfect,' Eloise said, gazing down at the rose. 'Even this flower. It is so beautiful but it has no fragrance.'

'No, and that makes it a false bloom to my way of thinking. I cannot stand subterfuge, Ellen. Lies and duplicity kill affection and destroy relationships.' His voice cracked with emotion, but as if he realised that he had revealed too much of his innermost self, he made a valiant attempt at a smile. 'Next summer I will see that the house is filled with honest to goodness garden roses.'

'I hope I will be here to enjoy them, sir.'

'Don't worry on that score, Ellen. Now that Maria and I have found you, we will do our best to make you stay.'

Although his smile was warm, Eloise felt as

though a chill breeze had swept through the room. His apparent kindness and concern for her were, as she had feared, just a ploy to persuade her to stay on and look after his child. For a moment, when he had given her the rose, it had seemed that they were about to enter into a more personal relationship. Now they were back on master and servant terms and she had to struggle to hide her disappointment. 'I will do my best for Maria, sir.'

'Yes, I know that,' Caine said abruptly. 'I'll tell Jessie to send Maria to you, but I have a meeting to attend and I must leave now.' He left the room without a backward glance.

Eloise looked up at the portrait on the wall and a shiver ran down her spine. There was a touch of self-assurance in Rosamund Caine's expression and a hint of mockery in her lovely smile, as if she were daring Eloise to vie for her husband's affections. It felt as though Caine's dead wife was speaking to her from the grave and issuing a challenge. 'You don't have to worry,' Eloise murmured. 'I know I cannot compete with you.'

'Who are you talking to, Ellen?'

Maria's childish voice made Eloise spin round. She had not realised that she had spoken her thoughts out loud. She covered her confusion by changing the subject. 'Why, Maria, that is a really pretty bonnet. Is it new?'

Maria did a twirl, holding out the full skirt of

her scarlet merino coat and tilting her head at an angle. 'Yes, it is. Papa bought it for me this morning. We went in a hansom cab all the way to Oxford Street to a new emporium; I think it was called D. H. Evans, or something. Anyway, it is very grand and he should really take you there and buy you some new clothes, for yours are horribly shabby, if you don't mind my saying so.'

Eloise let this pass. She glanced ruefully down at her drab serge skirt and the frayed cuffs of her white cotton blouse. It was true, of course, she did look like a drudge, and in truth that was what she had become. No wonder Barton Caine had barely given her a second glance. Compared to Rosamund in her blue silk gown trimmed lavishly with Brussels lace, Ellen Monk must appear like a scarecrow. She stifled a sigh. 'You look extremely fine, Maria. Where would you like to go this afternoon? That is if you don't mind being seen out with this shabby person.'

Maria chuckled responsively and her dimples deepened. 'I don't care how you look, Ellen. You have a lovely face in spite of the scar, and you are kind. I shall tell Papa to buy you some new clothes. He always does what I ask.'

'It's not the same for me, Maria. I am just an employee. Please don't say any such thing to your father.'

'All right,' Maria said grudgingly. 'Can we go back to the museum?'

'Of course we can. What did you enjoy most yesterday?'

'Being seen by lots of people, and today they will have a chance to admire my new clothes.'

It was not the best reason Eloise had ever heard for visiting a place which housed the most precious artefacts and classical statues in the land, but she had to give credit to Maria for being honest. They spent an agreeable couple of hours in the museum, and when they returned home Eloise read to Maria until it was time for tea. It was Mrs Dean who bustled into the morning parlour with the heavily laden tray and Eloise jumped to her feet to help her.

'Thank you, Miss Monk,' Mrs Dean said, placing the tray on the table and straightening up with a grunt of pain. 'My rheumatics are playing me up today. It's a sure sign that winter is on its way. We'll have rain before the night is out.'

'Mrs Dean is a martyr to her rheumatics,' Maria said, seizing an iced fairy cake and popping it into her mouth.

'You should eat your bread and butter first, miss,' Mrs Dean said severely. 'She's wayward, Miss Monk, just like Miss Rosamund was at that age.'

With a warning frown, Eloise offered Maria the bread and butter plate, and waited until she took a slice. 'Remember your manners, Maria.'

'Yes, remember your manners, miss,' Mrs Dean

echoed, showing no signs of wanting to leave the room. 'I was with Miss Rosamund's family since she was a baby and I watched her grow up. I was a kitchen maid at the big house to begin with, then I worked my way up to be cook.'

'My mama lived in a mansion,' Maria said proudly. 'They had lots of servants and my grandpapa was very rich.'

Mrs Dean nodded her head. 'Made his money in the West Indies. Sugar and slaves, you know the sort of thing. Not that I would want to boast about such, but times change.'

'Yes, indeed. We have to thank Mr Wilberforce for his successful campaign against slavery,' Eloise murmured automatically, but she was puzzled. Rosamund Caine might have been an heiress, but, apart from the oil painting, which must have been done by a master, there was little evidence of wealth in Caine's establishment.

Mrs Dean folded her arms across her bosom with a judgemental scowl. 'I don't hold with money gained from the suffering of others, and they say that hens come home to roost. They certainly did in that family.' She lowered her voice. 'Lost the lot he did. Miss Rosamund's father, I'm talking about. Gambled it all away and fled the country leaving behind all manner of debts. His wife died of a fever, although in my opinion it was a broken heart, and Miss Rosamund died giving birth to Maria.'

'How tragic,' Eloise said with feeling. 'She was so beautiful, and everyone in the hospital speaks so highly of her.'

'Oh, she was popular all right. Miss Rosamund could charm the birds out of the trees if she put her mind to it, but she had inherited the bad streak that ran through the family. Her brother killed a man in a duel and he had to flee for his life, and Miss Rosamund, well, I don't like to speak ill of the dead.'

'What does speak ill mean?' Maria demanded with her mouth full.

'Children should be seen and not heard,' Mrs Dean said severely. 'And don't speak with your mouth full. It's bad manners.' She turned to Eloise. 'You will need to be strict with that one, Miss Monk. She's just like her ma. In a few years' time she'll be a heart-breaker and probably just as flighty. Then the master will have to watch out. There'll be a string of young chaps knocking on the door. Just like the old days.'

Eloise grappled silently with this information. Her saintly image of Rosamund Caine was suddenly tarnished. Perhaps Caine's marriage had not been as blissfully happy as she had imagined. She knew it was unworthy of her but she couldn't help feeling relieved. 'Eat up, Maria,' she said cheerfully. 'Then you can have another cake.'

Eloise did not see Caine again that day. She returned to the nursery only to find it in chaos.

All the children were crying and Phoebe was vainly attempting to quieten Joss who was in the throes of a tantrum. Eloise rushed over to her and snatched Joss from her arms. 'What happened? Why is he in this state?'

'He bit William,' Phoebe cried angrily. 'And I slapped him, the little bugger. There weren't no cause for that sort of behaviour.' She stomped off to pick up William who was sitting on the floor, bawling. 'There, there, William. Did that nasty boy bite you?'

Eloise rocked Joss in her arms. 'I'm sure he didn't mean to hurt William. He must have done something to Joss to make him fight back.'

'I told you he's a wild one,' Phoebe said sulkily. 'I'm going to report him to Mr Caine and have him sent off to a school for imbecile children. There's no dealing with a nipper like him.'

'No,' Eloise shouted. 'That's not fair. There's nothing wrong with Joss.'

'What do you care?' Phoebe demanded crossly. 'He's just one of the many. There's dozens more to fill his place. We can't afford to have feelings for them.'

Joss began to quieten down a little but his whole body was racked with great, heaving sobs. 'Oh, my baby, I shouldn't have left you,' Eloise whispered into his damp hair. She reached out her hand to touch Beth who was clinging to the bars of her cot and whimpering. 'Don't cry, Beth, sweetheart.'

'Mama,' Beth sobbed. 'Mama.'

'Mama,' Joss echoed, twining his arms around his mother's neck. 'Mama.'

'Blimey! Did he just speak?' Phoebe set William down with a pat on his head, but as she came nearer to Joss he flapped his small hand at her.

'Go 'way!' he roared. 'Nasty lady.'

'Hush, Joss,' Eloise said, holding him tightly as if she was afraid that Phoebe might snatch him from her arms. 'It's all over now. Be a good boy.'

'He spoke,' Phoebe chortled. 'Well I'm blowed.' Then her smile faded and she stared suspiciously at Eloise. 'He called you his ma, as well as young Beth. Is there something you ain't telling me, Ellen? Are they your kids?'

Cold fingers of panic clutched at Eloise's stomach. She liked Phoebe well enough but she did not trust her to keep silent. She shook her head vehemently. 'No. As you say, they all want their mothers. Perhaps I remind them of theirs, I don't know.'

'You would tell me if you was, wouldn't you? I mean, we are friends and you wouldn't lie to me.'

'No, of course not.' Eloise rose hastily to her feet. 'We must get these children washed and changed into their nightshirts. I can finish up here if you like, Phoebe. Why don't you go to the kitchen and get yourself something to eat? I'm sure you could do with a cup of tea after all that commotion.'

'Well, if you insist, then I will. I've had enough of other people's kids today. But you watch out for that Joss. He might turn nasty again and bite you.' She ambled across the room, muttering to herself. 'I'd bite him back if the little devil attacked me. I certainly would.'

As the door closed on her, Eloise kissed Joss on the cheek. 'You know who I am, Joss, darling?'

He tugged at a lock of her hair that had escaped from the confines of the knot at the back of her head. 'Mama.'

Tears of joy ran down her cheeks, but her relief was tempered by fear. Now Joss had found his voice it would be even more difficult to keep their secret. Eloise made him ready for bed, and when she had settled all the infants in their cots she sang to them until the last one had fallen asleep.

She was too fraught to want food and so she skipped supper and went straight to her room, where she took her writing case from under the mattress and settled down to write a letter to her mother. Quite what had prompted her change of heart, she did not know. Perhaps it was in part due to what Barton Caine had said about the destructive power of lies, or perhaps it was simply that the time had come to tell her mother the truth about her situation. She knew that Mama would understand why she had run away from the Cribbs, and perhaps she would be able to persuade Papa that sending them to Yorkshire had been a mistake. She was not asking for help, as she knew that there was nothing that either of her parents could do from a distance of several thousand miles, but she just wanted everything to be out in the open. She laid out the facts simply and plainly, giving her present address and stating that she had been employed by Mr Barton Caine, the governor of the Foundling Hospital, to look after his little daughter, and that Joss and Beth were being cared for in the nursery. She omitted the fact that they had been admitted as foundlings; that was a piece of information best kept to herself for the present, but she assured Mama that they were all well and looking forward to the day when they were reunited. She signed the letter, blotted it and placed it in an envelope. Tomorrow she would take Maria for a walk to the post office in Holborn, and the letter would be sent on its long journey to Africa.

Next morning when Eloise went to the nursery Joss greeted her with shouts of glee, holding his arms out and calling to her from his cot.

'That boy is doolally tap,' Phoebe grumbled. 'He's been calling out for his ma ever since I come on duty. The night nurse said he was babbling on and on from first light. First he doesn't say a word and now we can't shut him up. Just look at him. He thinks you really are his mum.'

Eloise hurried over to Joss and lifted him from his cot. He clung to her, kissing her cheeks and smiling up into her face. 'Joss, my baby,' Eloise whispered and was rewarded by a beaming smile and more kisses.

'It's what I've said all along,' Phoebe muttered. 'He's not right in the head. Either that or you've been telling me a pack of lies.'

Eloise set Joss on the floor next to Beth. 'If they want to think of me as their mother, I don't mind. They're just babies, Phoebe, like all the rest of them in here.'

'Yes, but they don't think you're their ma, now do they?' Phoebe picked up William and put him in a high chair at the table. 'I'm going to the kitchen to see what's happened to breakfast. Anyway, I'm dying for a cup of tea.'

As Phoebe left the nursery, Eloise knelt down beside Joss and Beth. In a low voice she attempted to convince Joss that they were playing a game where she was called Ellen and not Mama.

'Want to go home,' Joss said, his eyes filling with tears. 'Phoebe nasty lady.'

'And we will go home, very soon, my darling. But for a while we must continue with the game. Beth is too little to understand, but you're a big boy now, Joss. Do you think you can remember to call me Ellen?'

Joss eyed her warily. 'Ellie.'

'That will do,' Eloise said, smiling. 'You're a clever boy.'

The rest of the morning passed off uneventfully enough. Phoebe's attention was diverted by a new baby brought in by Miss Marchant, and she left Eloise to see to the other infants and toddlers. The nursery was full to capacity and some of the older girls from the Foundling Hospital came in to help with feeding, washing and changing the infants. These girls were destined to go into private homes as nursery maids and they were eager to gain experience, and, for the most part, had a genuine desire to look after little children. When the time came for Eloise to leave, however, Joss saw her putting on her bonnet and shawl and he began to howl. Of course Beth joined in and soon there was a chorus of sobbing.

'It's no use,' Phoebe snapped. 'We'll have to send him away. That brat is a bloody pest.'

'Don't say that, Phoebe,' Eloise cried, torn between wanting to comfort Joss and Beth and the desire to keep up the pretence that she was unrelated to them. 'He's just a baby.'

'I'll play with him, miss.' A copper-haired little girl of about twelve ran to Joss and began tickling him. This made him sob even louder and he threw himself down on his face, drumming his feet on the floor. Eloise tore off her bonnet and flew across the room to seize him in her arms. He quietened almost immediately and plugged his thumb in his mouth, staring up at her with tears trickling down his cheeks. Beth clung to Eloise's skirts but she had also stopped crying. In the general pandemonium they went unnoticed as the girl helpers sought to pacify the other children.

'Remember what I said, Joss,' Eloise whispered. 'This is just a game. Mama has to go out to work this afternoon, but I'll be back in time to put you to bed.' She beckoned to the red-headed child. 'What's your name, dear?'

'Phyllis, miss.'

'This is Phyllis, Joss. She's going to look after you this afternoon. You will be a good boy for her, won't you?'

Joss nodded silently. Handing him into Phyllis's young arms was like cutting off a limb, but Eloise knew she must be strong, for all their sakes. With a last kiss and a cuddle for Beth, Eloise forced herself to leave the nursery.

It had been raining and the damp earth had the rich smell of Christmas pudding. Her feet crunched on the piles of wet leaves that had been torn from the trees by a storm the previous night as Eloise crossed the yard to the governor's house. She was still upset by Joss's tantrum and shaking inwardly as she waited to be admitted. If Caine opened the door she was afraid she might disgrace herself by bursting into tears, but it was Jessie who let her into the house. 'Miss Maria's got her coat on already, miss. She's waiting for you in the parlour.'

Clutching her reticule with the letter to her mother tucked away inside it, Eloise went to fetch Maria and they set off for the main post office in Holborn. Maria wanted to stop at a sweet shop on the way back, and she spent a long time choosing what she would buy with the twopence her father had given her. Eloise stood by patiently waiting for the all-important decisions to be made. Was it going to be Indian toffee or peppermint creams? Sticky boiled sweets or a penny bar of chocolate? Sugary fondants or liquorice sticks? When Maria had eventually made her choice, the rain had started again in earnest, and by the time they reached the governor's house they were both soaked to the skin. Jessie took Maria up to her room straight away to change into dry clothes but Eloise was left shivering in the hallway. Her teeth were chattering and she was chilled to the marrow, but her only change of clothes was in the hospital laundry. She made her way to the kitchen intending to ask Mrs Dean for a cup of tea, or some hot chocolate, but when she saw the state Eloise was in Mrs Dean threw up her hands in horror. 'You'll need more than a cup of tea, my duck. You must get out of them wet things before you catch your death of cold. Come with me.'

Eloise followed her up the back stairs to the main part of the house and on again up two more flights to an attic room at the very top of the building. At first she thought it was Cook's own room, but on entering she discovered that it was a small room under the eaves where unused items were stored or simply abandoned. Mrs Dean went to a large steamer trunk and lifted the lid. She pulled out one garment after another, each one carefully wrapped in tissue paper. 'These belonged to Miss Rosamund,' she explained, holding up a pink silk afternoon gown. She shook her head, laying it down carefully. 'That's too fussy.' She took out another and shook out the folds.

Eloise held her breath. The style might be six years out of date, but the dove-grey silk was as good as new. 'I can't wear that, Mrs Dean. Please put it away.'

'Don't talk soft, girl. Do you want to die of lung fever?' Mrs Dean thrust the gown into her hands. 'Put it on and I'll take your wet things and dry them by the kitchen range. No one will see you in it, and the master won't be back until late this evening. He's gone off somewhere on business.'

Minutes later, Eloise made her way slowly downstairs to the drawing room where she could hear Eloise playing the pianoforte. On the first floor landing, she caught sight of her reflection in a long mirror and she gasped in surprise. The silk fell in shimmering folds to the floor and the fit was so perfect that it might have been made for her. The elegant gown emphasised her tiny waist and the gentle swell of her breasts was revealed by an embarrassingly low décolletage, totally unsuitable for afternoon wear, and certainly not the sort of gown to be worn by a servant. She tossed her head, and her damp hair fell loosely about her shoulders in a dark mantle. She felt once again like the old Eloise, the pretty, carefree girl who had captured the heart of a dashing seafarer. She smiled as she negotiated the last flight of stairs and she burst into the drawing room executing a twirl for Maria, but she stopped short at the sight of Barton Caine, who was standing by the piano staring at her with a look of astonishment on his face which rapidly turned to one of anger. 'What in heaven's name do you think you're playing at?' He strode across the floor to seize her by the shoulders and his fingers pressed into her soft flesh. 'Is this some sick joke, Ellen?'

Chapter Twenty

Maria crashed her hands down on the piano keys. 'Stop it, Papa. You mustn't be cross with Ellen.'

'Be quiet, Maria,' Caine snapped. 'This is between Miss Monk and me. Go to your room.'

'Don't shout at her,' Eloise said in a low voice. 'This has nothing to do with Maria. It was my mistake.' Biting back tears of humiliation, she turned to go but Caine sidestepped her, barring her exit.

'You can't just walk away this time. I want an explanation. Why are you wearing my wife's gown?'

Maria slammed down the lid of the pianoforte. 'You're not being fair, Papa. We got caught in the rain and Jessie made me change my clothes too.'

There was no escape and Eloise raised her eyes to his face. The cold look she received chilled her to the marrow but it also made her angry. 'I am sorry if I've offended you, sir. It was not intentional. I thought you would not return home until late this evening.'

'I had to come back to collect some papers, but

that does not give you leave to masquerade in a dead woman's clothes.' Caine's voice was controlled but Eloise could see a pulse throbbing at his temple, and white lines were etched from his aquiline nose to the corners of his mouth.

She drew herself up to her full height. 'Don't use that tone of voice with me, Mr Caine. I didn't set out to masquerade, as you crudely put it. Mrs Dean took my clothes to the kitchen to dry, and there was nothing else for me to wear.'

'You could have gone back to the hospital to change,' Caine said stiffly.

'My only change of clothes is in the laundry, sir.'

'Nevertheless, you should not have taken Maria out on a day like this. It was foolish in the extreme.'

Maria tugged on his hand. 'We had to go out to post a letter to Ellen's mama and papa in Africa. They live there, you know.'

Caine stared down at his daughter and frowned. 'Go and ask Mrs Dean if Ellen's clothes are dry enough to wear.'

'Oh, Papa, I want to stay and make sure you don't bully poor Ellen.'

A wry smile curved his lips and Caine lifted Maria bodily out of the door. 'I am not a bully, Maria, and you have too much to say for yourself. Now do as I say, and you may ask Mrs Dean to give you a cup of milk and some cake.'

'Oh, all right.' Maria tossed her curls and stomped off towards the back stairs.

Caine closed the door. He stared thoughtfully at Eloise and she glared back at him. 'I have said I am sorry. It was a silly thing to do and I apologise for any hurt I have caused.'

'You told me that you had no family. How many other lies have you told me, Ellen Monk?'

'I have no family in England that is true. My father is a missionary in Africa.'

'So why didn't you tell me that in the first place?'

'Would it have made any difference?'

'Do you always answer a question with a question?'

Eloise shook her head. 'Not always. May I go now, sir?'

'No, not yet.' Caine walked slowly to a side table and reached for the brandy decanter. 'You look chilled to the bone.'

Eloise watched as he poured brandy into a glass and controlled her temper with difficulty. 'If that is for me, I don't want it.'

'You may not, but I do.' Caine poured a measure for himself and tossed it down in one gulp. 'Don't look at me like that, Ellen.'

'Like what, sir?'

'Questions, questions and never any answers.' He made a vague gesture towards a wingback chair by the hearth. 'Come and sit by the fire. My mother used to tell me that cold feet would lead to a chill or worse.'

It seemed useless to argue with him in this mood and Eloise went to sit by the fire. The full skirts of the borrowed gown billowed out around her like the petals of a flower. It had been so good to have pure silk next to her skin, and to feel like a pretty young woman again, but now it was all spoilt and she wished wholeheartedly that she had refused Mrs Dean's wellintentioned offer of help. She could think of nothing to say that would not make matters worse and the silence between them was as taut as the rope in a tug of war. She could not look at him, but she sensed that he was staring at her and when she could stand it no longer, she raised her eyes to his face. 'I am truly sorry that I have upset you by wearing your wife's gown. I can see that you must have loved her very much.'

'Loved her? You have no idea what my marriage was like.' Caine laughed, but there was no mirth in the sound. 'Yes, I did love her in the beginning. At least, it's true to say that I was infatuated with her and blinded by her beauty.'

The bitter tone in his voice shocked Eloise to the core and she stared at him in disbelief. 'I don't understand you, sir.'

'No, I don't suppose you do. Everyone thought we were the ideal couple, living the perfect life together. Rosamund was a consummate actress and she played her part well.'

'I don't think you should be telling me these things. Perhaps I should go,' Eloise murmured, rising to her feet.

'No, please stay.' Caine laid his hand on her shoulder and immediately snatched it away as if the touch of her flesh had burnt his fingers. 'I want you to stay, Ellen. I can't go on like this, and I must set things straight between us.'

'If it's about the gown, sir . . .'

'It's not about the bloody gown. I couldn't care less if you tear it into tatters and throw it on the fire. As a matter of fact I had no idea that Rosamund's clothes were still here. I gave orders for them to be disposed of shortly after her death, which really was a tragedy. Don't misunderstand me, I am truly sorry that she died giving birth to another man's child, but when I discovered how she had deceived me, our life together was over almost before it had begun.'

It was a shocking admission and Eloise felt her knees give way beneath her. She sank back onto the chair. 'Are you sure you want to tell me this, sir?'

Caine ran his fingers through his dark hair and a lock fell across his forehead, making him suddenly seem young and vulnerable. Eloise had to crush the impulse to throw her arms around him and hold him to her, comforting him in his anguish as she might comfort Joss. She sat quite still, clenching her hands in her lap as she witnessed his pain.

'I've revealed too much of my past to stop now. Bear with me, Ellen. I don't find it easy to talk about my disastrous marriage.'

'Then please don't, sir. Maybe it is better left where it belongs, in the past.'

'No, I have gone too far and I want you to know the truth.' Caine paced the floor, clasping his hands behind his back and staring down at the polished floorboards. 'I was just twenty-two when I met Rosamund Swan at a charity ball in the City. She was seventeen and the prettiest girl I had ever encountered, although until then my knowledge of women was limited to my mother and sisters. My father, coincidentally, was a country parson and poor as the proverbial church mouse. I was sent away to be educated at a church boarding school at the age of eight. Then I went on to theological college in Salisbury, destined, so I thought, to follow in my father's footsteps and enter the church. Meeting Rosamund changed everything. I was dazzled by her wit and charm and I couldn't understand why she chose me out of her many suitors, or why her father, who was a wealthy man, favoured the suit of a penniless young graduate who was about to take holy orders. In fact he encouraged me to vie for his daughter's hand,

and he offered me a position in his counting house at a very generous salary, which would enable us to marry straight away. I was young and green and did not see through the subterfuge. It was only on our honeymoon in Paris that I discovered my bride was pregnant by another man.' He paused, facing Eloise with a wry twist of his lips. 'Unwittingly I had made an honest woman of her. The father of her unborn child turned out to be a married man with whom she had been having an affair for several months. He was not her first lover and Mr Swan, who was apparently already in trouble financially, was eager to see his only daughter respectably married. Shortly after the wedding he was declared bankrupt and fled the country. I was then jobless and penniless, but a friend of my father's put me forward as assistant to the then governor of the Foundling Hospital, and I was glad to accept. When he retired, I was promoted to my present position. The rest you know.'

Eloise unclenched her hands and small crescent-shaped cuts on her palms oozed tiny spots of blood where she had dug her fingernails into her flesh as she listened to Caine's tortured admission of his unhappy past. She stared mutely at the wounds but she had felt no pain and she felt none now. The agony was in her heart, which was wrung with pity for the man she realised she had come to love with a passion that was both wonderful and alarming. This was not supposed to happen. She thought she had hardened her heart to all men, but somehow Barton Caine, whom she had thought to be cold, austere and arrogant, had changed her world forever. She met his eyes and immediately lowered her own, unable to bear the anguish she saw in their troubled blue depths.

'You have nothing to say,' Caine said bitterly. 'I can't say I blame you. It is a shocking tale and you must think poorly of me for my part in it.'

'No!' Eloise exclaimed vehemently. 'I have never thought badly of you, sir. I could not.'

'I don't deserve your good opinion, Ellen. I've been hard on you, I know, but my unfairness was born of frustration. You have not been honest with me, and I hate lies. I cannot abide deception of any sort.'

This made Eloise look up at him and she raised her chin with a defiant toss of her head. 'I had good reason for not telling the truth. You, it seems, acted out of pride.'

'You're right, of course. You saw through me from the start and I knew it,' Caine said slowly, fixing her with a penetrating gaze that seemed to bore into her soul. 'You must be aware that I have a deep regard for you, Ellen. When I first saw you in Miss Marchant's office, looking so young and vulnerable, so pale and frightened, I knew that you were not what you claimed to be.

I have tried to help you, and yet you have fought me all the way, preventing me from getting to know the real Ellen Monk, if that really is your name.'

Eloise hesitated. She was still trying to digest the truth about his marriage to Rosamund. She longed to tell him everything, but she was not certain how far she could trust him. Caine had been destined for the church, just like her father. If he knew to what depths she had sunk during the past agonising months he would not think so highly of her now. If he knew how she had suffered at the hands of Ephraim Hubble and that she had been on the brink of selling her body in order to support her children, and then had abandoned them on the steps of his own institution, his good opinion of her would be lost forever. Her deception was so great that he might never be able to forgive her. The intensity of his gaze seemed to strip her of everything except the need to admit the truth, or at least part of it. She licked her dry lips. 'My name is Eloise Cribb. My father is the Reverend Jacob Monkham, and as I've already told you, he is a missionary serving in Africa. I am a widow; that part is true also.'

'And what are you running away from, Eloise?'

'When my parents left for Africa I was sent to my late husband's family in Yorkshire. It was not what I wanted and I was miserable there, so I returned to London, hoping to find gainful employment, but it was not as easy as I had thought it would be. You saw me at my lowest ebb, and I am very grateful to you for giving me the opportunity to care for Maria.'

'Grateful?' Caine almost spat the word, and he knelt before her, taking her hands in his. 'I don't want gratitude, Eloise. Can't you understand that I have fallen in love with you? I have battled against it, but I cannot help my feelings.'

It would have been so easy to bridge the infinitesimal gap between them and to slide her arms around his neck so that their lips met in a kiss, and Eloise almost gave way to temptation. Every sinew in her body, every emotion screamed out at her to give him what he desired, but a small voice in her head warned her that this man had suffered much in the past at the hands of a deceitful woman. She wanted to tell him about Joss and Beth, but somehow she could not bring herself to trust him quite that far. Her children were her whole life. He had already been burdened with a daughter who was not his own flesh and blood, and he might look at her with quite different eyes if she admitted her deception. She laid her finger gently on his lips. 'Please don't, sir. You do not know me, really you do not.'

Caine recoiled as if she had slapped his face,

and he rose to his feet. 'I'm sorry, Ellen. I mean, Eloise. I should not have spoken so soon after revealing the sordid details of my personal life. It was tactless and clumsy of me. Please forget what I just said.'

Eloise stood up, brushing the creases out of the borrowed gown with shaking hands. 'Please, Mr Caine . . .'

A flicker of amusement made his eyes twinkle and his lips twisted into a rueful smile. 'I think we have crossed the bridge of formality, Eloise. At least in private I think you could call me Barton. It would make me feel less like a middle-aged roué and more like a valued friend.'

His smile was infectious and Eloise found herself responding even if her heart was aching. 'It might be better if you found someone else to look after Maria.'

'No, don't say that. You have established a rapport with her which no one else has been able to do. She is fond of you, and the poor child has had little enough affection in her short life. I try, I do try, Eloise, but every time I look at her I catch a glimpse of Rosamund and I relive that past betrayal. I do my best to conceal my feelings from Maria, and I get round it by spoiling her. I know I am not a good father, but I am genuinely fond of her. I care deeply for her and I do my best.'

'I know you do, Barton,' Eloise said softly. 'And she loves you, I know she does.'

481

'But you do not – love me?'

Eloise hardened her heart. It would be so easy to tell him that she returned his love tenfold, but she dreaded seeing the hurt and disappointment in his eyes when he learned the truth about her. She knew that she ought to walk away now, but she could not leave him. If she stayed it would be a mixture of heaven and hell, but she would rather be miserable with him than without him. She chose her words carefully. 'My husband is not long dead. My heart is not given easily.'

To her astonishment, Caine lifted her hand to his lips and brushed it with a kiss.

'I respect you all the more for that, Eloise. I'm begging you to stay on, if only for Maria's sake.'

'I will,' Eloise murmured. 'I will stay as long as she needs me.'

'I can't ask more than that, my dear. I promise I won't say or do anything to make you feel uncomfortable, but may I suggest that you move into Miss Trinder's old room, which is next to Maria's? You would be so much more comfortable living here and it would make Maria happy.'

Becky and Tibbie's warning came forcibly to mind. She did not really believe that Caine would try to force himself upon her, but she was no longer the innocent and trusting girl she had once been. She snatched her hand away. 'No, thank you, that wouldn't be right. Miss Marchant would not approve and I still have duties in the nursery. I think we will do better to continue as we are.'

He walked away and she could not see his face. He went over to his desk to pick up a sheaf of papers and when he spoke his tone was non-committal. 'Very well, whatever suits you best. Now, I really must get to that meeting or they will think I am not coming.' As Caine walked past her, he paused to touch her cheek with the tips of his fingers. 'I will never speak of this again, but if you should change your mind . . .'

She was drowning in the depths of his eyes. The temptation to give way to her emotions was so strong that Eloise felt herself swaying towards him. To feel his arms around her and his lips on hers would be her idea of pure heaven, but she stopped herself just in time and she moved away from him. 'You'd best hurry, or you will be very late for your appointment.'

'I just want you to know that you look ten times lovelier in that gown than Rosamund ever did. Please don't wear it again.' He left the room and the door swung shut, leaving Eloise staring at the wooden panels with her emotions so raw that she wanted to scream.

At first she thought it was going to be impossible to carry on as before. Caine's admission of his love for her had shaken her to the core. Her instinctive response to him had made it agonisingly hard not to give way to her feelings, but Joss and Beth must always come first. No matter how much she loved Barton Caine, she could never enter into a relationship with him if he did not accept her children. It was a heart-breaking decision, but after their last meeting Eloise tried to distance herself from him, and she spent every minute that she could in the nursery.

Now that Joss had regained his voice and his memory, it was increasingly hard to keep up the pretence that they were unrelated, and Phoebe was growing more suspicious every day. It had been particularly difficult on Beth's first birthday. Eloise had bought her a wooden doll with shiny black painted hair and rosy cheeks. She had smuggled it into the nursery under her apron and it had been a joy to see Beth's eyes light up as she clutched the doll in her chubby starfish fingers, but then Phoebe had demanded to know why Eloise had singled her out for a present, and she had pretended that a well-wisher had donated the gift. Beth was the only girl child big enough to appreciate a dolly, Eloise had said hastily. The boys would simply tear it to pieces. A tricky moment had passed, helped by the arrival of Matron on her ward round which had diverted Phoebe's attention.

At night in her narrow bed in the attic room, Eloise mulled over the possibility of confiding in Phoebe, but if she did that she might as well write it on the blackboard in the schoolroom for everyone to see. Phoebe was a notorious gossip, and although listening to her tittle-tattle made for an entertaining break in the daily routine, Eloise did not want to become the main topic of discussion amongst the staff in the Foundling Hospital.

As the days passed and October gave way to a cold and foggy November, Eloise found it harder than ever to leave her children, and the feelings of guilt that she experienced were as sharp as any of the pains she had suffered in giving birth to them. Her yearning to be with Caine, even if it was just for a few minutes each day, was a torment in itself, but added to the constant fear of her deception being discovered, she felt as though she was being torn apart. Maria had grown dependent upon her and demanded more and more of her attention, making it difficult for Eloise to spend as much time as she would like with Joss and Beth.

Normally on a Sunday Eloise would spend the afternoon in the nursery, enabling her to be alone with her children and allowing Phoebe the opportunity of passing some time at home, but on this particular day Eloise had been invited for tea at the governor's house at Maria's special request. Once again, she felt as though she was being pulled both ways. One part of her was locked in the nursery with her babies while her other self was desperate to spend a few precious moments with Barton. Since the fateful day when he had declared his love for her, their relationship had been fragile. They had not been alone together since that time, and, although Eloise had never sought Caine's company, she was always intensely aware of his presence. Sometimes, when he was near, she felt that her heart was beating to the same rhythm as his, and she always knew if his eyes were upon her. She had only to turn her head and meet his gaze to know that she was as much in his thoughts as he was in hers. It was agony and it was ecstasy but she knew that it could not go on forever. One day their feelings would bubble to the surface like molten larva, and there would be nothing that either of them could do to prevent the inevitable eruption of suppressed emotions.

When it was time for her to leave the nursery, Eloise gave Beth a last kiss and a cuddle. She had already explained to Joss that she would have to leave them for a while, and since he was busy playing with William she chose that moment to slip away. But as she closed the door, she heard Joss's voice raised in protest. He was screaming for his mama and she could hear his small feet drumming on the bare floorboards. If his attention was not diverted, he would soon be in the throes of another tantrum, but Eloise had to close her ears to his screams. She was tempted to send word to Barton excusing herself from joining them for tea, but he would demand to know the reason for her absence, and that would be difficult to explain. Eloise hurried on, covering her ears with her hands. She could only hope and pray that Phoebe would be kind and understanding to a deeply distressed small boy. Outside, the hospital was shrouded in fog which was rapidly turning yellow; a sure sign that by dusk it would have developed into a choking pea-souper. The damp, swirling mist wrapped itself around her and she could barely make out the edges of the path, but she knew the route to the governor's house blindfold and she quickened her step. Sounds were muted by the fog, but suddenly a small figure loomed in front of Eloise and they almost collided.

'Oh, Ellen, it's you!' Annie flung her arms around Eloise's neck and began to sob hysterically.

'You gave me such a fright,' Eloise gasped. As she put her arm around Annie's shoulders she realised that she had neither coat nor shawl and the back of her dress was wet and torn. Eloise withdrew her hand and was horrified to see blood on her fingers. 'Annie, what happened? Who did this to you?'

'It was her, the old cow,' Annie sobbed. 'She beat me black and blue for breaking a plate. It were an accident. I never meant to drop it, but she took a cane and thrashed me until I was sick.

I've runned away and I'm never going back there. Never!'

Eloise took off her own shawl and wrapped it round Annie's thin shoulders. 'We must get you indoors and see to those cuts on your back. That woman has gone too far this time.'

'I ain't going back,' Annie cried, clinging desperately to Eloise. 'Maybe they'll take me in here, just until me mum comes for me.'

'The first thing is to get you inside and out of the cold,' Eloise said, thinking quickly. She dared not take Annie to Matron, who would probably send her straight to the workhouse since she was too old to remain in the Foundling Hospital. 'We'll go to Mr Caine's house.' She took Annie by the hand, and they made their way through the fog to the tradesmen's entrance of the governor's house. Eloise hoped to smuggle Annie into the kitchen and rely on Mrs Dean's kind heart and discretion. If Barton knew of Annie's fate he would have to act responsibly and possibly return her to her employer. That, Eloise decided, must not happen. Queenie King was a monster in tight stays, quite unfit to run a bordello, let alone a lodging house.

In the kitchen, Mrs Dean was just putting the finishing touches to an iced cake and Jessie was licking out the mixing bowl with evident relish. They both stared at Annie as if she were a stray dog that Eloise had found roaming the streets.

'What's all this?' Mrs Dean demanded.

'This is Annie,' Eloise said, pushing her gently onto the seat of a chair. 'She is a friend of mine who has been badly used by her employer.' Eloise peeled her shawl off Annie's shoulders to reveal the wheals, cuts and bruises on her exposed back.

Mrs Dean winced and Jessie put the bowl down, wiping her mouth on the back of her hand. 'Blimey, she ain't half took a bashing. Her back looks like raw beefsteak.'

'Hush, Jessie,' Mrs Dean said, frowning. 'Fetch some clean linen and a bowl of warm water.'

Annie shivered, looking from one to the other. 'I'll be all right, missis. Me mum will come for me directly.'

Mrs Dean met Eloise's eyes with a questioning look, and Eloise shook her head. She patted Annie on an uninjured part of her shoulder. 'You won't want your mum to see you looking like you've been in a fight with Tom Cribb, now would you, Annie?'

Annie grinned and shook her head. 'Dunno who Tom Cribb is, but I wouldn't want to frighten her off, not after all this time. I must be twelve soon, although I dunno when me birthday is. Ma forgot to put it on the label she tied round me wrist when she left me on the doorstep.'

Mrs Dean clicked her tongue against her teeth

and raised her eyes to heaven. 'Dear Lord, what are we coming to?'

Jessie came in from the scullery carrying some rags and she poured water from the kettle into a bowl, which she placed on the table in front of Eloise. 'Poor little soul,' she murmured. 'She looks done in.'

'Oy!' Annie cried, bristling. 'Less of your lip, you. I bet I'm the same age as you, or even older, so don't give me none of your sauce.'

Eloise dipped a rag in the water, and having wrung it out she started to bathe Annie's back. She had to grit her teeth in order to touch the damaged flesh and she bit back an angry tirade against Queenie King for inflicting such injuries on a mere child, but Annie bore it all bravely, stifling her groans by stuffing her hand in her mouth. Just as Eloise was finishing, one of the bells from above stairs jingled on its spring.

Mrs Dean glanced up at the board. 'It's the master. Go and see what he wants, Jessie.'

Eloise wiped her hands on her apron. 'No, it's all right, Jessie. I'll go. He's expecting me anyway and so is Maria.'

Caine looked up as Eloise entered the drawing room and her heart did a bunny hop inside her breast at the smile of genuine delight on his face. He rose to his feet but Maria forestalled him by leaping up from a footstool by the fire and running to Eloise to give her a hug. 'I thought you weren't coming, Ellen,' she said, taking her by the hand. 'Papa was going to come looking for you. We thought you might be lost in the fog.'

'For heaven's sake, give Miss Monk a chance to catch her breath.' Caine ruffled Maria's hair, but his gaze was fixed on Eloise's face and there was an unspoken question in his eyes.

'I'm sorry I'm late,' Eloise said, smiling and hoping that Caine could not hear the frantic beating of her heart, and that he would assume her breathlessness was due to exertion. 'I came across a young girl in distress and I took her to the kitchen where I knew Mrs Dean would look after her.'

'She ought to be taken straight to Matron,' Caine said dismissively. 'I'll send her over with Jessie.'

'No!' Eloise laid her hand on his sleeve. 'No, sir. You don't understand.'

'Don't I?' He covered her hand with his. 'What don't I understand, Eloise?'

'Oh, Pa. You are silly,' Maria said, giggling. 'You know her name is Ellen. Why do you call her Eloise?'

'It's a secret between the three of us,' Eloise said hastily. 'You may call me Eloise if you like, or Ellie, if that is easier.'

Maria cocked her head on one side. 'I think I like Ellie best. It is halfway between Ellen and

Eloise. I shall call you Ellie. May I go and see the girl downstairs, Papa?'

Caine shook his head. 'You'd best stay up here in case she is suffering from some infectious disease. Come, Eloise. We'll go and see her together.'

'Annie is not sick,' Eloise protested as Caine followed her downstairs to the kitchen. 'She has been beaten to within an inch of her life by her employer.'

'It happens,' Caine said grimly.

Warm air scented with the appetising smell of baking wafted from the kitchen as Eloise opened the door. Annie leapt to her feet and ran to meet Caine. 'Sir, do you remember me now? You never said nothing when you last saw me in the gardens with Ellie, but I'm Annie. I was raised here in the Foundling Hospital.'

Caine stared at her for a moment and then he smiled. 'Of course I remember you, Annie. You were always in trouble, as I recall. You came before me in my office many times and nearly drove poor Matron out of her mind.'

'That wouldn't be difficult,' Mrs Dean muttered.

Caine frowned at her. 'Thank you, Mrs Dean. Perhaps you would be kind enough to give Annie some food and see if you can find something suitable for her to wear. We must have something tucked away somewhere. Something perhaps that Jessie has outgrown.' He turned his attention to Annie. 'Come and see me before you leave, Annie. I may be able to help you find alternative employment and I'll give you enough money for a night's lodging and an address where you can trust the landlady not to cheat you.'

'But, sir,' Eloise protested. 'You can't think of sending the child out on a night like this. It's almost dark and the fog is getting worse.'

'Let me stay here, guv?' Annie pleaded. 'I can work in the hospital laundry or scrub floors. I'm a strong girl and willing.'

'We'll sort something out later,' Caine told her firmly. 'In the meantime you do as Mrs Dean says.'

Annie subsided onto a chair. 'Yes, sir. You can rely on me.'

'We'll take tea in the drawing room now, Mrs Dean, if you please.' Caine opened the door and stepped outside into the passage leading to the back stairs. 'Come along, Miss Monk,' he called. 'Maria will be getting impatient.'

Eloise hesitated and she patted Annie on the arm with a sympathetic smile. 'Don't worry, dear. I won't let him send you out on a night like this.'

'I don't fancy your chances,' Mrs Dean said, eyeing the doorway as if she expected Caine to be listening at the keyhole. 'I've never known the master change his mind once it's made up.'

'We'll see about that.' Eloise hurried after Caine and caught him up on the stairs. 'You surely can't be thinking of sending Annie back onto the streets. She certainly can't go back to that awful Mrs King and she's just a child. Anything could happen to her.'

Caine paused on the top step and he gave her a searching glance. 'How do you know so much about Annie?'

'I – I . . .' Eloise struggled to think of a simple explanation. It had not occurred to her until this moment that Annie could reveal a lot more about her than she wanted Barton to know. Annie had only to enquire after Joss and Beth and the truth would out.

'You have no answer to that,' Caine said coldly. 'Is this another secret from your past that you have kept hidden from me?'

Chapter Twenty-one

'I think I hear Maria calling to us,' Eloise cried, slipping past him and making her way across the entrance hall to the drawing room. She thrust the door open only to discover Maria sitting quietly by the fire, studying the pictures in a book of fairy tales.

Caine was so close behind her that Eloise could feel his warm breath on the back of her neck. 'It seems you were mistaken.' He caught her by the wrist and spun her round to face him. 'What is it that you are not telling me?'

She snatched her hand away. 'I stayed at Mrs King's lodging house in Nile Street for a few days on my return to London. That is how I met Annie. Are you satisfied now, or must I account for every day of my life before I came to work for you, sir?'

'You are being mean to Ellie again, Pa.' Maria rushed to her side. 'Stop it, I say.'

Caine gave Eloise a despairing glance and his eyes were as bleak as the winter sky. 'As you are so quick to remind me, Eloise, it is really none of my business.'

'I'm hungry,' Maria said, stamping her foot. 'I want my tea.'

Eloise reached out to brush a lock of golden hair from Maria's forehead and she gave her an encouraging smile. 'Why don't you go downstairs to the kitchen and help Jessie? Then we can have tea straight away.'

'And I can see the strange girl,' Maria said delightedly, and ran from the room, slamming the door behind her.

Eloise went over to Caine who was standing by the window, staring out into the nothingness of the fog. She touched him tentatively on the arm. 'I did not mean to offend you, but you are right, sir. What I did before I came to the Foundling Hospital is my concern. We have agreed that there can be nothing between us . . .'

Caine turned on her with his eyes snapping angrily. 'You wanted that, not I. I agreed never to speak of my feelings for you again, but it is you who have built a brick wall between us.'

Eloise lowered her gaze, unable to bear the hurt and anguish which she knew were the cause of his frustration and anger. 'I am just an employee here, sir. Until my parents return from their mission I cannot afford to lose my position, but perhaps it would be better if I returned to working full time in the hospital. It's obvious to me that we can't get along, and we're just upsetting Maria.'

With a groan that could have been an exclamation of impatience or a cry of pain, he took her by the shoulders, and his eyes seemed to bore into her soul. 'My God, Eloise, you know how to turn the knife in a man's guts. I don't want you to go back to scrubbing floors and cleaning out privies. I want you here where I know you are treated with respect.' He ran his finger lightly down the thin silver scar on her cheek. 'And where this sort of thing cannot happen again. If I cannot have you then at least I want to be certain you are out of harm's way.'

Her lips trembled and she could not speak. Tears sprang to her eyes and she tried to break free but Caine only tightened his grip. His eyes darkened and he bent his head and kissed her with a ferocity that took her breath away. He wrapped his arms around her, running his fingers through her hair so that it fell freely about her shoulders. She struggled, but even as she tried to push him away her treacherous body responded to his embrace and she parted her lips with a sigh. Time seemed to stand still. She could hear nothing but the pounding of her heart, or was it his? She simply could not tell. The touch and taste of him were as intoxicating as the finest wine and her whole body was aflame with desire.

The sound of childish laughter shattered the moment and Caine released her just as the door opened and Maria danced into the room carrying a plate of cakes, followed closely by Jessie with the tea tray. Caine placed himself squarely in front of Eloise, giving her a chance to adjust her clothing and tidy her hair. Her hands were shaking so much that she could scarcely make her fingers work, but Caine had taken charge and he was directing Jessie to set the tea things out on a small rosewood table in the window, while Maria sampled one of the cakes. Staring dazedly at her reflection in a gilt-framed wall mirror, Eloise pinned up her hair and pinched her cheeks to bring back the colour. Taking a deep breath in an attempt to calm herself, she moved slowly to the fireplace where she made a pretence of warming her hands.

'I've seen the strange girl,' Maria said with her mouth full of cake. 'Her name is Annie and she likes cake too. Mrs Dean said she was glad she had made so many as they were all disappearing like morning mist. Do you want one, Ellie?'

Eloise straightened up, shaking her head. 'No thank you, Maria dear, but a cup of tea would be lovely.' As Maria skipped over to the tea table, Eloise looked across the room and met Caine's steady gaze. There was no denying her love for him now. She had given herself away completely and he knew it. There was no going back, but neither was there a way forward. Somehow she managed to drink a cup of tea and nibble at a slice of bread and butter, while Maria kept up a constant chatter and Caine answered in monosyllables. All through the tortuous meal, Caine's eyes hardly left Eloise's face. She tried to avoid his steady gaze but every time she looked up her eyes were drawn to him, and it was as if their long embrace continued even though they were seated far apart.

When Maria had eaten the last crumb of cake on her plate, Eloise rose to her feet. 'It's time I was going. Thank you for inviting me to tea, Maria.'

Maria smiled and yawned. 'I'm glad that Papa is being nice to you now. I don't like quarrels.'

Caine stood up and reached for the bell pull. 'It's time you were in bed, young lady.'

'Oh, Papa. Can't I stay up a bit longer?' Maria's bottom lip stuck out and her fair brows drew together in an ominous frown.

Eloise recognised the signs of an approaching tantrum and she placed her arm around Maria's shoulders, dropping a kiss on her upturned face. 'Go to bed like a good girl and I will see you tomorrow afternoon. Perhaps you can give me a piano lesson?' She did not add that she could already play, and the suggestion brought a smile back to Maria's face.

'Oh, yes. That would be fun. I love you, Ellie.'

'And I love you, poppet.' Eloise realised with a shock that she actually meant it. She had come to love the spoilt but unwanted child. For all her faults, Maria was a generous and affectionate little girl, who just needed love and attention tempered with gentle discipline to make her a much nicer child.

Caine went to the door and opened it just as Jessie came hurrying in response to his summons. He sent Maria to bed with a pat on the head and instructions to be a good girl and to remember to say her prayers. 'I will, Papa but only if you promise to come up to my room and kiss me goodnight.' She waited for his reply but when he remained silent she uttered a small sigh and blew a kiss to Eloise as she followed Jessie from the room.

'Don't look at me like that, Eloise,' Caine said abruptly. 'I do my best for the child. I can't pretend love where I feel none, and the reverse is true, as you know.'

'I have to go,' Eloise said hastily. 'It's late and I always help Phoebe to put the babies to bed.'

'Is that how we are going to part? You are going to run away again?'

'I shouldn't have let you kiss me.'

'But you did, and whatever you say, I know that you return my feelings. Why won't you admit it? What is it that you aren't telling me?'

'I have nothing to say. Please allow me to leave, sir?'

'You know that you are free to come and go as

you please, but I'll see you to the hospital door. The fog is so thick that you could lose your way even in such a short distance.' He opened the door for her. 'You did not come without a coat or a shawl, did you?'

'I gave it to Annie. She had nothing to cover her wounds and she was frozen to the marrow. What will become of her, sir?'

A grim smile lit his eyes. 'If you persist in calling me sir, I'll throw her out on the street right now.'

'I'm serious, Barton. Whatever has passed between us has nothing to do with Annie. Will you allow her to stay here for tonight at least?'

'She can have Miss Trinder's old room but only for tonight. Tomorrow I will try to find her a suitable position in a respectable household.' He crossed the hall and plucking a man's greatcoat from the coat stand, he wrapped it around her shoulders. 'You'll need this. It's bitterly cold outside.'

Eloise did not argue. She slipped it on and breathed in the scent of him that lingered in the satin lining of the cashmere coat. As he opened the door a plume of yellowish-green, evil-smelling fog curled into the entrance hall. Outside there was nothing but the pea-souper and silence. Caine offered Eloise his arm. She leaned against him as they picked their way carefully along the path, more by instinct than by good judgement. The fog was so thick that Eloise could barely make out her feet, and Caine's outline was blurred even though she was clinging to his arm. When they finally reached the hospital entrance, Caine drew her into his arms and kissed her long and hard. There was a hint of desperation in his embrace, a lick of anger and frustration and an intensity of passion that both thrilled and frightened Eloise. In the strange other-worldly atmosphere of the amorphous, swirling miasma, she responded eagerly to his embrace, but in her heart she knew that this must be goodbye. Annie's sudden arrival, together with Joss having found his voice, would make it impossible for her to keep up the pretence that her children were foundlings. Even if she extracted a promise of secrecy from Annie, Eloise knew her well enough to realise that one day she would blurt out the truth, and then Caine would realise just how much she had deceived him.

'Go inside, my love,' Caine murmured, punctuating his words with soft kisses. 'I can hardly bear to let you go, but we will talk things over tomorrow.'

'Goodnight, Barton.' She allowed herself one last glorious moment in his arms, closing her eyes and revelling in the nearness of the man she had come to love with all her heart. Tearing herself away from him was sheer agony, and as she slipped off the protective mantle of his overcoat she knew she was relinquishing his love and protection forever. But there was another voice calling to her, or rather two small voices – her helpless babies who were locked inside the austere walls of the Foundling Hospital. As soon as the door closed on her and she was alone in the vast, echoing entrance hall, all her senses were alert. There was something wrong. She picked up her skirts and raced across the hall to the staircase. She was out of breath and filled with inexplicable dread as she entered the nursery.

Phoebe was tucking the last infant into his cot and she looked up and smiled. 'You're late. Got lost in the fog, did you?' She winked and chuckled. 'Did the governor make you stay in after class?'

Ignoring the innuendo, Eloise hurried to the cots at the end of the room. She heaved a sigh of relief at the sight of Beth sleeping peacefully, but when she went to check on Joss she found that the cot was empty. 'Joss! Where is he?'

'Don't take on, Ellen. I know you had a soft spot for the kid, but he got hisself into such a state when you left that I had to send for Matron.' Phoebe paused, shaking her head. 'Don't look at me like that. I had no choice; he was upsetting all of the kids and he was going blue in the face. I thought he'd do hisself an injury.'

Eloise managed to control her voice with difficulty. 'Where did she take him?'

'She put him in a room on his own where he can't hurt hisself. If it weren't for the fog she said she'd have sent him to the school for imbecile children this evening, but he'll be packed off there first thing in the morning. Good riddance, I say.'

'What have you done, you stupid, stupid girl?' Eloise grabbed Phoebe's hands. 'Where is he? Where is my baby?'

'Have you gone doolally too? For Gawd's sake, Ellen, get a hold of yourself. You'll wake all the little bastards and I only just got them off to sleep.'

'You don't understand. Joss is my son and Beth is my daughter. I am their mother.'

'No!' Phoebe's eyes opened wide in disbelief and she shook her head. 'Don't talk daft, Ellen.'

'It's true. I must find Joss. I can't explain but I've got to leave here tonight and I'm taking my children with me. You must help me, Phoebe. Please help me.'

'I can't, ducks. If Matron found out she'd sack me on the spot.'

'Just tell me where Joss is, then.'

'Look, love, I can see you're in a state, but you can't take them little 'uns out on a night like this. Won't it wait until morning?'

Eloise shook her head vehemently. 'No. We must go now. Please tell me where Joss is.'

'All right, if you're determined to go through

with this, I'll show you where he is.' Hooking a nurse's cape off the back of the door, Phoebe handed it to Eloise. 'Take this. It's a spare anyway, and with a bit of luck the old dragon won't notice it's gone. You can't go out on a night like this without something to keep out the cold and damp.'

'Thank you, Phoebe. You're a good friend.'

With the sleeping Beth wrapped in a shawl, and Joss's warm clothes in a bundle beneath her arm, Eloise followed the light of Phoebe's lamp through the maze of corridors. Phoebe opened a door and stood aside to allow Eloise to pass. 'I can't do no more, Ellen. I got to get back to the nursery.'

'Yes, yes, do what you must, Phoebe. And thank you. I won't forget what you've done for me tonight.'

Phoebe pulled a face. 'You won't thank me when you get lost in the pea-souper. I wish you'd change your mind, girl.'

'I can't risk it. If you will just hold Beth for me for a moment, I'll get Joss and we'll be off.' Without waiting for a reply, Eloise thrust Beth into Phoebe's arms and she crept into the room. In the pale shaft of lamplight she could see Joss lying in a high-sided cot sound asleep with his curls tumbled over his tear-stained face. She called his name softly as she lifted him from the bed and he opened his eyes, recognising her instantly with a sunny smile which brought tears to her eyes. She hugged him to her breast, rocking his small body in her arms. 'Joss, my baby. We'll never be parted again, sweetheart. Mama promises you that.'

'Hurry up and get him dressed,' Phoebe whispered. 'Old Marchant will be doing her rounds soon.' She pulled a small purse from her pocket and thrust it into Eloise's hand. 'Here, take this. It's not much but it's all I got. I were only going to spend it on a new bonnet, so I reckon it'll be better spent looking after you and the nippers.'

'I'll pay you back every penny as soon as I can,' Eloise said, slipping a woollen jumper over Joss's head. 'Thank you, Phoebe. Thanks for everything. I will miss you.'

'Get on with you, or we'll both end up crying like babies.' Phoebe gave her a watery smile. 'Good luck, girl. You'll need it.'

It was surprisingly easy to leave the hospital unseen. The older children were at supper in the refectory, and it seemed that most of the staff were occupied in completing the last tasks of the day before retiring for their own meal or going home. For once, Eloise was grateful for the thick blanket of fog which covered their tracks the moment they stepped outside the building. Holding Joss by the hand, and with Beth hitched over her shoulder, Eloise made her way slowly out of the hospital grounds.

Keeping close to the railings, she turned east, feeling her way along Guildford Street until she reached Gray's Inn Road, where she headed north towards King's Cross station. It was the only place where she could be certain that there would be warmth and light and it would be easy to get lost in the crowd. It was not very far to the station but Joss was tired, and although Eloise was grateful that Beth was asleep, it made her a dead weight and difficult to carry. They had to keep stopping to rest in doorways, often disturbing a sleeping vagrant or tripping over the inert bodies of drunks sleeping off an excess of alcohol.

The only sounds to penetrate the eerie silence were the occasional clip-clop of horses' hooves and the rumble of cartwheels on cobblestones. It felt to Eloise that they were alone in a strange, yellowish-green world of stinking fog, but at last she heard the plaintive whistle of a steam train. The lights of the station filtered through the haze in shredded strands, but it was a little clearer inside the main concourse and Eloise found a coffee stall which was still open for business, where she bought a cup of hot coffee for herself and some milk for the children. There was a fire burning brightly in the ladies' waiting room and she sat down on the wooden bench with Joss at her side and Beth cuddled in the crook of her arm. A porter came in to attend to the fire and he eyed them curiously. 'There ain't no more trains tonight, ma'am.'

'I must have missed my train,' Eloise said, attempting a smile. 'Could we wait here until morning?'

'I'm locking up, ma'am. I'm afraid you'll have to leave.'

'But we've come a long way and my children are tired.'

'Sorry, ma'am, but that ain't my problem. Now I'll have to ask you to find somewhere else to spend the night. There's plenty of cheap doss houses round here, although I ain't too sure they'll take in a woman with nippers, but you might be lucky.'

They were out on the street again, and there was no sign of the fog lifting.

'I'm tired, Mama,' Joss murmured.

Eloise clutched his small hand and gave his fingers an encouraging squeeze. 'We'll find somewhere soon, darling.' She started walking northwards. If they could get as far as the dust yard, perhaps the Tranters would give them shelter for the night. They had only gone a few paces when a figure loomed out of the fog, almost colliding with them.

'Watch out, lady.' A huge man, wearing a battered top hat and smelling worse than the pea-souper, held a lantern close to Eloise's face. 'Ellie! Is that you?'

'Mick? Mick Fowler – Peg's gentleman friend?'

'The very same. Gawd's strewth, girl. What are you doing out in this and with them nippers? And why did you run off like that with nary a word to Peg and her ma? They was frantic with worry, and then that detective fellow come looking for you too. What's been going on, Ellie?'

Eloise shook her head. 'Oh, Mick. You don't know how good it is to see a friendly face. I'll explain everything, but do you think you could take us to the Tranters' house? I must get the children out of this dreadful pea-souper.'

Mick hoisted Joss onto his shoulders. 'Hang on to me jacket, ducks. I know me way blindfold.'

Clutching the tail of Mick's coarse fustian jacket, Eloise stumbled after him with tears of relief pouring down her cheeks. Just when she had thought they would have to spend the night out in the cold, Mick had appeared before them like an angel from heaven. Perhaps there was a god after all. When her father returned from his mission, Eloise vowed silently to pay more attention to his sermons.

Peg and Gertie were at first incredulous and then overjoyed to see Eloise and the children. Gertie couldn't get over how much Joss and Beth had grown in the past few months and Peg patted her swollen belly, announcing with pride that there would soon be another little Tranter to help in the dust yard. It would be a Fowler, Mick said, hooking his arm around her shoulders. Just as soon as the banns were read he was determined to make an honest woman of his Peg. Then Cyril, Jimmy and Danny arrived home and the sound of their voices awakened Daisy and Cora, who came in sleepy-eyed from the bedroom to join in the reunion. Mick and Cyril went out to the pie shop and returned with hot pies, pease pudding, mashed potatoes and a jug of gravy, and the family crowded round the kitchen table or squatted on the floor to eat.

Later that night, when everyone had gone to bed, Eloise lay in her old place on a straw palliasse in front of the kitchen range, with Joss and Beth sleeping peacefully at her side. They were safe for now at least, but her heart ached for the man she had given up in order to protect her children. She had not believed that love would come again to her after Ronnie's death, but she realised now that she had been mistaken. Loving Barton did not diminish the feelings she had had for Ronnie, but that was another life, locked away in a separate compartment of her heart and encapsulated in her adoration of their children. Nothing could take that away from her, but if she was honest with herself, she knew that Ronnie's profligate spending habits and selfishness would have eventually destroyed their happiness.

But the sad truth was that she had walked away

from the man whom she loved with all her heart. Barton Caine could have been her future but for the circumstances that had forced her to live a lie. Once he knew the truth, he would never want to see her again, but at least she would be spared the sight of his accusing face and the hurt expression in his eyes when he discovered her deception. She curled her arms around the warm bodies of her children and closed her eyes. Whatever tomorrow might bring, she would keep them safe. She would do anything necessary to see that they did not suffer.

Next morning there was the familiar and comforting hustle and bustle of the family rising early for work. After a hasty breakfast of bread and jam, Cora had taken Daisy to the ragged school, and the men had gone off to work with their hunks of bread and dripping wrapped in newspaper, and bottles of water to wash the dust from their throats. Gertie and Peg stayed behind to talk to Eloise. Last night there had only been time for the briefest of explanations as to why she had disappeared so completely, but now she was able to furnish them with the details. When she had finished, Peg and Gertie exchanged worried glances.

'You can stay here for as long as you like, ducks,' Gertie said. 'But that Pike fellow might still be searching for you, and he knows you were here.'

Eloise glanced at Joss and Beth, who were on the floor playing with a stray kitten that had wandered into the cottage. She sighed. 'I don't think the Cribbs will give up easily. In some ways I think it might be best if I went up to Yorkshire and had it out with them once and for all. Perhaps I have been too selfish in denying Joss the education and upbringing that the Cribbs could give him so easily.'

Peg threw up her hands in horror. 'But you can't be thinking of giving him over to them, not after what you've told us about Mrs Cribb and her horrible sister.'

Eloise shook her head. 'What alternative do I have now, Peg? You'll soon be a mother and then you'll understand that you would do anything for your children – anything at all. But I would insist on staying at Cribb's Hall so that I could be with them every day, even if it meant being treated like a servant. I won't be parted from my babies. I'd die first.'

Gertie refilled their teacups from the old brown china teapot with half the handle missing. She frowned. 'Are you sure about this, Ellie? Don't you think you ought to give your fellah a chance to speak for hisself? If he loves you, he'll understand why you done what you done.'

'If I thought that I wouldn't have run away. No, Barton is a fine man, but he'll never get over the way his wife tricked him into marrying her when she was expecting another man's child.'

'But it's not the same with you, Ellie,' Peg protested hotly. 'You was forced into acting the way you did.'

'It's true, I never meant to deceive him, but I doubt if he will see it that way. And if I should remarry, I would have to be certain that the man could love my children as well as he loved me. Poor little mites, they have suffered enough on my account. I must do what I think is best for them.'

'But that may not be best for you, Ellie,' Peg said gently. 'Stay here for a few days at least and think things over before you do anything silly.'

'Yes, ducks,' Gertie agreed, nodding her head. 'Peg's right. You're worn out with worry and you need time to think. We missed you and the nippers when you took off like that. Stay here with us until you're sure that you're doing the right thing.'

'And if that Pike bloke comes sniffing round just let him watch out.' Peg jumped to her feet and fisted her hands, dancing about like a prize fighter. 'My Mick and the boys will sort him out good and proper. We know how to look after our own in Magpie Alley. Let Pike come here and he'll find hisself buried at the bottom of a dust heap.'

Joss and Beth leapt to their feet and began dancing around with Peg while the kitten flew up the curtains and hung there, its fur sticking out all over its tiny body as it hissed with fright.

Eloise couldn't help laughing. 'I will stay for a day or two, and thank you with all my heart for your kindness.'

'Oh, tosh!' Gertie said, getting up from the table and reaching for her dusty jacket and bonnet. 'You're one of us, ducks. I'm off to work and you stay put, or I'll have something to say about it.'

Despite the cramped living conditions, Eloise did stay put for the best part of a week. She did not go back to work in the dust yard, but she kept the house clean, did the shopping and cooked meals for the whole family in an effort to repay the Tranters for their hospitality. Keeping busy prevented her from brooding too much about what she had lost, but every night Barton Caine invaded her dreams, which inevitably turned into nightmares as he learned the truth about her, and when she awakened she found her pillow was wet with tears.

As the days went by Eloise became more and more convinced that she must take the children back to Yorkshire. It was not a decision to be taken lightly, but with her parents thousands of miles away, and nowhere else to go, she knew she had little option but to throw herself on the mercy of the Cribbs. After all, Harcourt was a kindly soul, even if he was under petticoat rule, and Hilda must have a heart buried somewhere beneath that massive bosom. Eloise tried to convince herself and failed miserably, but she also knew that she could not impose on the Tranters for very much longer, and it was only a matter of time before Pike discovered their whereabouts.

On a particularly wet and dismal Friday morning, Eloise had finally and most reluctantly made up her mind to return to Yorkshire. She would break the news to the family when they returned from work that evening. She was standing at the kitchen table, kneading bread dough, when someone tapped on the cottage door. 'My hands are covered in flour. Can you reach the latch, Joss darling?'

Joss toddled over to the door and stood on tiptoe to push up the latch.

'Hello,' he said cheerfully.

Eloise had her back to the door and she was wiping the sticky dough from her fingers. 'Who is it, darling?' She turned her head just in time to see Joss swept up in the arms of a lady whose face was hidden beneath the wide brim of a fur-trimmed bonnet.

Chapter Twenty-two

'Mama?' Eloise said faintly. Although it was morning, it was dark outside and torrential rain was lashing down, but she would have recognised the figure silhouetted in the doorway anywhere. For a second, Eloise thought that she was dreaming, but when Grace raised her tear-stained face she was smiling with joy.

'Oh, Ellie, darling. I thought I'd never find you.'

'Mama!' Eloise ran to her, wrapping her arms around her mother and hugging her with Joss sandwiched in between them until he protested. Eloise loosened her grasp just enough to let Joss down safely, but she held on to her mother's hand, gripping it tightly for fear that she might suddenly disappear again, and this would all prove to be a dream. 'Mama, I can't believe it. You're really here. How – I don't understand . . .'

'Don't cry, Mama,' Joss said in a very grown-up manner. 'It's my nana.'

'He remembers me. I thought he would have forgotten his nana.' Grace smiled through her tears. She reached into her reticule and pulled out two lace-edged handkerchiefs. She gave one to Eloise. 'I came prepared, my love. I knew you wouldn't have one of your own.'

Halfway between tears and laughter, Eloise clutched the scrap of lace and cotton to her face and inhaled the familiar scent of lavender. 'Oh, Mama! This is too good to be true. Is Papa with you? How did you find me? Why aren't you in Africa? Oh, I'm so happy to see you.' Still clutching her mother's hand, Eloise led her to a chair by the fire. 'Let me take your cape and bonnet, they're soaking wet. Sit down, darling Mama. Tell me everything.'

Grace wiped flour and remnants of bread dough from her hand. 'All in good time, my love.' She took off her bonnet and cape and passed them to Eloise. 'Let me look at you, Ellie. Are you well, darling? You look so pale and thin.'

'I'm fine, Mama.' A shaft of fear clutched Eloise's heart. Her mother's lovely face was thinner and there were fine lines radiating from the corners of her eyes. 'You're not ill, are you? Is that why you came home so unexpectedly?'

Grace sank down on the chair and lifted Beth off the floor, sitting her on her knee. She glanced up at Eloise with a reassuring smile. 'No, I'm not ill. By some miracle I escaped the disease that laid your father and Janet so low.' She chuckled as Beth made a grab for her earrings and she covered her granddaughter's face with kisses. 'My little darling, how you've grown. You were just a baby when we left England, and now look at you.'

'Me too,' Joss said, climbing onto her lap. 'I'm a big boy, Nana.'

'You are a very big boy, Joss. Just wait until your grandpa sees you. He will get a surprise.'

Eloise drew up a stool and sat at her mother's side. She had to touch her again, just to make certain she was real. 'I can hardly believe this, Mama. I've missed you so much.'

'You couldn't have missed me any more than I have missed you, my darling,' Grace said tenderly. 'You were in my thoughts night and day.'

'And now you've come home. But why, Mama? Why have you come back to London so soon and how did you find us?'

'I'll explain everything; just give me a few moments to enjoy cuddling my grandchildren.' Grace was still smiling, but there was concern in her pansy-brown eyes as they scanned Eloise's face. 'I can see that you have had a hard time, Ellie.'

'I'm fine now that you're here, but I still can't quite take it in.' Eloise stood up and reached for the kettle. She could never keep anything secret from her mother for long, but she was not yet ready to tell all. 'I'll make us some tea while you tell me what miracle brought you to Magpie Alley.'

'Kitten, Nana,' Joss cried, leaping off her lap and making a grab for the unfortunate kitten, which had just woken up and was stretching and yawning, exposing a pink tongue and pointed white teeth. It dangled helplessly from Joss's grasp as he thrust it in front of his grandmother's face, and Beth struggled to get off her lap, holding her hands out in a vain attempt to snatch the unhappy animal.

'It's a lovely kitten,' Grace said, setting Beth back on the floor. 'Why don't you play with him while I talk to your mama?'

Eloise set the tea to brew and she returned to her seat. 'Well, Mama?'

'It took so long for your letters to reach me, Ellie. And when I read them I knew something was wrong. Oddly enough it was Hilda who alerted me to your plight. I don't think she meant to do you any favours, but she wrote a long and garbled letter about your ingratitude, and how you had run away from Cribb's Hall, abducting Joan's daughter who later died whilst in your care. She said that you had gone back to the fleshpots of London and that you were a disgrace to the name of Cribb. Of course I knew that it was a farrago of lies, and I also knew that you must be in dire straits, especially when she added that she had sent a private detective to seek you out.'

'And so you came home, Mama?'

'It was not easy to persuade your papa, but I stood my ground, Ellie. I told him that you and the children were more important to me than the entire population of Africa. Anyway, he had been terribly ill with malaria, and suffered recurrent bouts of fever so that sometimes I feared for his life. I sent a messenger to the senior missionary in Mombasa, and when he saw how ill your father was he agreed with me that we should get him back to England as soon as possible.'

'And he is here in London too?'

'He had to stay on for a while to settle in the new man, but Janet is with him and they will travel to England as soon as your papa can book a passage.'

'And you travelled all that way on your own?'

Grace smiled and clasped Eloise's hands. 'Darling, when I knew you were in trouble nothing could have made me stay in Africa. I would have walked home if necessary.'

Eloise raised her mother's hand to her cheek. 'Oh, Mama, I've missed you so.'

'And I you, dearest girl. I thought of you and the children constantly, and your father had to agree that he was mistaken in sending you to stay with the Cribbs. Can you imagine your papa actually admitting that he was in the wrong?'

'No, Mama. Never.'

'Where's that tea, Ellie? I am parched.'

Reluctantly, Eloise let go of her mother's hand and she poured the tea. She gave Joss and Beth cups of milk, and, at Joss's insistence, poured a little drop in a saucer for the kitten.

'I still don't know how you found us here of all places, Mama,' Eloise said, handing her mother the only cup in the Tranters' household which did not have a chip out of it or a broken handle.

'When I reached London I booked into a small hotel in Bloomsbury, and then I went straight to the Missionary Society. They gave me the address that you had left with them, and so I went to the Foundling Hospital and had a very interesting meeting with your Mr Caine.'

Eloise almost dropped her teacup, spilling some of the contents on her lap. She jumped to her feet, covering her confusion by grabbing a piece of rag and mopping at her skirt. 'He's not my Mr Caine, Mama. He was kind enough to give me a job when I needed one.'

'You always were a poor liar, darling. He told me everything, or at least as far as he knew your story. Unless I'm very much mistaken, my dear, Barton Caine is head over heels in love with you.'

'Did you – did you tell him about Joss and Beth?'

'It came out in conversation.'

'And now he must hate me. You don't know the whole story, Mama. There were reasons why

521

I couldn't tell him that Joss and Beth were my children.'

'I think you should have trusted him, darling. I can understand why you did what you did, but I think you underestimated Mr Caine.'

'Did he tell you about Maria's mother?'

'As I said, we had a long talk. He is a most remarkable man, Ellie. I don't wonder that you fell in love with him.'

Eloise covered her hot cheeks with her hands. 'I never said so, Mama.'

'You didn't have to, darling. But you will have a chance to tell him so yourself when he calls at our hotel this evening.'

'I – I don't understand.'

'I've reserved a room for you and the children at my hotel. Barton wanted to come with me this morning, but I insisted that it was best if I saw you on my own. He will have his chance later.'

'To tell me that it was all a mistake, no doubt,' Eloise said bitterly. 'Why did you say I would see him, Mama? And I can't afford to stay in a hotel. Just look at me . . .' She glanced down at her shabby blouse and skirt. 'These are all the clothes I have to wear. I left the Foundling Hospital in such a hurry that I left everything behind. I even had to borrow a nurse's cape, which I must return at some point.' She waved her hands in front of her mother. 'Look at them – they're the hands of a charwoman. I'm a mess, Mama.

What man in his right mind would look at me now?'

'Don't be ridiculous, Ellie. Your hands will soon heal and a little pampering together with some new clothes will work wonders. Your father has given me a generous amount of money to keep us until he returns to England. I think his illness and his experiences in the African bush have made him see many things in a quite different light.'

'You won't have to go back there, will you, Mama?'

'No, darling. Your father hopes to be installed in a country parish very soon and then we will be a family again.' Grace stood up, taking Eloise by the shoulders and giving her a gentle shake. 'Now, back to the present, Ellie. The first thing we will do is get you fitted out with a new wardrobe. Although you are so thin now that I fear we might have difficulty in finding anything ready-made that will fit. We will take the children shopping, and buy them some new clothes too.' Grace smiled down at Joss and Beth as they played with the kitten. 'And I will buy them each a birthday present, even if it is a little late.'

'I can't just walk out of here, Mama. The Tranters have been kindness itself to me.'

'Of course you can't. I owe them a huge debt of gratitude, and when we are settled we must invite them all round for tea, but for now, I think you ought to go and find them and tell them of our plans. I'll wait here for you.'

'Oh, Mama, it is so good to have you home.' Eloise flung her arms around her mother's neck and hugged her. 'Just one thing, though. How did Barton know where to find me?'

'He didn't, Ellie. It was that strange little waif called Annie. Apparently you insisted that he took her in and he had given her a job helping Mrs Dean in the kitchen. She brought a tray of tea into the drawing room and was clearing it away when she must have overheard part of our conversation. She was only too happy to fill in the gaps. She told us all she knew of your terrible time in Clerkenwell Green and about Pike, the hateful detective. She said that you had once taken shelter with a family called Tranter who worked a dust heap near King's Cross, and we thought it was worth a try. I wonder that Barton had not thought to interrogate Annie when you first went missing, but my guess is that he was so beside himself with worry that he was not thinking straight. That man clearly adores you, Ellie. Do give him a chance to prove it.'

Eloise stooped to pick up Beth who was attempting to climb up her skirt. She rubbed her cheek against her daughter's curly head. 'I have to be certain, Mama. I have to put my children first.'

Grace smiled. 'Quite right, but don't forget you are talking about a man who has raised a child who was not his own. He could have put Maria out for adoption, but he did not. And Maria misses you terribly, she told me so several times.'

Eloise nodded her head, but her throat was constricted with tears and she could not speak. Too many emotions were raging in her breast to allow her to think clearly.

'I know, darling,' Grace said, patting her on the arm. 'Everything will be all right. Trust Mama.'

'I – I still can't quite believe that you're here. I'm afraid I might wake up any moment and find that I am dreaming.'

With a gurgle of laughter, Grace pinched Eloise's cheek. 'There, that proves that you are wide awake, my darling. Now go and find those wonderful friends of yours and tell them that you and your mama are going shopping.'

Minutes later, Eloise stood in the entrance of the dust yard, where puddles of rainwater had enlarged to the size of small ponds. The great glowering heaps towered above her and the workers looked like an army of ants as they sifted, sorted and carted away anything of value from London's mountain of rubbish. With Beth in her arms and Joss scampering on ahead as if he had spent all his life on a dust heap, Eloise went in search of Gertie and Peg.

'You will come back and see us, won't you?'

Peg asked with tears sparkling on the ends of her eyelashes and slithering down her cheeks leaving snail trails in the grime. 'You won't forget us, will you, Ellie?'

Eloise hugged her regardless of the thin film of grit which covered Peg from head to toe. 'Of course not, Peg. I'll be godmother to your baby if you will let me.'

Gertie wiped her nose on her sleeve and sniffed. 'If she'll let you? She'll have me to deal with if she don't. You come back any time, girl. If your man don't treat you right you can always come and live with us in Magpie Alley.'

Eloise felt the blood rush to her cheeks. 'It isn't certain – I mean – I don't know if Barton will . . .'

Peg slapped her on the back. 'Course he will, ducks. The man would be a bloody fool if he didn't go down on his knees and beg you to marry him.'

'If he don't come up to scratch we'll send Mick and Cyril round with the rest of the lads,' Gertie said, folding her arms across her chest. 'We'll see he does right by you, girl.'

Eloise hugged them both and she called to Joss who was standing on top of a heap of breeze crowing like one of the cockerels that stalked about amongst the hens.

'He'd make a good hill man,' Gertie said with a gap-toothed grin. 'We can always find work for an able lad.'

With a last loud crow, Joss ran down the heap, sending up a cloud of dust. Eloise beckoned to him, telling him to follow her, but he danced on ahead, jumping the puddles and occasionally landing in the middle of one with a hoot of laughter. Despite his wet boots and socks, Eloise couldn't help laughing at his antics. When she reached the entrance, she put Beth down on the ground and watched her toddle off after Joss who was chasing a rather tatty-looking chicken. Mick was standing by his cart, waiting for it to be unloaded. 'What's this, girl?' he demanded, grinning. 'Are you looking for work?'

'No, Mick. I've come to say goodbye. It's a complete miracle but my mother has returned from Africa and she's come to fetch us.'

Mick embraced her with a hug that almost stopped her breathing. 'I'm glad for your sake, Ellie. But we'll miss you and the nippers.'

'I'll bring them to see you. We won't lose touch,' Eloise said, when she caught her breath. 'Look after Peg; she's a wonderful girl and a dear friend.'

'And I knows it. My Peg's one of the best, and she's very fond of you. If our little 'un is a girl, we'll call her Ellie.'

'I'd be honoured, Mick. If it hadn't been for you we might have perished on the streets. I'll always remember what you did for me and my children.'

'Aw. It weren't nothing, girl.' Mick's weather-beaten face flushed a dull brick red. 'If there's anything else I can do for you . . .'

Eloise reached up and kissed him on the cheek. 'I'd be more than grateful if you could find us a cab, Mick. My mother is waiting for me at the Tranters' house.'

Later that evening, when Joss and Beth were fed, bathed and tucked up in their beds at the hotel, Eloise and Grace were sitting in their private parlour waiting for Barton to arrive. Eloise kept glancing at the black marble clock on the mantelshelf. Her stomach felt as though it was full of butterflies flapping madly around, and her mouth was dry. She got up every now and then to pace the floor, and to take yet another look in the mirror above the fireplace to make certain that her hair had not escaped from the elaborate style that Grace had fashioned. Curled and pomaded, her gleaming brown hair was piled on top of her head like a coronet. Her new satin-striped blue silk gown fitted her slim figure to perfection, and waterfalls of lace at the neckline and cuffs only served to emphasise her slender neck and wrists. The small train, lined with frills, swirled around her feet and ankles as she moved, revealing the occasional glimpse of blue satin high-heeled slippers.

'You look beautiful, Ellie,' Grace said, smiling

happily. 'Your papa will have a fit when he receives the bill but it will be worth every penny just to see the look on Barton's face when he walks through that door.'

'He might be coming to tell me that everything is over between us, Mama,' Eloise said, nervously fingering her fan. 'You did tell me all that he said, didn't you?'

'Stop fretting, darling. I told you that we had a full and frank conversation. Now it's up to you to decide how you feel about him. Much as I liked him, I don't think life would be easy with a man like Barton Caine. You wouldn't get everything your own way, and bringing up another woman's child would be a challenge.' Grace rose to her feet. 'I hear someone coming. Now take my advice, Ellie. Follow your heart. Your babies are safe and well and no further harm will come to them, I promise you.'

Before Eloise had a chance to reply, the door opened and Barton Caine entered the room carrying a huge bunch of red roses. Eloise stood quite still, hardly daring to breathe as he formally greeted her mother, bowing over her hand and raising it to his lips. He was dressed in a well-cut black evening suit that emphasised his broad shoulders and slim waist, and at the neck of his starched white evening shirt he wore a wine-coloured cravat. To Eloise's dazzled eyes he looked breathtakingly handsome and completely unattainable. When he turned to her, she saw her own feelings mirrored in his eyes. His lips curved in a tentative smile as he held the bouquet out to her. 'I remembered your love of roses,' he murmured, 'but I'm afraid that they are from a hothouse and have no scent.'

Eloise took the flowers, and she met his gaze with a wobbly smile. 'They are beautiful, but not as honest and down to earth as garden roses.'

'In the summer I will fill the house with roses from the garden,' he said softly.

Grace rose to her feet. 'I think I ought to go and check on the children, Ellie.'

Barton moved swiftly to open the door for her.

'Take your time,' Grace murmured. 'Dinner can wait.' She gave him a brilliant smile as she left the room, closing the door softly behind her.

'I trust that I find you well, Eloise?' Barton made a move towards her and then hesitated, eyeing her warily.

Eloise was startled to realise that he was as nervous and tongue-tied as she was herself and she made a vague movement with her hand, indicating the sofa. 'Won't you sit down, sir?'

The sound of her voice seemed to trigger off an instantaneous response and he strode across the floor, taking the bouquet from her hands and tossing it onto the floor. 'Damn it, woman. Do you always answer a question with a question?'

He took her by the shoulders, looking deeply into her eyes.

A small sigh escaped her lips. 'No, sir.'

'You know my name, Eloise. Can't you bear to say it?'

'Why did you come here tonight, Barton?'

He answered her by drawing her none too gently into his arms and kissing her with all the ferocity of long pent-up emotions. She closed her eyes, parting her lips, and allowed her senses to revel in the taste of him as his tongue claimed her mouth, his teeth grazed her lips and his hands caressed her body. She felt herself melting into him until they were as one person, and she knew that she had come home. When he finally released her lips, he still held her in his arms, as if he would never let her go. 'I came to do just that, my darling. I came to tell you that I've been a complete fool all these weeks. I knew from the first moment I saw you that I loved you and yet I risked losing you by allowing my stupid fears and prejudices to rule my heart.'

'I lied to you about my children, but it was not from choice.'

He traced the outline of her cheek with the tip of his forefinger and a smile lit his eyes, turning them from the colour of a winter sky to the blue of midsummer. 'I know that now, of course. But until you ran away I had no idea that Joss and Beth belonged to you.'

'Did Phoebe tell you that?'

He nodded. 'Yes, of course. She had little choice, poor girl, when Matron questioned her about the missing children.'

'I'm sorry,' Eloise murmured.

'If only you had trusted me and told me the truth from the start.'

'You might have sent me back to Yorkshire. I feared that you would think as my father thought.'

He kissed her again, slowly and languorously, until she relaxed against him. 'I was a stiff-necked fool,' he whispered as he nuzzled her neck. 'I might have thought that way once, but not any more. I love you to distraction, Eloise. This past week has been sheer torment. I thought I had lost you forever, and I was out of my mind with worry, until Grace turned up on my door-step like an angel from heaven.' He cupped her face in his hands. 'I can see where you get your beauty, my love. Your mother is not only beauti-ful but she is a very special lady.'

Eloise blinked away a tear, but this time it was happiness that was making her cry. 'You'd better stop there, Barton, or I might be jealous of my own mother.'

He kissed her on the forehead, the tip of her nose and he brushed the teardrops from her eyelashes with his lips. 'There will never be another woman for me as long as I live, Eloise. I love you – no – I adore you. I'm asking you, most humbly, to be my wife. I want you and your children too, my dearest love.'

She drew away from him just far enough to look into his eyes. 'Do you really mean that, Barton? You already have one child who is not your own. You admitted freely that you cannot love Maria as you should. How would you feel about Joss and Beth?'

'I would love them because they are a part of you, my dearest girl. And I was wrong about Maria; I do love the little scamp. I suppose I always did, but I was afraid to admit it even to myself. My heart was closed and shuttered until I met you, Eloise. Now I see the world through quite different eyes.'

'Oh, Barton . . .'

He sealed her lips with a kiss. 'I so nearly lost you, Ellie. Don't ever leave me again.'

Eloise wound her arms around his neck and drew his head down so that their lips met. 'I'll never leave you.'

'Will you marry me, Ellie? I will do my best to make you happy, even though I cannot offer you much in the way of . . .'

She laid her finger on his lips. 'I don't care about material things, Barton. Once, I did. But if there's one thing I've learnt in the past months, it's that the only thing in life that matters is people. Love and family are more important to me than money. I would marry you if you were a dustman working the dust yard at King's Cross.'

'I am not alone, Eloise. There is always Maria.'

'And I will love her just as much as Joss and Beth, and our own children if we are blessed with a family. And most important of all, Barton Caine, I love you with all my heart and soul.'

'I wouldn't want to change anything about you, my dearest Eloise,' Barton said with a tender smile in his eyes. 'But I think that a mother's love is the most powerful of all.'

ALSO AVAILABLE IN ARROW

The Cockney Sparrow

Dilly Court

She sang with the voice of a nightingale . . .

Gifted with a beautiful soprano voice, young Clemency Skinner is forced to work as a pickpocket in order to support her crippled brother, Jack. Their feckless mother, Edith, has fallen into the clutches of an unscupulous pimp, whose evil presence threatens their daily existence.

Befriended by Ned Hawkes and his kindly mother, Nell, Clemency struggles to escape from life in the slums of Stew Lane. She finds work with a troupe of buskers and is spotted by the manager of the Strand Theare. Clemency looks set for operatic stardom, but a chance meeting with the mysterious Jared Stone brings danger and intrigue and threatens to change her life forevermore . . .

arrow books

ALSO AVAILABLE IN ARROW

The Best of Sisters

Dilly Court

Would fate ever bring him back to her?

Twelve-year-old Eliza Bragg has known little in life but the cold, comfortless banks of the Thames. Living above her uncle's chandlery she has grown accustomed to a life of penury and servitude, her only comfort the love and protection of her older brother, Bart.

But one day Bart accidentally kills a man and is forced to flee to New Zealand. Alone, barefoot, beaten down and at the mercy of her cruel uncle, Eliza realises that her very survival is at stake . . .

arrow books